Cold Steel Rail

An Inspector Vignoles Mystery

Stephen Done

The Vignoles Press

British Library Cataloguing in Publication Data:
A catalogue record for this book is available from the British Library
ISBN 978-1-9164010-0-6

Published 2018

The Vignoles Press
Stephen.done@gmail.com
FB: The Vignoles Press
www.inspectorvignoles.ukwriters.net

Set in Garamond
Cover design & layout: Bill Citrine
Editor: Peter Elson
Printed in Poland by booksfactory.co.uk

For Peter
Who has supported Vignoles from the start

Author's Note

The Leicester & Swannington Railway was one of the earliest railways and traces still remain today as a cycle and footpath. George & Robert Stephenson did build a very narrow tunnel at Glenfield and subsequently knocked the chimney off their locomotive on the inaugural run! The tunnel remained a limiting factor throughout the life of the line which saw quite heavy coal and stone traffic, although passenger services ceased in the 1930s. The 'Premier Brick & Terra Cotta Works' is real, although I have invented the persons working there.

There was never a crossing at Black Spinney, but I played with the geography to imagine a cottage and gates matching those that existed at Ratby and Glenfield. There was never a locomotive shed at Desford Junction, but it was needed for the story and I envisioned it as a small 'sub' shed able to house just two small locomotives.

The story is inspired by the real 'Durran Hill Murder' that took place near Carlisle in 1861. The man judged guilty, an engine driver called Richard Charlton, was the last person to be publically hanged in the UK. However, reading the readily available reports of the investigation and trial, I found a number of anomalies that were not, to my mind, sufficiently explained. Whilst Charlton would appear to be guilty, there are unexplained aspects of this sorry tale that suggest other possibilities.

So here is my own interpretation. It is not a 'New Tricks' cold case reinvestigation, and aside from retaining the names of a number of characters and revisiting some of their actions, this is a work of complete fiction bearing no intended resemblance to persons live or dead.

Stephen Done
New Brighton, August 2018

Prologue

It starts with two men, Kane and Abel. More specifically, Louis Kane and Jesse Abel, both resident in London.

Just two seemingly regular guys (as they say in the States). Smart and polite, clean-cut and served well by their expensive tailors, they look a proper pair of swells riding the cushions in their first class compartment (as they are often wont to do) with a reservation at a table for two in the dining car for later. They like to sit facing each other, beside the window, broadsheet newspapers neatly folded for ease of reading, notebooks filled with equally neat columns of numbers and meticulous jottings that nobody except the writer has ever read; polished leather luggage carefully stowed and expensive woollen coats neatly folded on the racks above their heads. They have classy tastes in smoking materials and display good watches on their wrists that keep impeccable time. These are men who command respect and show enough politeness and humility in return to offend nobody.

Decent fellows! Businessmen, of course. Travelling up, down and criss-crossing the country as they attend what must be important meetings and enjoying lengthy business lunches. To the more astute observer, Kane might be judged a self-made man with just a touch of the working class Londoner still lingering around his accent; but he presents himself well enough to win over even the most fastidious of golf club secretaries - for surely these two must slot in the odd round when time and weather allows? Kane probably honed his ability to lead men and make decisions in the war – that pale scar on his face coupled with his strong, erect, athletic build and striped regimental tie (easily bought on the black market...) aid silent recognition and admiration for a man who put his life on the line to protect the nation. Who could begrudge a former Commando his later good fortune in business?

Abel surely comes from a family with money. *Nouveaux riche* from the stockbroker belt of Surrey most probably, perhaps with an allowance from 'Pater' or a generous inheritance to ease the loss of family from early deaths.

Highly educated (one's bet is on Harrow) with Cambridge following as a matter of course. He probably did something secretive and terribly intellectual to help beat the Luftwaffe or U-boats. You can tell he was a back-room boy – in every sense of the word – by his effete mannerisms, the excessive use of lavender scent and his glossy hair parted with a line sharper than a razor's edge and by the almost feminine choice of colour and weave of his suiting and by his precise and meticulous movements. No scars on his face and hands soft and smooth with impeccable nails. The monocle is an outrageous affectation and a throw-back to a different age. It perhaps goes with the paperback of Christopher Isherwood's more outrageous writing he likes to slip into his coat pocket. But it takes all sorts to make the World go around. Of course (whisper it quietly, with a discreet tap on the side of the nose), he's probably one of *those* sort of men, but he's not alone, least of all around Whitehall, and he's avoided scandal at all costs - and that's what matters. Besides, his smile is warm, his manners positively charming and his tips generous. Live and let live, eh? What a chap does behind closed doors is nobody's business and besides, if a retired Commando can take him as a business partner then he must be a decent cove.

They are The Debt Collectors.

They are the men who collect. Who coax the unwilling, the obstinate, the lying and the down-right aggressive into paying up. It's really no use hiding, it's futile to run. Indeed, there is nowhere to run from these two. Evasion merely delays the inevitable, because Kane and Abel are patient and careful - and able.

They don't rush in like blundering fools, but take their time to study their quarry with a meticulousness close to obsessive. They then choose their timing with unsettling precision, striking just when their prey is most vulnerable. If they take on a job, they deliver, but do so in their own time. And they never fail. Payment, even if not quite in the form expected, is always extracted.

Because nobody refuses The Debt Collectors.

If the first sweetly worded request from these swell fellows is foolishly rebuffed, then their final demand will be exacted in a manner that inflicts the maximum pain and executed with a degree of unfeeling cruelty that would impress Dr Mengele. No matter how dearly their victims might wish to cling to this precious life on earth, they always end up begging for the final curtain to fall and the blessed relief of death.

However, despite their chilling notoriety, Kane and Abel are not on any wanted list. Not by name or description at least, although the unidentified perpetrators of their many sickening crimes are sought by many a bamboozled detective. Nobody has ever offered up their descriptions. Not once. Perhaps they are just too polite, well-mannered and obviously engrossed in their important work of business to warrant more than a cursory glance? By rights they should be unforgettable, and yet, somehow, inexplicably, they have the uncanny ability to blend into a crowd whenever they choose; to quietly melt away and like a rapidly fading dream, vanish into thin air, forever elusive and impossible to bring back into focus. Although preferring to travel by train or the occasional car (carefully liberated thanks to an extensive bunch of skeleton keys) and they often walk the streets, day or night, their faces never quite lodge in the minds of those enthusiastic witnesses eager to help the puzzled police. When asked to recall anyone 'acting suspiciously', the descriptions of Kane and Abel never appear.

Suspicious? Those two? Ridiculous...

And so, like two Scarlet Pimpernels, they travel without recourse to skulking in grimy shadows, going about their evil business with a clinical calm that is legendary amongst those who commission their services. The select few in the know call on their help from their cells deep in the more notorious prisons across the land. The Debt Collectors are the eyes and ears of these greedy, callous and power-hungry men, all of whom in their own domains like to think of themselves as the 'Mr Big'. These men are prisoners in name only. The lags who rule their prisons with more fear, authority and power than even the Governors would dare admit. They run rackets and make fortunes whilst the public mistakenly believes they are banged up in a cramped cell recanting their miscreant ways. Every so often these men wish to reach out and keep in check those on the outside entrusted with holding safe the fruits of violent robberies, extortion, racketeering and drug dealing, ensuring that their hard-won percentages remain safe, that nobody 'takes the Mickey' and thinks to run off with Mr Big's excessively large share. After all, crooks are crooks, and the idea of honour amongst thieves is pure fiction and each and every 'Mr Big' knows it. People get ideas, and they need timely reminders to ensure all is as it should be. Sometimes word gets back that someone's playing hard to get, that they've gone missing without leave or claiming any number of reasons why the loot they were trusted with protecting is strangely unavailable. Or gone missing.

And that's when The Debt Collectors get back on the road.

Chapter One

It also starts on Saturday 27th November 1954, with a man and a woman and a debt that needs paying...

The air was bracing, the sky a wintery bluey-white as cold as porcelain, the smell of baking bricks sharp on the nose from the smoking chimney.

'You know what you have to do?'

'Of course! We've talked it over enough.'

'There's no need to be irritable with me.' She brushed the lapel of his jacket. It was an intimate gesture. She needed him compliant - for now. 'When will you do it?'

'Thursday. Thursday evening, after she's closed the section down.'

'Hmm. That makes sense.' She smiled. Her lips bright red with 'Gipsy Kiss' lipstick, matching her nails. 'A nice touch, I like it.' She judged he probably needed an approving look, and dutifully obliged. She was standing very close, although he resolutely kept his arms at his side, making him both look and feel awkward.

'What do you mean?'

'I mean, Thursday's long enough after me going away. Nobody could think I'm involved. How could I be, as I'll be miles away?'

'That's the whole point.' He sounded annoyed.

'Come on...' She reached forward to part his jacket and slide her fingers through the opening on his Vyella shirt, but he recoiled from her painted nails as if from an electric shock. 'What is it, tiger?' Her eyes looked up at him under fluttering lashes. 'Not getting cold feet, I hope? That's not like you...'

'No! Of course not.' But his voice suggested otherwise, and she eased back, a slight frown forming on her smooth brow.

'You have to do it. There's no going back. Not now. You understand that?'

'I'm not bloody stupid.' He breathed out a stream of pale vapour as if he'd been holding his breath. 'Look, I've been thinking it over again, perhaps there's another way? Something less...?'

'No!' Her eyes flashed as she cut him off mid-sentence. Now she was annoyed, both by his cursing and even more so by the seeds of doubt in his voice. 'We've agreed the plan. We've worked it out, so don't even think about letting me down.' Her eyes narrowed and took on a cold, mean glint.

'I won't. It's just that I had an idea -.'

'Oh, I know all about your ideas.' She wagged a finger at him. 'And I've let you indulge them often enough.' Her voice was still firm, but there was a playful edge creeping back. She had to mollify him as she still needed him on her side. 'Half an hour on Thursday night and your debt's paid. In full. That's a promise.' Her voice was heavy with meaning and her eyes provocative. 'Not a bad deal, even if I say it myself.' She stepped closer again and this time he didn't draw back. He could smell her perfume, her body. 'Hardly a lot to ask in return for what you've had from me -.'

She gripped one of his wrists and suddenly pushed his hand hard against the swell of her left breast, pressing his palm against a hardening nipple. 'You have to agree?' She massaged his palm into the warm soft flesh beneath the unseasonably thin dress she'd deliberately chosen. 'You can't say it's not worth it.'

'Nooo... Stop!' He closed his eyes for a moment. 'We said it was the end. No more.' His breath was shallow and fast. 'It's got to stop.' He should pull his hand away, but his resistance was failing and his words lacked conviction.

'A shame. Oh, well.' She gave him that cheeky half-smile that always made her look even more girlish and which drove him wild. 'But you still need to pay for what you've already had.' She pulled his hand from her warm body and let it drop then re-arranged her dress and pulled her coat tightly closed. 'Think of that as a little extra to keep your mind on the job.'

She laughed, then turned to walk away, hips deliberately swaying suggestively, knowing that his eyes would be drinking in the sight. She suddenly stopped and looked over her shoulder in a coquettish manner. 'You've had your credit and now I'm asking you to balance the books. Remember, folk 'round here won't take kindly to hearing what you've been doing to me. Repeatedly -,' She lifted a perfectly pencilled eyebrow, 'All behind your *dear* wife's back.' She blew him a kiss, and was gone.

He collapsed against the rough brick wall and closed his eyes, heart pounding. He rubbed his eyes furiously as if trying to eradicate her image. But though he made stars and colours flash behind his eyelids with his knuckles he could not erase the scent of the 'White Fire' perfume he'd secretly bought her for her last birthday – at no little expense. Seventeen precious shillings for a tiny bottle of clear liquid! But now, just the slightest whiff of this scent brought images flooding back of the delicious heat and touch of her young body.

He stood up straight and quickly looked around to see if anyone had seen them. It looked as though he was alone in the brick yard. The Terracotta Works was under-staffed and this remote part of the dilapidated complex was usually deserted. There was something to be said for these short and dark winter days. You could hide a multitude of sins under the cloak of this rapidly encroaching gloom.

He turned and slapped the brick wall hard with the palms of his hands, welcoming the sharp stinging pain, hoping the shock might cauterise the desire inside. He was desperately trying to convince himself that once he'd done as they'd agreed, he could walk away and forget about her - forever. He would return to the family that, for now at least, was still in place, even if it was hanging by the slenderest of threads.

Chapter Two

Thursday 2nd December.

Thomas Leach strode purposefully through the echoing concourse of Marylebone station. He was on time. When he had a job to do he planned ahead and allowed more than sufficient time for each stage of the journey. A man anxiously checking the hands on his watch and cursing traffic snarl-ups and trains held at red signals, was a man liable to make mistakes. Leach enjoyed a carefully plotted schedule. That way he could take time and not lose his cool by rushing and becoming flustered. These basic tenets had seen him right so far, and he saw no reason to change now.

He would arrive in Leicester Central with bags of time on his hands and, as per usual, would stroll along to The Great Central Hotel and check in. He would take a beer or two in the bar and quietly while away the evening. He'd retire to his room before eleven, but not before first settling his account so he could slip out in the early hours with just a 'goodbye' to the night porter, and step into his waiting taxi.

Yes, he was an early riser, but nobody in The Great Central Hotel found that strange. It was doubtful anyone noticed, and besides, it was a seedy sort of place that saw all manner of night travellers come and go, including those furtive fellows who slunk away in the dead of night back to their sleeping wives, urgently wiping away the last traces of scent and lipstick and with lighter and slimmer wallets in their jackets. Leach was far less interesting. Just another unremarkable journeyman salesman who needed to be up and about even before the lamplighters started attending to the city's remaining gas lamps. His regular taxi driver never asked questions. A gent who tipped that generously and regularly, was a man to look after. Leach was a decent fellow with nothing to say for himself, and if he wanted a short ride out of town at God-knows-what-hour, so be it. And besides, the taxi driver didn't want someone else muscling in on a good fare - so he kept his trap shut.

Leach stopped and looked across at the W H Smith stall which was bathed in warm electric light that illuminated the many multi-coloured magazines, paperbacks and newspapers arrayed along the front. Why not pick up something to read? It would while away the journey and the evening wait. He could put it on expenses. That made him smile. He strolled across and grazed for a few moments whilst the proprietor hovered behind the counter feeling confident that this gent, who was surely catching the Manchester train, was going to buy.

Leach selected one of the last copies of the The Times, but then changed his mind and put it back before reaching for a green and white covered Penguin. A murder mystery.

'That's fresh in, sir. Been quite popular.'

'Yes?' Leach casually inspected the cover. 'Red is for Killing. Where do they dream up these titles?' He laughed as he fished out the two and six for the book.

'Should help the time pass on the train, sir.'

'Absolutely. One gets so tired of the news. Just full of moaning and complaining and accounts of yet another war.'

'Gets yer down at times, don't it? Best stick to a good murder, eh?' The proprietor winked, good naturedly.

Leach laughed and declining a paper bag, clutched the new paperback in a gloved hand and walked towards his waiting train. He settled back in a window seat in one of the modern coaches now becoming thankfully more common on the bigger express trains. The compartment was clean and the seat well-sprung and the lights actually worked. He noticed that his carriage was also just a step away from the dining car. Excellent. There was a warm smell of gravy wafting his way and his tummy growled enthusiastically. Leach gently patted the bulging brown envelope tucked deep inside the buttoned closed inside pocket of his suit jacket to give himself the reassurance that it was still where it should be, and lit up a first cigarette, the new paperback resting on his right leg now crossed over the other.

The Manchester express powered into life, huffing and chuffing deeply as the heavily laden train strained into action. The locomotive was sending great clouds of smoke and steam into the bitter London air where it mingled with the filthy smog crouching low over the sickly-yellow brick London houses and crept around the utilitarian blocks of flats that were springing up like new-season bulbs. It was going to be a cold and unhealthy night.

Leach was cosy in his compartment with the steam heating on full. The other two gentlemen sharing the space were silently and efficiently studying their evening papers and taking no interest in him, nor in each other.

He opened his book and started to read.

As the powerful engine, the curved nameplates on each side declaring it to be named 'Sir Frederick Banbury', hurried north, little did Leach know that despite his best laid plans, he would not live long enough to discover exactly why Red was for Killing, nor how Inspector Schmidt solved the puzzle.

* * * *

The sun had dropped low enough to kiss the gentle rise of the distant hills. In a last hurrah before nightfall, its golden rays felt their honeyed way through untidy hawthorn hedgerows and cast long filigrees of shadow across fields already collecting mist in their hollows. It had not snowed yet, but the night frosts were hardening and taking longer to thaw each short, sharp day. Where field gates opened, the water collected in rutted cart and tyre tracks had become ice, whilst the frost-rimed mud and cow dung was crunchy underfoot like sugary fudge. Sheep huddled beneath the gnarled woody canopy of an ancient oak, staring with puzzled expressions at the hardening grass, their breath puffing white clouds around their muzzles. A number of carrion crows strutted and hopped in the distance, cocking watchful eyes towards the men. By rights they should soon be cawing and croaking their way to roost, but they knew that a fresh and bountiful late meal would soon be served. It was worth staying up for.

An express locomotive hauled a trainload of passengers along the main line nestling low in a cutting. 'Sir Frederick Banbury' was releasing a stream of steam from between its whirring wheels as great billows of hot cumulous nimbus poured rhythmically from the chimney, only to be tossed backwards along the carriage roofs and ripped into fluffy white balls on fences and hedgerows or smashed soundlessly against a bridge parapet.

On the locomotive footplate, the crew were glad of the incandescent heat from the firebox and the fireman was uncomplaining about the relentless shovelling their hungry beast demanded. The work kept his limbs warm and supple. When he clambered into the tender to pull more coal forwards, he was instantly struck by the penetrating cold as the wind seared through the cotton of his engine-man's 'blues' and heavy donkey jacket, ramming chilling fingers down his collar and stinging his ears as if they'd been pinched. He had to worry away at the coal with a strong metal bar in order to break apart the lumps fused together by the attentions of Jack Frost the night before. It was as though each piece of coal was welded together by an over-zealous shipbuilder.

The driver, perched on his padded wooden seat kept his eyes narrowed like slits against the flashes of dying sunlight between fence posts and tree trunks that made the light flicker on his face in an irritating manner. He was staring ahead through a soot-stained spectacle plate because experience told him not to lean out of the cab for a clearer view as the bitter air would make his eyes run and torment him all the way down to Manchester Central. But he knew the road like the back of his hand and sitting like this this he could soak up more of the welcome warmth radiating from the boiler backplate.

His eye suddenly caught a small group of men gathered near a gate in a field, bathed in the sun's dying embers. They were carrying tools and heavy sticks and standing in a loose huddle. One was clapping his hands to get the circulation moving. Even in that momentary glimpse the driver sensed there was a reluctance about their gathering, a deliberate dawdling in finishing their cigarettes before moving on. The land suddenly swelled upwards around the railway and the view was gone. The driver brought his eyes back to the line ahead, then pulled the chain in the cab roof and the locomotive issued a wailing whistle as they hurtled into Ashby Magna tunnel.

* * * *

The men shuffled their booted feet. A cigarette butt was tossed, still smoking, on the pale grass and fizzled with a tiny sound for a moment before giving up the ghost with a tiny thread of smoke. Hats and caps were pulled down harder, collars turned up. Gloves readjusted.

'This is the best time. Just before it gets too dark to see.'

There was a mumbled response and pickaxe handles and spades were hefted in cold hands. Tested for weight and balance.

'What's up wi' you?' The eldest, and clearly the leader of this motley crew, noticed that the youngest of the pack was holding back, his spade clutched in both hands across his chest as if afraid he might drop it. The lad's face was paler than the others, made all the more obvious by his red and drippy nose.

'Just do it! Hesitate, and you'll make it worse.'

The young man nodded vigorously.

'Step up - and splat!' The speaker demonstrated by thwacking a particularly fat tussock of grass. 'Anyways, you've got a spade, so go for the neck. Straight down. Then move on.'

'Right.' The young man swallowed and the thin scarf about his neck showed the movement of his Adam's apple.

There was a sickening thump that reverberated across the field above the diminishing sound of the passing train. One of the men had barely broken stride whilst delivering the death blow and was already walking on, eyes searching, the wooden stave lifted ready for the next victim.

The young man licked his drying lips.

'Come on! I can't waste more time.'

They spread wide and walked in a loose line across the rolling field. There was the occasional exchange between the men, but otherwise all were silent. This was not work that invited banter. Breath clouded around the scarves bound across their mouths. Thump. Whack. Sometimes a crack of bone.

'Just kill it, for Chrissake!' Their gang master was impatient with the youth.

The young man raised the spade, took aim, then shut his eyes. He struck with all the force he could muster, channelling the embarrassment and humiliation he was feeling into striking downwards. He knew they would be watching. He heard how their relentless tread on the crunchy grass momentarily fell silent. The spade cut through something that offered little resistance then juddered to a halt on the steely soil below, sending a small vibration through his arms.

He heard one of the men shout 'Bravo!' and there was a trickle of sour laughter.

'Good lad. Now the next.' The older man's voice was quieter now. 'You'll come back after and pick 'em up, then burn 'em.'

The young man, just an acne-faced boy really, gave a glance downwards to avoid standing on the headless corpse, then looked away instantly and walked on. The first was always the worst, so they told him.

The raking light picked out a string of ruby red globules caught in rows on the white crystals of ice coating the long arching forms of the rough field grass. A startling sprinkling of red on green. But these were not holly berries, nor even alluring deadly nightshade. They were liquid, and one glassy bead slowly changed shape and slipped from its frosty resting place to drip onto the hard earth. A mass of fur, shattered bone and muscle leaked warm steaming blood and gore onto the ground.

Two carrion crows cackled and croaked as they fluttered to the ground. With a stiff-legged gait, they strode closer, heads cocking to one side, the better to spy their warm meal. They jumped and skipped and stalked nearer. Eager, yet their natural caution not allowing them to rush in, beady eyes watching the steadily diminishing shapes of the men patrolling the field. More ragged shapes of crows were now circling overhead, their cracking cries carrying far and wide, calling the roost to come and gorge...

Chapter Three

Eddie Earnshaw checked his fire, clanged the heavy fire door shut then leaned his shovel against the cab side. He gave the floor a quick look over and picked up a piece of small coal that had strayed onto the worn wooden boards of the ancient Midland Railway locomotive he was firing. He looked everything over and felt content there was nothing amiss. Engine number 58148 was getting rather long in the tooth, and both he and his driver, Robert Ashbourne, were careful to do everything they could to keep her looking trim and tidy and, more importantly, to keep her steaming.

Driver Ashbourne was leaning casually on the far cab side sheet, an unlit cigarette in the corner of his mouth, one hand resting on the regulator as they pulled away from Desford Junction towards Leicester. He gave a lift of his free hand as they passed the signal box to acknowledge the solitary figure inside watching their progress.

The past six months of routinely working the West Bridge Branch 'link' had taught Earnshaw that Ashbourne's unlit ciggie would remain where it was, precariously balanced in defiance of Newton's Law, until they reached Black Spinney Crossing, at which point Ashbourne would slow their train and perhaps draw to an unscheduled halt if he was in a conversational mood. The white painted wooden gates would already be drawn across Rothley Lane offering them a clear run through. However, road traffic was always light on the lane and they could easily afford to sit for a couple of minutes and exchange pleasantries with Mrs Palmer, the elderly crossing keeper, without causing any undue friction with road users. If the occasional vehicle did draw up to the closed gates, it was usually driven by a local who knew Old Janey just as well as they and might well wind a window down and call out a greeting and get a wave in return, all whilst the old-fashioned Victorian-era engine gurgled quietly to herself. Such a pause at Black Spinney was the cue for Ashbourne's ciggie to be lit, accompanied by friendly banter between the old crossing keeper and driver.

For that was the nature of the line. Or at least along this historic stub of of what had once been the Leicester and Swannington Railway, running east from Desford Junction past the tiny clusters of houses that formed Ratby and Glenfield, before rabbiting its way down an implausibly constricted tunnel to reappear in the heart of Leicester, where the tracks fanned out at the considerable expanse of the West Bridge wharf beside the River Soar. There was a timetable, of sorts, but the actual timings were somewhat fluid in practice and the printed document was treated more as a sequence rather than something to be closely monitored with a watch. There was never going to be a bottleneck of impatiently steaming engines champing at their bits, as the unfeasibly tiny Glenfield Tunnel had ensured that only one type of antiquated locomotive could squeeze down it. Nothing much else would fit and there were usually only ever two of the class in service on most days, although there was talk to trying out one of the new diesel shunters for size.

So, if they drew to a stand whilst a wicker basket brimming full of vegetables from Old Janey's allotment garden was handed up to the footplate whilst a small churn of milk was dropped off the guard's van for her use, or if driver Ashbourne handed over a greaseproof packet of sausages or a few rashers of bacon, then what harm was done?

'Janey's stuck there, day in, day out and never a chance to go to the shops. So we look out for her, Eddie. We all do. She works all hours without complaint, but she's in her seventies and whilst tough as an old boot, that's not to say she wouldn't mind a bit of help every so often.' He shook his head slowly as if unable to believe her age. 'I know she's got her daughter and family all living in – but even so.' Ashbourne pulled the regulator wider and the engine responded with some gentle chuffs and picked up speed. 'Me and the missus always like to buy a little extra and hand it across.'

'She does grow lovely vegetables.' Earnshaw had constantly marvelled at the sheer size and perfect forms of the produce crammed into the heavy basket placed in a corner of the footplate after some of their stops. He'd sometimes had a few beetroots or a monster head of cabbage or some delicious carrots to take home and enjoy with his aunty Maud, with whom he was currently lodging, in Leicester.

'Aye, you're not wrong there, Ed. And she does most of the work on that allotment an' all. OK, so Richie Charlton lends a hand on the heavy stuff every so often. He's good like that. Digging it over at the back end of the year - like he's been doing this last week or two. But everything else she does herself.' He gave Earnshaw a glance across the cab to emphasise the point. 'Her daughter Sarah's not much of a gardener, and as for her granddaughter...' He gave a contemptuous snort. 'As far as I can see, Rachel spends her time doing her nails and prettifying herself. She couldn't lift a bag of spuds even if her life depended on it, let alone dig 'em up.' He gave a contemptuous snort.

'Rachel also has a little girl to look after?'

'Daisy. Well, that's true,' conceded Ashbourne.

'That must be a handful, and she goes to work some days on top.' Earnshaw knew this was so, because sometimes they would see her being helped into the guard's van in order to could give her a lift the short way to the Terra Cotta Works in Glenfield. Wearing heels, a fashionably flared skirt and skin-tight sweater, she was a sight for sore eyes.

Earnshaw had caught glimpses of the whole extended family from the footplate as they passed to and fro along the line and could find little complaint in regard to the obvious attractions of the young mother. Despite that, Rachel and her mother Sarah and little Daisy were still little more than fleeting impressions caught through a window, in the back garden or, yes, clambering into the guard's van with perhaps more than just a glimpse of stocking. Rachel was certainly a pleasing sight, but even so, she was put firmly in the shade by the strong and characterful personality of Jane Palmer herself.

Ashbourne shut the regulator off and their elderly six-coupled goods engine gently wheezed and panted to little more than a crawl as they approached the level crossing some distance ahead, illuminated in the rapidly encroaching dusk by two oil lamps of considerable vintage. Earnshaw glanced back along their train of laden four-wheeled coal wagons and could see guard Timmerman leaning expectantly on the side of the verandah of his van at the end. Looking forwards again, Earnshaw could see light spilling from two small downstairs windows in the attractive octagonal shaped two-story cottage set slightly back from the road. This was Old Janey's home, and with its steeply sloping roof and tall cluster of chimneys and pale lime washed walls it looked a snug and comforting home. Their sedate approach made this pretty Hansel and Gretel cottage appear to glide towards them in a curious trick of the eye, as though sliding through the winter dark like a pale apparition against the Bible blackness of the surrounding fields. There were no street lights on the narrow lanes about and the distant village of Ratby was little more than pin pricks of light between the skeletons of trees on the horizon. A tiny square of light half a mile or more away suggested a solitary farm house, but otherwise Black Spinney Crossing was an isolated place and especially so in winter. Earnshaw didn't fancy being stuck out here. He suddenly shivered as the cold air caressed his shoulders.

The distinctive figure of the crossing keeper was standing at ground level facing them with a torch in one hand, although she was not using this to signal an instruction, but to illuminate her path as she found her way from opening the gates. There was no platform, just a rough path of compacted cinders and a dribble of tarmac probably left over from another job, serving as a rudimentary walkway. This was a place where the crossing gates were opened and closed and signals rose and dipped with a heavy metallic clunk at the top of their wooden posts controlled by wires that ran all the way back to the signal box at Desford Junction.

Palmer was dressed, as usual, in a long railway issue greatcoat over a black uniform of heavy woollen material worn with a long skirt, thick woollen leggings and stout boots. What was instantly distinctive about her however, even in the dark and from distance, was that she was wearing a military helmet. This was painted glossy black with 'W' clearly visible in white stencilled letters on the front. It had been issued to her in 1940 when, together with her late husband Emmerson, they had taken up additional fire-watching duties alongside minding the crossing. Jane Palmer had enthusiastically taken to wearing it at all times, declaring that 'one needed to be prepared as you never knew what might fall out of the sky at any moment.' When Emmerson died in 1948 and she took over his job as crossing keeper, she was still steadfastly wearing this anachronistic piece of headgear and ignoring any suggestions it be replaced by a British Railways cap. Old Janey was used to it, felt safe in it and was not going to change her ways any day soon.

'You can't be too careful working near goods trains. Things might fall off and with me standing down here, well that wouldn't do me no good, would it, me duck? I've a crossing to mind. What'd happen if I banged my head and saw stars and forgot to open the blummin' gates?'

Perhaps she had a point. Especially with the train crews passing things down to her and sometimes whilst their train was still in motion. So the pen pushers in higher authority decided to overlook this peculiarity, not because of any particular favouritism towards Mrs Palmer, but because this was a poorly paid position in an isolated spot with no amenities to hand. It was an unattractive posting in this modern 'jet age' of De Havilland 'Comets' roaring across the sky - and sometimes falling out - of scientists busy splitting atoms and designing robots to help around the home and any number of new labour-saving devices. Replacing her would be hard. Nobody wanted to be posted out in the sticks in a damp cottage with awkward shaped rooms with little more than an outside privy and a tin bath on a hook in the kitchen. Those in Marylebone House soon ignored her choice of headgear and let her get on with it. She was unfailingly reliable, had never once reported a single day's sickness and despite her advanced years was fully *compis mentus* and showing no sign of retiring. Added to which, like every other woman still working on the railway, she was paid barely half the wages of a man. It was commonly agreed the railway would struggle to replace her when the time came, and all things being equal, a tin hat on her head was hardly cause for concern.

'Evening, Mr Ashbourne! Evening, Master Earnshaw!' Palmer was always pedantically formal in her greetings. 'There's a wicked wind getting up. It'll blow some tonight.'

'Reckon you're not wrong there, Janey. There could be snow on the hills. You got enough coal for your fire?'

'I've got plenty, but thank you for asking all the same.'

'So how you finding it, you being here all on your tod? It must be getting a bit lonely.'

'Don't you worry about me, Mr Ashbourne. I'm snug as a bug in my little cottage and whilst I miss my Sarah and the young un's, I can't say as I mind having some space to myself, if I'm honest. I can get on with things without them under my feet all day.'

Her daughter Sarah, grand-daughter Rachel and great-grandaughter Daisy had all travelled by train to Liverpool the previous Saturday. Sarah's husband, Derek Lake, was back in the port after four months away at sea for a short spell of shore leave.

'You heard from Sarah?'

'A postcard. They're all having a lovely time. Not that they say much on a postcard, mind.' They both laughed. 'Well, it's nice for them to get together as a proper family once in a while. They've taken two rooms for the duration while he's back in Liverpool. It's better that way.'

'They're not coming over here?' Earnshaw asked.

'No, me duck. Derek's got to be back out again in just over a week or so. It's not worth their while. And besides...' She made a significant pause as her eyes met Earnshaw's. 'There's no space here for him and Sarah. No privacy - if you take my meaning. Remember he's not had his hands on Sarah for months!' She winked. 'Not that you'd know anything about any of that, Master Earnshaw!' She and Ashbourne laughed, and Earnshaw felt his cheeks burn.

'So, are you courting yet? Don't tell me you haven't seen a pretty girl to catch your eye.' Palmer grinned, showing a row of wonky nicotine-stained teeth in the gloom. She had a rollie tucked behind an ear but was notoriously mean in her smoking habits and despite Ashbourne lighting up, she declined to join him.

'Well, I, um...'

'Oh, get away with you! A strapping lad like you should have all the girls fighting over you. You need to get yourself scrubbed up and a decent hair cut and get out on a Friday night.' Despite her advanced years, her voice was strong and carried considerable force as she stood beside the steps of their engine, head uplifted, white curly hair framed surprisingly elegantly by the round metal form of the helmet, the strap secured tightly around a narrow but strongly defined chin. There was a playful twinkle in her eyes around which crows foot creases crinkled, implying this was a face well-used to smiling. The set of her mouth however, suggested he take heed of her advice.

'I do. That is, I go out and -,' Earnshaw felt a sudden urge to blurt out a secret as yet untold - even to his best friend Simon. He felt a curious connection between himself and Old Janey, specifically because of her jibes about his lack of a girlfriend, and he knew that when the time was right he would gladly share the news with her almost before he did with anyone else. Discretion sensibly kicked in however, and he held his tongue. It was too soon to go broadcasting a word about the lovely bus conductress working the route that took him to and from work.

'Nothing to report yet, Mrs Palmer!' Earnshaw hoped his reply was firm enough to put a lid on this line of questioning and he was grateful for the distraction of guard Timmerman approaching along the side of the track with a carton of eggs and a pack of butter to pass across. He retreated back into the cab to check his water levels.

Two visits to the cinema with Miss Candy Darling was not information to be shared with a chatterbox crossing keeper. Her disarmingly charming name alone was enough to send a delightful shiver down his spine. Miss Darling lived up to her name too, with bright blue eyes and her blond ponytail worn with a cap at a jaunty angle and that well-tailored conductress' uniform that hinted at the delights of her young body beneath. He felt his heart quicken at the memory of his hand slipping into Candy's for the first time. He felt a sudden jab of frustration that his driver was almost certainly going to dawdle here a few minutes longer. Earnshaw was itching to be back on shed as soon as possible and disposing of the engine, then cycling back home like the wind to wash and scrub himself as clean of as much coal dust, oil and grease as warm water and Swarfega would allow, before meeting Miss Darling for a quick drink. But only if they could beat last orders and it was going to be tight.

A few minutes later, driver Ashbourne gave a little 'pop' on the whistle and the old engine hissed into motion and gently chuffed across the road for their last wagon drop of the day. They would return about an hour later with a train of empties, but Earnshaw silently cheered when he heard his driver tell Old Janey they'd steam straight through on the way home so she was not standing about in the cold wind longer than needed.

He still might make that rendezvous.

Chapter Four

Richard Charlton looked at his watch for what must have been the hundredth time. Was it possible for the minutes to pass so slowly? The watch was a reliable timekeeper, because every driver needed a watch that kept good time, but he was starting to wonder if it was running slow. His stomach churned unpleasantly. There was a taste of bile in his throat. The waiting was getting to him and the longer this went on, the more tense he was becoming. It would be better to just get it over and done with.

Charlton walked around his engine one more time, idly fiddling with corks securing oiling points that needed no attention, testing drain cocks that required no testing. Deploying an oily rag for no purpose other than to look busy. He had to act naturally. Do nothing unusual. Just do what he always did, so nobody would suspect a thing. He kept repeating this like a rosary, and yet the more he tried to look relaxed and at ease, the more forced and artificial he was convinced he appeared. He'd not felt this self-conscious since standing before the altar of St Martin's church dressed in a new suit and a shirt with a starched collar that rubbed his neck, whilst he anxiously awaited the arrival of Miss Lucy Barwell and her father. That was ten years ago now, but he'd soon relaxed afterwards with a few pints and a slap-up meal with his blushing bride beside him. He felt a rush of guilt and fear as he realised he could still smell the scent of that other young body and her perfume. He couldn't seem to mask that maddening scent that drove him wild with desire no matter how much his clothes reeked of steam engine and heavy machine oils, no matter what his scrubbed and rubbed into his skin to cleanse it. Why could he not bring to mind the soft smell of his wife's freshly washed hair or remember her perfume?

He scowled and aggressively attacked a greasy stain for no reason other than something to do, but then impatiently tossed the oily rag aside with a low curse and glanced at the big Potts clock high on the shed wall, seeking a second opinion to his wristwatch. Two minutes gone. By rights he should clock off and get on his way home. He was on earlies tomorrow and there was no reason to linger. He'd had a long day on the footplate of his faithful old engine and would be back with her before he knew it. Another knot twisted in his gut as he realised that the next time he put his hand on the regulator of number 58143, he'd have done it. For better or worse.

Quite possibly for worse.

He cursed himself yet again for his foolishness. He should forget the whole stupid idea and hurry home to sit contentedly by the fire with the paper, whilst Paloma and Billy entertained them both with tales of their day at school and his missus made them dinner. He closed his eyes for a moment, but instead of a vision of this blissful domestic scene, all he could see was the almost naked body of a quite different young mother.

He shook his head, trying, but failing, to rid himself of this memory. If he shied away now, there would be consequences. He'd been made very much aware of what would happen. Of course, he could try to deny everything; deny he'd done little more than foolishly flirt and perhaps exchange an unwise kiss or two with a lonely young woman desperate for company – it was nothing! He would deny everything else. Lucy would be furious of course, but the storm would blow over. He would insist it was just a momentary lapse of reason and hope that would be the end of it. He was a senior driver with a spotless record. He was a popular family man about town, with a decent house kept perfectly by his diligent and hard-working wife. Surely, they would believe his denials and trust his testimony against that of a foolish girl who already had a babe in arms and a husband who'd walked out on her? Look how she dressed! She was tease – a flirt! He was confident there were plenty in the town who disapproved of the way she dressed - even if they spent long enough eyeing her up in forensic detail in order to strengthen their belief she dressed 'shamelessly'.

Charlton leaned his back against his engine and closed his eyes. He knew he was deluding himself. He was guilty. He was an older, supposedly wiser, family man who'd taken what he'd wanted from a vulnerable young woman right under the noses of her mother and grandmother – family friends who'd trusted him. They'd throw the book at him. Lucy would turn him out of the house and who'd argue she was wrong to do so? If he failed in his task tonight, then his secret would be out and his whole world would collapse beyond repair.

He'd made a promise, and it was too late to waver now. Actions had already been set in motion and he could do nothing to stop it now. He just needed to concentrate on how best to do what they'd agreed.

The trouble was, he felt almost helplessly indecisive and it was making him nearly ill. If he was not careful, he might retch his lunch up on the shed floor. *Get a bloody grip, man!* Just walk straight home to the wife and kids. It was what was expected. It was usual and normal and would not arouse suspicion.

Was he able to hide his nerves from the people who knew his moods better than anyone else? Lucy would know straight away something was wrong. She'd ask him what was up and he'd deny there was anything, and in so doing she'd know he really was lying and press the matter further. This would just make everything worse and put him under yet more stress. Having Lucy jumpy would make what he had to do later that bit harder. She'd be suspicious - and watchful. And that was exactly what he was trying to avoid.

Perhaps the pleasant fug of alcohol might help. He sometimes stepped into The Lancaster Arms for a pint and a game of doms with one or other of the lads on the way home. It held a certain appeal, but could he trust himself to handle sitting in public view talking about the coming Saturday football fixtures? A pint might help quieten his stomach, but he was sure he'd betray his jangling nerves to his mates.

He heaved himself into action and checked the sand boxes whilst he prevaricated. One of these was a little low on dry sand. If it was icy or damp tomorrow they might be thankful of a full supply. A walk to the sand drying house behind the shed would buy him a few minutes of activity while he tried to decide how to play out the next hours of waiting.

At that moment his fireman appeared from around the back of the engine. 'A bit low?'

It took Charlton a second to realise that fireman Mitchell was referring to the sand, not his mood. 'A bit. Best be on the safe side.' He lifted the heavy wheel barrow and made as though to push this across the yard, but his fireman intervened.

'I'll do it!' Mitchell stepped closer. 'I asked one of the fitters to take a look at the injector when he gets a chance. It stuck a couple of times today.'

'Aye, I noticed.' Charlton envied the man's ability to look and sound so normal and at ease.

'You get on. I've put her to bed.' Mitchell was referring to their engine. Coaled, watered, smokebox cleaned out and the fire raked to a thin bed and left to maintain a little gentle heat ready to be fired up for action when they clocked back on at 3.40am tomorrow.

Charlton hesitated, feeling foolishly annoyed at having this job snatched from his grasp at a time when he was desperate for something purposeful to hide his mental torment. But Mitchell was right. The fireman could hump the heavy barrow laden with metal canisters across the yard to collect the hot and dry sand. That was what he did most days and he could jolly well do it now. It made little sense forcing the issue, and once again Charlton had to remind himself not to do anything to arouse suspicion. He gave a grunt and lowered the barrow down to the ground.

'See yer tomorrow.'

Charlton made a non-committal answer and sloped off.

Chapter Five

The Reverend Vignoles took a moment to choose a walking stick from a collection jumbled amongst a number of furled umbrellas standing in a highly-polished brass shell case by the vicarage front door. This was a relic from the Great War and yet it managed to sit comfortably within the quiet domestic setting of the vicarage hallway without introducing too discordant a note. He'd once managed to force a slightly stilted sermon out of seeing the old thing gleaming in the corner of their hall, arguing there was a lesson to be learned in turning a weapon of destruction into, if not quite a ploughshare, then at least a harmless domestic object.

The Rev Vignoles didn't really need a stick to aid walking as he was still fit and could easily manage the four or so miles he and his son Charles were about to embark upon. However, he liked a nicely weighted stick in his hand to mark the beat of his stride and to swish away stands of stinging nettles or the over-reaching arms of thorns. In late summer, he might use it to help draw down enticing clumps of blackberries on otherwise out-of-reach fronds, and at any time of year would use it to point out landmarks or distant buzzards circling above the woods.

'The fox, today I think.' He felt the smooth polished wood of the carved fox head at the end of what had been intended for use as a shepherd's crook. He'd taken a fancy to it on a stall at a County Show before the last war. 'It's probably my favourite.'

Charles Vignoles smiled whilst wrapping a woollen scarf around his neck and buttoned his woollen coat tight. With gloves on and hat in place, he opened the front door to let his father through, but as an afterthought, swiped up another stick for his own use. This one was more ostentatious in a black hardwood with a silver ferrule and moulded boss. It was narrow and more like something a staff sergeant might take on parade, but Vignoles felt in the mood to join his father in some swishing of undergrowth.

They headed towards a favourite footpath at the bottom of the village of Dunton Bassett, where the former Great Central Railway drove its straight, double-tracked way along the bottom of the gently rolling vale and where soft violet mists were gathering between the hedgerows and copses of trees and pooling near the entrance to a tunnel. It was raw, and gusts of wind were tossing the high branches of the trees around the church and sending loose papery leaves scuttling about, but both men needed a breath of bracing air and were used to winter walks in failing light.

'I can see a tell-tale drift of steam, Charles.' The foxy stick got its first use almost before they'd lost sight of the vicarage front gate as the almost luminescent glow of steam was pointed out. 'We might strike the bridge in time to see what's on the front!'

'Righty-o.' Vignoles was only too happy to set off downhill at a good pace, not only to get the circulation going, but because he wanted to at least identify the class of locomotive if perhaps not to collect the number in the failing light.

They stepped onto Station Road in time to hear the engine churning away on the front of a very long train of four-wheeled open wagons.

'One of those new Standard Class 5's, if I'm not mistaken.' Like most English vicars, the Reverend Vignoles took a healthy interest in all things railway related. His ability to identify a class of engine or the origins of ancient coaching stock rivalled, indeed continually informed, his son's. 'Quite handsome in a rugged, utilitarian sort of way. I didn't much take to their appearance at first, feeling them a bit 'European' to my taste, but I find I'm slowly warming to their brutish form.'

'Same here. They're proving powerful and capable engines. *The Railway Magazine* have been quite complimentary and my chum Tim over at Woodford shed is positively drooling over the few he's got close to.' Vignoles stood beside the wooden fence at the side of the road leading up to the over bridge and watched as the green engine stormed beneath, both locomotive and train briefly cocooned in billows of steam pushed down and around the locomotive.

Chapter Five

The two men crossed the bridge to the sound of the rumble and roar and metallic clattering of the apparently numberless empty coal wagons, the sudden bangs and booms they made sounding like a series of explosions inside a metal box. They looked down on Ashby Magna station where a trail of smoke from a chimney pot suggested the station master had a welcoming fire burning in his office and could be guaranteed to have a great pot of tea brewing. They didn't turn down the steps to approach but instead threaded their way through a kissing gate leading into another frost-tinted field behind Dunton Bassett station building, walking a well-trodden path parallel to the main line railway.

Charles had tramped this particular path more times than he'd had hot dinners since he was about seven years old, when his father had first taken up the sinecure at All Saint's. Almost immediately after moving in, the young Vignoles, sometimes with sister Gwen and younger brother Jack in tow, had made this his favourite haunt. He'd spent countless hours in and around the little station and along the path at the top of the embankment watching the regular succession of rumbling freight trains and wailing expresses. It was the perfect vantage point. It was not long before the whole family had discovered this delightful walk that also offered the bonus of extended opportunities for watching passing trains, so both father and son knew the route well and encroaching night caused them little concern with Charles' torch being only occasionally deployed at the trickiest points. They climbed a stile and struck off at an angle from the railway towards the delightfully named hamlet of Willoughby Waterless.

'I wonder what they're burning over there?' Vignoles pointed his polished black stick towards a flickering glow of a bonfire behind some trees.

'Ah. Now I can tell you about that.' the Rev. Vignoles stopped and leaned heavily upon the carved fox as if suddenly weary, even though they had barely started their walk. 'Farmer Wilcox and his men have been busy. That's Waterless Manor Farm land. They've been at it for weeks. I do feel for them.'

Vignoles had just finished wiping his glasses with a clean hankie and was now squinting at the distant fire. 'Busy making bonfires?'

'Pyres more like. Poor mites. It's the rabbits. You may have read about the terrible affliction that is sweeping the land like a plague?'

'Myxomatosis?'

'That's it.' They continued walking as they talked, it being too cold to stand for long. 'The diseased ones are blind or close to it and have the most unpleasant sores and disfigurements. Its rather stomach turning when you see one with their white milky eyes. They struggle to feed and so they just sit and wait to die. They seem to prefer not to return to their burrows. I suppose they somehow know not to spread the hideous disease to the others.'

'It's highly contagious?'

'Very much so. It's set to wipe out millions of them in the next year or two. So they just sit there. Slowly dying in abject misery. Even the foxes don't want to pick off diseased animals. It's a slow and ugly death.'

Vignoles could smell the fire on the air. A curious blend of charring meat and burning fur. 'They're collecting the corpses and disposing of them?'

'Not only collecting. Farmer Wilcox and his lads hurry the inevitable process along. They put the things out of their misery every evening.' Rev Vignoles looked at Charles. 'They're country folk and used to beasts and their slaughtering, and I suppose they have to be pretty dispassionate about life and death, but this Mixy business is grim.'

Vignoles was silent. They were closer now and he could see the silhouette of a thin young man with a pitch fork turn the bonfire over, releasing tall fingers of flame and a stronger stench of burning bunny as he did so. 'There are so many?'

'Hundreds. Perhaps thousands around here alone. They say there are millions infected all over the land, so you can see why the farmers cannot just let them rot in the fields.'

'The buzzards must be thriving.'

'A fringe benefit. If only we still had the red kites around here...'

The two men walked on, both silent and thoughtful for a few minutes. They continued towards Willoughby Waterless with an increased pace, eager to leave the burning behind them. A distant wail of another train gave an excuse to swap a few gentle observations about the railway, but inevitably, the subject of the death of Michael Darlow forced itself back.

It was impossible to escape the tragic loss that had so recently visited their family.

Mike Darlow had married Gwen, the eldest of the three Vignoles children, and was father to Maurice, now a somewhat withdrawn and confused fourteen-year old struggling to come to terms with the sudden loss of his father through cancer. Mother and son were presently staying at the Vicarage whilst the funeral arrangements were made for the coming Saturday, and the family had rallied around to help Gwen and Maurice face up to their new situation. It was going to be a desperately muted Christmas with a heavy cloud hanging above the vicarage, but all had agreed they would do their level best to make this festive season – usually anticipated with considerable pleasure and excitement by Vignoles's and Darlows alike – as uplifting as was decently possible. Mike would expect nothing less. Indeed, he had almost commanded both wife and son in his last hours on this earth that they don't let his passing 'ruin their Christmas'. It was going to take a truly super-human effort by all to fulfil that tear-stained promise.

Attempting to rise to the challenge however, Anna Vignoles who had travelled down with her husband, had decreed that since 'Stir-it-up-Sunday was fast approaching', they would set to work making 'the biggest and best Christmas pudding the vicarage has ever seen!' She was last observed busy marshalling the others into action in the kitchen, with even a reluctant Maurice enticed to join them with the promise of aromatic pudding making and other edible delights, working their spell. The pudding might end up untouched on Christmas day, but that wasn't the point. Doing something pleasing and in a group in the warmth of the vicarage kitchen was what was needed at this moment. Both Vignoles and his father felt it wise to make their excuses and leave them to it.

As they passed through a kissing gate, they could see house lights twinkling around the little hamlet of Willoughby Waterless, with one already displaying a red, yellow and blue necklace of Christmas fairy lights draped around a tree.

'Gwen seems to be bearing up pretty well.' The tread of feet on grass starting to harden with frost punctuated the Rev. Vignoles' words. 'She's a strong girl, but I worry it's just not properly hit home yet.'

Vignoles agreed. 'I don't suppose any of us have quite taken it in.

There's still that sensation of adrenaline coursing through one's veins that the shock of death causes.'

'I thought he'd make until next spring at least. He seemed to rally a few weeks back and I suppose we all got our hopes up. It'll be sometime in the middle of January when the blues - for want of a better medical term - take hold of Gwen. We need to keep an eye on your sister and be ready to help.'

'And need to be careful not to appear nannying. Gwen won't like that. Not one bit of it. She's an independent spirit and won't have us fussing. Saying that, Anna and I can offer other kinds of help. With emergency funds if needed.' Another swish of his stick to swipe away arching fronds of brambles that were threatening to hook into their clothes. 'Just to help tidy her over until she can find work and get herself straight. We don't want her worrying about money. That's the last thing she needs at a time like this.'

'I'm surprised she agreed to that, Charles.'

'She hasn't exactly,' Vignoles replied. 'We've not quite broached the subject yet.' They'd stopped for a moment whilst he filled his pipe. He continued to speak whilst giving the now glowing tobacco a few puffs to get it properly burning. 'We'll talk it all through once we get past the funeral - and Christmas.' Vignoles was sounding less confident the longer he spoke. He could cross-question a villain but talking to his sister about financial help filled him with dread.

'Good luck with that!' The Rev. Vignoles smiled. 'But it's kind of you both. We'll do the same, of course. Even if she rebuffs us all, at least she knows we're here as a back stop.' There was a companionable silence to a few moments, as they listened to a hooting tawny owl. 'I'm perhaps more concerned about Maurice. He's awfully withdrawn. Almost silent at times.'

'Only to be expected. It's been a beastly time for him. He'll come around given a little time and support.' Vignoles was all too familiar with the symptoms shown by people receiving a nasty shock. He'd knocked on too many doors and seen their anxious faces lose hope watched as a greyness and almost deathly stillness take hold as he delivered the news nobody wants to hear. 'Is it going to be strange taking the service on Saturday?'

They were now leaving the hamlet having walked a virtual semi-circle around the few streets. The pungent smell of winter silage and warm beasts was emanating from an ancient brick barn.

'No, I think I shall be fine. I can pretty much take it in my stride. It's part and parcel of my job and I've done my share of them for people I've known and cared about. I'm grateful to be able to do one last thing for Mike. To be perfectly frank, having to take the service is a kind of blessing. I can handle meeting his parents and relatives that bit more easily in my pastoral role. It means I have a job to do, so I'm not just standing about eating sandwiches and feeling awkward and gloomy.' The Rev. Vignoles nonetheless sighed perceptibly and gave a little shake of the head. 'I have a suspicion we've lost an unsung hero.' He gave Vignoles a sidelong glance before continuing. 'Mike would never talk about his war work. But from the little scraps he allowed, I got the impression he did some important stuff. He was one of those secretive chaps working away on things about which we knew nothing, but which helped us win the war.'

'One of those Marlene Dietrich sang about,' Vignoles added. 'I tried to get him to open up a number of times, but he said he'd signed the Official Secrets Act and this was binding, and that was that. Not even with family. I think it was something in Radar and aircraft detection. It's a darned shame none of us will ever know now, especially Maurice. Now he'll take his story to the grave.'

They were heading across another set of fields towards Ashby Magna where they would then walk back up to the vicarage along the gas lit main road.

'And how is your work, Charles?'

'All quiet on the Western Front at the moment, which means I can take some time away from the office and not fret they need me. They're just down the line, so I can soon be back in if needed. But anything landing on my desk can be handled by the more than capable Trinder.'

'He's a good egg, your sergeant.'

'He is. Just the man to have minding one's back.'

'You'd miss him if he left.'

Vignoles darted a sudden look at his father. 'I will. He'll be a hard man to replace.' He swatted some dank grasses aside with his stick. 'It will do him no harm to hold the fort for now. Let him gain confidence directing the team and only call me in if he needs a higher authority to sanction something. So far I've not heard a dicky bird.' Vignoles puffed on his pipe and grinned. 'Righty-o, should we head straight back and see how that pudding is shaping up, or do we have time for a swift pint in the 'Arms'?'

Chapter Six

Mickey McMullen walked with the measured tread of a man who spent his life moving relentlessly from one unfixed abode to another. Going nowhere and with nowhere in particular to go and unable to stay for long when he found a place to lay his head. No matter how much his tired feet complained, no matter how much he wanted rest, he was continually moved along. If on occasion he received a friendly greeting or an offer of a cup of tea or – happy, happy day – a bowl of warm soup and a place to sleep, he was still expected to be gone as soon as possible in the morning. Don't linger. Just the one night, mind, then leave and don't darken these doors again.

So he tramped the endless days, up and down and around the same weary circuit, carefully judging how frequently he could reappear without becoming an active nuisance. If he was at least tolerated (which usually meant being studiously ignored rather than actively abused) he knew not to lean too hard on folk. They soon tired of his craggy and weather-beaten face, of his nicotine-stained beard and greasy hair and of his bad teeth and foul breath. When folk tired of a tramp, they turned spiteful. They neglected to keep the fiercer dogs tied up as he passed by, content to let the snarling beasts do an unpleasant job on their behalf, sending him running, his already tattered clothes ripped by sharp teeth.

Other times, tell-tale stones skipped on the ground near his feet, tossed by children taught to mistrust beggars. They lacked the courage to aim for the back of his head, but their eyes still launched daggers of displeasure and fear. No such luck with the gangs of young men who called out vile names and sometimes squared up to him, goading him to retaliate so they could show how brave they were to the girls who stood and watched. It was worse in the night when these arrogant youths rolled back from the pub and were all too quick to throw punches and try to trip him over so his head could become a football to kick. There was no explaining why his sleeping body should be a convenient place to urinate...

McMullen often tramped along the little railway. Day or night, as this way he ensured the minimum of human contact until he was ready to turn off the line and head into a township. He was particularly familiar with the sleepy 'Swanney' and knew, even without a watch that worked (for the scratched old thing on his wrist permanently declared it was nine forty-six) when each infrequent train was due. At the approach of a train he would step well aside and sit or lean against the fence that edged the single track to let it pass. In the summer he might choose to lounge amongst the tall fragrant grasses and flowers and watch the trains for want of anything better to do. As long as he was not obviously encroaching on the running line as they trundled by, the crews tolerated his presence. One of two would even sometimes toss a stick of chewing gum or a cigarette in his direction or at least offer a friendly greeting. It was not much, but any act of kindness counted.

'Stand well clear and don't let us *ever* see you walking on the line. That way we'll act like we didn't notice. Keep out of harm's way and don't even *think* about tampering with anything or else the Transport Police will be down on you like a ton of bloody bricks!' That was what one of the more senior guards had once told him, and McMullen knew not to chance his luck. A homeless man who once hailed from the Emerald Isle and had so far survived several winters with what he called the 'Luck of the Irish', knew how fragile a thing luck could be.

And so, his feet felt their way onto each greying wooden sleeper of the line as the dark of night slipped down the embankments in an icy draft and crept silently across the fields to lurk amongst the bushes, leaving just the stones of the permanent way to act as his guide; a pale greyness by which to steer him onwards. The awkwardly spaced sleepers required short and uncomfortable strides, but McMullan was used to the shuffling gait it demanded because his boots could no longer take the pounding on the sharp stones of the ballast. With no particular destination in mind and nobody waiting for his arrival, he ambled slowly, mechanically, as if in a daze. The very act of moving each complaining leg was all that mattered.

Left, right, left, right... Each painful step staved off the insidious cold that was snapping at his toes through paper thin and loosening soles.

Old Janey might stand me a cup of something warm.

McMullen was talking softly as he walked, as if maintaining a dialogue with an invisible friend.

I'm sure she would. And if she's in the right frame of mind, she'll maybe see her way to a slice of bread and a bit of cheese. Ah, she's a good old girl at heart. It's just a shame she never took up smoking, more's the pity of it!

Because I could murder for a fag.

Correction.

He actually stopped for a moment, as if wanting to reinforce the point he was making to his imaginary companion. *I could, as God's my witness, actually murder for a pint of beer and a fag. Sitting beside a warm fire. Although thinking on, if God was watching, murder would be a mighty foolish thing to do...*

He recommenced his slow, agonising walk.

It might be worth a try though... Now, when was it you last supped some beer?

His voice was soft and did not carry far, qualities that probably served to prolong his prospects of survival, because if few enough people loved a tramp, none liked a tramp who talked to himself. But it helped pass the time as he plodded his way towards the distant pinpoints of lights that marked Black Spinney Crossing.

All alone on a single line. Up ahead, just two white-painted crossing gates and a solitary house set within a swathe of undulating fields backing onto the mass of trees that formed the Black Spinney itself whilst the serpentine meanderings of Rothley brook, burbled quietly some distance away on the other side. Apart from the occasional rumble of heavy coal trains passing on the far busier Burton to Leicester line that curved away on its raised embankment far beyond the brook, there was little to disturb the peace. The Sparkenhoe Manure works in the far distance cast a glimmer of light into the night sky, but otherwise there was nothing but black night all around. The lane that crossed the line at Black Spinney was infrequently travelled and then usually only by lorries during the day coming to collect bags of manure. Hours might pass with barely more than a GPO van or the district nurse doing her rounds in a grey Morris Minor.

So quiet was this stretch of goods line in deepest Leicestershire, that McMullen jumped, as if he'd inadvertently touched an electric fence, when the dark shape of a figure moved some way ahead.

Jesus! He nearly frightened the very life out of me!

His finely-honed survival instincts kicked in and McMullen had barely spoken the words aloud. It was possible he'd not yet betrayed himself.

It was the slight glimmer of light from the manure works that allowed him to observe the movement. Someone had shifted their weight from one foot to another. Whoever it was had stopped moving now and could easily be mistaken for a slim shrub or sapling.

But then came the tell-tale glow of a cigarette.

Now why would he be standin' there of all places?

McMullen was keeping his thoughts to himself as he edged closer, taking gentle, measured steps on the wooden sleepers.

It was a man wearing a hat as he could just make out the sharp angle of the brim. The hat wearer was smoking whilst apparently waiting for someone or something. True, there was train due, but these hadn't carried passengers along this section of line since before the war, so the man was going to be mightily disappointed if he'd expected to get aboard. Even if they did take passengers, this was a strange place to wait. A long a stretch of open line with no obvious landmarks, let alone a platform, and in the pitchy dark. Perhaps the hat wearer knew one of the crew and this was a pre-arranged rendezvous? But then why not wait beside the crossing gates, as that way old Janey could flag the train down with her lamp.

No. The man could not be waiting for the train and was not expecting to be seen by the crew.

So what *was* he doing?

McMullen's flapping boot sole caught a stone and it pinged away with a sound like cut glass. The watcher instantly turned his indistinct face towards the sound, like the swivelling of an owl's head.

'Who's there?'

'Just me, mindin' my own business.' There was little point in pretence now he'd given the game away and McMullen had little choice but to face the stranger head on and hope for the best.

Silence. The cigarette glowed and then came the sigh of breath being exhaled.

To Hell with it. The man might offer him a smoke at least. But McMullen steeled himself for abuse as he drew close. He sensed tension in the air. Or was that just his own sour body and clothes reeking? 'It's a cold night to be standing by the railway!'

The man's face was just a pale oval. 'And for walking a railway line.' His voice was flat and emotionless. Cautious.

'And I'd rather be inside, beside a nice warm fire with a pint in my hand if I had the choice.' The man didn't answer. The trees creaked as the wind started to gust through the branches. Dried leaves skittered across the stones. 'Now you wouldn't have another cigarette on you by any chance?'

The man still said nothing, but there was the sound of a carton being opened and then a thin pale shape was touched to the end of his own lighted cigarette. The man dragged it into life then handed it across, but the tiny red glow threw insufficient light for McMullen to get any idea of what the man looked like. He took his first delicious inhalation of smoke. 'Are you alone?'

'Of course.' The response was instant.

There was no 'of course' about it. McMullen was no fool and his mind was quick and sensed something was wrong. 'So what brings you here then?'

'None of your business.'

'Suit yourself. Waiting for someone?'

'What if I am?'

'Not for a train I hope!' McMullen laughed, hoping to lighten the mood.

'Of course not.'

'Do I know you at all? Your voice is somehow familiar.'

'You don't. I've never been here before.'

McMullen sensed the man was deliberately altering the timbre of his voice. Trying to disguise it. 'I just feel like I know your voice. It reminds me of someone - but I can't quite bring them to mind.' McMullen was staring at the indistinct pale blur of the man's face, but this was now part turned away and he could not recognise the features.

'Some people would do well to be less nosey.'

'I meant no harm, I'm sure.' McMullen took the hint but was intrigued.

A few moments of silence fell in which they both smoked. 'I've got friends on the farm coming across with a tractor and trailer to meet me.' The man didn't elucidate further as to why they would be doing this; nor why they had chosen this most curious spot; nor why he'd chosen to climb over the fence and stand near the railway where he would surely be out of their sight.

'Then I'd be walking to their farmhouse. It beats standin' here. One field looks much like another in the dark and they might miss you,' McMullen chuckled. The nicotine was putting him in a good mood. What did he care why the man wanted to stand in the wind or make his voice sound funny.

'Where are you going?'

'To find somewhere to sleep. A barn or a nice cosy hedge.'

'It's not a night to be out.' Something about his voice made this sound more like a warning than friendly advice. The waiting man's cigarette was tossed aside, still alight and far from burned to a stub. McMullen carefully eyed where it landed. It was enough for an emergency fix later.

'I'll be off.'

'You do that.' Again, the comment did not feel reassuring.

McMullen peered into the gloom as the man faded away into the shadows. Nothing about his story made sense. It sounded like a pack of lies. His survival instincts told him to be wary of people who acted oddly and lied. Most people were surprisingly straight forward in their actions and he found it easy to anticipate what they would do next. But this man was a puzzle, and he was sure he'd met him before, but couldn't think where. Nothing about this encounter was right and McMullen wondered if the mysterious hat wearer was alone. That was an alarming thought. He could perhaps handle one man if he turned nasty, but two was a different story. It really was time to hurry on and get away. He'd give the chance of a mug of tea with Old Janey a miss for tonight and press on and find somewhere to get out of the weather and get his head down.

His luck was wafer thin at the best of times and now was not the time to test it.

Chapter Seven

The Gorse, in the railway town of Woodford Halse was a favourite for detective sergeant John Trinder and his wife Violet on the rare occasions they could come out together. It was a large mock-Tudor construction with the lower walls built of golden local ironstone and the upper storey black-painted exposed timbers and white plaster in-fill and diamond paned windows, built at the height of Edwardian optimism in a mock-Elizabethan style. It contained many rooms and a couple of bars and formed the railwaymen's social club, and as such was the primary social hub of the town.

Getting 'down the Gorsey' was not as easy as had once been possible for the Trinders, as their four-year old son Robbie demanded that one of them remain at home. A night out was only possible if they could call upon Violet's daughter Jenny to come over and babysit, and this evening, both Jenny and her husband, Tom Rigby had been more than happy to oblige.

'It's kind of you to both to offer. With you expecting, it won't be possible to make the most of your services once you have your own babe in arms, eh!' Violet had made this observation whilst greeting the young couple and inviting them into their cosy back kitchen.

'Don't worry, we'll just ask for the same in return,' Jenny replied, cheekily. Violet laughed, but her husband momentarily had a strange look in his eyes as if something was troubling him. However, in the excited bustle of the young couple's arrival and their own preparations for leaving, nobody noticed, and it passed.

'Robbie's asleep, but if he wakes you can get some practice for the even more demanding toddler phase...'

'Mother, *please*! Slow down. There's another six months to go yet before this one's even born, let alone toddling!'

'The time will soon fly,' Violet smiled.

'Although maybe not as quickly as you might wish it to when awakened in the middle of the night...' observed Trinder, with a knowing wink towards Tom Rigby. The young man was already filling the kettle to make some tea for Jenny whilst gratefully eyeing up the bottle of beer, bottle opener and clean glass neatly laid out on the table for his enjoyment.

'An evening out together and some music laid on too!'

Trinder was delighted, as he raised his pint glass to Violet a short while later. The bar was pleasantly full, but they managed to get good seats close to the well-banked fire (courtesy of the abundant coal supplies in a small town graced with a huge locomotive depot). He supped his beer and savoured the taste as Violet did the same with a double G & T.

'Much as I dote on Robbie, it'll be nice when he's old enough to let us do this more often.'

'There's a while to wait yet, John.'

'True. I sometimes think this place could take a more relaxed attitude to allowing little one's inside in the evenings.'

'You're not questioning the rule of law, are you?' Violet laughed.

'I follow the rules right enough, but there's no harm in wondering if some laws couldn't do with modifying.'

'The law's an ass. Now who said that?'

'Not sure. I bet the Guv'nor would know.'

Violet took another sip of gin whilst the musicians settled themselves down and check the tunings of their acoustic instruments. It was going to be a night of traditional folk music. 'I really must give Anna a telephone call. It feels like simply ages since we spoke properly. I wonder how they are doing? A death in the family is always hard.'

'You know how he is. He seems to take everything in his stride and doesn't give much away.'

'I imagine he feels different to how he appears on the surface.'

'Fair comment.' Trinder paused and reflected a moment before carrying on. 'His taking time off work is unusual. It's unheard of. Apart from summer and Christmas holidays, of course.'

'I think that says a lot. Don't be too quick to assume he's unaffected just because he maintains an air of professionalism. Gwen and he are close, and whilst I never got the impression Charles had an awful lot in common with his brother-in-law, he'll still feel it. Then there's the son.' Violet paused and gave a little shake of the head. 'What age is he now?'

'Fourteen, I think.'

'And already without a father. Its desperately sad.'

They both exchanged glances and thoughtfully supped more of their drinks whilst the fiddle player launched into a series of jaunty jigs, the others joining in as they warmed themselves and everyone else up for the main event.

'I can't remember exactly, but Gwen's husband can't have been much over fifty?' Trinder tried to remember. 'Probably less, come to think of it. It puts everything into perspective. We have to take what we can from life.'

'I'll drink to that. *Carpe diem*!'

They raised their glasses. 'Here's to making the most of every moment.'

'As we are now.' Violet smiled and settled deeper into her chair.

'I just hope I don't get a call out.' Trinder frowned momentarily. 'I've given Blencowe and Benson the number here - just in case. They can hold the defences until tomorrow, I'm sure.'

'So, you're in charge!' Violet smiled. 'You won't disturb Charles even if there is a shout?'

'No fear. He said only to bother him before next Tuesday if there was a murder!' Trinder replied, with a laugh.

'Thankfully, they're thin on the ground.'

'My only concern is fending off the Badger if he makes one of his surprise visits or demands me on the telephone.'

'Just do what your Guvnor does and pretend to listen, agree to everything and then carry on as usual,' Violet replied.

Trinder laughed again, took a deep draught of beer then carefully set his pint on a small table. He sat up straight, took a breath and looked as though he was about to say something important, but at that moment there was a ripple of applause as the singer walked to centre stage whilst the band ended their set of up-tempo jigs and reels.

She was a young and slender woman with long brown hair worn in a ponytail and dressed in a figure-hugging black roll-neck sweater and an ankle length skirt of heavy green velvet. Silver-coloured metal jewellery brought a dash of the chic to her look, suggesting that when she was not participating in the folk revival movement, she could be just as happy singing jazz in a trendy night club. The double bass player was also dressed in black and had glasses with heavy rectangular frames, which was again a nod to the jazzier side of the musical divide. The fiddle and squeezebox players were more obviously men of the folk tradition being older, grizzlier and looking as though they'd just spent a hard day ploughing. Or thwacking diseased rabbits. Perhaps both.

Violet had noticed her husband's actions prior to this intervention and raised a questioning eyebrow towards him whilst the band started their first proper song of the evening. Her husband however seemed to have lost interest in whatever he was going to say and stood up. 'There's a gap at the bar. I'll refresh our drinks and then we can sit tight and enjoy the set.'

As he placed his order, the young singer caught his attention by mentioning that the first song they were going to perform was notable for being the earliest attempt to describing something close to a murder investigation.

Intriguing. He met Violet's eyes across the pub as she silently mouthed 'how appropriate,' and rolled her eyes. The band stuck up.

It was Hankey the Squire as I've heard men say,
Who rode out a-hunting on one Saturday.
They hunted all day but nothing they found,
But a poor murdered woman laid on the cold ground.

About eight o'clock, boys, our dogs they throwed off,
On Leatherhead Common, and that was the spot.
They tried all the bushes but nothing they found,
But a poor murdered woman laid on the cold ground...

It was slow and sombre but had a good rhythm and the melody was strangely alluring. The singer's voice was tremulous and not as rich as Trinder would have preferred, but she was a compelling performer and managed to convey the mood of the sinister discovery. The unfolding story was also catching the ears of those crowded around the bar and slowly all chatter subsided as faces turned to watch the young woman weave her spell. Hands gripped pints held half raised, but nobody supped. The barmaid quietly poured a pint whilst Trinder's police mind was already wondering what Hankey the Squire would do next.

...They tried all the bushes but nothing they found,
But a poor murdered woman laid on the cold ground.

They mounted their horses and they rode off the ground,
They rode to the village and alarmed it all around.
"It is late in the evening, I'm sorry to say,
She cannot be removed until the next day..."

Trinder quietly returned to his seat. He loved his music but had never completely fallen for English folk, preferring dance bands and the swing beat of jazz and recently discovered the exciting strains of a wild new sound from the States. However, this song was getting under his skin.

The next Sunday morning about eight o'clock,
Some hundreds of people to the spot they did flock,
For to see that poor creature, your hearts would have bled,
Some cold and some violence came into their heads...'

Violet and he exchanged looks. The songwriter had perfectly painted a scene of sightseers wanting the thrill of viewing the corpse of this poor creature. Trinder hoped the squire had at least ensured she was covered by a blanket as she lay through the night. Typical of a policeman to think of the practicalities. And then there was the swell of anger and the urge for retribution amongst those ghoulish gawpers who'd come to stare at the unfortunate victim. He'd witnessed all of this himself in some of the more unpleasant investigations he'd worked on.

So now I'll conclude and I'll finish my song

And those that have done it shall find themselves wrong.
For the last day of Judgement the trumpet shall sound
And their souls not in Heaven I'm afraid won't be found.

The applause was loud.

'That was quite a song.' Violet enjoyed it as much as Trinder. 'Although I have to say Hankey the Squire didn't do very well with his murder enquiry!'

'He didn't have modern forensics.'

'True. He needed dear old Blencowe to make maps and diagrams and plot movements of potential suspects.'

'And Jane and Lucy doing the footslogging.'

'And DCI Vignoles aided and abetted by his trusty sergeant,' Violet gave her husband a cheeky smile across the top of her glass.

'I'm not so sure about the last part.'

'False modesty doesn't suit you, John. You're every bit the detective these days and you're doing well on those training courses. Have you got the exam results yet?'

'No. Not yet.' He sounded oddly flustered but quickly recovered. 'They're rather slow. But I can wait.'

'I'm sure you did brilliantly. You studied hard enough.'

'We'll see.' But Trinder looked strangely ill at ease and was drumming his fingers on the arm of his chair as if nervous. Whatever had caused the shift in mood, it was surely not the fault of the band as they were now busy with an uplifting and slightly rude song about saucy sailors that was causing ripples of laughter around the room. 'I'd be lost without the Guvnor, if I'm honest. I get so far along the line and then hit the buffers. I don't know how he does it, but he looks everything over and finds the way forward, finds that clue that I've completely missed. You have to hand it to him.'

'You need to have more faith in yourself. Trust your intuition and not rely on Charles.'

'It's how it works, Vi. He's the boss. You pass on your findings, he processes it, then acts.'

'Then here's your chance whilst he's on leave. Act on your own judgement and instruct the others and see it through.' Violet had drunk more gin than she was used to and was saying things that were surprising even herself. 'I don't wish anything too awful of course, but perhaps a tricky puzzle to solve these next few days might not be such a bad thing?'

'Careful what you wish for!'

However, Trinder's mind was drifting back to the envelope lying out of sight in his jacket pocket. It was already becoming tired from constant opening and closing as he secretly read and re-read the letter it contained. But he'd showed it to nobody.

Not even his wife.

But it would change their lives forever.

Chapter Eight

A few traces of engine smoke still lingered inside the kitchen and Jane Palmer could hear the locomotive huffing away into the distance as the last train of the day steamed urgently towards Coalville, the red lamp on the back of the guard's van winking as it flickered in the wintry wind. She'd exchanged a friendly wave with Guard Timmerman. Driver Ashbourne had given a short toot on the whistle, and they were gone.

Palmer now rang the block bells to inform the signal box at Desford Junction that the train had passed through. The delicate ting-tings of the bell answered in reply and she knew that Arnold Weatherall, who was on duty that evening, had taken notice. She then sent a different series of coded rings down the line and received another reply in acknowledgement. That was it. She'd signed off for the night. Palmer looked up at the clock on the wall and wrote the exact time in her log book in careful and legible handwriting using an expensive fountain pen filled with blue ink.

This pen was one of the few items in her keeper's cottage of obvious value. This particular writing instrument was one of her most treasured items from her married life and now, as a widow it had taken on even greater significance. A constant reminder of her late husband.

Emmerson Palmer had worked in the railways since leaving school; first as a clerk, then moving across into signalling. Minding a crossing was not one of the more popular jobs and it paid poorly, but when Emmerson married Jane, he found the job suited his temperament and that it was easier to bring up a family with everyone living so close to hand. Added to which, these crossing cottages sometimes came with a decent plot of land that enabled him to grow rows of fruit and vegetables to help keep the family provided for. Once settled in at Black Spinney, he could easily tend his prized veg between answering the bells commanding him to let the trains through. His work required the maintenance of accurate records of all train movements, activities and communications along the line, so a good pen was something he had set much store by. Jane Palmer could vividly recall that memorable Saturday early in their married life, when she and her husband had arranged for relief cover to allow the two to travel into Nottingham and purchase this fine instrument. Not as expensive as some other examples in the shop, but it had still needed the shop assistant to unlock the display cabinet to extract the pen of their choosing. It was certainly a tidy amount to count out on the counter top, their mouths slightly dry at the sight of nearly a week's wages being passed across. However, it came packaged in an elegant dark blue and silver cardboard box with a white satin lining which they had both admired all the way home and which survived to this day, even after nearly forty years of use.

Palmer now carefully replaced the cap on the pen and put it back in the box which always lay open above the ledger in which she recorded the day's workings. This would be the last time she would ever use it.

She gave a quick look out of the window to see if there were any tell-tale headlights of waiting cars held by the gates that barred the way, but as she expected, there were none. There was no need to rush, and so gave the old kettle a quick shake to check there was sufficient water inside and placed this on the hot iron range. By the time she had finished closing the gates across the railway and put away the oil lamps for the night, this would be merrily singing and she could make herself a nice cup of cocoa before turning in.

Palmer pulled on her gloves, and as habit decreed, reached for her trusty warden's helmet and placed it squarely upon her head. A strong gust of wind rattled around the cottage and moaned in the chimney and she thought she heard the garden gate bang. The latch was faulty and often refused to hold fast. Tightening an old and almost colourless scarf around her thin neck, she stepped outside. The wind slapped her in the face, but immediately pulled back as if apologetic for its unwarranted assault. It was a tricksy wind that came and went as it felt fit, the sort of wind that worried away at you and made you anxious to be inside.

She pulled her front door closed and used slightly bent nail retained for that specific use on a length of twine to hold it fast. Since she was in and out all day, this nail was a quick and simple way of ensuring the wind didn't blow the door open and send all her papers flying about. The kitchen, with its huge deal table beneath the window, also served as her office and was filled with neat piles of British Railways communications; working instructions, addendas to working timetables, handbooks, safety notices and all manner of other official documentation, the greater bulk of which had no relevance to herself, Black Spinney crossing, nor indeed to much of this stub of the old Leicester & Swannington branch. The majority of the accumulated paperwork dated back a great many years and was hopelessly out-dated. Palmer however, was a fastidious person and lived in constant fear of her rudimentary filing system being thrown into confusion by a swirling wind or perhaps one of the many wild farm cats straying in and tipping them on to the floor.

Nail in place, she walked towards the big wooden crossing gates that still guarded Rothley Lane. She would need to be careful tonight, as the gates were heavy and this unpredictable wind could pull or push them in an unexpected manner and she must not allow them to crash against the gate posts or send her falling on her back. She unhooked the gate furthest from the cottage and carefully swung it across the line, the long iron bar that locked it in place caught home with a satisfying clonk.

Palmer paused.

What was that?

A sound prompted her to turn and look around. The soft yellow light cast by the great oil lamps on their posts glinted on the cold steel rails leading off into the far distance. The train was long gone. The dusty tarmacadam of the road was also empty and yet she was sure she'd heard someone cough. The spinney trees to her right clattered their branches in the rushing wind. A piece of newspaper floated on the air like a magic carpet, up and down and around it flew before catching on the hedge. Palmer wrinkled her nose. She hated litter and walked across the road and plucked it off the hawthorn hedge. It smelt of fresh vinegar and chip fat. Someone had been eating their fish and chip supper and cast the greasy paper away. Ugh! She crumpled it into a ball and stood at the side of the road wondering what to do with it.

She didn't want to shove it in her coat pocket.

She sighed with impatience, the wind perhaps already putting her in a funny mood. Who had been eating their fish and chips in Rothley Lane on such a night? Irish Mick most likely. She'd seen him shuffling around a little while earlier. If he'd managed to get chips, then that might explain why he'd not knocked on the door as she'd expected him to. Palmer heaved the second gate back across the rails, and was about to secure it in place, when all thoughts of litter-bugging tramps were erased by the startling sight of a man standing between the railway line and her cottage.

His arms hung straight down beside his body with his hands in gloves. He was holding something. A platelayer's tool perhaps. It was hard to see exactly what. He was standing stock still with his back towards her as if he were staring after the long-departed Coalville train. Everything about his demeanour was unnatural and there was a palpable sense of menace about his presence.

Palmer let the gate go, not noticing that it was not quite locked into place.

'You're early!' She had to shout above the wind in the trees.

No answer.

She stood beside the strong gate post, drawing some comfort from its solidity. Not that she was easily scared. You couldn't be of a nervous disposition living and working in such a remote location as this, but even so, there was something not quite right about this man.

'Can I help you?' The figure looked odd. Not whom she'd expected. The way he stood there without moving was unsettling.

'What do you want?' She tried to peer into the night to get a better impression of the man but all she had was his back view. She walked closer. His stance and build seemed faintly familiar now.

'Mr Charlton? Is that you? You gave me quite a start, standing there like that!' She walked more briskly towards him, feeling foolish for her momentary nervousness.

The figure slowly turned around.

She took a sudden intake of breath. She was mistaken. Instead of the familiar face of the engine driver, she was looking at a cloud of white beard around the chin and two deep black, bottomless holes for eyes that bored into her head. He was laughing, but there was no sound or movement to his mouth, just a fixed, imbecilic grin.

'You can't stand there, sir!' This was not first time she'd had to move trespassers along. It was time to take control and sound authoritative.

His face was poorly illuminated by the lamp wicks tormented by the wind, but Palmer felt a queasy sensation of fear claw around her middle. Why was he inanely grinning at her. Perhaps he was crazy.

'Move along now, sir!' She took down one of the oil lamps, keen to appear unflustered, and besides she was getting cold. She wanted to be inside with her cocoa and not wasting time with this strange lunatic. Palmer was glad of her helmet. It gave her presence and offered protection. 'I must ask you to leave the railway premises immediately -.'

He stepped forward so the full glow of the oil lamp in her hand fell on his face which was still locked into an unnatural expression of excessive mirth. Palmer stared, immobilised for a tragic moment by surprise, followed by horror.

She was staring at a mask of Father Christmas. His garishly printed face laughing so his teeth were showing between red painted lips and froth of beard, deep crows foot creases forming at the corners of his eyes with the black punctured holes where his pupils should be.

'Ho, ho, ho!'

A gloved hand raised a wooden handled implement above his shoulder to one the side of his flat face with its stupid grin.

The kettle whistled a shrill warning from inside the kitchen.

Chapter Nine

Graham Hind turned the collar up on his British Railways issue donkey jacket, pulled his cap down harder and hunched his shoulders higher. Head bowed, he trudged at a good pace along the road, dreaming of owning a motorbike, as he did almost every time he made the walk from Ratby to Desford Junction shed. But a track-ganger's wages were meagre and saving anything by the end of the week was hard. On Friday or Saturday night, never both, another pint or maybe two with his mates was appealing, and besides, he deserved it having slogged all week on the railway, even if each precious shilling saved rather than spent on beer would take him that bit closer to buying a motorbike. At least Shank's pony was free...

However, there was talk of a big windfall coming his way. His pal George Baylock had recently got him into a little scheme to earn them both some extra spending money and if it proved to be as regular and the pay as half as good as promised, then he'd soon be able to afford a brand-new bike and more than a few beers on top. Happy days!

Inevitably there was some risk attached with this 'bit on the side', and that was a nagging worry. Georgie had assured him there was nothing to fear if he followed a few simple rules.

'Do as you're told. Don't ask questions and never, ever, discuss anything in public. Keep your head down and your mouth shut, and all will be fine and dandy!'

Fair enough. Hind grinned to himself. So far, it had been easy. A few small sealed packets of something unknown shoved into a sack of railway bolts they were hefting down the line swapped for an envelope of grubby notes at the pre-arranged place. Simple. All under the cover of darkness and with little fuss or bother. It was easy money.

Feeling chipper with these dreams of spending money, he approached Black Spinney Crossing, and was about to continue along Rothley Lane without crossing the railway, when his attention was caught by one of the crossing gates. The night was made yet darker by the heavy clouds threatening snow, but Hind's eyesight was good and had adjusted to the poor light, so the pale, almost ghostly framework of the gate seemed to glow in the dark as it stood at an odd angle, encroaching onto the road.

He slowed his pace and stared hard to make sure. Yes, the gate was swung about a quarter of its travel across the road and even as he watched, it emitted a low groan as the wind alternately tugged and pushed it on its hinges. Not like Old Janey to leave one of the gates unsecured. She was efficient and a stickler for doing things properly. A flicker of something close to apprehension made the hairs on his neck stand up. Something felt wrong.

Hind should just walk over and push it shut. It would take only a moment. All things considered, perhaps he owed Old Janey a favour. Shove it back into place, then hurry along to clock on. Yet something held him back. A sense of doubt and increasing unease was making his stomach flutter. Why was an unsecured gate having this effect? Perhaps because it was hard to believe the dependable crossing keeper had been so careless. The metallic complaint of the hinges was strangely disturbing, like someone moaning in pain. Perhaps it was better to just keep his head down and not meddle in things that were not his business, just as Georgie advised. And besides, he was late. He'd indulged in one too many drinks last night and overslept. No knock-up lad came around his place, as he was too low-down the pecking order for such attention. Worse still, this was not the first time he'd overslept. He was on a very short leash and in danger of getting a roasting - or worse. The foreman had threatened him with losing his job if he was late one more time, and a tale about closing an unsecured crossing gate might sound like a fib when the foreman studied his face and spotted the tell-tale signs of a night of beer and too little sleep. Palmer was surely about the last person likely to leave a gate loose, so that grumpy bastard of a foreman was never going to believe him.

Hind increased his pace and walked on. He needed the work, no matter how poor the pay and his newly found source of illicit income depended on him working on the line. He'd do well to look after himself first and let others take their chances. And besides, Georgie had ordered him to get on shed prompt, as he needed him to make a swift start that morning. There was some 'interesting' work to be done. All said with a nudge and a wink.

It was a deathly quiet road at this time and there'd be nobody driving along here much before Old Janey clocked on at 4am. That thought cheered him. There was no real danger, and now there really was no time to double back and still get to the shed on time. He rammed a ciggie in his mouth, but left it unlit, saving it until he could clock on and get into the shelter of the shed building.

* * * *

3.15am. Sammy Chambers was a scrawny lad with sticking out ears, prominent nose and pudding basin haircut that made him look like the runtish sibling of a Plantagenet king. His hob-nailed boots appeared too big, but actually pinched his unfeasibly large feet and neither the blue overalls and warm winter coat he was wearing seemed to fit properly. It was as if he'd been assembled late on a Friday afternoon shift by parents eager to get the weekend started.

Luckily, it was both dark and nobody was out and about to see this sartorial failure as he furiously peddled his bike that was too small for him with knees pointing outwards whilst hunched low over the handlebars to both help speed his progress and minimise the impact of the east wind. He was sucking the air in through his teeth which made the NHS fillings complain, but this was better than filling his lungs so they hurt. Yet despite the unpleasant hour and the physical discomforts, Chambers was a cheerful soul and was even trying to convert this air filtration system into a whistled version of "Young At Heart". His interpretation was not tuneful, but six months of being the 'knock up boy' had shown that his squeaking bike and his free-form whistling were as effective in stirring sleeping railwaymen as the little pieces of gravel he kept in the bulging and now permanently sagging coat pockets. He used this gravel to toss against the upstairs bedroom windows of each man he must ensure rose in time to make the early shift.

In practice, most railwaymen were so used to the routine they rarely needed waking. Even if they delayed to the last minute before turning on the bedside light and reluctantly pulled themselves away from their wives barely stirring beside them, they were already surfacing from sleep, senses tuning in to the sounds outside their upstairs sash windows, detecting like early warning radar, the distinctive squeak-squeak of his bike and the rattle of his loose rear mudguard and the plaintive rise and fall of whatever song he had chosen to murder that morning.

Clattering down Desford Station Road and onto the High Street without barely a glance to either side, Chambers was already looking for the tell-tale yellow rectangle of back-lit curtains at the upstairs window of Mr Charlton's house.

Richard Charlton was one of the more senior engine drivers and was held in high regard at Desford Junction Shed. It was only a small shed, in truth only a sub-shed to Coalville, but within the rigid hierarchy of footplatemen, Charlton was senior within this modest domaine. Experience had shown that Chambers never needed to deploy any of his small stones against the clean upper window of Charlton's trim little house made of red and dark brown brick in an attractive chequerboard pattern. Chambers was once again both unsurprised and a little relieved that this morning his job was going to be made that bit easier. It might be his duty but rousing a senior railwayman by hurling stones at window glass and calling from the street in the dead of night, felt like an impertinence.

He freewheeled closer with his eyes lifted to the first-floor bedroom window from which came a gentle glow from behind the curtains. He prepared to judge his approach so he could come to a momentary stop and give the heavy cast iron door knocker a quick, but gentle, double rap that would echo in the hallway but not awaken those who could be left to lie a little longer. Charlton had told him a few months back that this was acceptable if he could see the bedroom light was on. There was no need to risk sullying Mrs Charlton's immaculately clean windows unless it was imperative, nor indeed should he disturb her beauty sleep with his hollering.

However, this morning, to his surprise, Chambers could see the senior driver fully dressed and standing outside his closed front door, smoking with those short, almost aggressive, puffs that suggested a man who was anxious or impatient. There was a strange expression on the driver's face, almost one of being caught by surprise.

'Oh. It's you!'

Who else would it be? But Chambers kept this thought to himself. 'Good morning, Mr Charlton!'

The driver grunted and glared at the young man. He didn't seem pleased.

'You're up bright and early, Mr Charlton!'

'None of your business if I am.' The cigarette butt was dropped to the ground and firmly squashed by a heavy boot.

'I'll best be off then!' Time was tight, and Chambers had two more calls and some distance to cover, so he dutifully hurried away, peddling furiously and not unhappy to leave the strangely unfriendly stare of the driver.

If Charlton wanted a bright and early start, so be it. It warranted no further thought. Chambers however could not help but ponder on the look on the driver's face. He'd appeared tired and pale and yet also oddly flushed around the neck. And then there was that look in his eyes. A curious mixture of alarm and something akin to anger. Or fear. It was as if he'd been caught doing something he shouldn't. What could that be? Standing outside his house dressed exactly as usual and having a quick fag before leaving for his early shift - there was surely nothing strange about that.

Far more imperative was the need to dig hard into the pedals and push on to his next knock up and so Chambers pushed these idle thoughts out of his mind and returned to his futile attempt at whistling "Young at Heart".

Chapter Ten

Miss Laura Green parked her bike underneath the wooden steps of Desford Junction signal box and took a moment to readjust her clothes after her brisk cycle from Kirby Muxloe, where she now lived following her recent transfer. Her fingers were stiff and cold despite woollen gloves and moved clumsily, but even though keen to get into the snug warmth of the cabin above, she felt the wish to make herself look more presentable.

Mr Weatherall, whom she was relieving, was a senior signalman with over twenty-three years of experience, and like most of his profession, was a stickler for cleanliness and an almost fanatical attention to detail - and this naturally extended to personal appearance with no concessions allowed for inclement weather nor time of day – or night. It might be 3.30am and the end of a long shift for Weatherall, but his shirt would still look fresh, his tie would still be knotted perfectly and his heavy shoes would still be glinting with an enviable shine. There were no sagging pockets on his jacket and his cap looked as smart as the day it was issued. He would not take kindly to her trotting up the steps and arriving for work with her hair out of place and cap askew.

Fortunately, Laura was also a member of the 'Signalmen's Union' as they liked to unofficially call themselves and was more than willing to spend every spare moment in the 'box' cleaning what was already clean and dusting what didn't need dusting and tidying what was already perfectly tidy. All things considered, checking the lie of her coat collar before ascending the steps was the least she should do.

'Morning, Mr Weatherall!' Her voice was bright and breezy.

'Morning, Laura.' It was immediately apparent that her trim appearance met with his approval. 'Come on in, girl! Get yourself warm by the stove - you must be frozen.'

'It's cold enough out, that's for sure.' Laura Green was already standing beside the pot-bellied cast iron stove that radiated an intense heat, feeling her fingers tingle as the circulation returned. 'Anything to report?'

'No. All tickety-boo. There's tea in the pot.'

'Will you join me?' Green had noticed that two mugs were already neatly standing on the desk beside the stove awaiting filling.

'I think I shall. A bit of warmth inside me before I head home won't hurt.'

'I'd say so!'

She added milk and a teaspoon of sugar in each, a carefree indulgence neither of them had tired of since sugar rationing had ceased and took a grateful sip of hers. Removing her coat, she carefully placed it on an empty peg on the wall near the door, then started casting her eyes down the ledger that recorded every event and train movement of Weatherall's shift. Nothing stood out, just as he had reported and just as she expected.

'Any notices?' She was asking if they had been made aware of any special working arrangements that day.

'Not as I've heard.'

Weatherall checked the clock on the wall and belled a signal to the main box in Coalville. An immediate reply confirmed his communication that he had signed off. 'All yours.' He shrugged his coat on, then sipped some tea. Laura Green stepped to one side to allow Weatherall to record the end of his shift in the ledger, before she then added the exact time she took over the 'box. Green then stepped towards the bank of levers that controlled the points and signals and automatically picked up the cotton cloth that was draped over one of the brightly polished brass lever handles. This was used every time a lever was pulled, ostensibly to offer a better grip, but as much to ensure that not one finger mark ever blemished the almost dazzling shine of each heavy lever. No signalman or woman worth their salt would dare to pull a lever without this cloth.

The block instruments tinkled and Green glanced at the wall clock, responded with a few deft rings and then pulled a series of levers. Her limbs were still reluctant to work smoothly after the chilling bike ride and she knew she must take care not to tweak a muscle. A long shift of this hard graft would become unbearable if she put a back muscle out. Green and Weatherall both looked out of the cabin onto the glinting steel rails and waited, companionably, for the early parcels train that she'd just accepted from Leicester to hurry past on its way towards Coalville and beyond into the Midlands.

It would be a minute or so before it would arrive, so they sipped their tea and Green took time to take in the rakes of wagons in the sidings and mentally prepare herself for the likely shunting movements that lay ahead. The shunters working on the ground would organise where each wagon needed to go and when they needed to be collected and taken away, but in her commanding position in the cabin, she had ultimate control and must be sure that every train movement was safe before allowing it to proceed, and so in this brief hiatus in the dog hours before the railway fully awakened from its short sleep, it was good to take stock.

'Who's that over there?' Green stepped closer to the big glass windows.

Weatherall followed her glance and also moved forward from his respectful position near the unglazed rear of the cabin, as he was now just an observer, and no longer held authority over the running of the signal box. 'Looks like Richie Charlton.'

'He's due on shed!' Green took another glance at the wall clock. 'If anything, he's late.' Her breath steamed against the window pane. 'He's out at 4.20.'

'That's why he's fair hiking it down the line then!' Weatherall chuckled. Charlton would not be the first, nor indeed the last, engine man he'd seen trying to make up lost time to clock on before they incurred a ticking off by the shed foreman. 'But he's coming a funny way...'

'Mr Charlton's a Desford man, isn't he?'

'That's right, Laura. So why the Devil is he coming from down Ratby way? That makes no sense.'

Green slid open one of the windows and instantly got a blast of cold air in her face for doing so. Narrowing her eyes to stop the wind making them sting, she hailed the driver in a cheery voice. 'Hullo! Are going to be ok for the 4.20?'

They saw the hurrying figure jerk more upright in response to Green's hail, but he maintained his rapid pace without answering. He drew closer and, if anything, seemed to lower his head so his cap brim further obscured his face and they could see he a scarf wrapped around his mouth. A wise move on this raw night.

'Is everything all right?' Green tried another well-meaning question, but all they heard was a muffled response accompanied by a raised gloved hand.

Green shrugged her shoulders and gratefully closed the window. It was too cold to be leaning out and trying to illicit a response from uncommunicative engine drivers. She and Weatherall exchanged glances, but neither thought it worth further comment. Charlton was a seasoned driver and would soon be on the footplate of his merrily steaming engine they both could just see under the weak light cast by the ageing yard lamps.

Weatherall washed his mug out in the little sink and pulled on his hat and gloves whilst Green updated the ledger to record the passing of the parcels train, then gave the telegraph instrument some attention to allow a different train to pass towards Leicester on the main line and pulled and released a series of the heavy levers. She finished her tea and not long afterwards there was a sharp toot on a whistle. This was Charlton's engine which had eased forward as far as the little stubby ground signal, asking for permission to move off shed and into the yard to collect the first loaded coal train of the day for hauling down to West Bridge. Whatever the reason for his curious behaviour, the driver had wasted no time in getting back on the footplate and getting under way. No matter then, all was well.

Green wished Weatherall a 'goodnight' despite it being just after 4am, and once he'd closed the outside door, the signal box was truly all hers.

Chapter Eleven

As he swung the car around the corner, the headlamps of the police Rover illuminated a Standard Vanguard pulled up against the hedge and a uniformed constable standing beside an impressive roadblock formed from white painted trestles supporting a narrow crossbar banded in red and white. A matching set of trestles and bar could just be seen in the distant gloom on the far side of the crossing, again with the dark shape of another constable standing guard. The Leicestershire Constabulary had stepped up to the mark and cordoned off the area. DS Trinder was pleased. This was a vital first step in place and it was a promising start.

The constable had taken a step into the road as soon as he had seen them approach waving a hand lamp from side to side and lifting his other hand to command them to halt. He then expertly changed this gesture into a smart salute once he was close to the driver's side window and saw the warrant card being displayed. Trinder gave the constable a nod of acknowledgment and cut the engine. He liked the man's style.

Trinder had called in the constabulary immediately after learning about the serious incident reported at Black Spinney Crossing. He'd still been slightly groggy with sleep, standing in pyjamas and dressing gown in their kitchen at Woodford Halse after being woken by the jangling telephone bell. Trinder knew the Leicester boys would be able to deploy officers far more quickly than his smaller team, but perhaps more importantly, they would also have the authority to close Rothley Lane in the vicinity of the railway crossing and so protect the crime scene until the British Transport Police Detective Department team could get on site. This was a railway-related crime and fell squarely on their shoulders, but he needed the close co-operation of the constabulary. Such shared working was not always an easy mix, with both forces sometimes guilty of jealously guarding their own territory and being overly pedantic about who did what and where the bounds of jurisdiction lay. This bitter December morning, Trinder was more than a little relieved to see their presence. The area was cordoned off and it was now up to DS John Trinder to make sense of what they would find.

He felt a shiver of anticipation, mingled with a little dread. From what he'd already heard on the telephone, this was something to get the brain whirring and adrenaline pumping. But perhaps such a serious 'shout' could have waited until the Guvnor was back from leave. It was hard not having the experience and bloodhound qualities of DCI Vignoles to keep him on track. Trinder felt strangely exposed and on view as he sat behind the wheel of the car with just young PC467 Simon Howerth sitting in the front passenger seat, rather than the boss. He was glad to see the lad was looking bright and alert. He needed Howerth on top form this morning and couldn't have him yawning all over the place or whining he'd not had his breakfast.

As Trinder removed the keys from ignition he was reminded of his joking exchange with Violet last night in the Gorse. He would only call in Vignoles if there was a murder – and yet he had not done so, despite the ominous report he'd been given. Perhaps spurred on by Violet's advice, he'd taken the decision to react fast and get as strong a response in place as quickly as possible. It was imperative to get the basics in place, and quickly. Time was not a detective's friend. Trinder had already sent WPC Jane Benson ahead to start assessing the situation. She lived the closest of them all to the crime scene and would be there in about twenty minutes and so was the obvious choice. He also knew he could trust her to help ensure the area remained as undisturbed as possible. If anyone could be counted on to not wade in and destroy vital and fragile evidence, it was Benson, or perhaps her close friend and colleague WPC Lucy Lansdowne, who was holding the fort with PC Blencowe in the Leicester Central office. Trinder knew that in the time it had taken him to drive up from Woodford Halse, Benson would have put in the necessary telephone calls to hurry a doctor and police photographer on their way and so get the first stages of the investigation process underway. The smart green Vanguard might well be the doctor's.

Even as he was stepping out of the black Rover, he saw Benson in her long black police issue coat and neat little hat appear at the side of one of the massive gate posts from which the gates hung.

'Morning, sir.'

'What have we got?' Trinder stood by the car, not wanting to walk straight to the crime scene. He'd learned from Vignoles that taking a few moments to listen to the initial crime report, then take stock of the whole scene before closing in on the smaller details often paid dividends.

'A woman. Widowed. Mrs Jane Palmer, aged 72.' Trinder furrowed his brow as he heard her age and Benson noticed. 'She was long past retirement age but until this happened, was hale and hearty. She was the crossing keeper and with an excellent service record. It was her husband's position originally, and she took over after he died, some years back. I suggest she tried to foil a robbery and was fatally assaulted as a consequence.' Benson paused a beat. 'Its rather messy.'

Trinder gave a grim nod. 'There's no possibility she was struck by a passing train?'

'Accidental death looks unlikely from the nature of her injuries. The first train of the day came through without any report of an incident, although as yet nobody has spoken to crew or guard.'

'Then it's murder...'

Had he made the correct decision not to call DCI Vignoles? Earlier that week Vignoles had been adamant. *'You're in charge, John. Just think everything through with that analytical brain of yours. Don't prevaricate but double-check everything. Delegate and make the others do the leg work. Follow your instincts and ensure the facts fit like a glove, and you'll be fine.'* Trinder clearly remembered the curious twinkle in Vignoles' eye as he issued the instructions. It was almost as if Vignoles was sounding out his abilities as a leader. Trinder felt a strange cold finger run down his spine and his stomach tightened. It was one thing to be in charge, but a murder investigation was a world away from pilfering in the freight yards or an arson attack on a platelayer's hut, both of which were more typical fare.

Trinder glanced at his wrist watch. It was imperative they start the investigation without further delay. Kicking their heels whilst the DCI travelled up from Dunton Bassett made no sense.

'She lived alone?' Trinder asked Benson.

'Not usually, but I understand there was nobody else living here all this week. She shares the cottage with her married daughter, granddaughter and great granddaughter - who is about five or six years old.'

'Four generations under one roof? Interesting. The others have gone away?'

'They all went to Liverpool for an extended visit.'

'Visiting who?'

'I'm not sure as yet.'

'I'll need their names, ages and confirm their relationships and who are the husbands? I need to know when they left here - and why. And get me a number and address to contact the daughter, as she will be the next of kin.'

'Understood, sir.'

'I believe the body has been moved?'

'Correct. The two men who discovered her thought she was still alive and moved her inside the cottage into the warm to see if there was anything they could do. I think they tried to administer first aid, then called for help once they realised they were too late.'

Trinder had been prepared for this news, but having it confirmed in the cold pale dawn of day reminded him that they were going to be looking at a muddled set of clues, which would need careful untangling and interpreting. 'What time was she discovered?' Trinder and Benson were walking through the smaller gate at the side of the road reserved for pedestrians.

'About 5.30am.'

'Who found her?'

'Two platelayers. They were walking beside the track from Desford Junction which lies in that direction -' Benson helpfully pointed along the track. 'They were on their way towards Ratby to start oiling points and fishplates. They saw her lying on the ground outside. In this spot -,' Benson used her torch to indicate the location.

The ground was formed of a mixture of cinders, a smooth tarmac path and some soft mud. Copious dark stains of blood and some distinct footprints were immediately visible. Two large oil lamps lay on the ground, one of which had the glass smashed and splintered. There was a strong smell of lamp oil and a glossy stain in the mud. The twin rails of the single line lay like stripes of mercury on a dark landscape, the lines narrowing to a vanishing point some distance away where the faint glow of lights could just be seen behind a smudge of inky black trees.

'The two men rushed over to help and believing her to be still alive, albeit it in a bad way, lifted her inside,' Benson continued.

Trinder was studying the extensive blood stains clearly visible even in torch light. 'Their laudable actions complicate our task. What are their names?'

'George Baylock and Graham Hind. They're both back at Desford Junction now. I told them you'd want to speak with them and were not to leave the vicinity until you did. I sent them back to inform the shed foreman of our presence and communicate that the line must remain closed until further notice. I also felt we could do with fewer people in the area in the hope we might not trample over too many clues.'

'Good work. We need to get all this photographed...' Trinder indicated the blood stains and prints. 'Make plaster casts of any footprints in the mud. I have the forensic equipment case in the boot of the car. Take ink prints off every boot and shoe of anyone known to be here over the last 24 hours, starting with Baylock and Hind. Include ours for elimination purposes.'

Benson nodded she understood what was expected.

'Howerth. Get across to Desford Junction and take statements from Baylock and Hind. Get as much detail as you can from them about the position the body was lying in when they found her and exactly what they did upon arriving here. I want accurate timings. Once they've done that they can resume their duties, but I might want to speak to them again. I also want background information on the victim; her family, friends, her typical work routine; you know the drill. The signalman could be your best bet as the old lady was part of their field of operation.'

'Signal*woman*, Sarge. I know because Laura said she was on today – er, that's to say, Miss Green and I are - friends. That's why I know.' The fractional pause before he spoke the word 'friends' told Trinder all he needed.

'Understood.' Trinder hesitated a moment, wondering if the obvious romantic connection between the PC and signalwoman was an issue, but decided it was probably more help than hindrance. 'Get what you can from your friend. Maybe she can provide a means of contacting the victim's daughter, if so, advise me as soon as you do. That would save Benson a job, and it's urgent.'

Trinder felt a cold shiver travel through his body as he contemplated breaking this news. Vignoles always took on the unpleasant duty of contacting the next of kin. For a moment he wondered if he could pass this across, but immediately stamped that foolish idea out. He needed to confront this most testing of duties head on and not shirk responsibility.

'I need to know what trains passed here leading up to the victim signing off for the night and at what time, and the same again for this morning, if any. Tell me where these trains were going and who crewed them. We need to speak to the crews and their guards, in case they saw anything.'

'Wilco, Sarge!' The young constable looked delighted with the tasks he'd been set.

'Then hike around the vicinity and knock on doors.' Trinder had already noticed that the area seemed devoid of obvious habitation nearby and it struck him this task might not engage Howerth for long. 'I want to know who lives where; if they were out and about late last night or early this morning – dog walking perhaps - and if they saw anything suspicious. If any road vehicles pass, stop and question them too.'

'Righty-o.'

'If the constabulary have a car here, get one of them to ferry you to Desford Junction and they can assist with the leg work.' Howerth dutifully hurried off.

'Benson. Aside from the body being moved indoors, what else do we know?'

'Palmer signed off by ringing through to Desford Junction Box at 9.30pm last night.'

'This was normal?'

'Miss Green, who as you now know is in the box at present -.'

'Howerth's girlfriend.'

'The one and the same. She told me this is exactly as it should be and duly logged in the signal box ledger.

'You've already spoken with Green?'

'We talked briefly on the telephone to explain we needed to close the line, as you instructed.'

'There were no more trains along here after she closed down at 9.30pm, but did she reopen the line this morning?'

'Yes. And this is significant. Palmer signed back on as expected, at 3.45am and allowed the first – and so far the only – train through here at 4.30am on its way to Leicester West Wharf.'

'When was Palmer's body discovered?'

'At 5.30am. Hind and Baylock telephoned the signal box once they realised she was beyond their rudimentary first aid skills. That was about 5.45am.'

'Looking at these lamps, I'd say she'd opened the line, called the 1st train down and was attacked just afterwards. It's odd she had not got the lamps in place though.'

'I get the feeling this line is quiet and everyone knows each other and know the routine. They could probably trundle up and down with their eyes closed. As long as the gates were open, signal set, she could extinguish the lamps after.'

'Perhaps you're right. It's an anomaly. The testimony of Baylock and Hind as to how the body was positioned when they first saw her and in relation to those lamps, is crucial.'

Trinder now approached the cottage door, a slab of warm yellow light pouring out when he gave it a gentle prod with a gloved finger, careful not to touch it more than strictly necessary in case there should be finger prints that could be recovered. 'We're looking at her being assaulted between 4.30am and no later than, say, 5.20am this morning?' Trinder stepped inside the cottage as he was speaking.

'Not necessarily, Detective –.' The doctor looked up as he heard voices. His face was familiar to Trinder. Doctor Tomblin stood up from kneeling beside the body which was lying on a multi-coloured rag rug on the quarry tiled floor and his knees cracked as he did so. They took a moment to reintroduce themselves. Trinder remembered they had last met beside a narrow road bridge on the Mountsorrel mineral railway early last summer with another unfortunate corpse at their feet.

'I must do a proper examination on the slab as quickly as possible, sergeant. There are a number of puzzles I need to resolve. I must sound like a stuck record endlessly repeating myself, but there is of necessity some ambiguity about my initial observations and I am reluctant to offer much guidance at this juncture for fear of skewing your judgement.'

Trinder silently groaned. It was always tricky to get a doctor to offer direction on time of death at a crime scene, but he still dared to hope they might have something neat and tidy to work with.

'How so?'

'Let me talk you through what we have, sergeant. It's really quite interesting...' Trinder and Benson stood to one side with Doctor Tomblin on the other as they inspected the body lying between them. The old lady's face was distorted into a grimace of acute pain that was slowly locking into place as *rigor mortis* took hold. It was clear she had experienced acute suffering before the merciful release of death. It made difficult viewing.

One side of her face was covered with blood and slippery, stomach-churning, gore. An eyeball was missing, leaving a vile, gaping red hole and a smear of something sticky. 'The most obvious wound is to the face, as you can see. A nasty and powerful blow to the eye, delivered by a heavy and slightly pointed instrument, but it was not sharp. A metal bar, a stave or such like. It burst rather than pierced the eye ball and -'

'I get the point.' Trinder stopped the doctor. Benson was breathing slowly as she controlled her reaction. Trinder was also glad he had not eaten more than two hurried slices of dried toast. 'That blow is what killed her?' Trinder added.

'My first note of caution! I think it is what did for her, ultimately, but not instantly, despite the severity of the wound. I cannot yet be sure. The two men who found her thought she was showing faint signs of life and they could well be correct. I think the attacker assumed she was dead after delivering this blow. It almost certainly rendered her unconscious and presumably immobile, but it might have taken a little while for life to end as blood clearly flowed liberally as the staining on her face, clothing and on the ground outside testifies.'

'Once the heart stops the blood flow ceases?'

'Correct. There is even some slight pooling on this rug, which suggests the men were correct in their belief she showed signs of life, however this could just be spilled blood collected in the eye socket.' There was a sound of Benson taking a deep breath and holding it. 'But there's more -.'

Trinder also steeled himself as the doctor knelt down and slowly rolled the corpse forwards to reveal the back of her head. 'You see that helmet over there?' He nodded towards the glossy black helmet that had been placed on a wooden chair. 'She was wearing it when discovered outside.'

'Trinder exchanged a glance with Benson, who was busy making notes with a look of determined concentration on her face. She was succeeding in not revealing how the sight of the poor murdered woman was affecting her. 'How odd? Perhaps she suspected trouble and had it lying around since the war, as many people still do, and took the precaution of putting it on before going out to investigate?' Trinder was speaking rhetorically, not expecting a reply.

The doctor shrugged his shoulders. 'Whatever the reason, the fact she had this protective headgear caused the assailant problems. It looks as though she was first attacked from behind.' Dr Tomblin looked Trinder in the eye to ensure he had his full attention. 'I can detect the signs here – and here – of two blows to the lower neck and shoulders. The first blow I suspect landed on the back of the helmet, glanced off and made this mark on her shoulder. She probably staggered under the blow and the second struck her across the neck and ear. This would have been exceptionally painful, but not life-threatening.'

'Did she drop those lamps we saw outside as the blows landed?' Trinder looked at Benson, who nodded that this was a valid line of enquiry and made a note. 'Does she have defensive wounds to her hands?'

The doctor gave a slight uplift to the corner of his mouth to suggest he approved of Trinder's line of questioning. 'I don't think they are defensive, but there is a story to be discovered in studying her hands. Your suggestion about her carrying the lamps and therefore unable to immediately defend herself could be valid. But, there are marks on her fingers and a lot of fresh dirt under her nails.'

'Implying what?'

'I think once she was on the ground, badly concussed but still conscious she was clawing at the ground. In acute pain and yet unable to do much more.' Dr Tomblin shrugged his shoulders. 'However, this is speculation.'

Trinder frowned. 'She dropped to the ground, still alive but then was turned onto her back for the final and lethal attack?'

'A good working hypothesis at this stage.' The doctor grinned. He was rising to his task.

'Do you think the blows to the head and to her face were done by the same weapon as that which took out her eye?' Benson asked.

'Ah! Now here's the start of the complications.' The doctor looked at Benson and Trinder with something akin to excitement. A job such as this demanded that he find some measure of professional fascination in trying to untangle the riddles a dead body presented and was clearly revelling in the task. 'I'm not entirely sure they were done by the same implement. I want to study the wounds in more detail before pronouncing further in my report. Ideally, I would compare these wounds with any likely implements you may find.' He gave Trinder and Benson another eager look. 'My first inclination is to suggest you are looking for two different weapons, or a single weapon capable of inflicting very different types of wounds.'

'But that's rather curious isn't it?' Benson interjected. 'The assailant surely needed to move in fast – whack, whack - she drops to the ground, then perhaps turns face upwards and he moves in to deliver the death blow. Why would the attacker stop to choose an alternate weapon?'

'I agree.' Trinder was frowning as he turned the scenario over in his mind.

'The weapon perhaps had both a blunt and a sharp end?' The doctor offered.

'A two-sided weapon.' Benson made a note.

'However, that is not the end to the complications, I'm afraid. If anything, it is just the start!' Doctor Tomblin laid the body gently down on her back. 'I am concerned about the lividity of the wounds to the back and side of her head. They look to be a few hours older than the nasty gouge to her face. I cautiously suggest they were made some hours in advance of the blow to her face. Perhaps as long ago as early last evening.' Trinder looked startled and was interrupted before he could speak. 'I know, sergeant! This is important, and yet I cannot be more precise at this stage though I will try my level best to refine my observations once I get her on the slab.' Knowing that the detectives would need convincing of this surprising development the doctor went on to explain his thinking. 'Look here - there was bleeding from her ear, dribbling down. The blood flowed freely, so she was alive and it was being pumped by the heart, but this has then congealed and started to darken and form a crust.'

'No attempt to wipe it away?' Trinder observed.

'Top marks! She could have been unconscious for some time and unable to attend to her bleeding. There is blue-green bruising starting to form under the blood, and again this takes time. The blood on her face however is far fresher, still very wet and a brighter red, although steadily darkening as time passes. I can see a very marked difference. That is why I believe there is some time between the initial attack and the *coup de grace*.'

'Are you suggesting she was attacked twice – with quite a gap between?' Benson asked.

'I'm just stating facts. How they are interpreted is your part of the game.' Doctor Tomblin stood up. 'I suggest you consider the possibility of a period of time between assaults. I have to do some nifty calculations to have any chance of refining my timings. I've been making readings of the ambient temperature in this room, which is cosy and warm, and the perishing cold outside and also of the body. We base much of our estimates on time of death on body temperature and the rate of cooling. Bringing her inside will have skewed these and needs factoring in. Take what I say with a very big pinch of salt.'

There was the sound of voices and footsteps outside and a police photographer with a tripod and two very large suitcases appeared at the door, accompanied by one of the constables.

Trinder acknowledged their presence.

'Hurry along with your photographs of the body as I need to get her back to the mortuary as quickly as possible,' the doctor also addressed the photographer, who grunted in reply and was already setting down his equipment.

'Once we've removed the body, start on the blood stains and footprints outside. It should be lighter by then.' Trinder issued his own instructions and then stepped back outside the small kitchen into the now pale grey light of day, accompanied by Benson. 'Look at this. It's been damaged.'

They inspected the door frame, which had successfully resisted a number of hard blows against the wood, but fresh splinters were brightly visible low down on the outside jamb.

'And look, Sarge. The door has been kicked at least twice as if to try and open it.'

There were distinct muddy boot prints on the paintwork. 'A couple of hard kicks and a furious attack on the jamb to try and gain entry.' Trinder using a gloved hand gently pull the door closed. The attack had not done any significant harm to the door. 'See here. This lines up with a hole drilled into the door jamb.' A piece of garden twine held a long metal nail with a broad head from the bottom of a hefty metal loop screwed to the surface of the door. Trinder threaded this nail through the loop and it slid easily into the hole. 'A simple and effective lock that takes seconds to open and close.'

'But in the dark and if not aware of this pin, it might explain the frustration the attacker felt at not being able to get the door to open?'

'Perhaps...' Trinder unfastened the door again. 'There's also a mortice lock, but with Palmer outside handling the lamps, they would not have expected the door to be locked... and yet it still refused to budge due to her makeshift nail.'

'Hence the kicking.'

Trinder inspected the mortice lock in more detail. 'This is almost rusty with lack of use. Palmer probably used the nail to quickly pin the door closed when she stepped outside. The prints are a gift. Get all this photographed and try to match them with other prints on the ground.'

Benson made a note. They now carefully walked along the front of the cottage that faced the single line of track, searching for possible clues and taking great care not to disturb the softer ground.

'Have you seen this, Sarge? It looks like they tried to break in through the window.'

Part of the window frame had been given some attention, resulting in a smashed pane as if the burglar had meant to reach in and unhook the latch inside. A few flakes of grubby green paint had flaked off the frame reveal some maroon underneath as a result of the intruders rather wild and uncoordinated attentions. 'This makes even less sense. Why try a strongly made window when there's an unlocked door a yard away?'

'Perhaps the burglar thought nobody was in, started on the window. Palmer came out to investigate and he duly attacked her?'

'Would she have pinned the door shut behind her whilst rushing out to confront someone smashing her window?'

'And not carrying oil lamps.' Benson looked puzzled.

'What's this?' Trinder was swishing away some clumps of brown and faded vegetation below the window to reveal a hefty wooden-handled implement. He lifted it with his gloved hands being careful not to smear any potential finger prints. It had a cast metal head, one end pointed like on a pick axe, the other flattened out into a strong spade shape. 'A mattock. Used to break up hard and compacted earth with the pointed end, and the other to scrape and cut into earth. Was this used to break the window?'

'Is that blood?'

'I think it is.'

'The sharper end might have done that damage to her face.'

'Quite possible.' Trinder carefully put it back exactly as he found it. 'Photograph this in situ, then get it to the lab boys, but with extreme care so as not to disturb any evidence. And advise doctor Tomblin. Let him look at it before it leaves the site. He'll want to test it against the wounds in due course.'

Trinder stood up and looked around. He fished out a pack of Black Cat cigarettes and offered one to Benson, who hesitated before gratefully accepting. She'd been up and working for a good few hours and needed something to keep her mind sharp. Whilst they smoked in silence they both took a moment to consider what they had seen and what it implied. They had already gathered some strong clues and Trinder was starting to feel more confident it might not take too long to crack the case. He felt his shoulders relax and the knot in his stomach loosen.

'If this was an aggravated robbery then we need to establish what was stolen. The doctor and photographer should have finished with the body now, so let's go back inside and see what we can find.'

Chapter Twelve

Fireman Eddie Earnshaw was sweeping the cab floor, tidying up small lumps of coal that had fallen whilst he'd been getting up steam. There were still a few stray bits of wooden kindling and a tuft of cotton wadding blown into a corner left over from when Sammy Chambers had first lit the fire in the dog hours of the morning. He threw what he'd collected into the firebox, gave the fire another glance, then straightened up and checked the few basic gauges to be found in the utilitarian cab.

It was a working environment that made no concessions to comfort. This was an old engine, and the cab was almost startlingly basic compared with the ultra-modern 'Standard' classes of steam locomotive that were now coming out of the various British Railways locomotive works, some of which were virtually fully-enclosed against the elements, had cushioned seats with a back and ergonomically designed controls to ease the stresses and strains on the crew. What luxury!

The primitive gauge glass showed that there was plenty of water in the boiler and he had more than enough pressure. A touch too much perhaps, but Earnshaw had not expected that they would be still on shed due to this unexplained delay, and so he'd got dear old number 58148 all steamed up and ready to roll two hours ago. After an interminable wait for the signal that would let them move off shed to collect their waiting train of wagons, Mr Hodges the shed foreman had eventually hurried over and shouted up to them.

'There's a hold up! It's serious and could be a long 'un. Sit tight and wait for instructions!' Hodges looked anxious and frazzled but dashed off without further explanation or discussion.

Bringing an engine to a full head of steam and then being asked to 'sit tight' without moving was not ideal. It was now a tricky task to keep the old lady quietly burbling away without blowing the safety valves. Earnshaw had managed to squeeze a little more water in the boiler to quieten her down and raked his fire a little flatter to ease off on the heat, but even so, if they didn't move soon she was going to send a screaming jet of steam into the dawn sky.

Driver Ashbourne was too experienced to let this hiccough in their day overly concern him. He knew his engine was in fine fettle despite her age, and it was the fireman's problem to mind the steam. He'd probably give Earnshaw a cheeky wink when the safety valves duly popped and would ensure that the other lads knew all about it later when they were back on shed at the end of the working day. Footplate life was punctuated by such innocent leg-pulling and often resulting in nicknames being given that could linger long after the minor incidents that prompted their initial invention were forgotten. 'Froggy' Wilson had discovered one of these amphibians swimming around in a side tank and had got himself soaking wet trying to catch the slippery customer. That had been twenty years ago, and yet the name persisted. Poor old Pete 'Puffer' Jones had famously allowed his engine to run out of 'puff' and force his driver to sit glowering in a relief loop reserved for lumbering goods trains whilst their passengers grumbled and fumed in the carriages behind whilst his guard glowered at his pocket watch and cursed the crew. Again, this had happened such a long time ago that Puffer was now a senior link driver with a fine reputation, but the ignominious name persisted.

As for 'Steady' Ashbourne, he was an older gentleman who had long since given up any aspirations of securing one of the prestigious 'top links' that worked the express passenger trains. He was content with life on the 'Swanney', cosseting and caring for his 'old lady' and in the extended periods between trips reading the sporting pages of his paper or poring over a new seed catalogue. Choosing which type of root vegetable to plant was one of his special pleasures. Indeed, he was at this moment perched on the tiny piece of polished wood that served as a seat in the cab with one foot on a piece of pipe work whilst studying a list of next season's potatoes, already dreaming of placing an order in advance of the longer days and the distant promise of next spring. However, for all his apparent ease, 'Steady' Ashbourne was keeping half an eye on what was going on in the shed.

There was something wrong, that much was certain. He suspected an accident down the line, as he could see Mr Hodges and his assistant hurrying about with anxious looks on their faces, whilst various fitters and plate layers were gathered near the side of the shed, all taking turns looking down the empty line as if the twin steel rails would communicate with them, talking and smoking and looking uncomfortable. They were not being yelled at for slacking but could not enjoy the anxious wait to hear what the reason was for this odd and extended delay.

Ashbourne also heard the frequent clatter of telephones ringing in Mr Hodges' office and their frequency further suggested all was not well. A bell was a bell, and yet there were times when one could almost sense them heralding something ominous.

'I reckon Richie Charlton's had a problem down the line.'

Earnshaw was now polishing the copper pipework. 'You really think so?'

'Summat's up, and I reckon its down West Bridge way.' Ashbourne let his seed catalogue flop onto his lap and watched as a figure hurried down the steps from the signal box and ran towards the engine shed. 'Can't remember the last time I saw Hodges run!'

Earnshaw leaned from the cab and watched the shed foreman for himself. 'He does look worried.'

'Probably a derailment. Shouldn't be nothing too serious. Just blocking the line and darned awkward to shift.' Ashbourne's voice was perhaps more light-hearted than he felt inside.

Both men knew that the line speeds down to the West Wharf were slow and the chance of serious injury to the crew were minimal if their train jumped the tracks. In places the sleepers were so old and rotten it was quite possible the track had spread out of gauge allowing locomotive or wagons to drop down into the ballast. The spur to Groby quarry was even worse, and perhaps they'd dropped onto the cinders where they left the branch and were blocking the line. However, there was another far grimmer possibility, that someone had been struck on the line. In the dark, with greasy rails and a fully-laden coal train there would be no chance of stopping, even if only travelling at 15 miles an hour. A fatality was everyone's worst nightmare and the harried looks on the faces of Hodges and his assistant seemed to be implying the worst.

Ashbourne quietly folded his seed catalogue and stuffed it into his black leather engineman's bag and stood up. 'I don't like the look of that, Ed.'

Earnshaw followed his sightline and saw the black police car pull to a halt and the headlights turn off. Two policemen climbed out.

'That's Simon!'

'You know one of the coppers?'

'He's my best mate! He works for the railway detectives down at Central.'

'Then you can ask him what's going on.'

They watched as the two policemen talked with Mr Hodges. After a few shakes of the head and some gesticulating, they all walked inside the shed office. It was about ten minutes later that Mr Hodges approached their engine, walking with a determined stride and a grim set to his jaw. He looked ashen pale.

'I need a word.'

'What is it, Mr Hodges?'

'There's been a fatality.' The foreman coughed nervously. He was a tough man who rarely showed any emotion except if Derby County managed a win on a Saturday, but he looked visibly shaken as he looked up from the yard. 'They think its murder. It's Janey Palmer.'

There was a moment of silence, filled once again with the distant ringing of that telephone.

'Old Janey? Are you saying Old Janey's been murdered?'

'I'm afraid so.' A muscle twitched at the side of Hodges' jaw. 'The police think it could have been a robbery and she was attacked. She was found dead beside the track early this morning.'

'But Janey's not got 'owt to rob!' Ashbourne leaned heavily on the side of the cab shaking his head slowly in utter disbelief. He looked as though someone had just punched him in the stomach and winded him. 'Why would anyone do such a thing?'

'None of us can understand it. It was Georgie and Graham that found her. They were walking the line to Ratby. It was not long after Richie had taken his train down, either.'

Ashbourne blew air slowly out of his lips and stared down at the ash strewn ground.

Earnshaw was listening in mute silence. This was shocking news and the thrill he'd felt at seeing his chum Simon roll up in a police car, was instantly overridden by this devastating news. He was remembering how only last evening the elderly crossing keeper had been ribbing him about not having a girlfriend. Now he would never get to tell her about that pretty bus conductress he'd managed to spend an hour and half with last night. The delight of feeling the curve from her waist to the swell of her hips as he put his arm around her and walked her to her bus stop. The hurried kiss, followed by a second before Miss Darling bade him 'goodnight'. Selfishly, that realisation made his eyes sting. The shrill alarm of the safety valves finally releasing on his engine made them all jump but was the perfect excuse for Earnshaw to leap into action and get the injector on to force a little more water in the boiler to try and calm the engine down.

'They'll get the line open as soon as possible but it'll be another hour or more, I guess. We'll send you into the yard and you can crack on making up the midday goods to keep busy and use up some of that bloody steam.'

'I'll be happier with something to do.' Ashbourne had to shout over the screaming valves.

'The police want to question you when you finish making up that train.'

'We've been here the whole time. What can we tell them?'

'It's what they do, so don't argue!' The strain was getting to Hodges. 'Just answer their questions. Janey was one of us, so you to give 'em all the help you can to catch the murdering -.' The foreman's words were lost in the roar from the safety valves as he turned away.

Chapter Thirteen

'What are we looking for?

'We start from the presumption this was a robbery. Someone made obvious attempts to break in and it looks like they were rumbled by Palmer. There are anomalies that need explaining, but the broad sweep seems to fit violent robbery.' Trinder was casting his eyes around the kitchen parlour. The rag rug was still in place on the floor with its ugly blood stains, but he could now hear the sound of the van taking the body to the mortuary accelerate away outside. The photographer was busy working outside and Dr Tomblin had also packed up his doctor's bag and gone. They had the place to themselves.

Benson was standing beside the cast iron range which was still issuing some welcome heat. She gave the handle of the old metal kettle an exploratory touch then quickly recoiled and took up a tea towel to wrap around the handle. Using this, she the lifted the kettle off the range and gave it a shake, then sniffed it. It radiated intense heat and the smell of scorching metal.

'This has long boiled dry. If left here much longer the bottom would burn out.'

Trinder had been riffling through a pile of British Railways booklets on the kitchen table in the hope there might be something of interest between the pages and was now opening the table drawer. 'What does that suggest?'

'She put it on the hob to make a hot drink but was distracted. She went outside to investigate - and never came back.'

'There's no one living close enough to have heard it whistling. A pity. That could have been an indicator of the time she was attacked.' Trinder looked across at the Benson. 'We need to ask the men who found her if they heard the kettle or if it was already dry when they found her.'

'It had been moved off the actual ring, but this range kicks out some heat so was still very hot. It's going to be hard to estimate when it boiled dry.' Benson was not sure what this implied. She carefully placed the kettle on the quarry tiled floor then moved on to looking in a cupboard set into the side of the chimney breast. It held various food stuffs in packets and tins. 'She kept a good stock. I suppose being out here all day and every day, she needed to. There's no shop close to hand.'

Trinder was inspecting the log book and making a note of her last entries. 'Nothing after 9.30pm. You said a train came through in the early hours.'

'At 4.30. Is that not logged?'

'She called the train through...' Trinder was thinking aloud. 'She then put the kettle on for an early morning cuppa, intending to put the entry into the log. But was suddenly disturbed by someone outside – her assailant returning?'

'If the doctor is correct, then she had been attacked earlier in the night and would surely still be groggy. Maybe concussed and struggling to think straight?'

'In that state she was tardy in putting out the lamps, not hurrying to fill out the log.'

'Then why not alert the signal box or stop the train and tell the crew? Surely her first action in coming around would be to call for help?'

Silence as they pondered these questions.

'Look, sir. All these storage jars have loose lids, some have been left off and the packets are all open, and there are a lot of spillages. Its a complete shambles.'

Trinder looked across. 'Going by the way she maintained her log book and the neat stacks of official documents, she was an orderly and methodical person. This kitchen is commendably clean and tidy.'

'That suggests this has been searched.'

'Was somebody looking for something small enough to be hidden in there?' Trinder joined Benson and looked at the untidy cupboard.

'In a tin of cocoa or a packet of dried peas?' Benson was sceptical. It sounded far-fetched.

'House breakers are rarely that thorough. They grab high value items and scarper. Let's try upstairs.' Trinder lead the way.

'Ok, here we go.' He had stepped into the main bedroom and immediately could see the intruder had given attention to ransacking a chest of drawers. It was made from solid oak, recently polished and clearly the most substantial and impressive item of furniture they'd seen in the house and quite probably Palmer's pride and joy. The top draw had a brass escutcheon, and this had been violently attacked with the wood freshly gashed and wounded at the front until the lock could be disengaged and the draw dragged open. It was empty except for a muslin bag containing lavender that was spilling a little of its fragrant contents.

'They cleaned her out. Whatever she had of value was presumably kept here.'

'A more promising location than a tin of Cocoa.' Trinder was feeling more confident about how to interpret this information.

The two lower drawers did not have locks and had been only partially pushed back into place. Benson opened each one, handling the shining oak with care with her leather gloved hands, placing each drawer on the bed. Clothes and undergarments had been rudely lifted, searched, then dumped back, although it was obvious that they had once been meticulously folded and stacked and still retained something of their original order. 'Just clothes. If there was anything worth taking, then it's long gone.'

Trinder was peering in the wardrobe. A few shoe boxes had their lids lifted and not put back in place, but these still held shoes. All were old, but well cared for. 'I get the feeling they were getting desperate. All they got for their troubles were the belongings of an elderly and under-paid old lady. You said she had her daughter and family living here - perhaps they had something of more interest?'

The two other bedrooms told a similar tale, with drawers opened in bedside tables and chests of drawers and evidence that someone had quickly looked through the modest and unremarkable items lying there. There was nothing to suggest the intruder would have found much reward for their efforts.

'We'll need to ask the daughter and granddaughter if they can identify anything that's been taken, although I'm not expecting much. Look at the place. A humble abode with a few low-value possessions. Exactly what you'd expect. We need to know what was in the locked drawer. That has to be the main focus.'

'Older people do prefer cash stashed under the mattress or even a locked drawer to banks. There could have been some savings taken. It all feels opportunistic, Sir.' Benson's expression was despairing. 'Its obvious they lived a simple life. The furniture dates before the war – and I mean the first one.' She looked baffled. 'There's no justification for what happened to her, but somehow it's made even more repugnant for the sheer futility of being killed for...for nothing!'

'A life taken for a few quid stashed away. Get the photographer to record all this and I want the finger print team over the house like a rash. It's high time I gave the Guv a call.' Trinder looked at his wrist watch. 'He'll be finishing breakfast.'

'Lucky man.' Benson felt her tummy rumble.

* * * *

Trinder sat on a wooden kitchen chair and dialled the operator. It was fortunate that Palmer had a telephone in her cottage. She needed one as part of her job alongside the impressive array of block telegraph instruments that stood in a line along a shelf behind the table. These were the most unusual items in the room and indicated that for all it's simple domestic appearances, this cottage kitchen was actually a working railway office that played a vital role in controlling the movements along the line. Each instrument was brightly polished and dusted so the wood and metal parts were gleaming like soldiers on dress parade in the light cast from the overhead light bulb.

Whilst he waited for the operator to make the connection Trinder once again glanced at the messy food cupboard that Benson had been inspecting. This disorder was surely the result of a hasty search. But what on earth could they have been hoping to find? Who secreted valuables in a jar of dried peas, for God's sake? This was a discordant note and he was struggling to reconcile what it implied with the more easily interpreted aspects of the case.

'Your call is now connected,' the crisp tones of the operator cut across his musing.

'Sir? Trinder.'

'Good morning, John. Didn't take you long to get on the blower, eh?' Vignoles injected a light note into his voice. He knew it would be important if Trinder had called the vicarage at such an hour and he didn't want to make his sergeant feel awkward. If he was completely honest, Vignoles was feeling itchy to get back into work and didn't resent the intrusion one jot. He wasn't used to so much time away from the job and was suffering from cabin fever being cooped up in the vicarage.

'Sorry to disturb you, but something's come up and I'd appreciate your observations.'

'Fire away. We've breakfasted, and I was thinking about taking a stroll into the village and whiling away an hour with the stationmaster, so I have time on my hands. I presume it's serious?'

'A murder. A lady crossing keeper killed resisting what looks like robbery.'

Vignoles gripped the telephone receiver a bit harder. 'Are you calling from the crime scene? I didn't recognise the location nor number when the operator put you through.' Murder was as serious as it got. He felt a twinge of something like envy, but instantly pushed this aside. This was no time for foolish emotions.

Trinder explained where he was calling from. 'The shout came in very early and I thought it best to respond immediately. It felt imperative to get on site quickly and start the process.' Trinder's justification of his actions was as much to himself, as for Vignoles' benefit. 'We've cordoned off the area and the body's been inspected by a doctor, photographed and on the way to the morgue as I speak. The photographer is still on site and Benson will make some casts from a collection of strong footprints found close to the position the body was discovered. A finger print team should be here any minute. We might even have the murder weapon. It's certainly bloody and a possible match with some of the blows.'

'It sounds like you have everything under control. What can I do?'

'I wanted to make sure I've not missed anything obvious.'

'You're the lead detective at the crime scene and for now, that location is your jurisdiction. I'm standing in the hall with an unlit pipe, so you hold all the cards. Just remember, John, before you walk away, make sure you've inspected everything to your satisfaction. Make notes of even the most improbable things. Walk around, look and think through what actions are implied by every detail. Once you leave the site and everyone packs up their kit, you only have photographs, finger prints, those plaster casts and your personal observations and hunches to work with. Gather all you can.'

'Wilco, sir.' Trinder felt better already. A pep talk from the master was exactly what he needed. A cup of tea and a bacon roll wouldn't go amiss either, but they would have to wait.

There was the sound of a match striking and a brief pause as Vignoles got his pipe alight. Trinder took this to be a good sign. 'Run over what you've learned so far,' Vignoles continued after a quick pull on the pipe. 'What's on your radar?'

'On the surface, it looks pretty straightforward. An elderly lady crossing keeper living alone in a remote location is attacked outside her cottage in the dark, most probably whilst trying to resist a house-breaker.'

'Is she usually alone?'

'As a matter of fact, no. Her family have been away for the last week.'

'Do you think the robber would have been able to gain entry with the others in the house?'

'Unlikely. Quite a lot of force was used on the door and they also broke a pane of glass in a window. The cottage is small and when inside they smashed open a locked chest of drawers. All of which would take time and cause a lot of noise.'

'What does that tell you?'

'They knew she would be alone. Someone was aware of this fact and exploited it.'

'Or they struck lucky? Sometimes criminals can be astoundingly dim-witted. Anything else puzzling you?' There was another puff on the pipe, clearly audible along the line.

'The doctor is being cagey about time of death.'

'When are they not?' There was a sympathetic chuckle down the line.

'But it's not so much the actual time of death that's worrying me. We suspect she actually died about the same time she was discovered by two gangers walking the line. They tried to administer first aid, but she was too far gone and once she expired they raised the alarm. The problem is that the doc thinks there were two separate assaults upon her, with a gap of some hours in between.'

There was a moment's silence. 'That is significant. And curious. This needs careful consideration. And a good man working on the cadaver to interpret the science. Who's the doctor?'

'Doctor Tomblin.'

Vignoles took a moment to retrieve the name from his memory. 'OK. He did a thorough job on that Mountsorrel affair, if you remember? Sit in on the PM and try to get him to pin down the timings of these assaults. GBH resisting a house breaking, with the victim later expiring from their wounds, is one thing, but two quite separate attempts to kill or severely hurt the victim does not fit that bill. A house breaker never chooses to see the occupant, let alone attack them. Far too risky. They usually prove to be cowardly individuals who'd run a mile if seen, rather than square up and attack.'

'She was hit twice from behind. Which fits the scenario of trying to knock her out to give time to enter the house and avoid being identified. But she was later blinded in one eye using a different weapon, or possibly, using a different edge of a blood-stained garden mattock we discovered. She eventually died from this wound.'

'Blinded?' Vignoles thought this over. 'Concentrate on this aspect. Timings are going to be key. But just as critical is motive. This sounds pre-meditated. There is something vicious and cruel about what they did. Not at all like the actions of a cat-burglar. You have a lot to do, so I'll let you get on. I think it best I come to the office on Monday and we'll talk more.'

'Glad to hear it!' As Trinder put the receiver down he felt relieved. He'd not messed up - yet. He'd also got confirmation that there was something distinctly fishy about this robbery.

He was interrupted in his musings by the return of the constable at the door. 'Excuse me sir, but I've got a Mr Brian Toomey here. He's the relief signalman. He's come to man the crossing gates when you're ready to reopen the line.'

'Bring him in.' Trinder stood up and moments later shook hands with a thin man with round spectacles who was standing just inside the cordon.

'Miss Green called me in. I'm the relief. Standing in for sickness, holidays and for...other eventualities.' He coughed and looked at the floor, transfixed by the red staining on the rug. 'When you need me to take over, just say the word and I'll open the section.'

Trinder nodded. He could see that the photographer was packing up his camera and that Benson was starting to open up the forensic bag and set out some enamelled bowls ready to mix plaster of Paris to make casts of the various footprints. He also noted that a young man with a suitcase had just drawn up in a car. Trinder recognised his as one of the Leicester Constabulary finger print team. Everything was progressing swiftly and looked to be under control. There was surely no need to keep the line closed for much longer. Benson could do her work with just the occasional train passing at a walking pace, and likewise the finger print man would be working mostly around the door, windows and inside the cottage.

'Once we've checked the crossing gates for prints and around these block instruments, I shall inform the main signal box to start letting trains through and you can take over. A constable will remain on site until we finish all forensic examinations. You will touch nothing except what is strictly needed for you to do your job.'

'As you wish, sir.'

Trinder then advised the uniformed constable that once the forensics officer had checked the gates, he could dismantle the barriers across the road. 'If anyone drives past, flag them down and ask if they saw or heard anything between 9pm and 5am.'

Trinder then walked around the heavy wooden gates, peering closely at the white paint. It was rain stained and in places the wood underneath was showing where paint had flaked away and where the paint was unbroken the surface had lost its gloss and unlikely to retain clear print marks. Scuffs and abrasions abounded, but there were none that piqued his interest. He feared the print man was going to have a fruitless task with these.

As he turned away, his eye caught something tucked underneath the hawthorn hedge on the opposite side of the railway line to the cottage. It was red and white and seemed to made from thin cardboard. Just a bit of wind-blown litter, but when on a crime scene it paid to check everything. He walked over and pulled it free.

A mask of Father Christmas with a thin white elastic cord to hold it in place. It looked brand spanking new. He stared at the laughing face, wondering what this meant. It would soon be Christmas and Benson had explained there was a young girl usually living in the cottage, so perhaps one of the family have bought it in advance of acting out the charade of Santa visiting on Christmas eve. But why had it ended up under a hedge? The grown-ups were either away in Liverpool or working diligently at keeping the crossing not casually losing a Santa Claus mask. Had if blown out of the opened door of the cottage?

It was unlikely to be relevant but remembering the advice from Vignoles he decided it needed to be retained. Benson could bag it up and they could ask the family about it. It was probably nothing, but that was part of the detective's lot to seek answers to irrelevant questions.

Chapter Fourteen

Vignoles came back from the hall where the vicarage telephone was housed and met the quizzical glances of his wife and sister Gwen. Maurice was still sitting at the table near the window, kicking his heels and glowering in a sulky manner at the leaden sky outside.

Gwen's son was at a stage of life the more Liberal-minded educationalists were starting to call 'difficult.' In fairness, Maurice could be charming, polite and surprisingly pleasant company and bright with it, if perhaps not destined to be an atomic rocket scientist. However, these more promising periods were growing less frequent by the day. There were articles in the press and on the radio that tried to explain that young persons like Maurice were in the middle of a relatively new idea of being a 'teen-ager'. A description that seemed to confer its own special badges of belonging that including moodiness, reticence and an attitude towards his elders that swung dangerously close to insolence.

Vignoles recalled that back in his day there had been no such concept and someone of Maurice's age would already be hard at work in a factory or down a pit or learning the family trade or business. Those fortunate to evade hard labour through educational high achievement were expected to be swatting hard to prove they deserved the chance to grab a golden ticket to a better remunerated future and avoiding a life time of sweat and toil. A place in a University or Technical College would be beckoning for those fortunate to pass the relevant exams. Maurice however, was showing few of these attributes, despite the significant advantage of attending a decent (and expensive) grammar boarding school. His high-flying 11-plus pass seemed a long time ago, and his school performance was apparently slipping by the month. The lad was in danger of losing his way.

Vignoles however stifled the urge to berate Maurice for idling away his time with a sharp reminder that the poor chap had just lost his dad, and the dreaded funeral was still to be endured and weighing heavily upon his young shoulders. The lad had been rudely wrenched from school and the companionship of his close friends just at a time when the term was winding down for Christmas. This was always a popular time at boarding school, with many enjoyable activities and social events relating to the coming holiday, and whilst his academic achievements may have stalled, his enthusiasm for spending time with his school chums was at an all-time high. It had been a doubly cruel shock to be suddenly taken away from everyone he was perhaps closest too and thrust into the small and closeted world of his grandparent's house. Little wonder Maurice was struggling to know what best to do with himself.

'Was that John on the telephone?' Anna Vignoles asked.

'Yes. Something's cropped up. It sounds like he's on top of it. I shall leave him to it until Monday, then see how the land lies.'

'If you need to go into the office today, we have everything arranged and can manage.'

'No, Gwen, I'm happy to leave my sergeant in charge. He's an able detective, and besides, it will be interesting to see how he performs.'

'You make it sound like he's been set an exam,' Gwen smiled weakly. She looked grateful to have a different topic of conversation and was making an effort to open the subject up.

'Not exactly. He's probably sat enough of those over the past year, but he's certainly got himself a knotty piece of homework!' Vignoles gave Maurice a quick glance to see if the lad was responding, but there was no obvious reaction. Vignoles sat down in an armchair and started to clean his pipe. 'John's got flair for detection and is quick to spot things. He'll be all right, and I think he might like the idea of working without me breathing down his neck and watching every move.'

'Is it awfully serious?' Anna asked. 'I sensed from your tone of voice it was significant.'

'Not another awful railway accident, I hope?' Gwen interjected.

Vignoles looked first at Gwen, then Maurice, whilst he pondered whether to elaborate. He concentrated on his pipe to buy himself a few more moments. The mantle clock tick-tocked the time, filling the room with its relentless measure. If there was a subject likely to engage a sulky teenage boy, then a bloody murder probably fitted the bill. It was not exactly a subject for a household in the grip of mourning, but everyone was fully aware of the nature of his work and he was pretty sure it might spark a reaction.

'There's been a fatality. A woman working a railway crossing was found bludgeoned to death.'

That worked. Maurice sat bolt upright as his head snapped around to look at Vignoles like that of a hawk spotting prey. 'A real life murder?'

'Indeed. Although the juxtaposition of life and murder is perhaps unfortunate.' He gave Maurice a sly wink.

'Corr! Where did it happen?'

'Maurice!' Gwen snapped. 'This is not a subject for salacious enjoyment.'

'I think it best to be vague about the specifics, as much, because I have only the minimum of information to work with. I do however know that it was not far from Leicester in a remote rural location.'

'How awful. Does John have any idea why someone would do such a terrible thing?'

'He suspects a botched robbery, Anna. Maybe the robber thought nobody was home, but once he was discovered and she'd seen his face...'

'If she saw his face, then it was curtains! She'd pick him out in an identity parade in no time.' Maurice sounded excited. 'He'd have no choice. Bam!'

'I fear your analysis might be correct, even if put rather brutally.'

'How did he do it?' Maurice looked as animated as he'd been for days.

Whilst Vignoles could fully appreciate Gwen feeling unsure about her son sounding so excited about the direful news, he could understand the lad's reaction. Like most detectives, he could not help but feel a thrill of professional interest tingle through his body upon first hearing about such an incident. Perhaps it was more than a little ghoulish. If this thrill were to be expressed openly, it would indeed be unsettling, even revolting to an outsider, but working in a world of crime as Vignoles did, it was essential to be able to respond with energy, interest, even with a measure of excitement to the task of understanding and explaining even the most disturbing and shocking events. It was appalling that someone had been so brutally attacked and but there was also no mistaking the fact that the call to visit a murder site brought a strange sense of anticipation and interest. Unravelling the mystery of what had happened and bringing those responsible to account, was perhaps the ultimate task in his line of work.

Vignoles finished cleaning his pipe. He'd found something to properly stir the lad up. Something to take his mind off what was probably an increasingly stultifying experience of being holed up for days in a sleepy vicarage, with rooms filled with heavy furniture and unfashionable floral print wallpapers on the walls, creaky bedsteads, smoking chimneys and collections of giant potted plants in equally giant vases on dark wooden stands. He needed to keep the lad engaged and so took a calculated decision.

'I believe the crossing keeper was struck several times to the head.'

'Gosh. Do you have any idea who did it?'

'That is for my detective sergeant to try and determine. He's still collecting evidence at this stage as it is still only a few hours since the body was discovered.'

'Has he any suspects lined up to interview?' Maurice was hooked.

'He has a likely murder weapon which suggests he might not be too long in apprehending a suspect. But I have only the barest details.'

'Can we go and help? I'd be awfully interested to see how a real murder investigation was carried out.'

'I'm afraid not, Maurice.' Vignoles concentrated on opening a fresh packet of 'Three Nuns' tobacco. 'It's a specialised job collecting evidence. Some of this can be fragile and easily damaged and one must restrict the number of persons on site to ensure such evidence is not contaminated.' This was clearly an unrealistic request, but Vignoles tried to make his refusal at least a partial explanation of the processes involved.

'Contaminated?' Maurice chewed this thought over for a moment. 'We don't have colds. And we could wear scarves across our mouths just in case.'

Vignoles laughed. 'I don't mean contaminated as if with a contagious disease. We must collect any minute scrap of evidence that might tell us who was present at the time of the murder, but the challenge is that all the time we are on site we also run the risk of actually adding to what is there. The fewer persons on site, the better.'

Maurice looked thoughtful as he digested this information.

'I wonder if your sergeant has any interesting leads?' Gwen asked the question. She could see that the conversation was animating her son and felt grateful for this despite the gruesome subject matter.

'It's very early in the investigation.'

'You said he found a murder weapon. Is that not a lead?'

'It is.'

'Was it a knife?'

'He mentioned a gardening implement that seems to fit the bill.'

'How does he know? Was it covered in blood?' Maurice was leaning forwards and his voice was full of interest.

'From what I understood, I think it might be,' Vignoles replied.

Gwen gave him a look that suggested this was more than enough detail.

'If he found it so quickly, I'd say the attacker didn't do a very good job of trying to hide evidence of their crime,' Anna observed.

'He's not very clever.' Maurice was enjoying this. 'If it was me, I'd want to throw the weapon in a deep lake or river, or perhaps bury it, so you'd never find it.'

'I very much hope you'd do no such thing!' Gwen looked at her son in horror, then at her brother as if seeking his support.

'I understand what you are saying Maurice. You're trying to see the situation from the eyes of the perpetrator. Thinking through their actions, imagining what you might do in that situation. This can be helpful, even if perhaps unsettling to those outside of the investigation,' Vignoles gave his sister a reassuring smile through the cloud of blue aromatic smoke as he got his pipe lit. She remained tight-lipped.

'It sounds jolly interesting work. I think I'd be good at it. Imagining how the crime was committed, using the evidence.'

'What conclusion are you reaching based on what you've heard?' Vignoles asked.

'It suggests someone who is careless. Who's lashed out once they knew they'd been identified – they struck in fear, and then ran off like a coward, throwing the weapon away with little thought of how to conceal it.'

'A decent first analysis.' Vignoles gave a little nod of encouragement.

'I agree. This was an unplanned attack done in haste,' Anna added, hoping to make Gwen feel more at ease by joining in the debate. 'That suggests a person who will fail to properly cover their tracks.'

'I think we are in agreement on this point.' Vignoles blew a smoke ring.

'I bet you'll get him quickly if he's so slap dash. Perhaps you'll be able to trace him to a hideout, then flush him out. But maybe he'll escape and there'll be an exciting car chase!'

'Your uncle works on the railways, so I hardly think a car case is very likely,' Gwen added tartly.

'But you told me you had a Rover these days?' Maurice looked disappointed. He'd shown no especial interest in trains in recent months, but a soft topped Riley in racing green passing through the village with a roar and a wink from the leather flying-jacketed driver had briefly snapped him out of a gloomy reverie and got him talking about sports cars.

'We do have one, and my sergeant is rather fond of driving it.' Vignoles laughed at Maurice's observation. 'I rather hope we can avoid the kind of car chase you see in B Movies, but if the crime was reactive rather than pre-planned, then I would expect an arrest quite soon. But in my experience, it rarely works out that way.'

'You're not convinced?' Anna could tell.

Maurice was intrigued. 'Have you smelt a rat? Found something even more suspicious? Do tell, uncle!'

'It would be wrong to speculate based on so little information. There are a few points I learned from that short telephone conversation that don't tally. It's probable I misunderstood and got hold of the wrong end of the stick. Nonetheless, some points need clarifying. You see, every detail, no matter inconsequential, require an explanation.'

'What sort of details?'

'That a blood-stained murder weapon was so easily discovered. A convicted murderer can expect a death sentence, so making little attempt to properly hide the weapon was foolhardy in the extreme. The murderer should at least have thrown it into a nearby river or pond asyou suggested. Or even given it a darned good clean and put it away where it would attract little attention. No, it would not surprise me if there was more to this investigation than immediately meets the eye.'

Chapter Fifteen

It was nearly two hours after finally rolling off shed before Ashbourne and Earnshaw spoke with the police. They had pottered around the yard banging and bumping coal wagons and a variety of wooden box vans into a train ready for hauling away later. However, both crew and the shunters working the yard were unable to think of anything except the shocking news. They had struggled to properly knuckle down to the job and it had taken an inordinate amount of time to finish a relatively short and simple task. Adding to their discomfort, was a sky heavy with ominous snowy-laden clouds and a keen east wind which all conspired to make for a trying and miserable time.

As they clanked their way back to top up the tender with water, they saw Charlton and Mitchell finally bring their train back up from West Wharf, many hours later than scheduled. All eyes were on their arrival, their locomotive fortuitously illuminated by a solitary finger of golden light streaming down like a bolt from an accusatory finger from William Blake's painted deity, hidden out of sight above the cloud cover. Perhaps this uninvited natural spot light implied that these men could shed more light on the dreadful murder. From the little Ashboure and Earnshaw had been able to learn, it looked as though they were the last people to have seen Old Janey doing her job at the crossing. This gruesome fact lent a sense of weighty anticipation to their return and everyone stopped and watched the stately progress of the empty coal train with considerable interest. The two figures standing in the almost open cab of their locomotive seemed to be giving extra concentration on their job, as if trying to evade the many glances and stares in their direction.

Earnshaw gave them a slight wave with his gloved hand as he leaned on the side sheet of the cab. He thought the two footplate men looked strained and tired, whilst the guard remained out of sight in his van. Earnshaw would hopefully get a chance to talk to fireman Mitchell, whom he knew quite well, a little later and hopefully hear more about what they had witnessed.

However, Earnshaw was more eager to finally get to speak with his best friend PC Simon Howerth, who was now standing near the water crane, shading his eyes from the momentary shaft of bright sunlight as he too tracked the arrival of the train with intense scrutiny.

'Si!' He gave the uniformed constable a wave.

'Eddie?' PC Howerth cracked a warm smile. 'I was wondering if you'd be around or if you were out Coalville way.'

'Chance u'd be a fine thing! We've been kicking our heels here for hours with bugger all to do.' Ashbourne peered over the side to see who was speaking.

'It's a serious incident. I've been collecting statements from absolutely everyone. I need to ask you both some questions before you can get on with your work.'

'Let me get some water in here first.' Earnshaw was already jumping down on to the cinders underfoot and swinging the heavy arm of the water crane over the tender using a long chain, so the black canvas tube that looked not unlike an elephant's trunk, hung over the water filler. 'Just a quick top up.'

Driver Ashbourne fiddled with the engine for a few moments, then carefully climbed down the cab steps, removing his gloves and leaning against the top step of the engine as he rolled a cigarette. 'What can you tell us? We're all in the dark. We knew her, you see. Old Janey. We'd like to know what's going on.'

My DS won't want me blabbing out too much at this stage,' PC Howerth made an apologetic gesture. 'He's on his way here to talk to the men who've just come up from West Wharf. Perhaps I can tell you more after that.' The older driver just gave him a withering look. 'It looks like a violent robbery took place in the early hours and Mrs Palmer died as a result of the injuries she sustained. I cannot say more.'

Ashbourne nodded, but remained silent. The bush telegraph had already told him this much.

Earnshaw had got the water flowing into the tender and walked across to join them. 'Why would anyone think she had something worth stealing?'

'Can you say she didn't?'

'No-oo... I've never actually been inside her place, come to think of it.' Earnshaw fell silent. He needed to stick to facts, not groundless speculation. This was a serious investigation.

'How well exactly did you know Mrs Palmer?' The question was fired at them both, but Ashbourne answered.

'Well enough. Always said "hello" and sometimes passed the time of day for a few minutes or so. You know, talking about the weather, how the spuds are coming along. How's the family, and such like. That's about it.'

'Were you aware she was alone last night?'

'Oh aye. Most of us knew that.'

PC Howerth raised a questioning eyebrow.

'It's a quiet little line and we all know who's-who and pretty much what each other are up to. We take interest and keep an eye out for each other. Naturally we learned that her Sarah and the rest of the family are away and I checked Janey had everything she needed for the duration. Milk. Bread. A few coals for her fire.' The driver looked at his fireman. 'Even soft lad here can vouch for that. Old Janey ribbed him rotten about not having a fancy girl!' Ashbourne gave Earnshaw a wink. It helped lighten the deathly mood that was gnawing at them like the north wind that was bearing a few flakes of snow.

Earnshaw nodded, but remained silent. For the second time that morning he felt a constriction in his chest and a stinging in his eyes.

'When did you last see Mrs Palmer?' Howerth was making notes, although his fingers were freezing and complaining.

'Well it were last night of course. We took the last train through. It was 9.30pm as we rolled straight through on the way to Coalville and back here then on shed.'

'You were on time?'

'Spot on.' Ashbourne gave the young PC a steely look as if resenting the question.

'Did you speak to her?'

'No. We'd had a quick natter over the side of the engine on the way down, but it was a raw night and the wind was blowing up. Not a time for hanging around. But there she was, with her funny helmet on her head right beside the track.'

'Was anything different?'

'How do you mean?'

'Was anything not as it should be, or stood out as strange?'

'Not as I saw.' Ashbourne shook his head and looked at Earnshaw.

'It was pitch black, to be honest,' he replied. 'But I saw her standing close to the door of her cottage. I didn't see anything amiss. I wish I had something useful to say.'

'Was her front door open?'

'I think it was shut. There was light spilling from the kitchen window.' Earnshaw was trying his best to be as accurate as he could. 'She watched us pass, then I ducked back in the cab and that was that.' He felt a lump in his throat and managed to stop talking before his voice cracked. He remembered well enough. He'd seen her standing there and willed his driver to hammer on down with their train and hurry away to drop off their wagons. He had a date waiting, and only had thoughts for the lovely Miss Darling. He felt foolishly guilty.

'But on the way down to Leicester you did linger a while at her crossing?'

Ashbourne hesitated and eyed the PC's open police notebook. All this was going on record and that might not play out well. But he'd already admitted they'd spoken with Palmer and he had little choice but to elaborate. If there was going to be any come back from senior management then he'd just have to take it on the chin. 'Just a few moments, mind, nothing more. Just checking things were alright.'

'And were they?'

Ashbourne shrugged his shoulders. 'She was the same as she ever was.'

'Did she speak to you, Ed?'

'Not really.' He felt his cheeks glowing despite the icy wind. 'She asked if I had a girlfriend.'

'Really?' Howerth felt slightly disappointed despite this intriguing revelation about his best friend. It was inconsequential and irrelevant. He thought he'd found two perfect witnesses who were going to report something amiss so he could get the credit for helping crack the investigation open. Howerth tried one last roll of the dice. 'On your way down and especially on the last trip back last night, did either of you see anyone along the line or any unusual activity? I don't just mean at Black Spinney. Anything at all.'

Ashbourne finished his cigarette and threw the stub onto the ashy ground then very deliberately stood on it and twisted his boot so it was extinguished. His voice remained as quietly spoken as before. 'No, but if I had an inkling I knew who'd killed her, I wouldn't be standing here talking to you. I'd take a fire iron and give the murdering Devil a hiding to within an inch of his life - then let you finish him off.'

Howerth said nothing for a beat. The man's quiet and deliberate manner left him in no doubt he meant what he said. 'It would better if you passed on any suspicions you have and leave us to deal with it.'

'Aye...well.' Ashbourne gave a deep sigh. 'I might not show it, but it's made me quite sick. And bloody angry.'

Howerth looked at his friend who was clearly putting some consideration into his reply. 'I'm trying hard to think. You don't know you need to remember who was where and doing what or things that happened along the way, so it's hard to dig it out.'

'Even if it seems like nothing, it could still be useful.' Howerth looked back at the driver hoping for something more.

'I can't say I saw anything that had me wondering.' He paused. 'Well, of course, I saw Irish Mick, but he's always around and there's nothing odd in that. He wouldn't hurt a fly!'

'Who is Irish Mick?' Howerth instantly looked interested.

'A tramp. Michael Mc-Something. I dunno what. But no, no.' Ashbourne suddenly looked regretful and turned to his fireman for support. 'We all know him and he's just a harmless down and out. Forget I even said that. He'd never lift a finger to anyone.'

'I think Mr Ashbourne is right. He's a right character and could do with a bath and a shave, but I can't see him killing anyone.'

'There is every chance this was a spur of the moment robbery. Like you said - what had she to steal? So perhaps someone with nothing, not even a roof over their head, might try their luck?'

An icy silence fell around the engine as the wind whipped around them. More flakes of snow danced and flew about in the air.

'When and where did you see this tramp?' Howerth knew this information could not be ignored.

Ashbourne took a moment to answer. 'I think you're wasting your time, constable -.'

'The DS can decide about that. We need to speak to everyone and anyone in the area. And perhaps Irish Mick saw someone acting suspiciously. Where was he?'

Ashbourne cleared his throat. 'It was not far from the crossing as it happens. A hundred yards or so before we reached it.'

'When was this?'

'On our way back to Coalville.'

'You mean you saw him close to the crossing as near as makes no difference to 9.30pm?' This was even better than Howerth had dared hope.

'He was beside the track, because I saw his cigarette glowing and could just make out a pale face in the dark as we passed.'

'Beside the line? How close exactly?' Howerth was aghast. 'You mean the rail side of the fence?' Ashbourne's silence was confirmation enough.

'He was trespassing.'

'I suppose you could say that...'

'There's no supposing about it!'

'Constable, we turn a bit of a blind eye to him. He's harmless and never makes trouble.' Ashbourne could hardly bear to see all this being written in the PC's notebook. It was not going to make good reading.

'Most unconventional.' Howerth gave Earnshaw a strange look. It was clear he would be asking his friend more about this alarming piece of news over a pint, in private. 'Did you see him?'

'Not this time. I suppose I was on the wrong side of the engine.'

Howerth closed his notebook. 'Thank you. That was very helpful. I need to go and find out if your friend Irish Mick is really as harmless as you say. If nothing else, he can explain why he was on railway property.'

* * * *

The short minutes alone in the car whilst driving to the engine shed at Desford Junction gave Trinder a chance to reflect on what had already been a busy morning. He parked the car close to the back of the red brick shed building, cut the engine, then sat for a moment with his gloved hands on the wheel as he chewed things over.

Whilst still at Black Spinney Crossing, PC Howerth had provided the contact details of Mrs Sarah Lake, the deceased's daughter. She was staying in rented rooms in Liverpool with her husband Derek, their daughter Rachel and her own young child, Daisy. Not that Trinder was particularly interested in the little girl, nor indeed did he feel unduly exercised about any of the family, as they were a great distance away and could hardly be considered party to the crime. Once armed with this information he'd telephoned the office and despatched WPC Lansdowne to Liverpool on the first train she could find, with instructions to bring Sarah Lake and the family back that same day to make a formal identification of the body. This would then allow the post mortem to take place. Lake could also help ascertain what had been taken from their cottage.

Trinder had then stared at the number written in the big, schoolboyish hand of the young constable and tried to decide if a telephone call was really the way to break such desperate news. It was far from ideal. He was needed here to undertake more interviews of potential witnesses whilst everything was still fresh and could not afford to delay these whilst he made the long journey to Liverpool to tell the family in person. Neither could he expect Lansdowne to handle this traumatic duty. As each hour passed, there was the possibility that news would travel – as it always seemed to do – and the family might hear of what had happened before he had spoken with them.

Reluctantly, Trinder had dialled the number and waited anxiously as the operator connected him and a bell jangled in an unknown room somewhere on the banks of the Mersey.

It had been an odd exchange and not nearly as testing as he'd feared. If anything, it had been rather abrupt and oddly free of emotion. Mrs Lake was at first silent and suspicious of who was calling her, as one might expect. Then there had been a sharp intake of breath as he passed on the news. This was followed not with the sound of crying or other indications of emotional anguish, but instead with near silence as the phone line whined and whistled and crackled. Trinder had an unpleasant suspicion the operator was still listening in, but this might have been his imagination.

'How did she die?' Sarah Lake eventually asked.

'She was assaulted and struck a number of times. We think she perhaps surprised a burglar outside her – your – cottage.

'She was outside?'

'Yes. We think she was putting out the oil lamps that light the crossing.'

'I see. Yes, I know the routine. The man jumped out at her as she was preoccupied?'

'That is a possibility.'

Another pause filled with electrical noises.

'Did she die quickly?'

'I could not give an opinion on that. We must wait for the doctor's report.' He thought he heard a sharp intake of breath, perhaps the first clear sign that the news was hitting home, but Mrs Lake said nothing. 'I'm sorry, I know this is difficult, but I must ask you to come here today to identify the body. It must be done as soon as possible. I've already sent one of my female police constables to Liverpool to escort you and your family back here.'

'There was no need for that! I can make my own way. I'm quite capable.' She sounded fierce and irritable.

'I'm quite sure you are, but WPC Lansdowne will be there as soon as she is able. I think it best you have her escort you at this difficult time. Please await her arrival.'

'If I really must. But I'll come on my own, there's no need for everyone to trail across there. And besides, Derek is back out on his boat first thing Monday. He'll want to see more of his daughter and the little one. It won't help mum now, dragging them all back. We don't get much time together and what we get is precious.'

'I understand.'

'When will she be here, this lady policeman?'

'WPC Lansdowne will be there in the next few hours. I regret I don't have the train times to hand as everything has been arranged very quickly.'

'Tell her to call from the station when she arrives. Goodbye.'

And that was it. Trinder sat back in the leather seat of the car and pondered this exchange. Shock was a strange thing. It made people act out of character. They were liable to say and do things quite at odds with their usual way of being. Added to which, over the telephone, Sarah Lake was just a disembodied voice travelling along a wire without the advantage of facial and physical gestures and movements to help provide insight into how they were truly feeling. This made it hard to judge character, and Trinder was glad he'd sent Lansdowne to Liverpool. She would have a good few hours in her company and would be able to gain a far better impression. It would be good to hear her assessment, because despite making as many allowances as he could, his initial response was that Sarah Lake did not seem exactly distraught that her dear old mum was dead.

Trinder strode purposefully towards the locomotive that had recently chuffed its way up from West Bridge. He'd allowed the train through Black Spinney Crossing on the strict understanding they wouldn't stop along the way. They could drop off their train of wagons in the yard and then wait for him to finish up at the crime scene before he joined them for questioning. These three men were surely his strongest set of potential witnesses. Any one might have been the last to see Mrs Palmer alive before the assailant administered that dreadful wound. Trinder had sent Benson to quiz guard Timmerman, whilst he tackled the two footplate men.

He introduced himself and immediately asked for their names and addresses. These were given, but they both looked uneasy and spoke quietly as they did so. Charlton was pulling an ear lobe, Mitchell was fidgeting and shuffling his feet nervously. A visit from the police rarely induced an enthusiastic response. Trinder was long used to cagey looks and apprehension and knew not to be hasty in reading much into their behaviour in these opening exchanges.

'May I come aboard? It'll be warmer up there, I'm sure!' A little levity to break the ice as he clambered up the cab steps. Driver Charlton perched on the stub of wood that served as a seat, whilst fireman Mitchell leaned on his shovel near the open end of the tender, which was still near full of coal. One short trip to Leicester meant they had plenty in reserve. Trinder was glad to stand facing the two men in the other corner of the cab, soaking up some welcome heat from the boiler backhead. The snow was starting to fall faster now and the 'lazy wind' was doing what it did best - not bothering to go around his body but taking the straight and lazy route through the layers of clothing he was wearing and bite deep into his bones.

'You are probably aware that Mrs Jane Palmer has been killed outside her crossing gate cottage. We suspect foul play.' Both men grunted acknowledgement. 'She was discovered at about 5.50am this morning by two platelayers, George Baylock and Graham Hind. They thought she was still showing signs of life and moved her inside and tried to administer first aid...'

'Did she say owt?' Charlton asked, his arms crossed over his chest as he leaned back in something approximating repose. 'Before she died?'

'Why do you ask?'

'I wondered if she'd given a clue who'd done it, that's why.' Charlton's eyes were quick. Two dark pools reading Trinder's face with a level of scrutiny that Trinder found intriguing, perhaps even slightly unnerving.

'No such luck. She was just about alive when discovered but expired soon after without being able to offer any help in identifying her attacker. What time did you leave the shed this morning?'

'We rolled off at 4.20 or so. We backed on to our train which was waiting on the siding just across the way and were off no later than five minutes after.' Charlton looked across at Mitchell, who nodded agreement.

'Was there anything different about this morning? Anything not quite as usual?' Trinder was making notes as he spoke, the brim of his hat largely covering his face as he bowed his head. He thought Mitchell was about to speak but Charlton cut across him.

'Nothing. All normal.'

Trinder was sure Mitchell had intended to speak, so looked up and held the man's gaze until the fireman shifted his weight uneasily and darted the more senior man a guilty look. 'You had to rush back home, of course. You know, for your knife. Not that that's got anything to do with all this.'

Charlton's face darkened, and he gave Mitchell a filthy look. 'Of course it's got nothing to with it, stupid!' He looked at Trinder and reined in his anger, then laughed, but it sounded forced. 'I forgot this-.' he dug into his blue railwayman's jacket and pulled out a hasp knife, the blade of which was folded into the handle. 'I use it to slice bread and cut cheese for me lunch. With dirty hands it pays to use a knife. Bloody daft to forget it!'

Trinder made a note. 'You came on shed as per usual, but then realised you'd forgotten the knife and dashed back home to fetch it?'

'Aye, that's about right.'

'What time was it when you realised you'd forgotten the knife and returned towards home?'

'What does it even matter?' Charlton looked exasperated and gave Mitchell another angry glance. 'You'd be better spending time trying to catch who killed old Janey.'

'That's exactly what I am doing. I need to understand everything leading up to the discovery of her body.' Trinder was not in the least bit sure this line of questioning was serving any significant purpose and was eager to keep Charlton on side. He was a vital witness and he needed him to be cooperative. 'In nipping back home for your knife, did you see anyone?'

'Such as?'

'At that time of the morning there would not be many people up and about and I'd like to speak to anyone you can remember.'

'I didn't see no one.' He sounded defensive. 'Not unless you count the knock-up boy on his bike, and that wet rag won't be much use.'

Mitchell squinted across the cab at the gauge glasses and quietly moved past Trinder, who took his turn with his back to the falling snow. There was a soft whooshing sound and a gently gurgling as Mitchell put the injector on. It took only a few moments but seemed to calm Charlton down and he started talking in a quiet and moderate manner, somewhat at odds to his earlier outburst.

'Ok. I was knocked up by Chambers and came straight over. I was already up and dressed and having a first smoke outside my door. Some days you're up and ready and other times you need him hammering on the knocker. But this morning I felt quite alive -.' Charlton stopped and winced at his use of the word. Trinder just nodded and made notes. 'I met Wally in the shed about a quarter past three, and we were starting to get the engine ready when I realised I'd left me blessed knife back home. I set Wally onto oiling around the engine and nipped off.'

'You did as instructed?' Trinder addressed the fireman.

'Of course. I was hard at it 'an all, what with getting the fire ready and oiling around on top of that. This old thing drinks oil like I drink tea and a right pain in the backside to get to some of the oiling points.' Was there a hint of resentment in his voice? Trinder made a mental note.

'Mr Charlton, when did you get back on shed after collecting the forgotten knife?'

'About four, or as close as makes no odds. Like I said, its only a step back to Desford.'

'Can you confirm that?' Trinder asked Mitchell.

'What is this? An inquisition?' Charlton flared up again.

'Just procedure. I need to get all details clear and have them confirmed.'

'It was about four. Has to have been as we moved off shed and were in the yard soon after.' Mitchell shrugged his shoulders, 'I was underneath the engine with an oil can in my hand when I heard Richie come back. I don't have a watch.'

Trinder nodded. He'd spent more than enough time on this detail and it appeared to be offering nothing useful. 'Tell me about what happened once you'd set off along the line towards Leicester. Anything you can remember, no matter how trivial.'

'We rolled off the yard by twenty-five past and once we'd got the signal for the line, we proceeded towards Black Spinney, passing there on time at 4.30am sharp.'

'You're certain of this?' Trinder asked Charlton.

'It's only a few minutes away and besides, we were the first train down the line. I can calculate the passing of time by where we are on the line without even looking at this – which is hard on the footplate at that time.' Charlton tapped his watch and Mitchell nodded agreement.

'What did you see as you approached Black Spinney Crossing?'

'Nowt. It were dark!' Mitchell replied, quick as a flash.

'Not quite. There were Janey's lamps, don't forget.' Charlton's voice was softer now, encouraging rather than admonishing. 'Remember?'

'I didn't see 'em.'

'You must have, Wal! You need to eat a sack of carrots if you didn't!' Charlton shook his head in mock outrage, a smile of disbelief on his face. 'And don't tell me you didn't see Janey? I waved at her as we passed, remember?'

'I remember you waving your arms about. No, no come to think of it, you didn't wave. You remembered that wrong. You pointed at something. Down over my side. I wondered what the Hell had got into you. You said you'd seen something at the side of the track. Eyes reflecting light.'

'I did? Strewth, I'd quite forgotten.' He made a short laugh to make light of it. 'I was sure I waved at Janey.' Charlton looked momentarily flustered and wiped his brow with a red and white spotted neckscarf.

'I've got it clear now. First you pointed and said something about dying rabbits.' Mitchell's tone of voice was mildly mocking. 'Inspector, don't ask me to explain what all that was about, but there we were, steaming along nicely when he gets it into his skull to come over my side and point at something I can;t see for the life of me by the line. It's flippin' black as pitch and I can;t see a buggerin; thing. Next thing I know he's over the other side, waving or whatever to Janey as we pass, then gives a toot on the whistle just before we cross the road, and I'm back to checking my fire.'

'I expect that's why you couldn't see them,' Charlton responded. 'You're looking into the fire all the time and then into the dark. It burns onto the back of the eyes.'

By way of a reply, Mitchell clanged the firedoor open and white blinding heat leaped into Trinder's face. He recoiled momentarily from the inferno. The door clanged closed again leaving his eyes with two floating dots of colour swimming in front of them. 'Now imagine in the night trying to see some soddin' creature flopping about in an unlit field after looking into that!' They all laughed. The fireman was right.

'Mr Charlton, you saw Mrs Palmer at the crossing?'

'Correct.'

'What was she doing?'

He hesitated for a fraction too long for Trinder's liking. 'Just standing there.'

'You're quite sure about that?'

'We passed in a matter of moments. Then I saw something in the field and wanted to point it out which distracted me. I think they must have been rabbits. There's loads of them around.'

'Quite possibly,' Trinder's voice was cool. 'But my interest is in Mrs Palmer. Was she holding the oil lamps?'

'The lamps?' Charlton spoke the word as if the very idea of oil lamps was hard to comprehend. 'Um...' He shook his head. 'I can't rightly say. Not to swear by.' He looked apologetic. 'I think one was in place and perhaps...' He screwed up his face as he made an effort to remember. 'Yes, that's right, she was carrying the other. That makes sense as the one she was carrying would be the one on Wally's side of the line, except it wasn't in place, it was in her hand.' Charlton looked relieved. 'It's hard reconstructing what you've seen isn't it?'

'It can be.' Trinder wished to sound sympathetic but was trying to decide if Charlton was just an innocently unreliable witness, or a bare-faced liar. 'Anything else? Perhaps a car or a motorbike parked near the crossing?'

'I didn't see nothing.' Mitchell replied.

'Me neither.'

'How well did you both know Mrs Palmer?'

'I've known her for years. I help her and the family out from time to time,' Charlton offered.

'In what way?'

'In the garden. She's got a veg patch out the back. I come over and do the heavy digging and get the spuds planted or lifted, put up the bean canes. Just helping out.'

'You go frequently?'

'Not frequently, but I was there Monday, as I was off due to my shifts. I was in and out of the garden shed and digging out the back.'

'Did you go inside the house?'

'No. I usually have muddy boots on. Occasionally I'd take a mug of tea by the range for a bit of a warm up, but usually I drink it outside. Janey was long used to being outdoors and with me working on this old girl -,' He slapped the side of the almost vestigial cab and grinned. '- I'm not scared of the British weather. And besides, there was Sarah and the other girls inside. I'd be in the way. They don't need me hanging around.' Another tug on his ear lobe.

'In the main you worked on her garden?'

'Correct.'

'You know what a mattock is?'

'Yeah...'

'Did Mrs Palmer own one?'

'She kept it in the shed out back. Why do you ask?'

'Was it in the shed when you finished working on her veg patch last Monday?'

'I suppose so.' Charlton stared at Trinder, unblinking, holding his gaze. The look of a man confident and unruffled.

'Might you or Mrs Palmer have left it beneath the cottage window that looks out on to the railway?'

'Of course not. I'm always very particular with tools and put them back in their place after use. If you knew Janey and her girls you'd know they were the same. They never left things lying about.'

'Mr Mitchell, how well did you know Mrs Palmer? Did you help around the house?'

'Not me. Can't say I knew her like a friend. We chatted over the side of the engine and passed the time of day. Same as I do with others on the line, but I never called socially.' He suddenly looked deflated, a sadness in his eyes. He looked across at Charlton as if seeking help, but the older man was staring at the cab floor, lost in his own thoughts. 'I just can't credit it.' Mitchell gave a slight shake of the head. 'It's bewildering why someone would do such a thing.'

'Thank you for your time gentlemen. I ask that neither of you leave the country in case I need to talk with you again.' Charlton gave a short laugh upon hearing this and Mitchell managed a rueful lift of the corner of his mouth at the idea either of them could sail off to some far-off land. Trinder snapped his notebook shut.

'That will be all - for now.'

Chapter Sixteen

WPC Lucy Lansdowne had not been expecting Mrs Sarah Lake and her family to be enthusiastic about seeing her, nor for Mrs Lake to be anything other than miserable company on the long haul back to Leicester, however, as she was shown into a large bedroom in the Cunard Hotel she was surprised at the level of hostility that was almost palpably emanating from the Lakes.

Derek Lake was a strong and muscular man of medium height with close cropped hair and an angular face weather-beaten to a nut brown in sharp contrast to the pale, wintry faces that most people were already wearing. He was dressed in corduroy trousers held up with black braces and an open white and blue striped shirt in thick cotton that allowed a good view of a neck laced with taut sinews and a tattoo of a swallow in dark bluey-green ink. He betrayed no sign of feeling the chill in his open shirt with rolled up sleeves despite a meagre fire in the grate that was failing to make much impression on the chill in the room. A life on the North Atlantic had clearly toughened him up. It was his big and powerful hands that drew Lansdowne's attention, however. The knuckles bore the disturbing letters 'L.O.V.E' and 'H.A.T.E' tattooed on them in crude letters suggesting it had been done by an amateur. Perhaps he'd done it himself, although Lansdowne could not imagine what would prompt him to scar himself with such startling messages. As Derek Lake swung the door open, he leaned on the door jamb with one arm, gripping it tight so 'H.A.T.E.' was revealed like a menacing beacon on knuckles that grew pale with the force of his grip. He effectively barred the door as he challenged her.

'What can I do for yews, luv?' He didn't sound like he was trying to be helpful.

'WPC Lansdowne. I telephoned from the railway station -.'

He glared at her with a withering contempt she found disturbing. The face of a woman could be seen beyond his shoulder. She was standing in the centre of the room holding the hand of a little girl.

'Mr Lake?' He did not react, so Lansdowne tried to catch the eye of the woman. 'Mrs Lake - Sarah? May I come in a moment, please?'

The man gave her a look up and down, his eyes lingering for too long in so doing and didn't seem to particularly like what he saw, then reluctantly stepped aside. It was an invitation of sorts and Lansdowne took a breath and entered the room, feeling self-conscious as she squeezed past his sinewy body. She removed her policewoman's hat before speaking again.

'Mrs Lake, may I offer my sincere condolences. This must be the most awful shock for you – for you all.' Lansdowne meant what she said, even if it was convention and not personal knowledge prompting her words. Sarah Lake however, looked and her china blue irises - made all the more intense by the clear whites that betrayed no sign of red or puffiness from weeping - stared back with the coldness of a gannet eyeing prey below the waves.

'I think it's none of yours or other folk's business. I feel what I feel and don't share it with those I don't know. Especially the police.'

Sarah Lake was probably in her early fifties with light brown hair pulled back and held in place on one side by a glittering diamanté clip. Her figure was an enviable hourglass and the smart twin-set of turquoise tweed shot through with flecks of darker blues and grassy greens, looked perfectly tailored and flatteringly enhanced her shape. It was an elegant travel outfit that had clearly cost her husband deep in the purse. Lansdowne spied a pair of long gloves draped over the back of a chair and a matching hat on a table. Mrs Lake was at least prepared for a journey, if openly unenthusiastic about her travel companion.

Her husband was standing with his arms folded across his chest and the bulge of his biceps was straining the cotton fabric of his shirt. Without doing anything more, his presence was still intimidating. He shifted his weight whilst his wife was talking and made impatient breathing sounds. Lansdowne felt ill at ease, sensing this movement so close behind her back.

'There was no need for you to trail over here you know. I can find my way home perfectly well.' Sarah Lake's voice lacked emotion. 'Another waste of police time and money of course.' She snorted with contempt, then, having communicated her thoughts about police funding, looked down at the little girl. Lansdowne judged her to be about four-years-old and clutching a little velvet bag with a draw string in one sticky hand and what looked like a strawberry jam sandwich made with sliced white bread in the other. 'Mind you don't drip that all over the floor, Daisy!' Although admonishing the child, there was a marked change in Sarah Lake's tone and genuine affection in the way she looked at the girl.

'It felt heartless to ask you to make the journey without someone to accompany you.' There was a stony silence. 'Mr Lake, I understand you wish to remain in Liverpool?'

'I've got a ship to board. I've got to earn a living. Hong Kong and on to Shanghai, for the record, so I don't have time to be taking no train trips half-way across the country.'

It was Lansdowne's turn to remain silent. Mr Lake was intimidating, and she was not about to pass comment on his apparent lack of concern that his mother-in-law was dead.

'It sails when it sails, an' I won't be sticking around, so yews don't go giving me that look, girl!' Lansdowne felt her cheeks flush. Had she telegraphed her feelings that obviously? 'Sarah is a capable lady. She don't need no policewoman sitting with her.' Derek Lake was contemptuous, his local accent strong. 'In fact, that's about the last bloody thing she needs!'

'Mind the language!' Sarah Lake gave her husband a quick look. 'I've told you, not in front of the little one.' Having encouraged the child to resume eating the sandwich before it emptied more sticky red goo on the none-too-clean carpet, she straightened up and adjusted the lie of her jacket, then rested her hands on her shapely hips. 'I've packed a bag, so when do we leave?'

'We have an hour before the next departure from Lime Street. Will it be just yourself? As I explained on the telephone, I have rail passes for you all.'

'Derek's staying here with Rachel and Daisy.' There was a pause. 'Rachel's gone to fetch some ciggies, in case you were wondering.' Her voice seemed to admonish Lansdowne for trying to discreetly inspect the room for signs of the missing mother of little Daisy. 'She's upset and taken it badly. She didn't want to be here when you called.'

'I'm sorry. I have no wish to cause distress.'

'I'm only staying the one night. That's long enough?'

'For the identification, yes. However, you will need to be present for the inquest. Although we don't as yet know when that will be.'

'It had best be after I sail,' her husband growled. 'I get little enough time with me missus as it is.'

'I suppose it won't be for a few days or more,' Lansdowne replied. 'I'm sure the coroner will try to accommodate your personal situation if at all possible.' She offered an encouraging smile, but it generated no response.

'We'd best be getting along. Are you lot paying for the taxi?'

'Yes, Mrs Lake. All expenses will be met by us.'

'That's something at least. Go on – I'll join you in a moment.'

Derek Lake was already holding the door wide open and Lansdowne was under no illusions it was time to leave. As she walked down the creaky stairs and past a battered black painted door with the frosted glass that declared it led to the Saloon, she was already processing what she'd seen and heard.

Bereavement, particularly under such circumstances, could illicit many responses and the Lakes were expressing their unhappiness in their own way. They spent little time all together under one roof and having to be wrenched away at short notice could make even the most reasonable person resentful, factor in a hideous murder and it was hardly surprising there was an atmosphere. Lansdowne could also imagine that her presence as an authority figure was far from comforting. She was effectively reinforcing the shocking fact that Lake's mother had been taken away by a wanton act of violence. She would cut Mrs Lake some slack for her brusque manner.

The taxi was waiting as pre-arranged, the driver sitting with a neatly folded paper resting on the steering wheel whilst he read about the football on the back page. Lansdowne stood on the curb waiting for Mrs Lake to appear, hugging her coat tighter as the perishing wind hurtled off the Irish sea. The air smelt of salt and brine mingled with burning house coal and a strange amalgam of scents from all manner of goods being transhipped in the docks close by. There was a continual low hum and rumble and clatter of activity, punctuated by regular blasts on shrill steam locomotive whistles or the occasional ship's hooter booming with a deep bass tone. It was a world away from the lonely crossing cottage set deep in the heart of rural Leicestershire. She wondered how Mrs Lake and her daughter managed the transition between the quiet and barely altering rhythms of the countryside with the gentle passing of the occasional train and this noisy, lively, ever-changing bustling sea port, full of people and buses, trams, trains and glamorous ocean liners?

Chapter Seventeen

Trinder walked away from the locomotive, head bowed slightly against the falling snow. He couldn't put his finger on exactly why, but there was something about Charlton and Mitchell he was unsure about. Were they telling the truth or was this all carefully rehearsed? They'd had a long time on the footplate together to agree their stories, so it was a possibility he had to accommodate.

He stepped inside the open door of the small engine shed to gain shelter and cupped his hands together as he struck a match and fired up a cigarette. Standing tall and exhaling his first lung full of smoke he glanced back across the yard and was un-surprised to see both crew standing in the cab of their engine looking his way. Mitchell was drinking tea from the enamelled lid of his billy can but turned away the moment Trinder saw him. Charlton however, just stood with arms folded and stared back.

Trinder leaned against a heavy wooden work bench and continued to smoke. *All right, Mr Charlton, I can face you out any time of day.* He continued to observe the crew whilst turning over his interview with them. The immediate problem as far as Trinder could see it, was that these two men worked a regular link. Always together and probably with the same engine and he suspected for some considerable time. They might even be friends outside of work or just work colleagues, but either way railwaymen stuck together as a rule. As Trinder considered this fact he watched Charlton finally lose interest in the staring match and the two men quietly and efficiently worked on their engine, followed by a short toot on the whistle as the elderly machine trundled out of sight.

The question was, if one told a lie, would the other back it up?

Trinder's guess was that neither would deliberately snitch on the other. But if the lie was covering murder? Surely not. If both men were guilty of attacking Palmer – it was possible – then they would construct a joint story that could be hard to break down. But did these two men really do such a thing? He wasn't convinced. Two seasoned engine crew violently attacking a friend and colleague for a few pounds under a mattress? No. He didn't like that one bit.

When he thought about their odd tale it all felt oddly plausible for being faintly ridiculous. Charlton at moments had floundered a bit, but that was probably because he'd had to admit he'd caused a distraction so both men had effectively diverted their attention away at a vital moment instead of keeping watchful eyes on Palmer, the crossing gates and most importantly, a clear road ahead.

They were key witnesses, not lady killers, and Trinder reminded himself to keep his imagination firmly in check. This had been drilled into him over the last year on numerous training courses and it was time he started putting the theory into practice.

Charlton saw Palmer and claims she acknowledged the driver's wave from the cab. This suggested Palmer had recovered sufficiently from the first assault to go about her usual routine of opening the crossing. Like so many loyal railway workers, she was unlikely to shirk her responsibilities and so, still groggy and possibly concussed, she'd managed to open the gates. Palmer was probably working slowly and in a less organised manner than usual, hence the imperfectly displayed oil lamps. However sore she felt from the bash on the head and shoulders, she'd managed to let the first train of the day through. But what jarred was why she did not flag down their train and tell them what had happened? Charlton was a family friend and would surely have helped in her hour of need. Any crew would have. It was a consignment of loaded coal wagons, not a packed commuter train or crack express running to a tight schedule and there was no imperative to let them pass without even a brief mention of her distress. It made no sense. Not even a telephone call through to Miss Green. It was odd.

Trinder needed to learn more about Palmer, but he suspected she'd been a tough and uncomplaining sort. The kind of person who wouldn't make any fuss. A bang on the head was no reason to go waving her arms about and bringing the railway to a halt. She would get the trains running, make a nice cup of tea and then there would be time enough to advise her superiors of what had happened. If this scenario was correct, then it was soon after the train had passed that the assailant returned. Seeing she had recovered so well, he must have decided that he needed to silence her forever.

That at least narrowed the time band for when the fatal blow was delivered. He should concentrate his efforts on the period between the train passing and Baylock and Hind walking up the line. A shorter timespan was manna to a detective. If gave focus to an investigation.

'Sir?'

Trinder snapped out of his thoughts by WPC Benson and PC Howerth approaching.

'Did the guard have anything to report?'

'I'm afraid not, Sarge. He was busy making tea inside his van, and apart from a cursory glance through the ducket window on the side, he took little interest.'

'Did anyone on that train look where they were going!' Trinder felt a sudden flash of exasperation. 'Did he at least see Palmer?'

'He caught a fleeting glimpse of her back view – he recognised the outline of her tin hat so knew it was her. That was it.'

'More interested in his tea...'

Benson agreed.

'Nothing else? No suspicious murderers loitering with intent?'

'Er...No.' Benson gave Trinder a strange look.

PC Howerth had respectfully remained quiet during this exchange, but it was clear he was itching to speak.

'What is it, Howerth?'

'I've just discovered something. It's important.'

'Yes?'

'We might have a murder suspect.'

Trinder threw his cigarette away and stood upright. 'Go on.'

'A tramp. Called Irish Mick. He was seen in the area about 9.30pm last night...'

Chapter Eighteen

The taxi ride from Kirkdale to Lime Street passed in silence, both women staring out of their respective side windows at a city draped in smoke and sleet and encroaching darkness. It was a city of brooding buildings, warehouses and serried ranks of tall-storeyed Victorian dwellings with corner pubs and shops at street level, their windows throwing warm yellow light on the damp roads and pavements. A giant Christmas tree outside St George's Hall was festooned with garlands of coloured bulbs bringing a splash of much-needed colour in front of this monstrous classical edifice that was a uniform matt black of furry soot. The city was settling in for a night of filthy weather.

At Lime Street station the two women had to walk some distance along the central access road that allowed the black taxicabs to drive into the station and stop in the centre of the express train platforms. Their seats were booked in a carriage at the very front of the train, which due to the its length, poked out from beneath the glazed over-arching roof and was unprotected from sleet now falling in unpleasant splatters. This less than ideal location was perhaps indicative of the complementary nature of their travel arrangements.

Sarah Lake didn't seem to mind, perhaps relieved to move away from the curious eyes of porters and travellers milling around the portion of the train closest to the taxi rank. A number of curious bystanders were already throwing unsubtle glances their way, perhaps wondering why a smartly-dressed woman was being escorted to the train by a policewoman. It must look as though Lake was under arrest and this did nothing to improve her truculent mood. Not for the first time that day Lansdowne wished she'd had time to change from her uniform before setting off on this journey, but everything had happened so fast there had been no time.

As they approached their carmine and cream painted carriage, they hesitated a moment at the door, huddled under Lansdowne's umbrella that reverberated to the sound of thick icy rain. The grand locomotive coupled right next to their carriage chuntered quietly and something of its warm and powerful presence caught their attention. This gleaming sky blue-painted beast was steaming as though with sweat, the pale clouds of scented vapour curling softly around their legs before evaporating.

'Like a race horse after a gallop.' Lake stopped and appeared transfixed. 'I go to the races with my hubby. Not as often as we'd like, of course, as he's at sea so much. I like them after the race when they're steamy like this.'

Lansdowne smiled, pleased the silence between them was broken even though the sleet was starting to dampen her legs and she felt a shiver through her bones. Anything to lighten the mood and make their trip that bit easier. 'It does look like a working horse harnessed to its load and ready to start work.'

A barely audible wolf whistle from one of the crew leaning from the cab drew their attention.

Lake looked up at the smirking, thin-faced man with his peaked cap made glossy with drops of sleet and apparently balanced on ears which stuck out like Dumbo's. A pair of gloved hands rested on the polished cab side sheet. 'Mind your manners or she'll arrest you!' But Lake's voice was surprisingly light-hearted and there was a spark in her eyes that had previously been missing.

Lansdowne laughed gently, eager to encourage the thawing of the tension between them. 'Oh look, the engine's named 'City of Leicester'.'

'It's not the engine I'm looking at.' Lake's reply was surprising and not what Lansdowne had expected, but at least an improvement on stony silence.

'Going far, ladies?' The fireman had to raise his voice to be heard over the hiss of the locomotive and the crisply enunciated tones of the station Tannoy announcer.

'To the City of Leicester,' Lansdowne replied, taking a couple of steps closer to the engine, Lake joining her under the umbrella.

The man pulled a rueful expression. 'A shame, I'd love to take you all the way...'

'We're definitely getting out at Edge Hill!' Lake and the fireman both laughed with something flirtatious in the sound.

'Actually, we change at Stafford...' Lansdowne was puzzled.

'Another time then! Best get aboard ladies, we're all set.' The fireman stood upright. 'Enjoy the ride.' And with a toothy grin and an outrageously cheeky wink, he turned his attention back to his engine.

They took their seats in their empty compartment, but the mood had noticeably lifted and Lansdowne hoped they might manage to converse a little and make the time pass that bit quicker. She was eager to learn more about Lake's mother and their life together in the cottage. Any information gathered might prove instructive and perhaps offer a clue as to who could have committed the crime.

They settled facing each other in seats beside the grubby window smeared with streaks of soot and watched and listened as 'City of Leicester' made a series of slow volcanic eruptions as the heavily laden London train slowly eased into motion. Great swags of steam dropped into view as the engine started to bark more regularly and they observed a turntable nestling under a towering sandstone rock face. They watched as a sombre black tender engine that glistened with the wet as if newly varnished, slowly turned around about thanks to the efforts of the crew bent to their task in clothes darkened with the rain. Then everything went dark as they entered the first of a long series of tunnels and overbridges that spanned the unfeasibly deep and narrow cutting that commenced almost at the platform ends. All they could see were indistinct swirls of smoke pressed to the window glass, regularly illuminated by flashes of deep orange reflecting on the thick billows as the impertinent fireman hurled more coal into his locomotive's fiery belly. It felt like a vision from Dante. Fire and smoke and a pervading smell of sulphurous coal whilst the ricocheting bark of the engine reverberated around the compartment like repeating cannon fire. Smoke now started to seep into the compartment, illuminated by the weak electric lighting. Sarah Lake sat leaning forward, resting her chin on her hand staring at the window whilst a ghostly wreath of smoke curled around her as if she were smouldering. Her expression was intense and hard to read. Lansdowne thought she looked slightly demonic when the flashes of orange flickered on her pupils. It felt like a relief when the engine burst out of the dark into the lighter, albeit rapidly fading, daylight and with an almost joyful wail on the whistle tore through Edge Hill station as it gathered speed.

'It's an old joke. But not for polite company.'

'Sorry?'

'Getting out at Edge Hill.'

'Oh.' Lansdowne was non-the-wiser.

'It means not going all the way. You *know*.' Lake gave Lansdowne a salacious look. 'Telling your man to stop and get out before he does you-know-what down the dark tunnel.' Lake laughed at Lansdowne's horrified expression. She was used to policemen and railwaymen and their risqué jokes and bad language, but this was so unexpected it startled her.

'You *have* got a fella?'

'Of course.' Lansdowne felt mildly indignant but happy to allow the conversation to take this intriguing course. It might prove instructive.

'Then you know how it is, you sometimes let them have a bit of a fumble around, but then it's time to tell 'em to get out at Edge Hill. Ha ha!'

Lansdowne smiled. Mrs Lake was quite a character and evidently had learned some of the local jokes from her sailor husband. It was healthy Lake could laugh and make a joke on what must be a desperately difficult day. There was no harm in a few moments of ribald humour to take her mind off the depressing reason for their journey. However, it might also suggest indifference. Lansdowne's detecting instincts were on high alert as she moved the conversation on.

'Daisy is a sweet little girl. How old is she?'

'Nearly five. Mind, you saw her on a good day!' Lake smiled. 'But, she's a darling at heart and especially if she's something to eat to keep her quiet.'

'And your eldest is how old?'

Lake made a strange laughing sound, a mixture of mirth and surprise. 'Rachel is my daughter, but Daisy's not *mine*, me duck.'

'Daisy is Rachel's little girl?'

'Of course, but I'll take looking young enough to be her mum any day. Just wait until I tell Rachel.' Lake seemed to be enjoying the mistake.

'The father ran off soon after Daisy was born, leaving Rachel in the lurch. He was a good-for-nothing waste of time if ever I saw one.' She made a snorting sound that perhaps said far more than her words. 'Then he got himself run over by a delivery truck in Carlisle whilst staggering home drunk. Can't say it was any loss to the World.' She rootled in her handbag and fished out a packet of Peter Stuyvesant menthol cigarettes and placed one in her perfectly lipsticked mouth, but immediately removed it again as she spoke. 'They're both better off without him.' She noticed Lansdowne's expression. 'I know, there are plenty will say Daisy needs a mum and a dad but believe me he was good for absolutely nothing.' She replaced the cigarette and struck a match. 'Rachel and Daisy came to stay with me and -.' Lake stopped a moment as she took a deep drag on her cigarette, her hand shaking slightly, although she quickly stilled the motion by resting her arm on the rudimentary table that stuck out under the compartment window. '- and with mum.' She took another puff, then put her handbag away from her lap and smoothed her skirt across her shapely thighs and fiddled with the buttons down the front of the perfectly tailored jacket clinging to the curve of her ample bust. These were the first open demonstrations of her bereavement Lansdowne had witnessed.

'I can imagine your mother loved having you all there. All girls together. Four generations under one roof. It must be special.'

'Crowded and noisy, more like. Sorry, duck, I was not thinking -.' Lake offered the pack of cigarettes to Lansdowne, who declined whilst deciding that now was not the time to mention it was a non-smoking compartment. Getting Lake talking was important and she didn't want to do anything to break the flow or spoil the fragile alliance that seemed to be building. They were alone, so a little smoke might be overlooked just this once.

''We get under each other's feet to be honest. It's a tiny place. Have you seen it?'

'No. I came straight from the office.'

Lake studied Lansdowne for a few moments as she smoked. 'It's not made for so many. There was a time when it was normal to have everyone crowded in on top of each other of course. You should see some of the places in Liverpool and how they have to live. Bombing those slums was a blessing.' Lansdowne was unfamiliar with life in such a big city but could appreciate the point being made. 'But you expect better these days, don't you?' Lake exhaled smoke in a slow, extended breath. 'I'd love a house on one of those new estates. All bright and clean and modern and with an electric cooker with a eye-level grill. Imagine that! New shops with those new strip lights and good roads and maybe even a little car on the drive. I can dream. Anyway, with Derek at sea most of the time, it just made sense us being all together with mum. We muddle through.'

'Do Rachel and you both work?'

'Of course. We can't all live on a crossing-keeper's pay!' She snorted derisively. 'Rachel's part time over at the brick works. Does a bit of office work. I don't think the business is doing well so they can't offer her full time, but that suits for the moment as she's got the little one.'

'And yourself?'

'I'm in sales.' Lake said it proudly and paused a moment, perhaps hoping for a positive reaction, but Lansdowne remained silent. 'I travel and promote beauty products. I'm with a very good company that offers good prospects. They're an international brand.' Her bosom swelled with pride. 'They reward good monthly sales with bonuses.'

'Travel?'

'Yes. Around the county. Well...my sales area is focussed more on the villages close to our place.'

Lansdowne suddenly recognised the twin set as uniform, not a private choice. 'You're an Avon Lady?'

'That's right.'

'I suppose the work means you keep irregular hours.'

'Late afternoons and some evenings. It works well, as I help mind Daisy whilst Rachel is out. Evenings are the best time to find the lady of the house at home.' She made it sound like she only visited country estates and significant houses rather than the suburban outskirts of Leicester and insignificant villages.

'You have a car?'

'No such luck.' There was a nervous pull on the cigarette. 'Not yet. I cycle.' She said the word as if embarrassed. 'We hope to get a Morris Minor.'

'I always use a bike or the bus,' Lansdowne replied.

'I've a case of samples to carry and the villages around about are scattered wide so it's hard in the bad weather. And slow. I might live next to the railway, but those trains are no use, worst luck.'

'Were you and your mother close?' Lansdowne suddenly changed tack.

'She was my mother.' A long drag on the cigarette followed. It was an open-ended statement that offered no insight.

'Rachel and Daisy got along well with her?'

'Look, I know it's your job, but you could cut the personal stuff now. You're a pretty thing and probably nice enough, but I feel like I'm on trial.'

'Sorry. Asking questions comes naturally to those in my profession.'

Lake smoked in silence for a while and stared out of the window at the River Mersey that glimmered between the diamond patterns of the steel latticework of a long railway bridge they were crossing. Lights were sprinkled across both banks of the river and a freighter lit up as if with candles, inched its way along the Manchester Ship Canal. She stubbed out the cigarette, took a deep breath and looked at Lansdowne.

'I didn't mean to sound harsh. You've a job to do. So, come on, what can you tell me? Let's get it over with. I'm going to have to face the facts at some point, aren't I?'

'I'm afraid so. I'll try to make this as easy as possible.'

'Forget the soft soap, duck. There's nothing you can say or do to change things. She's dead. That's it. And we're going to be evicted as quick as you can say the word because the cottage is tied to the job. And before you ask, no, I don't fancy opening and closing gates for the rest of my life. Let's not shilly-shally around and pretend it's going to be easy, because it won't be.'

Lansdowne swallowed in the face of this harsh assessment. She then recounted the bare facts of the crime as she understood it. A summary by DS Trinder over the telephone had given her a fair understanding of the situation. 'We're treating this as an aggravated break in. A robbery that went wrong.'

'Of course it is! Nobody would want to just kill her. Sometimes I feel like I could strangle her, but that's just families. Don't give me that look, I don't mean it, it's just something you say. For goodness' sake, why would anyone want to kill *her*?' Lake sounded exasperated. 'What did they take?'

'We're hoping you can tell us. DS Trinder wants you to look around and tell us what's missing.'

'There's nothing. Mum only had a few little things to her name and got paid a pittance for working all hours. They won't have found much.'

'Did your mother have savings in the house? People of her generation are not keen on using a bank and often prefer putting money under a mattress or in an old biscuit tin.'

'She had some savings. She and my old dad put money aside. They were careful. Thrifty. A lifetime of saving and she had a couple of hundred pounds. Maybe more. I don't exactly know.'

'A significant sum to keep in the house.' Lansdowne was shocked.

'There was no telling her. She'd never trust it to a bank.'

'Perhaps someone heard about this money? It would be a serious temptation.'

'She never talked about her savings and kept it locked away. That's why I'm not sure about what she had.'

'She could have let something slip. Perhaps whilst chatting to a close friend or acquaintance? People talk, they pass on what they've heard. It's all too easy to accidentally let the cat out of the bag.'

'You think this was done by someone we know? A friend?' Lake gave Lansdowne a searching look.

'The majority of all crimes are committed by people known to the victim. Not always close friends or family, but someone who knew your mother was alone that night. With all of you at home, I think it unlikely anyone would have risked a break in.'

'I see.'

'Can you think of anyone who might do such a thing?'

'Of course not! We don't socialise with murderers.' Lake sounded contemptuous and looked out of the window as a station flashed by the rain-streaked window.

'We think the robber was only interested in theft, but when your mother discovered them, they responded with force.'

'It was an accident?'

'That would be generous to the assailant. Anyone striking another with force intends to do serious harm. But we need to wait for the post mortem report and see what fresh evidence has turned up before further speculation.'

Lake seemed eager to speculate, nonetheless. 'People pass the crossing all the time.' She was narrowing her eyes as she spoke, as if bringing half remembered memories to mind. 'Some stop and pass the time of day. They could see how we live, observe our comings and goings. Learn our routine. Some of these people we know almost like friends, others are complete strangers. Any of them could easily have worked out that mother was alone.'

'Can you remember someone acting too inquisitively? One too many questions about you and the girls going to Liverpool?'

Lake stared at the little rivers of rain snaking their way down the window for a moment as she considered this question. 'Most folk are decent enough. But I've never had time for vagrants and gypsies. I never give them the time of day.' Lake nodded her head with conviction and some of the aggression first displayed in Liverpool returned. 'I bet one them did it!' Her eyes flashed with resentment as she looked at Lansdowne. 'That's it. It was a thieving – murdering gyppo! I'm telling you, that's who you should be looking for.'

Lansdowne did not react and kept her voice calm when she replied. 'Is there anyone in particular you are thinking of? Someone who has given you cause for concern?'

'One? They're all the same, aren't they? You can't trust any of 'em as far as you can throw 'em.' Her voice took on an unpleasantly hard edge that did not suit her as she dug into her handbag and pulled out another cigarette. 'One beggar looks like another. Dirty and scruffy and always looking to scrounge something.' She shrugged her shoulders dismissively.

'You are thinking of a homeless tramp, rather than a group of travelling gypsies?'

'What's the difference?' Her face was momentarily masked by a cloud of smoke as she exhaled with a hard sound. 'You need to round them up and thrown the bloody book at 'em.' Perhaps it was the smoke irritating her eyes, but they were narrowed to slits and held a strange, cold gleam that suggested a lack of generosity. Her face lost some of its charm and her stiff, jerky movements as she smoked and sharp exhalations of smoke made her even less attractive. Lansdowne was making mental notes.

'Alright. I'll tell you. There's a sneaky tramp who comes past all the time trying to cadge stuff off us. Always wants a fag or food or whatever else he can wheedle out of anyone soft enough to listen.' She waved a hand to suggest the unlisted requests. 'I shoo him away - of course. Fat chance of getting anything off me and I won't let him even look at Rachel! Ugh. But mum was too soft. I told her no good would come encouraging his sort.' Another drag on the cigarette. 'I even caught him in the kitchen once or twice, drinking *tea*!' She shook her head in disbelief. 'The biscuit tin was cleaned out by the time he left.'

'He was invited in by your mother. Why would he abuse her hospitality?'

Lake snorted contemptuously. 'Because that's what they do. At least once a month he comes around. Sometimes more often, maybe when I'm out at work. The perfect opportunity for the thieving so-and-so to sniff around whilst she was busy minding her instruments and the gates. It adds up. You'd best tell your sergeant to arrest the good for nothing and empty his pockets' She gave Lansdowne a look that suggested she'd already as good as solved the crime.

'City of Leicester' wailed a warning note as the sleet battered against the glass like so many grains of rice tossed against a wedding car window.

* * * *

Thomas Leach was standing beside the buffer stops at the end of the platform. He was just a few steps away from the sleet-stained locomotive that had recently hauled his train into the vast Victorian Gothic edifice of St Pancras. He felt tiny amidst the great walls of fantastically sculpted terracotta and smoky red Victorian brick set beneath a giant vaulting train shed that seemed to drain all the light from the many lamps dangling from lengthy chains. Filthy smog mingled with locomotive smoke and sickly air that made people cough and hold handkerchiefs to their mouths or breath through scarves wrapped across their faces.

He stood like an immovable rock amidst a wave of happy weekenders heading to the West End and buffeting their way against the opposing tidal flow of workers eager to get aboard their packed trains, slamming the many doors of their carriages almost in unison as the guards urgently whistled them away to start their weekends in the northern suburbs or in the Bedfordshire commuter belt. Leach was glad of the hustle and bustle. A single man in a hat and suit could easily get lost far in the madding crowd of impatient pen pushers and overly-perfumed office girls - and he had a strong desire not to be discovered.

Leach had deliberately taken a Midland Region train from Leicester London Road rather than travel back from Leicester Central. On the spur of the moment, he had broken his journey south at St Albans, where he'd hastened to find some much-needed sustenance at a café and then into a cosy pub for a pint or two. He'd needed the drink. He'd never been to St Albans before and was sure no-one would think to find him there and this knowledge gave him time to calm his nerves and start to think of a solution to the desperate bind he now found himself in.

Not that he'd got very far understanding what had happened or what he was going to do about it. A dead body was bad news, but the goods he'd been instructed to collect were missing, and that was actually far worse.

If those two facts were not bleak enough, he'd needed to use some of the considerable funds entrusted to him in the now slightly less fat envelope in his suit jacket pocket to help buy himself out of that tricky situation. Three awkward facts all demanding explanation.

Or perhaps not. His client wasn't a man much interested in listening to him whine about what went wrong. He wanted his property and had paid more than handsomely for it to be collected. If he didn't get what he wanted, then he expected action to be taken. Suitably severe punishment would be administered to the person or persons responsible for this aberration and Leach knew that he was included. You did not let this kind of man down and expect to get away with just a telling off. Failure to deliver was not an option.

Leach lit a cigarette. Even a swift return of the items in question might not be enough to save himself from a beating. A few hard slaps and kicks to keep him sharp and on his toes, but at least bruising and broken ribs healed. His reputation might cut him some slack. He charged 'top dollar' as the Yanks would say, and he did as he was instructed without fuss or bother. But if he stood any chance of saving his skin then he needed to act quickly. He needed to keep his head down under the radar to buy himself some time whilst he called in favours and asked awkward questions about dangerous men it was unwise to be inquisitive about. It was going to be a dangerous twenty-four hours or so, but he needed to know who had stolen a march on him and taken the goods in question.

He stared at the green and black steam engine that had hauled his train and noticed it bore a brass nameplate that declared it to be 'The Sapper'. What kind of a name was that? 'A Sucker', more like. He'd taken a sucker punch this morning, that much was for sure. Someone had muscled in and pissed on his chips, and he needed to find out who - and quickly. If they'd got some inside 'gen' on this tightly-kept secret, then they must be people with good connections not afraid to double-cross his client. That took courage. Leach whistled quietly and nervously between his teeth as he considered this startling fact. Anyone with the brass neck to pull that kind of a scam was going be a big player with a goon squad of heavy weight muscle to offer protection, and the only suspects he could think of were London boys.

First things first, he needed to alter his plans. Change his routine and avoid all the places he might be expected to visit. He best not return home tonight but find a hotel on the other side of town and get to work before they sent someone looking for him. It wouldn't take them long. He was already late for the pre-arranged rendezvous and every hour he didn't show up just increased the danger he was in. He'd need to square up to them at some point, but when he did so he needed to offer something as an olive branch. He needed a name at the very least, but the goods would surely save his neck. If he failed, he'd be fitted for a pair of concrete boots and left standing at the bottom of the Thames.

He felt an icy shiver through his body despite his expensive cashmere overcoat. He needed a brandy. A drink solved nothing, but fear and nerves were starting to take hold and he needed some Dutch courage, so he strode towards the crowded station bar filled with cheery Friday night commuters starting their weekend.

Two smartly dressed gentlemen decided at that same moment to also thread their way through the throng to the same bar. They didn't hurry and had the knack of slipping between moving people with the ease of big African cats through the brush of the savannah. And like cats homing in on their prey, their eyes never once lost sight of the back of Leach's head.

Chapter Nineteen

'Your mother's body was discovered here. It looks as though she was carrying one of the oil lamps at the time she was attacked,' Trinder elucidated. 'Did she always put them out and take them in at the same time?'

'Without fail,' Lake replied. 'Always before she rang in to the 'box in the morning, and immediately after ringing off in the evening. In the evening she'd snuff the flames out then bring them inside and put them on the scullery floor where they stank the house out if she didn't shut the door. I thought them a fire risk, but she was not having any of it, saying they were too valuable to leave outside. In the morning she'd get the range glowing again with a scoop of coal, put the kettle on, then light the lamps and hang them outside and nip back inside for the first brew of the day. She did it like clockwork.' Lake looked at Trinder. 'That means you know when she was killed.'

'We have a reasonable idea.' Trinder's concerns about exactly when Palmer had died were still nagging him and his lack of conviction was betrayed by his voice. Lake's analysis was sound. If Palmer maintained a strict timetable, and if she was putting the oil lamps out before signing on, then she must have been attacked just before 4am. Conversely, if she was collecting them in the evening, it must have been shortly after 9.30pm. The big fly in the ointment was that the doctor had been unable to support either time in his initial observations and hinted at a confusing gap between attacks. If Palmer was dead before 4am then how on earth could she have opened the section?

Perhaps something had happened that forced Palmer to alter her disciplined regime? A stranger approaching, attacking the window or the door. All plausible. Far harder to explain, was the testimony that Charlton had seen her outside the cottage and given her a wave and guard Timmerman's imperfect view of her from the back of his van about 4.30am. Nothing was adding up.

Conscious that Lake was staring at him with some impatience, he snapped out of further consideration of these contradictions. She looked tired. The visit to the morgue to identify the body had been mercifully brief and Lake had stoically taken just a few moments to identify her mother and not lingered looking at the mutilated corpse. Lake had stifled a sob, wiped a tear away, smoked two cigarettes in succession in the police car as they travelled across to the cottage, but otherwise said little and succeeded in hiding her emotions. Her face was pale and her hands trembling slightly, although the deepening cold was just as likely to be responsible for both symptoms. Trinder must press on then let her take some rest.

'I need you to see if anything is missing. We're working on the assumption this was a robbery.'

'I can't see why else anyone would do what they did. Though we've got nothing worth stealing.' Lake stepped inside and stood in the centre of the room and looked around, her face inscrutable. 'Did your men leave those cabinets in such a mess? They can jolly well put them straight! They're always neat and tidy.' She sounded annoyed.

'This is how we found them. It looks as though someone searched through all the tins and packets,' Lansdowne answered.

'Why would they do that?' Lake's voice was almost contemptuous. 'Surely they wanted valuables, not dried peas?'

Everyone was thinking the same thing.

'Can you see anything missing from this room?' Trinder enquired after Lake had slowly walked around, her hand occasionally reaching out towards a familiar object before pulling back at the last moment without touching it. She seemed respectful of their wish to preserve the crime scene intact.

'Not that I can see. I need to look upstairs.'

They stomped up the creaking wooden stairs covered with a thin runner that did little to deaden the sound of a loose board that let out an angry squeak and entered Palmer's bedroom. The damaged chest of drawers was immediately obvious, and Lake walked over to it.

'Mum kept her savings in here.' Lake indicated the draw with the forced lock.

'Was there much? Trinder asked.

'Quite a bit.' She paused as if debating whether to say more. 'I've been thinking this over, and there might have been as much as £500, but I can't be exact.' Trinder raised an eyebrow and Lake noticed, whilst Lansdowne stifled her sharp intake of breath. She could buy a Semi-detached house with a garden and a garage in Stoneygates for cash with a sum like that.

'I thought you said there was nothing worth stealing?'

'I am not sure exactly.' Lake looked flustered. 'I do know she and dad saved for literally years and years. All their working lives. They never went out. How could they, tied down to those ringing block bells and gates to open and shut every day?' She snorted. 'Look at this place. It's from the Ark. She never bought many clothes.' Lake did not sound as though she held any affection for the family home. 'She never spent anything on us.'

'Was there anything else in the drawer?'

'A few things she thought were important, but I can't remember what. Nothing interesting.' Lake stared at the gaping wound on the wooden surface where the lock had been forced and at the obviously empty draw. 'I know there was a set of silver teaspoons. A wedding present from some long-dead aunty. I don't suppose they were very valuable, but they meant a lot to her and of course, she never used them. And a few Irish linen napkins and a tablecloth.' Lake shook her head. 'Jesus. You really think she was killed for a tablecloth and a set of spoons?'

'No.' Trinder's response was instant. 'She was most probably killed for that substantial cache of money.' Trinder was intrigued that Lake chose to focus on the low value items. 'It would be like robbing a post office or local bank branch - but far easier. The other items could be useful in identifying the perpetrator, however. If you could give us detailed descriptions, we can get our officers looking out for someone trying to sell or pawn them.'

Lake nodded acquiescence and continued her walk around the upper floor. There was nothing to note, except that in her own bedroom a small box in which she kept a few items of jewellery had been opened and emptied, but the contents were discovered lying on the floor behind the dresser, perhaps contemptuously swept aside in frustration once they realised they were of low value.

'Do you not find that odd?' Lake challenged Trinder. 'They don't want the jewellery but take a few stupid tea spoons?'

'I do. The money was a good haul and hard to trace. A far better prospect than jewellery - or spoons.'

'Perhaps by the time they got to this room the robber was feeling his nerves jangling and realised that these items could be traced, so abandoned the search and escaped?' Lansdowne offered.

Lake glanced at her and nodded. She accepted the explanation.

'I would like you to walk around the outside of the property and see if anything is not as it should be.'

'If I must,' Lake agreed, and they made their way outside, turning up collars and pressing down hats against the snow. They had to narrow their eyes against the stinging flakes.

'What are those?' Lake pointed at a row of white plaster blocks standing in a row on a piece of tarpaulin with sacking laid on top.

'One of my officers has been making plaster casts of boot prints in the mud,' Trinder explained. 'WPC Benson is also taking ink prints of everyone's footwear so we can eliminate those we might expect to find here – we will need to do yours.' He looked at Lake's expensive shoes with smooth soles, singularly unsuitable for the wintry conditions. These, and her fine twin-set looked at odds with the almost Spartan cottage interior. Her appearance was in stark contrast with the tired interior and unremarkable items within. 'We need to obtain a print of your husband's boots for elimination purposes.'

'Well that's another waste of time, as he's not been over here in a year.'

'So long?' Trinder wondered if they could also pass over on chasing that up. It would mean another haul over to Liverpool.

'Can I see the prints in the mud?' Lake asked.

'Of course. Mind how you walk. Just here – and here.' He and Lansdowne shone their torches. Snow was already starting to gather in the impressions, further highlighting the detail and making them more clearly defined than before. 'Do you recognise this tread? It's quite distinctive.'

Lake stared at the prints for a while and looked as though she was going to speak, but then shook her head. 'Just boots. Most of the men around here wear boots. As did mum.'

'Which is why we are checking everyone's footwear to see if we find a match,' Trinder replied. 'Did you own a mattock?'

'Is that a garden implement?'

'Yes, with a short, pointed end and the other for digging hard ground.'

'We've many garden tools in the shed. We might have one in there. Why?'

'We believe a mattock was used to damage the window frame - as you can see here.' Trinder indicated the fresh scars of the assault on the window. 'We think it was also used to kill your mother.' There was silence for a beat and they could hear the wind rushing through the branches of the spinney. 'The mattock was found lying underneath this window.'

Lake went even more pale. 'I see.' She pushed a strand of hair away from her face and wiped some snowflakes from her cheek. 'You think there are clues on it - something to tell you who did it?'

'We hope so. Can you show me where it was usually kept?'

Lake nodded and chewed on the inside of her lower lip as they walked around the cottage and through the neat vegetable patch towards a green-painted wooden shed. She expertly unpinned the door, held fast by yet another nail in the manner the family seemed to favour, and opened the door wide. Rows of old, but well-maintained tools were neatly arrayed along one wall. The other side was taken up with a heavy bench stacked with small terracotta plant pots, trays filled with tiny brown packets of seeds, bundles of twine, a pair of work gloves and all the other paraphernalia of the amateur market gardener. Everything looked in place and there was no evidence that someone had disturbed the contents.

'I think it was stored there.' She pointed to a gap between a fork and a spade.

'Who used this shed?'

'Mum mainly. I sometimes helped her, but I'm not much of a gardener. In my line, selling cosmetics, I have to keep my hands and nails looking immaculate. It would never do to turn up with chipped nails, would it? I can tell you that Rachel has no interest at all and wouldn't know a spade from a fork.'

'Anyone else?'

'Richie Charlton was in and out of here, of course. He comes over to help sometimes.'

'Richard Charlton, the engine driver?' Trinder asked.

'He's a family friend. Mum's friend, any road. We're used to him coming and going as he pleases and...' She stopped mid-sentence and stared at Trinder as if in disbelief.

'Presumably Mr Charlton would know about the mattock kept in here?'

'Obviously. But sergeant, you can't seriously think he would do such a thing? That's ridiculous! Why would he? Mum and he got along well.' Lake's voice and expression were incredulous. 'Why would he kill her for Heaven's sake?' She paused as the image of a drawer once filled with money appeared to come to mind. 'Look, he was in and out of the place all the time and if he really wanted to steal her savings he could have done it without any of us noticing! He could nip upstairs and be in and out of that drawer in moments. It was hardly a secret where mum kept the key!'

It was a valid point.

Lake slapped a hand impatiently against her expensive coat. 'As I told your lady constable on the train, it's not decent folk like Richie you should be pointing the finger at. You need to talk to those filthy scroungers who come sniffing about our door begging and thieving all the time.'

'You've had other thefts?' Trinder asked, his interest piqued since PC Howerth had reported the sighting of an Irish tramp in the area.

'Not as *such*. But come on, everyone knows what they're like! They'd steal as quick as they'd look you in the face. You have to watch them like a hawk - or else they'd strip the place clean!' She gave a disapproving sniff. 'You read all sorts in the papers about the gyppos. They must have heard about mum's savings.'

Trinder said nothing. This was mere speculation based upon her own prejudicial attitude towards gypsies, tramps and thieves and not backed up by anything that sounded remotely like evidence. Nevertheless, it chimed with the sighting of just such a character the night before, so he would put a call out along the railway and across the county that same evening. It was time to haul Irish Mick in for questioning.

Chapter Twenty

PC 1870 Steven Bacon of the Leicestershire Constabulary was cycling (he would later describe this in his report as "proceeding") at a leisurely pace, aware that his rear tyre was in need of more air, made worse by the near freezing cold, and was wondering if he should stop and deploy his bicycle pump. He was not feeling especially eager to kneel at the side of the road and get his stiff fingers into action fiddling with the dust cap on the inner-tube valve and so he gently pedalled on, concentrating on avoiding the worst pot holes to help protect his tyre.

The snow was not yet settling with any great enthusiasm, but there were wind-blown gatherings of white at the margins of the road and it was collecting in the plough furrowed fields above which, lapwings wheeled, making the idea of pulling over and stopping even less appealing.

Oh, for a hot cup of tea! But it being Sunday the little cafe in Glenfield was closed. However, despite his ruminations on sweet tea and optimum tyre pressures, PC Bacon was a diligent officer and had taken careful note of the briefing his sergeant had given them the day before about keeping his eyes peeled for suspicious characters. He was to make sure he quizzed all and sundry he encountered to see if they could help the British Transport Police with their enquiries. Everyone in the station had talked of little else but the Black Spinney murder and there was a desire to do all they could to help the investigation. Instructions had come down to specifically look for vagrants, and for one particular individual who should be brought in for immediate questioning. Bacon had dutifully made notes, but better still, he thought he knew the tramp the sergeant said they wanted to talk to, and PC Bacon was sure he could track the little rascal down. It was therefore with slightly more enthusiasm than normal, he had pedalled off to start his day whilst hoping that his squishy tyre would not prove a hindrance.

Murder. Around these parts? Heck, that was hard to fathom. PC Bacon's head was almost spinning with the news. He just couldn't stop thinking about it. Even if he was destined to play only a minor role in the case, if he put in the time and effort, he might be the man who found the witness who would offer up a vital clue. This thought alone ensured that the next day or two could potentially be more exciting for PC Bacon than the last few years taken together.

His gentle beat around the sleepy villages and business premises of this part of Leicestershire, whilst undoubtedly an important civic duty had resulted in few tangible results. It was hardly a hot bed of crime around here. Any sense of fulfilment was based upon the demonstrable fact that almost nothing ever occurred here beyond the odd incident of petty pilfering, a few drunken fisticuffs on Friday nights or youths trying to push a railway wagon along a siding. Whether this was a direct result of his pedalling and freewheeling along quiet lanes on his trusty bike was hard to say, but he could at least take some comfort in believing that his presence was an active deterrent. However, this weekend, things had notched up a few gears. He'd already passed the crime scene a number times since the murder as it lay at the heart of his beat, and he'd conversed with whichever constable was on duty at the time.

Today, his good chum PC Rouse was on duty, even though the corpse and the finger print boys were long gone. DS Trinder of the British Railways Detective Department had made it clear he wished to maintain a low-level presence on site for some days following the murder to protect the cottage from thrill seeking onlookers and the press corps and also in the hope that somebody might stop and offer information about what had happened.

Constables Bacon and Rouse had avidly discussed the crime and the rumours and theories already spreading like wildfire. The sums of money stolen from the chest of drawers was now varying wildly from a few hundred to many thousands. Bacon was no longer sure of the officially quoted figure, but both men agreed that this incredible sum was explanation enough, and even the threat of hanging would not deter some folk from the idea of getting their hands on a thousand pounds or more of used and untraceable bank notes. They were also in agreement that someone local must had got wind of the fact the old lady was alone that week and decided that this would be a good time to rob her lifetime's savings. It stood to reason. It was obvious that is what had happened. Old Janey had let her tongue wag once too often (and let's face it she loved to chat and gossip) and she'd let the cat out of the bag and there you go. If that was not proof enough in the minds of Bacon and Rouse, then the spoons were surely the deciding factor that declared this the work of an amateur, albeit one with streak of violence and temper. Both constables had chewed over the fact that Irish Mick needed bringing in for questioning. His was perhaps a surprising name on the wanted list as the tramp had never been especially troublesome before now, but they both agreed that there was no knowing what a man might do when he was hungry and under the influence of drink.'

'It was crying shame, but there you go.'

'Money and drink working their worst...'

'There's no knowing folk. They can just snap one day...'

'It was just too much of a temptation...'

'Aye, you're not wrong there...'

They shook their heads meaningfully and felt confident they had the case sewn up.

It was with this conversation still ringing in his ears that PC Bacon saw Mickey McMullen, aka 'Irish Mick' seated on a newspaper in the lee of a blackthorn hedge. The man was fiddling with some metallic objects resting on a piece of fabric opened on his knee, and Bacon's suspicions were instantly aroused.

He freewheeled closer and as McMullen heard the tick-tick-tick of his bike and looked up, Bacon noted the tiny clinking sounds as the cloth was hurriedly wrapped around whatever it was that was sufficiently interesting for the vagrant to sit in a hedge in a developing snowstorm. The bundle was pushed into one of the pockets of his filthy coat.

'What have you got there, Mick?' PC Bacon felt his pulse race. He must take this slowly, falling back on the drills he'd learned years before during his training.

'Nothin'. I've got nothin' at all. And isn't that that the story of me life?' The tramp gave a toothy smile and beamed at the policeman with an expression of complete innocence. 'Now you wouldn't by any chance have a wee cigarette...'

'No, I haven't! And I've told you before about cadging things.' PC Bacon dismounted and carefully propped his bike on its stand. 'I want to see what you've got in your coat pocket.'

'I've got nothing in there!'

Bacon lifted a sceptical eyebrow and held McMullen's gaze. He wasn't accepting that.

'And why can't a poor hungry fella just sit here and mind his own business? What's it to you what I have in my pocket, anyway?' McMullen was looking put out, but he was stalling for time. The inevitable shake down was coming.

'Ah, so you do have something. Let me see.'

'It just a few wee things. Nothin' of any interest to you, nor anyone else expect.' McMullen was already slowly reaching into his pocket knowing that resistance was futile.

Bacon waggled the fingers of his gloved hand with impatience. 'Come on, I haven't got all day.'

The tramp regretfully unrolled the square of yellow and red handkerchief to reveal six small teaspoons. They were bright with an almost bluey-silver quality in the flat, snowy light of day. Polished and clean, they glimmered against the fabric. Somebody had taken great care of these.

'Where did you get those?'

'I found them.'

'A likely story.'

'I did - as God's my witness!'

'If we find a witness who saw you steal them from where I think these came from, you'll need more than God on your side!'

'I've nothing to hide.' McMullen was frustrated, but he knew his options were limited. 'I saw them lying there at the side of the road just mindin' their own business and that's no word of a lie.'

'Or you took these from inside Black Spinney Crossing cottage.' Bacon gave his sternest stare at the filthy tramp who was giving off a powerful odour of unwashed body, bad breath and drink. PC Bacon was grateful for the wind gusting some of this foetid aroma away. 'You stole these from

Mrs Palmer.'

The wind however seemed to have gone from McMullen's sails. His mouth moved open and closed a couple of times like a beached fish before he managed to answer. 'I never! That's a scandalous lie. I swear on Mary, Joseph, Jesus and all the -.'

'Save your breath, I get the picture.' PC Bacon waved the man to be quiet. 'You protest too much and that makes me even less inclined to believe you.'

'I'd never rob Old Janey. She was always good to me.'

'You admit to knowing Mrs Palmer?'

'Everyone knows Janey! God knows, she was about the only person who had time for me.' McMullen's cheeky humour faded in an instant and he looked like a tired and hungry man, old before his time, eyes red-rimmed and watery. A shabby figure without hope, forced to sit on a newspaper in the snow at the side of the road. A miserable life you'd not wish on your enemies.

PC Bacon gave the slight figure a searching stare. Did he really look like a brutal killer? 'If you didn't break into Mrs Palmer's house and take these spoons, then where did you find them?'

'Like I told you, I found them in the hedge. A wee while ago and I couldn't hardly believe my luck.' His eyes were anxiously roving up and down the lane as if he expected someone to appear. Someone he was reluctant to meet. 'There they were, all wrapped up in this cloth.'

'Where was this, exactly?'

'On Rothley Lane.' McMullen's face suddenly took on an eager look, and he ceased searching the lane and held his gaze with the constable. 'Now it's funny you mention Black Spinney, because it were just a few steps along from there.'

'And that curious coincidence has me wondering again why I should believe you.' PC Bacon narrowed his eyes and took a few moments to study both the tramp and the gleaming spoons laid out in a row once more. He had no detailed information about whether the spoons reported taken from Mrs Palmer's house came wrapped in such a bright piece of cloth, nor did he have any specific information about their design, but he knew that six had been taken and apparently were the poor murdered woman's pride and joy. He was sure these were one and the same.

'Give them to me,' PC Bacon held out his gloved hand.

McMullen recoiled. 'I found 'em! If someone wants to go leaving them at the side of the road, I don't see why I can't be keeping them.'

'They're not yours to keep. Now hand them over then show me exactly where you claim they were lying. Point out the spot.' He paused to give the vagrant a hard stare. 'Tell me the truth, otherwise things could get very serious for you.'

'They're just old spoons. I had the idea that seeing as nobody was wanting them, what with them lying unloved and unwanted by the side of the road, I might get ten bob for them in a pawn shop...'

'Ten years more like – or worse.' There was a hint of real menace in his voice. PC Bacon gave McMullen a steely look. The tramp was trying to flannel him with all his jokey Irish repartee and it was starting to grate. He was not prepared to humour him any longer.

'For those?'

'For murdering Mrs Palmer and stealing her property.' Bacon carefully rolled up silver spoons and pocketed them. 'You're coming down the nick to answer some questions.'

McMullen scrambled to his feet. 'You can't arrest me for taking these out of a hedge!'

'I'm not arresting you. I'm asking you to accompany me to the station where we can discuss this in the warm. Now, you can walk with me and stop bellyaching about wrongful arrest or I can telephone the lads to drive over in the Black Maria and slam you in the back. The choice is yours.'

McMullen grumbled and regretfully eyed the bundle now being secured in the constable's bicycle bag. They could have bought him many a hot meal, a warmer coat and some new gloves. 'Will I be gettin' a mug of tea and a ciggie? And a biscuit or two on top? For co-operating.'

'I'm sure we can stretch to that. Now move along.' Bacon was feeling the cold and snow was starting to tumble heavier from the leaden sky. He knew the tramp, having encountered the cheeky rascal more often than he'd prefer, but he'd never once seen the vagrant act violently nor indeed be mixed up in any serious monkey business. But that little bundle looked mightily suspicious. Surely it was too fanciful for two sets of silver teaspoons were knocking around these quiet lanes? That was for the detectives to decide, of course, but he would take the credit for bringing in a chief suspect.

He allowed a quite smile. Despite the cold and the snow, this was shaping up to be a good day at work.

Chapter Twenty-One

DCI Vignoles was seated behind his desk in Leicester Central station, pipe smoking in one hand and a steaming cup of deliciously strong coffee (thanks to his father-in-law finding a supply of good beans) perched on the one clear space on his customarily untidy desk. He was feeling almost guilty about how much he was enjoying being back in the office.

He'd taken last week off and was not due back in until tomorrow, but if he was brutally frank, he'd been going stir crazy at the vicarage, and was itching to get his feet back under his desk to riffle through the papers steadily piling up. Even if he chose to put aside most of this paperwork for another day, he could, at the very least, look out onto the bustling platforms of Central. Even now he could see the tell-tale signs of a fireman busy preparing his B12 type engine for imminent departure, with the blower raising a little stain of dark smoke from the chimney as the overall-clad figure threw on a round of coal.

Gwen and Maurice would need plenty of support in the coming months and he would do his best to be there as and when they needed him. However, there was a limit to what else one could say or do after a week of being cooped up together. His continuing presence was not going to bring Mike back from the all-too freshly covered grave nor significantly lessen their pain of loss. If anything, he suspected both Gwen and Maurice were finding the constant attention suffocating. The simple truth was, they were going to have to face the inescapable reality in their own way and in their own time. Everyone now needed some breathing space after the ordeal of the funeral last Saturday and Vignoles felt it would be in everyone's best interest if he took himself away for a few days. Sunday had been perhaps the worst day so far; dragging interminably, each of them lacking energy and inspiration as the awful come-down after the funeral took hold. They'd done their best, talked too much about subjects that didn't interest them, drank and eaten too much for no other reason than something to do and taken aspirins and liver salts to reduce the head and bellyaches that followed. There had been nothing left to say except endlessly repeat how 'it had gone well' and agree 'they had done him proud', but nerves were starting to fray and they constantly got under each other's feet and the danger of someone inadvertently causing upset and tears was never far away. Maurice in particular had been irreversibly sulky, and his glowering expression and monosyllabic responses had tested even the Reverend Vignoles' reserves of patience.

The call to arms prompted by a murder investigation was exactly the excuse Vignoles needed. Anna had also leapt at the opportunity afforded by her husband's need to return to the office by suggesting she take Gwen and Maurice into Leicester for some Christmas 'window-shopping' - although really just an excuse to get into the distractions of the city, eat homemade pasta and unseasonal ice cream at Carelli's where they would be thoroughly over-indulged by Anna's parents. As a consequence, they had all travelled in together by train that morning in surprisingly high spirits. Better still, Anna and Vignoles would return to their home that evening, which was an appealing prospect for both.

Vignoles was eager to see how Trinder had managed with the investigation. Murder was a grim business, and whilst he had every confidence in Trinder's acute abilities, Vignoles could not afford for this case to come off the rails. They had a responsibility to do right by the poor murdered woman and Vignoles needed to run his experienced eye over proceedings. His rank and presence back at work demanded he take ultimate control, but even so, Vignoles was going to allow Trinder a freer rein than usual. He wanted to see how his DS handled the responsibility. Was he testing Trinder? Perhaps he was...

Trinder had passed across a sheaf of carefully typed case notes for him to read the moment Vignoles had entered the Detective Department offices that morning. This had been accompanied by the intriguing information that a possible suspect was already waiting in the holding cell ready for when they were ready to question him.

'Looks like you've been busy, John. Let me run my eyes over this one more time whilst I smoke a pipe and ruminate on what you've discovered, then we'll take it from there.'

The perfect syntax and lack of correction fluid in these case notes betrayed the swift and able hand of WPC Lansdowne, who was meticulous to a fault on the typewriter and in her command of the English language. Trinder, bless him, was forever crossing words and sentences out with any colour of pen that was to hand, blotting words and letters with liberal applications of the sticky white fluid that tended to congeal into a lumpy smear or just adding his (many) corrections between the lines of type in a cramped hand that was hard to decipher. The content was usually acceptable and incisive, but the presentation fell short. Trinder was obviously learning how to delegate and it made for easier comprehension.

Vignoles took another swig of coffee and watched for a moment as a gleaming new British Railways 'Standard 5' engine trundled to a halt outside his window with the down Manchester stopper. These were still sufficiently rare for its arrival to demand a moment's attention. Doors banged as small wheeled sack trucks ground their way across the platform hauled by porters hefting luggage and parcels to and from the train. Like so many worker ants, scurrying about all with jobs to do and working together in a complex but not easily discernable pattern, that on the surface, looked like chaos. With pipe jutting from the side of his mouth he steepled his fingers and lost himself in thought, now barely watching the animated scene before him as Vignoles turned his mind to considering what he'd just read.

There were aspects of the report to commend and Trinder had demonstrated a methodical response; making swift and important decisions from the start. Requesting close cooperation with the Leicestershire Constabulary had been wise and handled with assurance. The rivalry between County Constabulary and Transport Police was ever-present and needed careful management. The older and far larger force considered themselves infinitely superior to 'The Train Boys' as they liked to call them, and rarely lost any opportunity to score points or make irritating jibes about them 'playing trains' and not being 'proper' policemen. Well, this was a murder of a railway worker on railway property and Vignoles was going to make sure his team saw it through and didn't suffer the humiliation of having it handed across to the 'civvies' as they in turn liked to call the constabulary. His team were more than capable of handling a murder investigation and proven themselves on numerous occasions before and they were not going to fail this time.

To that end, good efforts had been made to gather a wide selection of forensic information, some of which still needed detailed analysis. A hefty set of statements had been collected and carefully sifted and processed. There was a pencilled footnote from Trinder advising him to expect a raft of photographs from the lab later in the day, showing the crime scene and victim, together with the all-important results from the post mortem which might well push the case forward significantly. Added to which, there was the homeless tramp pulled off the street and presently biding his time in a tolerably warm cell with breakfast and a mug of tea on to keep him amenable. He was currently prime suspect in DS Trinder's opinion.

Vignoles agreed it was essential they interviewed this character and the decision to pull him in and hold him was wise. Any eagerness he felt to commence the interview was, however, being tempered by the fact there lay a rather serious problem at the heart of this case, as presented. There were a number of problems, in fact, and these had not been satisfactorily addressed. Vignoles needed to work these through using the information he had, hoping to offer some explanation for the apparent anomalies. The problem was, the more he considered the facts, the more puzzled he was becoming.

He re-read the report for the third time, then let the papers drop to his lap as he stared once again at the platform outside his window. The Palmer case was shaping up to be a proper puzzle. This was going to be a tough nut to crack and promised to exercise his mind. He was glad he'd made the decision to come back to work.

* * * *

DS Trinder meanwhile was seated at his desk towards the rear of the larger of the two rooms that formed the Detective Department offices. From this vantage point he could survey the others at their desks and see Mavis Green stationed behind her monstrous typewriter like a gate guardian, forbidding entry to anyone unless they met with her approval. WPC Benson had her head down working on her own separate report. She was presently comparing ink prints taken from the boots McMullen had been wearing when he'd been brought in, with a print taken from one of the plaster casts she had made at the crime scene. Both appeared identical and she was eager to have this significant piece of evidence ready to be shown to Vignoles.

WPC Lansdowne was talking on the telephone to the Leicestershire Constabulary, following up some details thrown up by their door to door enquiries, whilst PC Blencowe was standing before a large-scale O.S. map of the area surrounding Black Spinney Crossing and carefully pinning small flags indicating where those they had interviewed were placed at the time Palmer's body was first discovered. It was an impressive piece of work, but no matter how hard Trinder stared at it, the little flags were not persuading him either way about Micky McMullen's guilt, nor were they helping him untangle the problematic issue of when exactly the crime took place.

In fact, Trinder was struggling to concentrate on this pressing matter. He was due to report to Vignoles any moment and needed to get his thoughts in order before they both tackled McMullen, but instead of his usual clarity of thought, he was distracted by an envelope he was slowly turning in his hands away from the sight of the others.

It had been, somewhat fortuitously, handed to him directly by the postman instead of landing on their doormat where Violet might have found it. When delivered a few days ago the envelope had been fresh, white and crisp, but now was already showing signs of wear and tear. Repeated handling and extraction of the letter inside had taken its toll. But no amount of re-reading the letter or turning the envelope around was improving his state of mind. Why could he not just face up to the facts and deal with them? Instead, he stupidly stared at the envelope in the vain hope that one last look might give him the courage to admit to what the letter inside demanded of him. Trinder felt his stomach churn. Perhaps he was sickening for something. He tried to convince himself it was not his own weakness and an attack of nerves causing this sensation. A cold was quite possible. The snow falls over the weekend had brought a sudden change in temperature and the train journey in to work had been in a sweaty, overheated compartment filled with cigarette smoke and body odour poorly concealed by various after shaves and perfumes and the reek of damp wool. This unappealing reek had forced him to escape the claustrophobic atmosphere of his compartment and lower a drop light on one of the doors in the corridor to get some fresher, but bitterly cold air. Catching a chill was preferable to enduring a moment more of that foetid air.

He shivered, then impatiently thrust the letter back into the jacket pocket where it had lain for the last week.

Pull yourself together! Just blurt it out and deal with the consequences!

His internal dialogue was no less intense for being silent. Lansdowne, looking up at that same moment and met his gaze.

'Everything alright, sir?'

'Of course.' His voice was uncharacteristically brusque and he impatiently stood up and adjusted his suit jacket with a slight cough to clear his throat. 'I'm wanted.' He could hear the new-fangled intercom buzzing on Mavis Green's desk. Vignoles was summoning him.

* * * *

'The vagrant McMullen is your chief suspect. What's your thinking?'

'One of the interviews picked up his name. He was seen beside the railway not far from Black Spinney at about 9.30pm by driver Ashbourne and fireman Earnshaw as they were returning towards Desford Junction moments before they passed through the crossing. Mrs Palmer's daughter, Sarah Lake, also offered his name as a likely candidate.'

'Did she elucidate as to why?'

'No. It was a bit of rant, to be honest. An attack on anyone who lives on the road and ordinarily I'd not give much credence to it.'

'But you have something more concrete?'

'Plaster, actually.' Trinder risked a slight smile. 'The most compelling evidence comes from Benson. She's been analysing the various boot and shoe prints found at the crime scene and discovered that the boots McMullen was wearing when he was picked up on Sunday are an exact match to some fresh and clear prints at the crime scene. McMullen's boot prints were found on the front door where it had been kicked, adjacent to the spot we understand the body was lying and also leading to and from the tool shed where the probable murder weapon usually resided. It makes for a compelling argument that McMullen is our man.'

'It suggests McMullen kicked the door – for whatever reason - and walked past Palmer as she lay on the ground. It could however be argued that he coincidentally was there a short while before a crime was committed. I accept the boot prints place him there, but at what time, and doing what?'

Trinder took a sharp intake of breath but said nothing.

'Are you satisfied about his motive for killing her?'

'He's hungry and without money. Palmer had a very substantial amount squirrelled away.'

Vignoles gave his pipe some attention. 'You're standing by the idea this was an opportunist robbery that spun out of control during which, Palmer was assaulted and later killed in order to protect the intruder's identity?'

'Ye-es.' Trinder sounded cautious. 'I think the robber had prior knowledge that Palmer was alone that week. McMullen could have gained that information quite easily as he was apparently a regular passing the cottage.'

Vignoles nodded. 'Which introduces pre-meditation into the equation. Have you been able to corroborate Sarah Lake's estimation that £500 was taken?'

'No. We have to take her word for it and she was only able to offer her own guess.'

'That's unfortunate. A very substantial sum if correct and motivation enough for violent robbery. Why might Lake lie?'

'I was not aware Mrs Lake has lied?'

'You cannot be sure she did not. We're forced to take what she says on trust and this puts us at a disadvantage whilst allowing Lake to introduce a powerful motivator for a violent crime. However, what concerns me is that I find it hard to believe that even with a life time of scrimping and saving, Palmer could have amassed anything like that much.'

'I was rather taken aback.'

'McMullen did not intend murder?'

'I think the assailant did not go there intending to cause her death.

Perhaps he first tried for a knock-out blow to buy time whilst he rifled through her belongings.'

'A reasonable assumption.' Vignoles flicked through the report to find the relevant point. 'But I'm puzzled about when this knock-out, as you call it, took place. The doctor seems to be suggesting Palmer was attacked twice - with an interval of some hours. What do you make of that?'

'That point has nagged away at me over the weekend. We're awaiting the full post mortem report which hopefully will clarify the matter. On the day, the doctor showed me older bruises to her neck and shoulders that suggest a severe blow, or perhaps two blows, sometime between nine and midnight-.'

'Presumably when Palmer was closing down the crossing for the night.'

'Yes. However, the blow that ultimately killed her, seems to have been delivered sometime after 4.30am, once the first train passed through, crewed by Charlton and Mitchell.'

'Charlton claims he saw her alive as that time.'

'That is true, but their testimony is confused on that aspect.'

Vignoles puffed on his pipe for a moment. 'Are we saying this opportunist thief, this hungry and homeless vagrant, either took most of the night to find what he was looking for before administering a parting blow or else he returned later to deliver the *coup de grace* at considerable risk to himself and delivered with a chilling level of violence. Both versions sit oddly with me.'

'The first scenario cannot work, because Palmer opened up the section to let the train through, so she could not have been dead before 4.30. Unless she was held hostage and made to open the line and then murdered.'

'An interesting idea.' Vignoles was puffing on his pipe, 'but I too find that hard to believe and certainly not by a half-starved tramp.'

'I think she was temporarily incapacitated by the first attack thus allowing McMullen to get into the cottage and take what he could find. She then roused herself and managed to open up her section and bell through to allow the first train to pass down the line.'

'And the tramp saw this? The train steamed past him perhaps and he realised that Palmer was right as rain and possibly able to identify him, so he decided to come back to finish her off.'

'It could work.'

'I hope so, because otherwise it feels like we're fishing in the dark. Come along, let's see if our friend from the Emerald Isle can offer some illumination'.

* * * *

'Mr McMullen. I am DCI Vignoles, and you already know DS Trinder.'

'We became acquainted yesterday when he kindly invited me to enjoy your marvellous hospitality here,' this accompanied by a cheeky wink. McMullen looked better for a hot bath, a sleep on a hard bed with a blanket followed by fried eggs and toast for breakfast. He was leaning back in his chair with his feet encased in unappealing socks of an indeterminate colour, with the look of a man who'd just enjoyed a stay in a classy hotel.

'I trust you've been adequately looked after?'

'Perfectly! A night in a bed even if it as narrow as a plank of wood and just as hard, is a rare pleasure.' He leaned forwards as Vignoles and Trinder took their seats on the other side of the table. 'But they're a bit stingy with the tea. Could you see your way to rustling up another wee drop?' Another wink.

'All in good time. Mr McMullen, you are not under arrest and stayed here last night, voluntarily, because we urgently needed to speak to you and as you have no fixed abode, we needed to ensure we could easily find you. We need to ask you about a very serious matter, Mr McMullen, but if you answer these questions to our satisfaction then you will be free to leave.'

'I was rather hoping I could stay for another night,' McMullen looked crestfallen. 'Or at least until they serve lunch!'

'This is not a boarding house,' Trinder interjected sharply.

McMullen folded his arms across his chest. 'Alright then, another mug of tea and I'll answer all your questions.'

Vignoles nodded to Trinder who instructed PC Howerth who was standing beside the door, to go and refill the tin mug.

'Your full name please?' Trinder lead the questioning, as they had agreed.

'Micky McMullen. Michael. Mick. It's all the same to me, though nobody's called me Michael in years.'

'Where were you born?'

'Londonderry.'

'How old are you?'

'I've not been counting and no-one's been remembering, but the last time I checked I must have been 45. Give or take.'

'How long have you been in England?'

He shrugged. 'Years. Days, months. They don't mean much when you walk the streets begging for a crust to eat.' He tapped his broken watch. 'It's always the same time! I like it like that. A cold night or a wee rainy day can feel like a lifetime so it's better not to see the minutes crawl.'

'What did you do before you were homeless?'

'Ah, well now... It's all an age ago. It was another lifetime. And talking of lifetimes, he's taking a Devil of a while making that tea!'

'You do remember what you did before you ended up like this?' Vignoles pressed the point.

'I might, but I don't much care to talk about it.'

'We need an answer,' Trinder wasn't accepting that.

'I was in the Army. I got demobbed and I never found my way back into things.'

'Why was that?' Vignoles asked.

McMullen shrugged. 'Things happen or they don't happen and then one day your luck runs out. One day you find your wife's run off with another man and taken all you ever owned with her. And alright, perhaps I liked a drop or two of the old drink – and I don't mean the tea that's coming me way now, thanks be to God!'

McMullen's mood noticeably lifted as he eagerly slurped the steaming liquid, the sound setting Vignoles' teeth on edge.

'You walk the lanes around Desford, Coalville and Glenfield regularly?'

'Don't forget the railway! It's safer. Quieter. I get left alone.'

Vignoles made a pained expression. He'd read this alarming point in the statement made by driver Ashbourne. 'So I hear.' He gave McMullen a look that suggested this practice was going to end with immediate effect. 'Walking the West Bridge Line as apparently you do, would ensure you passed Black Spinney Crossing. You must know Mrs Palmer, Mrs Lake and the others?'

'I know them to wave to, but the younger girls run away from me like I had the plague - more's the pity. That Rachel's a pretty young thing!' He chuckled. 'Don't look alarmed. I never got even close to them. It was only old Janey who had the good manners to return a greeting and put the kettle on.'

'Did you go inside their cottage?' Trinder asked.

'Sometimes. Mostly not.' He winked at Trinder, 'Old Janey probably thought I'd steal something.' He laughed openly whilst Trinder gave him a stony stare in return.

'And when you went inside, where did you go?'

'The kitchen, where else? Just a wee step inside the door and its warm and there was always a chance of a biscuit or a rind of the loaf with some beef dripping coming my way.'

'Did Mrs Palmer ever talk about her possessions?'

'Now why would she do that?'

'She might have been making conversation and mentioned things she owned.' Trinder asked. 'For example, did she ever mention a set of silver teaspoons exactly like those found in your possession.'

'I found them! I never knew they were hers and that's the God's honest truth. They were at the side of the road in a hedge.'

'Did you go to Black Spinney Crossing on the night Mrs Palmer was attacked?'

'I walked past, but I didn't step in.'

'You didn't knock on the door and ask for a cup of tea?' Vignoles added.

'No. The idea crossed my mind, but I was in an awful hurry.'

'Why was that?' Trinder was intrigued.

'It was windy and bitter raw and I needed somewhere to kip. A man in my place soon learns to get me head down when its dark and snowy.'

'Did you see Mrs Palmer as you passed by on the way to finding somewhere to sleep?' Vignoles asked.

'She was inside, but with her back turned. If she'd seen me I might have tried my luck with a knock at the door. Listen, sergeant inspector, I'm no fool. I don't trouble folk in the dark. They get frightened and can turn nasty.'

'Is that what happened? You startled Mrs Palmer and she came out. Feeling alarmed, she was not as friendly as usual? She told you to leave in no uncertain terms and it made you angry?'

'No!'

'Did you strike her? Perhaps she annoyed you and made you angry and resentful. I can understand how that could happen.' Vignoles added, his voice soft and sympathetic.

'I never.'

'Perhaps you didn't mean to really hurt her, but you were arguing and you knocked her down.'

McMullen remained silent.

'Did you return to the crossing later that morning?' Trinder asked. 'In the early hours before it got light.'

'Why would I do that? I was sleeping in a farm shed for as long as my rumbling tummy would allow. Then I was up to Coalville and back yesterday. That's when I heard what had happened. It's a cryin' bloody shame, that's what it is. McMullen shook his head, sadly.

Vignoles moved the questioning on. 'You had a decent pair of boots on when you were brought in. I'd say they were not much more than six months old. Or less. How did a man in your position come by these?'

'Now that was a piece of luck.' More tea was slurped in preparation for launching into a fulsome explanation. 'I had a pair that were falling off me feet. They didn't stop the damp nor the wet and were good for nothing. It's bad enough walking all day, but in boots falling apart it's a living Hell. Have you ever tried walking on stones with loose soles flapping -.'

'Get on with it.' Trinder was impatient.

'I would, but me old boots won't let me! Ha ha!' McMullen laughed, but seeing the solemn faces opposite, he stopped short. 'It was the other day when I was near Coalville. After the night at the farm. The day before that Bacon fella pulled me over and took those nice shiny spoons off me. Well, that was when I got 'em.'

'PC Bacon brought you in yesterday, which was Sunday, so you're talking about Saturday?' Trinder was making notes.

'That'll be it, you're a bright lad! Glad we got that cleared up. Well it was the Saturday morning, if that's the day you say it was, when that nice gentleman Mr Richie, handed them over. Hopped off his engine and came over with them wrapped in a piece of sack. He said it was nearly Christmas, so he'd give me those boots by way of a wee present. Now wasn't that a kindly thing? And best of all, they fit almost perfectly. Just a scrunch of newspaper at the toe end.'

'Who is Mr Richie?' Vignoles asked.

McMullen shrugged his shoulders. 'He's on the railway. He drives the little wee engines and he's one of the lads that takes the time to give me a wave and ask how I'm doing.'

Trinder was busy flipping through his notebook, checking names. 'There's no Mr Richie that I can find... Not that we've interviewed the Coalville shed crews yet. What's his first name?'

'Richie! I'm telling you.'

'Do you mean Richard *Somebody*?' Trinder worked it out. 'And you say he's a driver on the line that goes past Mrs Palmer's crossing and through Glenfield Tunnel?'

'That's what I'm tellin' you. He's a decent fella, to be sure. I often see him lending a hand with the heavy stuff for Old Janey.'

'Richard Charlton.' Trinder jabbed his finger on a name in his notebook. 'Known as Richie to friends.'

Vignoles looked at where Trinder was pointing, frowned a moment as he took in the name and considered what this implied, then looked back at McMullen. 'Just to get this straight, Mr Richard Charlton, the engine driver gave you those boots as an early Christmas present on the morning of Saturday the 4th?'

'Hooray, you got it! Now, I was thinking a digestive would go well with what's left of this tea...'

Chapter Twenty-Two

'McMullen has an uncorroborated alibi. He admits to passing Black Spinney somewhere around about 9.30pm on Thursday night, placing him in the right place to have attacked Mrs Palmer.' Trinder was setting out the case to the assembled team with Vignoles seated beside him. Blencowe's map was close to hand and he reinforced his message by indicating the location of the crime. 'He claims he walked down the line, glimpsing Palmer who he claims was still alive and well inside the cottage, as he passed. He claims he carried on along the line for some distance, then found himself a farm outbuilding to sleep in.'

'We need to find where he stayed that night,' Vignoles added.

'He could be in trouble,' Blencowe interjected. 'He was caught red-handed with some items lifted from Palmer's cottage.'

'A set of silver spoons. On the face of it that makes him odds on favourite. But, there's a problem.' Trinder indicated a cardboard box with a pair of black work boots standing inside. 'These are the boots McMullen was wearing when we pulled him in yesterday. They match exactly the prints we found in the mud around the cottage and the perfect muddy mark on the door.'

'Boots presumably worn by Palmer's assailant?' Benson asked.

'It's possible they were.'

'Specifically, these are the boots worn by someone who kicked the cottage door in what looks like an attempt to force it open, walked close to where we understand the body lay and left a trail to and from the tool shed,' Vignoles elaborated. 'They do not in themselves prove the wearer was the killer.'

'If not the killer, then why was this boot wearer kicking the door and going to the tool shed?' Lansdowne asked.

'That's one of the questions we need to answer,' Trinder replied.

'But, Sarge, if McMullen was wearing these boots and was caught with stolen goods he surely has to be the killer?' PC Howerth interjected.

'Slow down. There's a fly in the ointment. A bloody great bluebottle, to be precise. McMullen claims he was wearing a quite *different* pair of boots on Thursday night. Boots that were falling apart. Presumably showing signs of considerable wear. Unfortunately, McMullen has thrown these away and unless the boots can be retrieved we cannot now confidently place him at the crime scene. He started wearing these boots you see here on Saturday morning. I'll come on to that point in a moment. Benson, are there any prints so far unaccounted for that might fit McMullen's life-expired pair?'

'There are four fresh and distinct tread patterns I've been able to capture in plaster, plus a great number of scuffed, damaged and indistinct marks that are probably ours and others that have necessarily been on site for legitimate reasons over, say the last week or longer. One set were Palmer's as expected. Two others match the boots worn by Baylock and Hind, the two platelayers who found her body and there is the intriguing set that match the boots we took off McMullen. These treads do seem to follow a trail to and from the tool shed, although incomplete and one print was found on the opposite side of the railway line, suggesting the wearer was standing by the hedge observing the cottage. I have two clear prints of what looks like a shoe, quite a good quality one with little wear, but so far have not matched this. But there is nothing that I can categorically say is from McMullen's worn out boot.'

'That means we can't even place him there for sure? The tramp is now innocent?' Howerth interjected.

'No quite, but it is awkward. What is perhaps more interesting is that McMullen claims he was given these boots he was wearing on the Saturday morning in Coalville, by Richard Charlton the engine driver.' There was an intake of breath and glances were exchanged. This was a surprising revelation.

'Charlton's statement confirms that he was driving the only train that passed through the crossing on that fateful Friday morning, at 4.30am.

Charlton claims to have seem Palmer, apparently fit and well outside her cottage as they passed. His fireman, Mr Mitchell, cannot corroborate his claim.'

'Does that make Charlton a suspect?' Benson asked.

'He's on the list. His decision to buy a new pair of boots - on the spur of the moment apparently - and give away a perfectly serviceable pair that can be placed at the crime scene, is curious behaviour that needs a proper explanation,' Trinder replied. 'We need to learn all we can about Charlton. Benson – check his service history; see if there are any incidents, anything anomalous, violent or unexpected. Investigate his finances. Maybe he's strapped for cash? Has a gambling habit?'

'Aye aye.' Benson responded.

'Sir?' PC Howerth piped up. 'I was talking with Laura last night in the pub'. Blencowe laughed and Howerth stopped, realising that this was perhaps information he needn't share with the room. The young constable cleared his throat and started again, trying to sound more formal this time. 'Miss Laura Green is the signal woman who was controlling the line on the morning Mrs Palmer was discovered. She mentioned something about driver Charlton. It sounded nothing very much last night, but now I'm wondering if it's important.'

'Then share it with us,' Vignoles was encouraging. Past experience had shown that PC Howerth was a quick-witted young man with a nose for detection. Even as a young and precocious schoolboy he'd shown a remarkable aptitude for the detecting profession. Qualities that persuaded Vignoles to chance his arm and take him onto the team in the face of stern criticism by others who felt less forgiving of some of Howerth's youthful antics.

'Laura said she arrived in the box to take over from Mr Weatherall. She'd signed in and taken control of the box and they were having a mug of tea each, when the two of them saw someone hurrying along the cess at the side of the track. He was coming from the direction of Leicester, which of course means from the direction of Black Spinney Crossing. When we talked this over we realised that the crossing would be the closest place this man could easily get onto the track. They watched him draw close and realised it was driver Charlton. She said he was in a real hurry.'

'Did Miss Green challenge him?' Vignoles asked.

'She did. She slid a window open and called his name, but he had his head down and just waved back at them as he trotted on to the shed and said nothing. It was bitter cold with the window open, so she closed it again and left it at that.'

'Miss Green is sure it was Charlton?'

'Both she and Mr Weatherall were positive it was him.'

'Do we know where Charlton lives?' Vignoles asked the assembled group.

'Desford,' Blencowe replied instantly. 'If Charlton was coming along the line from the direction of Black Spinney then he was way off target. Totally wrong direction.' The set of his jaw suggested he was already suspicious about Charlton.

Trinder indicated the small township of Desford on the map then traced the course Charlton was seen taking along the line on the map for all to see. 'That *is* curious. What time was this, Howerth?'

'4.00am or a minute or two after. It was clear he was late getting on shed and that probably explained why he was hurrying. She didn't think much more about it because by twenty past four, Charlton was steaming away towards West Bridge and on time.'

'We need to pay a call on Charlton,' Vignoles stated. 'Lansdowne, I want you to concentrate on his family. We're looking into his work life and found nothing so far but see what you can find. Do the same with his fireman – what was his name?'

'Mitchell, John Mitchell.' Trinder replied.

'I want background checks on both men and their families. Ask around their home towns and the engine shed. I don't mind if they get wind of you nosing about. Ruffling a few feathers might be instructive,' Vignoles fired out the instructions. 'Howerth - get statements from both Miss Green and Mr Weatherall about what they saw.'

'Yes sir.'

'Blencowe – when we can expect that PM report? We need to see it by the time we're back.' Vignoles stood up and the others followed suit with a mass scraping of chair legs. 'You're driving, sergeant. We're going to Desford shed.'

* * * *

They were seated in the cramped mess room at the back of Desford Junction engine shed. It was filthy. A motley collection of stained tin mugs and cracked plates had collected in a sink that looked as though it had last been cleaned about the time the railways were Nationalised. The walls had once been painted a glossy cream but were now stained varying shades of nicotine brown and streaked by rivulets of condensation. A cast iron stove was roaring in a corner with items of damp workwear hung around it pegged out on thin rope criss-crossing the ceiling as a washing line. The glass in the metal framed windows along one wall was so milky white and opaque it was almost impossible to see out, except through a triangular piece missing from one pane. The icy blast entering through this opening offered some fresher air into the squalid, noxious and stiflingly hot atmosphere.

Richard Charlton was seated on a hard kitchen chair with his own legs stretched out so he could tilt the chair onto its back legs. He pulled a tin of tobacco out of his blue cotton jacket and rested it on his flat stomach. He was making a convincing attempt of looking relaxed despite having just been invited to step inside the mess room by Vignoles and Trinder for questioning.

Vignoles chose a tolerably clean chair to sit on, but not before first placing a copy of the Daily Herald on the seat to protect his clothes, whilst Trinder elected to remain standing to one side, forcing Charlton to twist his head in order to look at or speak to either man. Trinder didn't want the driver to feel at ease, despite having the advantage of being on his own territory.

'Mr Charlton, we need to ask you some more questions in relation to the death of Mrs Jane Palmer.'

'I thought you'd arrested the bugger as did it?' Charlton's piercing eyes fixed on Vignoles, never looking away or blinking even as he skilfully started to assemble a cigarette.

'Word spreads quickly,' Vignoles replied.

'It's a small world. A small shed. We get to hear everything that's going on.'

'Being that well informed, I feel sure you'll be able to offer us further assistance.' Trinder responded, forcing Charlton to turn and look at him.

'Since you mention it, we did interview someone in relation to the investigation, but they were released without charge.' Vignoles added.

'Why'd you do that?' Charlton looked surprised, his eyes searched Vignoles' face for clues. 'Irish Mick was guilty. The murdering little sod!'

'How do you know that he is?' Trinder retorted.

'Stands to reason - from what I heard, anyway.'

'What have you heard?'

'He was there the same time Old Janey was killed. Everyone's saying so! Some of the lads saw him, don't forget. If they'd just stopped the train and scared him away.' Charlton shook his head as if gripped with remorse. Trinder's face suggested he was not convinced. 'They should've been on to him. I mean, he's just the sort that would want to thieve her money, 'cos he was so hard up. He was caught red-handed with her stuff, at least, so I heard.' His look challenged Trinder as he licked the cigarette paper and sealed it.

'Let me get this straight, Michael McMullen, otherwise known as 'Irish Mick, is the man you consider guilty of killing Jane Palmer?' Trinder made a point of writing in his notebook.

'Yeah. The one and the same.' Charlton lit his rollie and masked his face with a cloud of smoke.

'Interesting.' Vignoles interjected, forcing Charlton to look at him. 'You see, Mr Charlton, we're here as a result of something we learned from our conversation with your mate the tramp.'

'He's no blasted mate of mine!'

'No?'

'Come off it, you can't trust anything a stinking old drunk tells you!'

'Since you mention it, he was lucid and gave a surprisingly clear testimony. However, I'm more surprised at your obvious contempt for Mr McMullen and denials of friendship. You remind me of St Peter...' Vignoles deliberately kept Charlton hanging on with a withering smile. 'Of course, beggars and their like can sometimes struggle to win the sympathy of hard-working family men like yourself -,' Vignoles again paused deliberately, allowing Charlton time to give his cigarette yet more determined attention, his look of puzzlement increasing. 'But you do know Mr McMullen, and not only that, you feel some sympathy for his situation.'

'Who says?' Charlton shrugged his shoulders dismissively. 'What I mean is, one tramp looks like another.'

'I don't think they do. Let me jog your memory. You and fireman Mitchell worked a train from Desford Junction to Coalville on the morning of Saturday the 4th. Is that correct?'

'What if we did?' Charlton seemed to be having problems with his perfectly rolled cigarette and was fiddling with it, avoiding eye contact.

'Whilst you were laying over in the yard at Coalville you spotted McMullen – Irish Mick – if you prefer. You were pleased to see him. You had prepared a little surprise for McMullen. A surprise that required you to make yet more excuses to your fireman and leave your engine and hurry into Coalville, where you purchased a new pair of work boots. Putting these on, you returned to your engine after your intriguing shopping spree and duly presented this tramp – the very same one you apparently consider to be a killer and who looks just like any other - with the pair of boots you'd been wearing that morning. And wearing the evening before.' Vignoles and Trinder both made a point of looking at the evidently brand-new boots on Charlton's feet. Charlton instinctively reacted and withdrew his feet so they were tucked under his chair, which tipped forward and forced him to grab his tobacco tin before it fell from his tummy. He looked flustered and started to cough after taking a hurried inhalation of smoke.

'Wrapped in sacking as well. A nice touch.' Trinder sounded mocking. 'A heart-warming early Christmas present.'

'A most generous gift.' Vignoles added.

'What if I did?' Charlton looked up at Vignoles, having finally ceased coughing.

'You gave a decent pair of boots to a man you claim you can hardly even remember and have nothing but contempt for. Why would you do that?'

Charlton shrugged his shoulders. 'I felt sorry for him. I'd seen him struggling. The soles were flapping loose on what he was wearing.'

'Heart-warming.' Trinder grinned. 'Do you make a habit of giving away such expensive items? I don't suppose your wages are extravagant.'

'I do alright. I keep my missus and the kids in food and clothes.'

'Does your wife know you bought a new pair on Saturday?'

'What's that got to do with anything? It's my wages.' The two detectives remained silent. They wanted him to keep talking. The longer someone talked the more likely they were to betray themselves. 'Look, I felt sorry for him, alright? Like you said, we'd worked an early train up to Coalville and had time to spare. It was going to be a long lay over. I told Mitch to mind the engine whilst I nipped into the town. There's a place where I get decent boots. It's real handy. Just a few minutes from the yard, across the road. Lots of the lads use it.'

'It was a spur of the moment decision?' Vignoles asked.

'I saw him hobbling about and it got me thinking how I could help. It was starting to snow and...'

'You felt an overwhelming urge to do your bit. Goodwill to all men and all that?' Trinder's voice was sarcastic.

'Being kind's not a crime. More folk should try it.'

'Trying to dispose of evidence from a crime scene, is a crime, however.' Vignoles gave the driver a stern look. 'Can you tell me why the boots you generously gave to Mr McMullen exactly match the prints we collected from around the spot Mrs Palmer was attacked between Thursday night and early Friday morning? There is also clear imprint on the door into Mrs Palmer's cottage that exactly matches the left boot of the pair you gave McMullen on Saturday. Do you know how that got there?'

Charlton opened his tobacco tin again. Paused, then stared back at Vignoles. The silence was punctuated only by a distant clanging sound of a fitter working on a locomotive in the shed close by and the sharp toot of a whistle in the goods yard.

'All right, I was there. What of it? I'm often there because she was a friend. All the girls living there knew me. Ask my missus and she'll say it's so. Old Janey had a decent veg plot – bigger than we have - so in return for helping on it and odd jobs and whatever, she'd give us some veg. It helps feed the family.' He looked pleased with his explanation and expectantly waited for a positive reaction, but the detectives observed him impassively. 'Obviously my boot prints would be all over. Stands to reason.' Another silence. 'I'd called over. Early evening like. On the Thursday, but I was away long before she rung off working for the night and was attacked.' He looked even more satisfied as his story unfolded and gave an almost arrogant puff on this cigarette.

'You're confirming that you were at Black Spinney Crossing, in and around the front door and the garden shed on Thursday evening and wearing the boots you subsequently presented to Irish Mick on the Saturday?' Trinder was pointedly taking notes.

'That's what I said.'

'What time were you there? Precisely.' Trinder was waiting with pencil poised.

'Five or six. Perhaps a bit later.' Charlton was assembling another cigarette, his hands seemed less steady than before. 'After I'd clocked off I swung around to see how she was. To see if she needed any jobs doing.'

'In December - in the dark?' Vignoles was sceptical.

'You arrived sometime after 5pm. How long were you there?' Trinder continued.

'About an hour or so. I'm not exactly sure. Then I was home for me tea.' He pulled at his jacket sleeve in a casual manner as if trying to conceal his wrist watch.

'Every engine driver I have met is an excellent and almost instinctive timekeeper. It becomes second nature. They also tend to invest in reliable watches,' Vignoles gave Charlton a knowing smile.

'I know I was there about six and home by eight.' He gave a nervous laugh before once again licking the cigarette paper. 'I cannot say better than that as I was not checking. There was no need. I was back home in time to see my kids and wish them goodnight.'

You arrived later and stayed for longer than the hour you first suggested, thought Vignoles who saw Trinder shift his weight from one foot to another as he reacted to the same realisation. Charlton was perhaps deliberately confusing the timings. He was trying to conceal something.

'Did you have reason to go to the garden shed whilst at Mrs Palmer's that evening?' Trinder asked.

Charlton looked at each man in turn, as if weighing something up. 'I tidied up the tools. Cleaning them and putting them neat for the winter.' Having perhaps struck upon a valid excuse for being there, his voice regained some of its earlier confidence.

'In the dark and cold?' Vignoles was sceptical.

'I had a torch.'

'Did you see a mattock - whilst doing your tidying?' Trinder's voice was icy. 'By your torch light.'

A pause. 'Yes.' Charlton took time to light his second cigarette. 'As it happens, I used it. She gets invaded by those blasted rabbits. And some of them are sick. It's horrible. All covered in sores and blisters and with white eyes and they just sit their dying in the dark. I went over to kill them.' He stared at Vignoles defiantly. He looked like a man who'd found the alibi he was seeking.

'We might expect to find your prints on this mattock?'

'Of course. And blood and hair.' He gave a slight upturn to the corner of his mouth as exhaled a long stream of smoke. 'From the rabbits.' He almost smirked.

'Did you put the mattock away in the shed once you'd finished slaughtering bunnies?' Trinder asked.

'Yes.'

'What did you do with the corpses of the rabbits you kindly put out of their misery?' Vignoles asked.

'Threw them on the compost heap.'

'Would that not make a terrible smell?'

'I was going to go back and burn them. Later. On another day, that is. But it was getting late and it being so cold it could wait. The cold would stop them smelling.'

'Are you aware that Mrs Palmer had a lot of money in the house?' Vignoles suddenly shifted the subject.

'Why would I?'

'A simple yes or no will do,' Trinder demanded.

'She might have mentioned something, but I wouldn't know how much or where she kept it.'

'Mrs Palmer never showed you the locked drawer in her dressing table, or talked about the considerable amount she had saved?'

'Are you accusing me of something, Sergeant?'

'Of what might I be accusing you?' Trinder gave him an innocent look.

'Of hitting and robbing her!' Charlton's voice rose, and he looked agitated. He suddenly went pale. 'Oh, come on! You don't think I *killed* her?' He removed his engineman's cap and ran a hand through his hair in an urgent manner. 'Never. I swear on my children's lives. I never done that.' He was shaking his head and his hand was quivering slightly.

'Your wife will be able to confirm that you came home sometime around eight-o-clock on Thursday evening?'

'Leave her out of this!'

'That's not possible. If she can corroborate your story, that will go a long way to reassuring us of your innocence. It would be wise to be completely frank with us at this moment,' Vignoles responded, mildly. 'Perhaps you have something you wish to tell us. It can be enormously beneficial to your situation if you choose to be candid.'

'As it happens, both she and the kids can tell you I was home about eight, just like I said.' He sounded unrepentant and aggressive.

'You did not leave the house again until it was time to go to work?'

Charlton narrowed his eyes and gave the DS an odd look. 'Why would I do that?'

'You tell us.' Trinder held his gaze, searching the driver's face for clues.

'When do you usually leave your house to go on shed in the morning?' Vignoles broke the stand-off.

'Three thirty or as near as makes no odds. The knock up boy can confirm that.' Trinder made a note. He was someone they needed to interview. 'I'm always up before he arrives so he can see the light in the hall and only knocks on the door softly, so as not to wake the wife and kids.'

'And on Friday morning you left your house at the normal time?'

'I was a bit on the early side, as it happens.' Charlton laughed, as if at the foolishness of getting up earlier than needed. 'Just after three twenty.'

'Any reason for your enthusiasm to be out and about on a raw night?' Vignoles smiled.

'I just woke early.'

'Can you tell us why you were seen hurrying along the line from the direction of Black Spinney Crossing towards Desford Junction a few minutes before four?'

Charlton picked at a stray piece of tobacco between his teeth before replying. 'I was a late. I had to hurry home, proper quick like, as I'd stupidly forgot my clasp knife. I use it for cutting my cheese in my snap tin. And peeling my apple. I can't stand the peel on an apple and always take it off.'

'You went home? When was this?'

'I came on shed about three forty or so. Said hello to Mitch and saw our engine was already steaming up pretty well, but then I realised I'd forgotten my knife, so I told Mitch to oil around the engine for me as well as get up steam and I ran back.'

'To Desford?'

'Where else would I be going?'

'You were seen coming from almost the opposite direction.' Trinder appeared to be reading from an entry in his black notebook. 'Hurrying along at the side of the railway line away from Black Spinney Crossing and seen from the signal box. How is that could a quicker way back from Desford.'

Silence.

'It was quite a diversion. I'd like you to explain how and why you took that very long route,' Vignoles added.

'Whoever said that I was there was mistaken. I jumped on the shed bike and peddled to my house like the wind. I was never near Black Spinney. Obviously.'

'You said you ran back to your house.'

'Ran. Peddled. Cycled. You know what I mean.'

'We have two witnesses who say differently.'

'Different to what?'

'That you were on foot and hurrying towards this engine shed from the direction of Black Spinney Crossing close to 4am.'

Charlton stamped his fresh rollie out, despite being only partially smoked with an aggressive twist of his new boot. 'They're lying. It was a black night and as you can see I wear dark overalls and jacket and a cap pulled down just like everyone does. They saw someone else, if they saw anyone.'

No, you're lying. But you're no fool either. The defence council will stress the poor visibility and the fact that most railwaymen dress the same. They will challenge Miss Green and her colleague aggressively, quite possibly winning the point in court. Vignoles kept his thoughts silent.

'Am I under arrest? Because otherwise, gentlemen, I'd like to get back to my job.' Charlton stood up, carelessly knocking over his chair as he did so. This had the unfortunate effect of drawing some of the sting from his outburst, as he turned away to set it up right again.

'You are free to go. For now. But we shall speak to you again. I ask that you remain in the area, except when your specific railway business takes you further afield.' Vignoles tipped his hat to the discomfited driver, then he and Trinder stepped back out in the winter air.

Chapter Twenty-Three

There was little illumination beside the railway lines to cut through the misty dark of a wintry London night. Some distance away an array of electric coloured lights was held high above the rails on a signal gantry, their brilliant points of scarlet glinting on the mercury silver rails like linear spills of fresh blood. A bitter wind was whipping around the gantry lattice work with a ghostly moan whilst buffeting between the high cutting walls on the far side of the tracks and the collection of ugly factory and warehouse backs on the other. A scrunched ball of ageing newsprint bounced between the lines like the tumbleweed loved by directors of western films.

This wasn't the mid-west in the time of cowboys and Indians, but a nondescript stretch of quadruple track in south-east London. Once the lights had been switched off in the warehouses and the drilling machines stilled in the machine workshops that smelt of lubricating oil and metal shavings, and the last drop of sump oil had been drained from Mr Carter's Ford Popular in one of the squalid back street garages, the area fell silent as a graveyard. On an unwelcoming night in December there could be little reason to walk these ugly streets of locked doors and blank windows, where even the foxes steered clear.

There was even less reason for anyone to notice the loosened panel in the tall wooden railway fencing topped with curls of barbed wire now festooned with captured scraps of litter. Nobody peered through the gap left where the panel had been imperfectly replaced to witness the sight of three men stumbling down the low embankment of unhealthy grass to stand close beside the busy lines carrying trains that offered little warning of their speeding approach. Just a low whine and a whoosh and they were gone leaving a whiff of electricity, brake dust and toilets. There was the occasional blue flash like lightning as an electric pick up shoe briefly disengaged and arc'd back to the single electric rail that mirrored the curve of each running track. This third rail was an unassuming and yet silent menace. A high-voltage presence in the pitchy gloom. It would be easy to overlook this infinitely patient assassin.

No one was watching. But if some hardy soul had braved this desolate location their attention might have been caught by this odd group of three now beside the thrumming lines, they might have noticed that one of the men appeared to be with there under duress and had tried to resist and break away. His struggle was over in moments, expertly quelled by his captors as this strange scene took on an increasingly disturbing quality as he was first felled, then pinned on his back, to the stony ground.

As he lay partially winded with the strong creosote smell of railway lines filling his nostrils, Michael Leach wondered why they'd brought him here of all places. He knew very little about railways other than they were cold, hard dangerous places to be on a night like this. He recognised a steam engine, of course, and knew they worked like coal-fired kettles on wheels, but that was about the limit of his interest and understanding. His mis-spent youth had not been spent at the end of platforms underlining numbers. He'd grown up learning how to swindle and steal and make shady deals and avoid doing an honest day's work. Consequently, he knew a lot about money and probably too much about the shadowy underworld and had become adept at avoiding the newly-formed Flying Squad. Leach was, however, vaguely aware that in and around London many of the trains he rode (invariably without paying) looked like they were missing a locomotive up front and the green-painted carriages whined and whirred and produced a strange smell that reminded him of rubbed geranium leaves. He'd never taken time to consider from where these unremarkable trains took their current. Even if he had learned that these stealthy machines were fed from that extra third rail raised on a succession of porcelain insulators that looked like rows of white gloved hands cupping the rail, it was too late for this information to help him.

Because Michael Leach was about to be given an object lesson in just how dangerous it was to get too close to high voltage third rails.

He'd been slammed to the ground in a move that even his heightened survival instincts had not seen coming. Here was the man who prided himself on his stealth and craft and ability to avoid trouble, pinned down and cornered. He'd been convinced that taking a grubby room in a 3rd rate hotel would ensure his safety for at least a night or two, but at no point had he realised that he'd been stalked by two men who were true pro's. Hired killers. Men who knew every trick in the book and they'd out foxed him, good and proper. He was in deep trouble. The hard ballast was unpleasant and unforgiving across his shoulders and digging into the back of his head which was throbbing and sending darts of bright coloured pain through his temples whenever he tried to move from side to side or, worse still, lift it off the ground to get a better view of his tormentors.

Leach had been given no time to regain his breath or make any serious move to escape before he was expertly trussed like a joint of beef and his futile attempts to free his hands or feet had demonstrated that he was up against two men who knew a knot when they tied one. They must have been bloody Boy Scouts. Or sailors. The sort of people who learned how to whip a cord around arms and legs and have them tied so they didn't come undone. Bastards! He wanted to spit the accusation out, find a way to vent the intense feeling of anger, humiliation and fear now coursing through his veins. The gag across his mouth was just as expertly tied and all he could do was make vague moaning sounds between his short intakes and exhalations of breath. This sucking, moaning, wheezing sound making him sound like a faulty Hoover.

'Take slower breaths or you'll hyper ventilate.'

'He needs to calm down. He'll do himself an injury what with thrashing about and breathing like an asthmatic.'

'Now, you just listen to what Kane says. Lie nice and still now.'

Leach's eyes widened, trying to communicate as much hate and anger as he could muster, the air still hissing through the cotton gag.

'This is how it works. I'm going to ask you once again. Nice and slow so you understand the question and don't go getting the wrong end of the stick and telling us a load of nonsense. You had to go flying off the handle and cursing and swearing and talking a load of rubbish, so we've had to tie you up like a Christmas turkey. It's your choice.'

'That smack you gave him is coming up with a proper shiner! That eye is going to be a really nice colour.'

Leach's gasping, blowing and sucking sound grew in volume accompanied by an even stronger animal whine of distress.

'I'll smack him again if he doesn't give this a rest.' Kane glowered.

'I bet you would. Now, Mr Leach, you're getting yourself all worked up again. That won't help one bit. Now be a good fellow and do as we say.'

'Abe, I'm going to have to hurry you along. We don't have all night...'

'Too true, Kane. Time, tide and electric trains wait for nobody.' Abel chuckled, then leaned over Leach and peered at him closely. Leach could smell his aftershave. Lavender or violets blended into something sickly. 'Now be a good chap and listen.' The air sucked in and out of the gag in stentorian gasps. 'I'm going to ask you a question, then remove the gag. You will not shout, attempt to bite me or otherwise misbehave.'

Leach stared daggers, the whites of his eyes bright around his dark pupils like a frightened horse.

'Kane, I fear he's not getting the message. He's going to act stupid again, I can just sense it.'

'We've got about eight minutes, so a dose of your medicine might coax him along.' Kane sounded coolly practical.

'Ooh! A quite excellent idea!' Abel looked almost childishly pleased as he swiftly picked up to two lengths of heavy duty copper wire sheathed in a thick rubber casing, each one attached to a piece of sawn off broom handle, the other ends of the two wires already clamped onto the live third rail using massive crocodile clips with hefty rubber grips. Abel started to pull on a pair of huge protective rubber gauntlets. He spoke whilst looking into Leach's bulging eyeballs. 'Can't be too careful. Nasty stuff electricity. You can get badly hurt messing around with this.'

Leach rolled his head from side to side in a frantic pantomime of fear and loathing. Cold sweat was beading on his forehead despite the freezing air.

'Now, once again. Where are the goods? You do know what we're talking about. The nice little bag of goodies you came to collect. We need the exact location - if you'll be so kind?' The cloth was pulled from Leach's mouth.

'I don't know! They were missing. I'm trying to find out! You've got to believe me -.' Kane's gloved hand clamped his mouth closed then replaced the gag.

'We know how it is. You thought you could sell a story about some tin pot house-breaker whilst quietly pocketing it for yourself and trying to pull a neat little stunt. It's human nature to be tempted -.'

'- like Eve. She just couldn't help herself!' Abel was now sporting round welding goggles and brandishing the wooden poles in each gauntlet'd hand, the ends of the copper wires hovering above Leach who was trying to push himself deeper into the immovable ballast, eyes fixed in horror on the copper wires.

'Nice analogy! Abe's quick like that, see. Makes the connections – ha ha – connections. Electrical connections. Get that Abe?'

'Droll, Kane, so droll.' He wavered the wires closer to Leach's groin.

'Now, once again. Tell us where and that's it.' Kane took over the grilling. 'And just so there's no misunderstanding, I'm talking about the little bag of very special, very expensive and very irreplaceable goods that you were paid handsomely to collect and deliver by a certain Mr Giggs. And seeing as the aforementioned Mr Giggs ain't best pleased with the non-appearance of the said goods, he sent us along to jog your memory.' Kane winked, then pulled the gag away. Leach gulped in the cold air, desperate to get some oxygen into his burning lungs, his eyes rolling painfully as they strained to monitor the encroaching copper wires. His chest was heaving and the words were suddenly hard to formulate.

'I was set up! It was a fix – an inside job. We can get them - together!' He gulped air. 'She was dead when I got there. The place was cleaned out!"

'Why don't I believe him, Abe?'

'You're too cynical, that's why, Kane. He needs a little teaser. A coaxing caress...'

'Nooooo!!!'

'Don't overdo it!'

'I'm a professional. I know how to handle this.'

The wires touched for a fraction of a second with a sickening snap and flash, leaving a twist of smoke and smell of burning meat and cloth. Leach screamed an agonising yell of pain, but the gag was clamped back and the powerful arms of Kane held it in place as Leach bucked and twisted in a desperate attempt to flee the appalling pain.

'Spill the beans old boy. We just need to collect the debt and then we'll be out of your hair.' Abel stared through the black mirrors of the goggles, Leach's contorted face reflecting back.

'Please God – aaaaagh – no – aaaaagh – I don't know! They killed-.' Leach writhed in pain, face distorted in agony.

'Times up. Train's due. I reckon that's his final word on the matter.' Kane shook his head solemnly.

'Much as we'd love to natter for longer, we've got to run along. Kane, be a good fellow and step back a touch. This might get a bit messy.'

The wires were held against Leach as the red signal light blinked to green. There was a long howl of pain that told of unimaginable suffering as his body bucked and cramped and flayed and burnt. Little blue flames licked around the wires and flickered in the impenetrable lenses of the welding goggles. Abel finally pulled the wires away, flipped his goggles on to his forehead, then casually stood up, stepping nimbly around the railway lines to carefully unclip the wires. He tossed these across to Kane who expertly caught them and rolled the wires neatly around the poles and placed both in the highly polished doctor's bag that stood close by, then clicked it shut. Abel lifted the twitching body with an ease that was surprising for such a slim man, then let it fall so the head lolled back over the nearest running rail to offer an expanse of clean neck to the approaching train. The smell of burning meat and singed hair was intense. Abel stepped away from the crumpled body and straightened up whilst slowly removing the gauntlets. These he folded around the googles which he also removed. Collecting his rather effete hat of pale lilac-grey that had been resting off the ground on a stand of strongly stemmed weeds, he replaced this on his head. He sniffed the air once or twice in an unhurried manner as he adjusted the cuffs of his Jermaine Street tailored shirt, cuff links catching the green signal light.

'Pork. Reminds me of your mother's Sunday roasts, Kane. My, she does a legendary roast.'

'The best!'

They walked unhurriedly up the bank towards the loosened fence panel, never once looking back, whilst casually making further minute adjustments to the lie of their clothes and buttoning up their expensive overcoats.

There was a blare of a horn. It was repeated, more urgently this time. Perhaps the motorman or his mate had seen there was something on the line, but they were rounding a curve and travelling too fast and with a green light showing and they had no chance of stopping. The application of the brakes could only minimise the speed of impact, but nothing more. There was barely a sound as a succession of yellow lighted carriage windows flickered past revealing late-night travellers dozing, kissing or drunk and blissfully unaware of the body being quietly sliced to pieces beneath them.

'Talking of my Ma's roasts, are you hungry? Cos' I'm bleedin' famished.'

Chapter Twenty-Four

'What do you make of Charlton?'

'He's lying,' Trinder replied.

'About what?'

'I'm not entirely sure. But he's hiding something and he's clever about it.'

'In what way?'

'In the way he admitted to being on site at some point that evening. He didn't attempt to deny he was wearing the same boots we later found on McMullen. Then his crazy story that he used the mattock that same evening to kill rabbits.' Trinder looked at Vignoles. 'What on earth was *that* about? Are we supposed to believe he was wandering around her garden trying to thwack rabbits after dark? They run too fast, for a start.'

'Healthy ones do and after dark they should be tucked up in their burrows. But perhaps not diseased ones.' Vignoles was chewing on the end of his unlit pipe talking from the side of his mouth. 'Blinded and crippled and disoriented - they're helpless,' Vignoles was hunching his shoulders against the cold, hands thrust deep in his coat pockets. 'They've got Myxomatosis. A vile disease introduced into the country by the Government in an attempt to decimate the rabbit population by using a form of biological warfare. Apparently, rabbits will eat all our market veg unless they are exterminated, or so the reasoning goes.'

'Really?' Trinder looked surprised. This was a news story he'd evidently missed.

'It's only what father tells me. A slow death and farmers are encouraged to kill the creatures when they see them and burn the corpses. I saw that first hand. The fields around Dunton were illuminated by bonfires last week.'

'Charlton could be telling the truth?'

'It's plausible. Or a clever ruse to explain away prints and blood and gore on the mattock.'

'Precisely!' Trinder was not giving up on Charlton. 'If he was wielding the mattock like a weapon against diseased bunnies, it would be easy for him to approach Palmer. She knew and trusted him as a friend and had no reason to feel threatened despite him holding a potential weapon. He could easily be standing close to her and deliver the blows from behind without warning.'

'Good point. We need to search for the rabbits he claimed he killed. Has anyone looked in the compost bin at the cottage?'

'I doubt it.'

'You've maintained a watch there?'

'Had a constable on site day and night.'

'Then Charlton should not have been able to return and throw a few corpses on the compost to reinforce his story.'

'Why would Charlton kick the cottage door and attempt to smash the window? He can explain away his boot prints on the ground and even the blood-stained mattock it seems, but kicking the door immediately strikes a suspicious note. Why would he set himself up like that?'

'I share your concerns. There's no obvious logic in either action. Smashing the window glass was pointless. A solid window frame with small panes was a poor means of entry at the best of times.'

'Doubly stupid as Charlton must know how the door was fastened with a nail and could just let himself in without any trace.'

'It's an anomaly. However, he has offered us a decent explanation for his boot prints,' Vignoles opened the car door. 'And that's why Charlton is walking free - for now.' They climbed inside the Rover. 'Back to the office and see if that PM report has arrived.'

Chapter Twenty-Five

Abel adjusted the lie of his pale lilac-grey suit trousers then flicked a speck of engine soot from his lapel. A blue silk tie was held in place by a silver and diamond tiepin held against an immaculate shirt of brilliant starched white. Bespoke and hand-sewn to order, the shirt was one of a set of seven that hung in Abel's fastidiously organised wardrobe in his Belsize Park apartment. His shoes gleamed like mirrors, no trace remaining of the recent midnight scramble down a shallow railway embankment. An expensive and aromatic cigarette smoked lazily in his right hand. His skin was pale and baby smooth with finger nails immaculately trimmed and polished as if lacquered. Abel always preferred to wear gloves or protective gauntlets when administering his infamously cruel punishments to ensure his nails remained perfect.

He was fussy like that.

Kane, sitting opposite him in their first-class compartment, flapped a more rugged hand in the air. 'What *are* you smokin'? They stink like bleedin' chewing gum!'

'Menthol, dear boy. Cleaner on the palate. You should give them a go.'

'Don't buy any more. It's like sitting in a bleedin' dentists waitin' room. Yeah, that's it. It smells like that red mouthwash they make you gargle.' Kane ripped open a carton of Navy Capstan and lit up. The hard smell of these untipped favourites of the Merchant Navy immediately competed with that of the menthol. 'Proper fags, these. *Men's* fags,' Kane laughed throatily, perhaps proof of the lung burning properties of his favourite drug. The pale scar showing on a weather-beaten cheek as he inhaled.

'Philistine!' Abel looked away in mock outrage.

When they had first boarded the Manchester express at St Pancras that morning, the train guard thought they looked like London stockbrokers, although upon reflection, neither man dressed in the obligatory uniform of striped trousers, black suit jacket, bowler and carrying tightly furled umbrellas and copies of the *Financial Times*. Perhaps they were salesmen. The guard modified his assessment and decided they were in the motor trade. He'd seen their type before. All flashy watches and diamond tie pins and show off clothes that cost too much with a cocky attitude on top. As he sat in his little compartment at the back of the train, the guard decided he didn't 'take' to either of them. Especially the one in that ghastly coloured suit. Ugh! He looked like one of those men the newspapers claimed hung around toilets at night.

Mind you, the other one, the one in the charcoal grey suit, he looked like he could handle himself. Short, wiry and with muscles showing even from under the suiting. He might have been a Commando. Or a fighter pilot. He had the little moustache and the sheepskin collar to his top coat that gave him the look. And the cold blue eyes of a man who when he lined up his gun to shoot made sure he didn't miss. A right pair of diamond geezers. Satisfied with his fictional impression, the guard promptly put them out of his mind and never gave them another thought.

The silence in the compartment was broken by Kane. 'What's your reckoning on that Leach fella? Was he playing us a straight bat?'

'Absolutely, old boy. He was clean as a whistle. 750 volts where it hurts does tend to focus the mind somewhat.'

'Or fry it.'

'It was not his *mind* we were frying.' Abel chuckled heartlessly.

'That means some smart Alec really has muscled in. Cleaned the place out and done a runner. That's not good. Not good at all.' Kane looked grim.

'Agreed. Palmer was one of the best. Only met her the one time, that I can remember, but she was steady. Came across as safe as houses.'

Kane shook his head sadly as he contemplated his acrid cigarette and the unfairness of life. 'Bad for business, an' all. Mr Giggs is not happy. 'Incandescent' was the word used. He won't be alone in losin' his rag. Bumping off Palmer and muscling in on other people's property will have half the lags in London getting proper steamed up. Leach was one of the trusties an' all. Us bumping him off might cause some friction.'

'Hmm. That is unfortunate. Once the word gets around, it'll kick off. Before we know it, we'll have too much work.'

'Or none at all if someone takes umbridge at Leach's demise...' Kane let that grim thought hang in the air a moment.

'Oh, surely not?'

'I don't give two hoots about Leach and we did what needed doing. But he turned out clean and we've been left looking exposed. I don't like that. That's why we need to see how the land lies and put a plan together to get this straightened out before someone starts talking and casting aspersions.'

'We have a reputation to uphold.'

'We do. And I don't like some jumped up little squirt steppin' on our toes, neither.'

'We'll have to put our foot down. Teach them a lesson.' Abel blew a smoke ring, with the look of a man contemplating something pleasing.

'Darned right!' Kane stubbed his cigarette out then reached into his jacket inside pocket and extracted a well-thumbed notebook. A metal propelling pencil was held against the book by an elastic band, and he slid this out and carefully turned the barrel to extend the lead. 'We'll review what we know is missing and consider who would be stupid enough to try it on. It's hard to fence and you need to be well-connected to handle stones that hot.'

'Or just stupid.'

'There's that an' all.'

'Remind me, what is the precise scale of the loss?'

'The best stone is reckoned at £500K. Add in the rest, and it's just shy of £800K.'

'Phew...'

'Men get killed for gems like that. We need to take control of this situation.' Kane was riffling through pages of neatly compiled lists. His biceps were bulging the suit jacket like a heavy weight boxer, but his handwriting was small and perfectly formed. 'We've never failed to collect.'

'The best in the trade. When The Debt Collectors come calling, you always pay in the end!'

'As Mr Leach discovered. It's just unfortunate he didn't have the goods to hand and nothing else to offer,' Kane sighed deeply and shook his head as if mildly exasperated by an unruly child as he studied his notes. 'He proffered no reasonable compensation. In fact, if my addition and subtraction is correct, he's even short-changed us by fifty smackers from that envelope in his jacket. Darned cheek.'

'Lost the goods and some of the collection money on top. Was there no end to his foolishness?' Abel frowned. 'Odd. Leach had a reputation for being a class act, but he fell short. Still -.' Abel's face brightened up. '- I don't know about you, but I've a feeling we might have to do some more persuading before long.' He raised an eyebrow whilst his perfectly manicured fingers rippled on the patent leather of the doctor's bag, the diamond ring on his finger sparkling in the pale winter sun streaming into the compartment.

Chapter Twenty-Six

Vignoles was on the telephone to Dr Tomblin. Trinder on the other side of the desk re-reading the post-mortem report, brow furrowed with puzzlement.

'Are you absolutely sure? I don't mean to call into question your abilities nor fault your concise and well-written report, but –'

'- you're questioning both.' There was a chuckle down the line.

'I know, but it's just these findings put a metaphorical cat well amongst the pigeons -,'

'More like a flippin' great tiger,' added Trinder, with an unhappy growl.

Dr Tomblin cut them both off. 'No need to apologise. I expected a call once you'd read it over. I appreciate the difficulties it throws up and hinted as much to DS Trinder on the night.'

Vignoles gave an appreciative grunt down the line.

'The facts speak clearly for themselves and are much as I suspected when I first inspected the body. She was attacked twice, in separate incidents. Whilst I cannot be more precise, my estimation is that she was first assaulted mid-evening, receiving a blow to the back of the skull and to her shoulders and back. These were powerful enough to potentially render her unconscious or at least temporarily incapacitated. She was then dealt the far more severe and unpleasantly disfiguring blow to her face some time later, this being the blow that ultimately finished her off. I will stake my reputation on that second blow coming between 2am and perhaps around an hour before she was declared dead by myself, at 5.05pm.'

'The second attack could have been administered by either Baylock or Hind prior to moving her inside?'

'Now, now inspector, you cannot expect me to answer that. It's your job to determine who did what. I cannot reasonably declare whether this final blow was administered prior to the body being moved or after it was moved inside, although I saw no traces of blood splatter where she lay on the kitchen rug and so I would suggest this is far less probable. You might want to get the forensic chaps to give the rag rug and floor another going over, just in case.'

'We already have and found nothing to suggest the blow took place indoors,' Vignoles replied. 'This first attack was done with a blunt instrument. Could this have been a wooden handle of some description?'

'It could, and the mattock the constabulary examined was brought across to the lab and the bruising is certainly consistent with something of the same size.'

'There was blood on the sharper end of the mattock head. Can you confirm this is Palmer's?'

'Now we're on tricky ground.'

'I feared you would say that. But could this tool have created that particular blow to her face?'

'It could. It is a good match. There was some bloody matter recovered from the pointed end that I feel confident is the remains of her pulverised eye.' Vignoles pulled a face. 'However, the blood and gore is hard to pin down. There was a tiny brown hair that I cannot as yet place, as Palmer had snowy white hair.'

'Could it be rabbit?'

'Interesting. Why do you think that?'

'We have a suspect who claims he used the tool to put mixy rabbits out of their misery.'

'I see. If you find a rabbit corpse on site I could use it to make a comparison.'

'We're looking.'

'That would be helpful, Vignoles. But I must warn you this development also adds to our problems. Medical science cannot as yet determine the difference between human blood and that of other animals - rabbits included. I will need to be even more cautious because the matter I thought to be human eye might now also be rabbit.'

'Ah...'

'However, the mattock in size, shape and weight is a strong contender for the murder weapon. I'm not prepared to go further than that.'

'Of course. Thank you doctor.'

Vignoles rang off. 'You probably got the jist of that?'

'I did.' Trinder tossed the report onto the desk. 'Hind and Baylock are in the frame?'

'I never liked the fact they moved her body despite their Good Samaritan intent. Are their statements to hand?'

Trinder riffled through the Murder File and extracted two short statements. He passed one across and Vignoles quickly reminded himself of the content. Trinder did the same, and they swapped reports.

'Your thoughts, John?'

'Two railway workers find a colleague in distress and try to help her as best they can. When she gives up the ghost despite their best efforts they notify the relevant agencies and await our arrival. On the face of it, there's nothing to raise suspicion.'

Vignoles was filling his pipe and Trinder felt minded to follow suit and flicked a Black Cat cigarette from a carton.

'But did they hasten Palmer's demise? Dr Tomblin suspects she died about the same time they were with her.'

'As they both claim. Another clever twist on the facts. Rather than offer succour, they killed her. A neat cover story. They severely disturb the crime scene and their prints are absolutely everywhere and our natural inclination is to admire their valiant efforts.' Trinder contemplated the office ceiling as he chewed the idea over. 'Poorly paid for a back-breaking job daubing oil on fishplates all day long or packing wobbly sleepers. They knew Palmer and her family and as a result got wind about the extraordinary stash of savings?'

'The spoils were worth splitting between them. They could both live like kings.'

'And easier for two to take Palmer by surprise. One distracts her, the other strikes.' Trinder still looked worried however. 'But why did it take them two attempts? Why not finish her off properly earlier in the evening?'

A locomotive whistled in the station behind where Vignoles was seated. It felt like a warning. A smoke ring drifted towards the ceiling as Vignoles pondered this puzzle. 'If I asked you to telephone the Badger and give him a run down on the case as it currently stands -.'

Trinder blanched.

'Don't worry, I shall do the honours in due course, but I want to hear how you would proceed if in my shoes. After all, I put you in charge and it's as much your case as mine, as far as I'm concerned.' Trinder smoked and listened, looking thoughtful. 'Badger won't take any flannel so you need to keep it snappy, but ensure you get approval for your next actions.' Vignoles gave Trinder a sideways look. 'Or at least ensure you've primed him for your actions, even if not *quite* secured tacit approval. There's a difference!'

'Righty-o.' Trinder sat upright in his chair and gave a few pages in his notebook a quick scan before continuing. 'I would start with a quick resume of the murder situation as found. List the initial actions taken and my belief this was probably an aggravated robbery of a substantial, no, surprising, sum of cash. Motivation enough for murder.'

'Badger will buy that. But do you?'

'I do. Whatever the exact amount, it appears to be in the hundreds. People have been killed for far less.'

'Agreed.'

'I would advise him of the timing issues raised by the PM report -.'

'He won't like that one bit. He'll tell you to give the doctor a bawling out for sitting on the fence in the belief that a raised voice down a telephone will get the doctor to give you a neater answer.' Vignoles gave a wry smile.

'You think Dr Tomblin is falling short?'

'Not in the least. But you'll need to make a decision which side of this fence you're on. Defend the doctor and stand your ground or take the easier option of pleasing your superior and run the risk of making facts fit where they don't.'

'But surely that would mean compromising the investigation?'

'It might. Or Badger, who for all his faults is actually a perceptive copper at heart, might be right? He can be a shrewd judge of character. Perhaps the doctor has misread the signs.'

Trinder looked stumped. 'I prefer to trust medical science.'

'Which even the doctor admits is flawed. He's using the information he can glean from a compromised situation and science cannot answer every question.'

'I can see the doctor's argument for putting forward the case he has. I'll stand my ground and back him.'

'A wise decision.' Vignoles was pleased.

'I'd tell Badger we have four potential suspects. McMullen, Charlton, Hind and Baylock.'

'He'll want that slimmed down - and you'll need to give good reason why each is in the frame.'

'I suggest we re-interview Hind and Baylock as a priority, specifically about their albis for Thursday evening after Palmer was closing down for the night and grill them separately about how they found Palmer and their subsequent actions up until the moment Benson arrived on the scene. I want to question Mrs Charlton as well. And search the Charlton house.'

'Why?'

'To see if we can find stolen goods or a pile of money.'

'Charlton's not been charged.'

'A search warrant might be tricky?'

'Soft soaping the magistrate and convincing Badger of the necessity, if only to help reduce then suspect list, will square that. Badger prefers action, so he'll jump at the chance. Whilst at it, get warrants for the two platelayers' houses.'

'Good thinking!'

'What else?'

'I'd like to speak to Mrs Lake's daughter, Rachel.'

'She was in Liverpool at the time. Explain your reasoning.'

'Crimes such as these most often start at home. We've been told the whole family were in Liverpool, but have we confirmed that as fact? Lansdowne did not see this Rachel when she collected Lake. On top of that, perhaps Rachel has a better idea of how much money was stolen? It will be interesting to see if mother and daughter tell a story that tallies.'

'I'm liking your cynical attitude. Take nothing for granted. Right, I'd best telephone Badger and pass on what you've told me.' Vignoles sounded unenthusiastic.

Trinder stood up and then opened his mouth as if to say something, his hand reaching almost instinctively inside his jacket pocket, but Vignoles was already dialling London. Trinder turned away and left the office.

Chapter Twenty-Seven

'A decent house. Vi would love a place like this.'

'Win promotion to D.I. and I'm sure you can buy her one,' Vignoles replied. Trinder reacted oddly to this response and opened his mouth but said nothing. 'You're right though,' Vignoles continued. 'Charlton's not on his uppers.'

They were approaching the Charlton house on the High Street in Desford. It was a two-storied end of terrace built in warm red brick with darker brown bricks placed at intervals to create a decorative pattern. The bottom three feet of the front wall was built from rubblestone and possibly the remains of a far older construction, whilst the roof looked to be of Welsh slate with an elegant chimney stack at each end. The glossy green door was central and opened straight off the pavement and there was a window on either side, the frames painted in light brown. The front step was of slate and spotlessly clean, looking all the more so by the sleet now slicking the surface with its icy sheen. Whilst no mansion, it was a cut above the typical cramped two-up, two-down Victorian brick terrace most railwaymen had to make do with and was well-cared for.

The cast iron door knocker was lead-blacked and in the shape of a grinning bearded man with a face surrounded by leaves and berries, enhanced by a Christmas wreath of holly and ivy entwined around woven hazel wands that was fastened above it. 'The Green Man,' Vignoles observed as he gave a single echoing knock. Moments later a fresh-faced woman opened the door, the action accompanied by a glorious waft of warm air scented by something aromatic and delicious from the kitchen. Mrs Charlton was wiping her hands on an apron, the sleeves on her dress rolled up to her elbows. There was a slight smudge of flour on her forehead.

'Yes?' Her voice was friendly and without suspicion, although her expression quickly changed to one of curious puzzlement.

'Mrs Charlton?' Vignoles introduced Trinder and himself. 'May we come in please? We would like to ask you a few questions.'

'Questions? What about?'

'If we could do so inside...'

'Oh, well...come in.' She stepped back to open the door wider and as she did so, looked over their shoulders at the two uniformed constables standing beside the police Rover, bidden to stay where they were by a deft hand movement from Trinder. This action did not escape Mrs Charlton's attention, however. 'Go through to the kitchen. I'm in the middle of baking and it's an awful muddle.' She was brushing flour from her hands on her apron.

'Apologies for intruding whilst you are busy,' Vignoles was speaking as they were ushered into a warm kitchen with a big deal table dusted with flour. The smells of hot spiced apple pie were intoxicating, rising from a dish resting on one end of the table whilst the range was issuing the aroma of a meat pie. Vignoles felt his stomach rumble. Both men removed their hats. A radio in the corner was playing "Mambo Italiano", the joyful music adding to the scene of comfortable domesticity.

'You will probably have heard about the death of Mrs Palmer?'

'Gosh, yes. Dreadful. Absolutely dreadful. Richie and I were shocked when we heard. We just can't believe it.' She gave the detectives a measured look, glancing at each in turn perhaps wondering why men in uniform were standing outside her house like sentinels. Trinder felt sure she had no idea why they were there.

'We would like to ask you about Mrs Palmer.'

'I hardly knew her, poor soul -.'

'And about the evening of Thursday the 2nd. Just to confirm a few facts.' Vignoles gave her a slight smile.

'Why would you want to do that? I mean, it's awful she's been killed but we were here at home, I can't see how -.' She stopped and placed a protective hand gently on the swell of her tummy. 'I'm not quite sure I understand. What facts need confirming?' She gave Trinder a hard stare and addressed her next question to him. 'And why are those men standing outside?'

'Perhaps you might like to sit down, Mrs Charlton?' Vignoles urged and he was relieved when she sat in the nearest chair. 'In the course of a murder investigation we must investigate everyone who may have been - perhaps inadvertently and innocently – in the vicinity of the victim around the time of their death. Your husband has admitted to calling upon Mrs Palmer that Thursday evening -.'

'- but he's not here right now. He's at work on his engine. If you call back, you can ask him then.'

'We wish to ask you a few questions. Without your husband here.' Trinder added, pointedly.

'It would be better to come back when he gets home. He's expected about six-o-clock.' Mrs Charlton looked flustered. 'Richie knew and worked with her, whereas I rarely met her. Just on the odd occasion, in passing. I could hardly say I knew her.'

'Just routine and less intrusive whilst your children are at school. May I?' Vignoles pulled another chair away from the table and sat down. He was making it clear in as firm but gentle manner as he could that the interview was going to proceed despite her protestations. 'Whilst we talk, my sergeant will instruct two constables to undertake a search of your house. They are under strict instructions to be careful and leave everything in order.' Vignoles was opening a document he had extracted from his pocket.

'What do you mean, search? You want to search our house?' Mrs Charlton looked flabbergasted and went worryingly pale.

'I have a warrant. Please don't be alarmed. It will be over as quickly as possible. But I must insist.' He passed the warrant across, but Mrs Charlton just stared at it sightlessly, her head shaking almost imperceptibly as she struggled to take in the shocking news. Trinder slipped out and they heard the front door open and his voice commanding the men.

'Why on earth do you need to do this?' She suddenly looked Vignoles in the eye, a smouldering anger and hurt burning there. 'You cannot possibly think my husband is involved in -,' she struggled to form the words. '- in doing *that*?'

'He is involved to some extent and told us as much. We just need to establish that what he told us is factually correct. If it is, then there is nothing to be alarmed about and we will leave you all in peace.'

A little clockwork timer jingled on the table and Mrs Charlton reached for it and stopped the sound. She ran her hands over her face, then stood up. The tread of heavy shoes could be heard on the stairs. 'The pie. I need to take it from the oven...' She sounded distracted, her voice flat and lifeless. 'It's steak and ale. My husband's favourite.'

'We can talk as you do so. I need to establish what time your husband came home last Thursday.'

A family-sized pie was lifted from the oven, a rich meaty smell adding to that of the apple pie. Steam rolled around the kitchen ceiling. Mrs Charlton placed it on the top of the stove and stared at it as if she had never seen it before. 'It was eight. Or eight-fifteen.' Her voice was flat.

'Was that normal?'

'No. Yes. I mean, it depends. It varies. He works different shifts and the times change.' She sat down rather heavily. 'He sometimes stops for a drink – just a glass, mind - he's no drinker!' She gave Vignoles a sharp look. 'He's a good husband. He never gambles and has just the occasional glass of beer. It's thirsty work on a footplate. He likes a game of dominoes played for matchsticks alongside a glass of ale with some chums. It's good for a man to have his own friends. I mean, look at the house. He's good to us.' She was defiant and Vignoles had to concede indoors was just as immaculate as outside. This was a well-organised home and Mrs Charlton looked fit and healthy and her baking prowess was not to be doubted. He did not, as yet, sense any undercurrent of tension.

'You were not surprised he came home around about eight?'

'Not in the least. He explained he had been to Old Janey's. He sometimes goes to look in on her.'

'So that evening he had not been for a drink?'

'Like I said, he does so only occasionally.'

'Did he say why he had gone to see Mrs Palmer?'

'He was helping in the allotment.'

'In December. After dark?'

'I wouldn't really know about that sort of thing. I'm not much of a gardener, to be honest.' The first flicker of doubt crossed her forehead. Two red spots formed on her cheeks. At least she was regaining some colour.

Trinder re-appeared at the doorway into the kitchen. He leaned against the jamb and remained silent as he looked and listened.

'Did he tell you about the rabbits?'

'What rabbits? I don't understand, I thought this was about the murder.'

'Did he tell you he was killing diseased rabbits on Thursday evening at Mrs Palmer's cottage.'

Mrs Charlton made a distasteful face. 'Ugh. He'd better not have been! Touching diseased animals and coming in here, what with me like this.' She looked more horrified than at any point so far.

'It affects only rabbits and is harmless to humans. He was not putting you or the baby at risk. What about his new boots?'

'Which new boots?'

Trinder adjusted his position as he observed. He was becoming interested.

'The boots your husband bought on Saturday morning in Coalville. Did he not tell you about them?'

'Why did he buy new ones? His work boots are fine.' She looked as though someone had winded her. 'That's to say I get him a new pair when they are quite worn out or sometimes the soles get melted by the heat and we get the cobbler to re-sole them. He always goes to work with serviceable boots.'

'You did not notice he had a new pair?'

'No. I-I didn't look. I had no need. I'm busy with the children, getting their breakfasts and dinners ready, or it's bath and bed time. He changes his boots and overalls in the wash room outside. Unless they need a really good clean he leaves them there for the next morning with some newspaper stuffed inside to ensure they are dry.'

Vignoles nodded. It was a convincing scenario. Charlton could perhaps have hoped to conceal his boots for some days until they were convincingly grimy and scuffed and hope she didn't notice.

'Did your husband go out again on Thursday evening?'

'Of course not. Why would he?'

Despite firing the reply back in a flash Vignoles noticed a slight hesitancy in her voice. Trinder had his notebook open, looking every bit the bloodhound detective and now chose to speak.

'You confirm that Mr Charlton did not leave the house under any pretext, for any length of time, from when he returned home from helping Mrs Palmer, which you believe was between 8 and 8.15 pm, until the time when he left to go on shed early on Friday morning?'

'Yes.' Her voice lacked conviction.

'At what time did he leave for work?' Trinder continued.

'At the usual time, I expect.'

'You expect, or you know?'

'He leaves about 3.30 or thereabouts most days. Sometimes a little earlier or a little later. The knock-up lad ensures he's up. Not me. Listen, as a railway driver's wife I'm long used to his early rising and have learned to sleep through. You have to. Especially with little ones to look after and getting them fed and off to school later and with me now in the family way. I need my sleep.'

'You cannot actually say what time your husband left for work?' Trinder was forcing the issue.

'Not precisely.'

'Did you hear him return home a short while later? Perhaps about ten minutes or so before 4am?'

'Why would he do that?' Her puzzlement was answer enough.

Vignoles picked up the questioning, in a gentler voice. 'I could imagine with two young ones keeping you busy and as an expectant mother, you might have fallen asleep quite early on Thursday night? A late night is the last thing you need.' He sounded sympathetic.

'Gosh yes! I get so sleepy these days.' She smiled. Both detectives smiled back, indulgently. 'I go out like a light.' She laughed nervously, then looked down and her cheeks burned. The sudden realisation she was discussing her sleeping habits with two strange detectives was embarrassing. 'I might have nodded off not long after 9.30. I seem to remember Richie urging me to go up to bed at some point, but I didn't look at the clock.' Her cheeks flushed red.'You went to sleep about 9.30pm and did not awaken when your husband left for work at, what we can only presume, was 3.30am?' Trinder was making notes.

'I suppose so...'

'Are you confirming that as correct?' Trinder fired the question back.

'I don't see why you are asking these impertinent questions. I'm trying my level best to be calm as you pry into my private life and on top of that your policemen stomp all over my house doing goodness know what with my personal things! It's outrageous.' A heavy footfall upstairs and a creaking floorboard perfectly illustrating her point. 'What is this about? Accusing my husband of...of killing some stupid rabbits and buying new boots! What does it matter if he bought new boots? I don't understand what you want!'

Vignoles gave Trinder a warning glance to remain cool. Now was not the time to pile on further pressure. 'I appreciate this is unnerving. No one is being accused of anything.' *At this stage.* 'Do you know of a tramp, a Northern Irishman by the name of Michael McMullen, otherwise known as Irish Mick?'

'Pardon?' She now looked even more perplexed. Her reaction appeared genuine. She rubbed her forehead in exasperation. 'I do not make a habit of socialising with tramps - wherever they come from.'

'You husband was kind enough to present Mr McMullen with his work boots. Specifically, the serviceable pair he replaced with the newly bought ones on Saturday 3rd. It sounds as though McMullen was somebody he cared about, and perhaps had discussed helping him?' The radio started playing a soft Christmassy number as the pleasant kitchen filled with the mouth-watering smells of baking, and yet a frostiness more in keeping with the sleet falling outside was now creeping around the table.

'I have no idea what you are talking about. I do not know this man,' Mrs Charlton pursed her lips. Her hands were entwined in her lap, the knuckles white. Her eyes had lost some of their sparkle.

The constables were now working their way around the front parlour. Vignoles stood up. 'DS Trinder will oversee the final stages of the search.' He replaced his hat with a polite nod as he did so. 'Thank you for your time.'

'Was-.' she hesitated. 'Was that what you wanted? Everything is all right, isn't it? It's ridiculous to think otherwise.' Her laugh was short and strained.

'Most helpful. One last thing. About Mrs Palmer - how well did you say you knew her and her family?'

'We walk past her place sometimes on a warm evening and stop and say a few words. Richie talks gardening for a few minutes. We were not friends, but it was perfectly companionable.'

'And her daughter, Sarah? And Rachel?'

'Why are you interested in them?' She frowned. They waited for her to continue. 'We waved a greeting or said a few words across the fence. The little girl Daisy is very cute. We never went inside, and they never came here.'

'You would say that your husband knew the family better than you?'

'Of course. He was a work colleague. He saw Mrs Palmer daily and like many railwaymen he is happy to assist another in practical things like turning over the allotment. What are you getting at?'

'Just seeking to understand the relationships. Your husband never talked about the others? About Sarah or Rachel?'

Mrs Charlton flushed angrily. 'Inspector, I'm not sure I like the tone of your questions. I'd be grateful if you would leave now. I'm tired of being interrogated. I need to rest.'

Vignoles and Trinder finally made to leave the kitchen, but once again, at the last moment Trinder stopped in the doorway. 'I see you've been getting ready for Christmas. I saw some boxes of decorations for a tree in the front parlour. Are they new?'

'Most of those we've had for years. Richie got them down from the loft. We're going with the children to buy a tree next weekend. They get so excited. We bought a few extras too. Silly little things. A couple of paper sacks for presents and some glitter, wrapping paper.' She gave a weak smile as if trying to recover some of the pleasure of thinking about a happy home filled with young children at Christmas.

'I always think the anticipation is better than the actual day. We have a little lad and he's already starting to get over-excited!' Trinder appeared to soften in his demeanour. 'I've decided this year I'm going to dress up as Father Christmas, even wearing a mask – you can get cardboard ones that look quite convincing – as I creep into my little boy's room. Just in case he wakes up, so I appear convincing!'

'How funny you should mention that? We've just bought one of those. My husband loves to play Father Christmas and he had the same idea.'

'When did you go shopping?' Trinder sounded casual, as though the question was purely for his own interest.

'Wednesday afternoon. My husband had a half day and we took the chance and we went into Coalville. Why?'

'No reason. Just curious,' Trinder turned to follow Vignoles. He quietly asked one of the constables to double-check something during their search. The Father Christmas mask was missing.

Chapter Twenty-Eight

The young police constable was rubbing his hands together and wincing as the maddening stinging and itching took hold. His hands had become damp with the digging and his joints now ached despite his gloves. After washing them in hot water, which on reflection was not the best idea, he was feeling the pain as the blood started to circulate again. His fingers glowed an angry pink before he'd jammed them back into his gloves. The sensation was now almost unbearable. He hoped he didn't get chilblains and stared miserably at the thin layer of snow that lay over Black Spinney Crossing as he stomped his feet.

He was in a sour mood. He'd been posted here for two days, tasked with standing about and feeling like a spare part with almost no passers-by and little activity on the railway as his only diversion. However, after hours of this intense tedium, he thought things were about to look up that morning. The telephone had rung inside the curious octagonal cottage and the taciturn relief crossing keeper had called him across.

'It's for you! Sounds serious.'

It had been his desk sergeant giving him some new instructions.

'Straight from the DS himself, no less! By heck, you're a lucky man PC2166.' There was a chortle down the phone that suggested the sergeant was not alone at the front desk and was sharing a joke at his expense. The young constable soon discovered what they'd found so amusing.

Dig out a bloody compost heap? To see if he could find some dead rabbits. If this was their idea of a joke, then he wasn't laughing. But desk sergeant Harris had been adamant this was a direct order and told him to 'jump to it!'. The constable was still struggling to comprehend why he'd been set this stupid task and why some clever dick detective thought dead rabbits were going to be on a compost heap. Dried leaves and grass cuttings, rotting cabbage leaves, egg shells and tea leaves and goodness knows what else all turning into a smelly mulch was what he was going to find. And he had. Spade loads of it.

But not one rabbit. Obviously.

So here he was, chilled to the bone with fingers stinging like merry Hell and desperately in need of a mug of tea and some hot food. If that wasn't bad enough, having reported back that his search had proven futile, Desk Sergeant Harris had grunted in a disappointed manner before offering him some better news. The detectives were finished with the place and handing it back to the family. There was no need to stand guard a moment longer. The bad news was, they were short of vehicles and it might be another hour or two, perhaps longer, before he could get someone out that way.

'Typical.' PC2166 grumbled aloud. 'I do what I'm told and make a decent fist of it and all I get in return is they say they've had enough of the place! What a waste of time.' There was nobody around to hear him and it helped to express the sense of frustration bottled inside by moaning aloud at one of the crossing gate posts. 'Leave me here on my tod with that grumpy old sod inside who never says a word. Yes, Sarge, no Sarge, I'm happy to stand here freezing my what's-its off with nothing to do. You could at least come and rescue me.'

His words sounded flat and muffled by the snow that now lay in a thin covering across Leicestershire. A delicate blanket pierced by tufts of grass and wayside weeds and by the texture of the ballast stones and the metal wheels, rods cranks and linkages that controlled the signals. It reminded him of the gossamer thin creations his mother had crocheted to lay over his little baby sister's cot.

Two magpies cracked and screeched in a tree and sent flakes of snow tumbling to the ground. 'Two for joy? You're pulling my leg.'

PC2166 heard the sound of a car approaching. This was sufficiently rare an occurrence that he took note, a tiny spark of hope flaring as he wondered if the lads down the station had felt sorry for him and motored out to rescue him. No, blast it. This car was a deep maroon and cream and far too nice for the cop shop. It was, however, slowing down and indicating it was going to stop just a stone's throw from the crossing gates presently closed across the railway line.

Two smartly-dressed gentlemen stepped out. Shoes glistening against the snow, expensive hats on their heads, a flash of a wrist watch that glinted in the weak daylight an was that a diamond tie pin? They looked out of place. Like a pair of jays on a Corporation tip.

'Can I help you, gentlemen?'

'Good afternoon, constable, and what a bracing day it is!' Abel gave his most heart-warming smile.

'That's one way of putting it.' PC 2166 was fighting back the urge to continue shaking and beating his stinging hands.

'Am I correct in thinking this where that awful incident took place last Friday?'

'Are you from the press?' The constable had been informed he could now leave the murder scene to the family and anyone else who cared to pass, but he remained wary. He was no lover of the London red top press and their accents suggested they'd come up from the 'Smoke'. That was surely the last thing the family needed; two prying gutter-snipes out to stir up salacious stories. Perhaps he should encourage them to leave.

'Nothing escapes you, constable. We'd best watch our step!'

PC2166 observed that the man speaking was dressed in a woollen overcoat of obvious quality and wearing a pale lilac-grey hat. There was a strong whiff of cologne. The speaker laughed and winked at his colleague.

'He's gonna go far. Seen right through us in a flash!' Kane gave an approving nod of his head, his startling blue eyes further reinforcing the young constable's idea that they reminded him of jays.

'Before you do your duty - and I am quite sure it *is* your duty – to rebuff our questions and send us on our way -,'

'I meant no offence -.'

'None taken!' Abel momentarily closed his eyes. 'I should explain that we fully appreciate your caution.' Abel read the bright silvered numbers on the constable's uniform, one eye squinting through his monocle. 'PC2166, I feel it only fair to explain that whilst we are members of the 'Fourth Estate', which can, we freely admit, draw the disapproval of many, we're from an altogether more elevated publication.' He said this with the most sugary of tongues, rolling each word and savouring it as though he were dining on the finest food.

The young constable was already wondering what on earth the man was blabbering on about. What was the Fourth Estate? Perhaps it was a city housing committee?

Kane stepped closer, the pale scar tissue down the side of his rugged face clearly visible. It looked as though he'd been on the receiving end of a nasty knife wound some years ago. 'What my colleague is takin' forever to say is, we're from *Picture Post*. Know it?'

'I should say! My mother has subscribed for years and we absolutely devour every copy.'

'Not literally, I hope...' Kane gave a wry smile, then turned away and made a show of using his hands to create a virtual picture frame as he tried out a few compositions.

'Your mother clearly appreciates photo journalism of the highest order,' Abel gushed, one of his eyes watering with the effort of focussing in the cold air and bright light reflecting off the snow. 'She must be a woman of taste!'

Kane darted his colleague a look that suggested he rein in some of the schmaltz. 'We don't do the cheap stuff you see in the ragtops.' Both Kane and Abel pulled faces suggesting they'd just smelt the fumes and slime from the bottom of the compost heap. 'We're more - considered. Respectful and discreet.' He went back to trying out some more imagined compositions using his strong hands, a look of intense concentration on his face.

PC2166 was transfixed. 'I do. Ma and I both agree about this. And the pictures really are good.'

'We uphold the very highest standards. My esteemed colleague here earned his stripes with his war work.' A wink. 'D-Day...'

The constable was impressed. That explained the scar. Kane was walking towards the cottage and managed to suppress a guffaw as he busied himself with another charade of imagining a possible photograph.

'As a man clearly of discerning taste, you'll appreciate that we have absolutely no interest in the actual crime, *per se*,' Abel added. 'That's a matter for the professionals - such as yourself.' His smile was sickly.

PC 2166 was about to admit he was nothing but a very junior constable, but the attention was flattering. Digging that pile of rotten vegetation was all part of the investigation. Unglamorous and filthy, but that's what crime-fighting professionals did; slogging away for hours in the cold in the name of crime-fighting. He straightened his back and clasped his gloved hands behind his back as if on parade.

'It's the tragic human story we explore.' Abel gave a sad look that spoke of sympathy and understanding. 'We compose a story from a few artfully chosen words – that's my forte – to accompany my colleague's finely photographs.' He stepped closer and dropped his voice to a stage whisper. 'For obvious reasons we don't broadcast the fact, but my friend over there is one of the best.' He raised an eyebrow. 'No names! But let's just say that we work as a double-act and in the office they call me Laurel...'

The young constable's eyes widened. 'Laurel and...*Bert* Hardy?'

'Shhh! Mum's the word!'

'Of course. I'll keep that under my hat. Helmet.' He felt his pulse quicken. Surely the greatest photo-journalist in Britain - perhaps in the whole of Europe – and he was here. Working right in front of him. Hardy's photographs filled a scrapbook in his bedroom. PC 2166 could not quite recall having ever seen a picture of Bert Hardy, but he knew he was a Londoner. The accent was spot on. He nodded appreciatively as he listened.

'With your kind permission, constable, my friend would like to explore a few angles inside the cottage and around the garden. Looking at how best to capture the once cheerful house now cruelly bereft of its elderly occupant.' Abel was hamming it up dreadfully.

'You'd best be quick as the others are all coming back sometime soon today. I was told only just now. They were away in Liverpool when it happened. It will be a terrible homecoming.' The constable started to open up. He wanted to help, and the cold and boredom and his itching fingers were now forgotten.

'Is that so, constable?' Kane gave him a piercing look even from a few yards away. 'Just ten, twenty minutes to have a little gander. I can get a feel for the place. I've not got my camera with me, of course. We'll come back another day and have a word with the family to see if they'd be willing to allow us to shoot a few frames.'

'Of course. Go ahead, the place is empty. Almost.' The constable was fascinated. His initial caution was being thrown to the wind by the minute. The chance to help the legendary Bert Hardy was too good to miss. They were now walking towards the cottage, the constable having to catch up.

'There's the relief signalman. He just sits near the instruments all day. He doesn't say much.'

'We'll not get in his way. I'll start upstairs.' Kane was already opening the front door and confidently stepping inside. Ignoring the look of surprise on the face of the morose man seated in the chair at the big kitchen table, he quickly stepped across the room and up the stairs.

The constable hurriedly explained their presence, which elicited a blank response from the relief signalman who muttered, 'Please yourselves, just keep out of my way,' and fell back to studying the sports pages of a tabloid paper. Abel rolled his eyes and silently indicated this reading matter, which forced the constable into almost laughing. He was enjoying the feeling of sharing a joke between them.

There was the sound of feet on wooden stairs testing out the treads, then a slight squeak of a wooden board being removed.

'What's your friend doing?'

Kane called down from around the bend on the stairs. 'Nothin' to worry about. Checking I can get a tripod set up, if I lift a tread. Dead easy.' His head appeared and he gave a cheeky smile. 'There's a good shot from here looking across the room, the opened door, a figure silhouetted against the snow...'

'Gosh, yes.' The constable nodded approval.

Kane disappeared and there were a few other sounds from various points above the ceiling.

Abel smiled indulgently. 'Sheer professionalism. He's always like this. A little recce in advance. Looking at angles, how best he can set up a picture. The lengths he goes to. It's best to do this in advance so we can work swiftly alongside the family when we turn up in earnest with the Leica loaded.'

'That makes sense.' The constable could hear something being moved across a floor upstairs. 'He's very thorough.'

'Has to be to stay at the top of his game.'

'But he won't take any photos today?' The constable was trying to hide his disappointment.

''fraid not. All the gear is back in the hotel. We would never presume to just turn up and snap away without prior approval.'

Ten minutes later and they were standing beside the tool shed. Kane was inside claiming he 'might get a decent shot through the cobwebby window' and got busy rearranging the tools. They left him to it.

'You said the family are returning home? Do you know their names?' Abel was holding a notebook open in his soft kid-leather gloved hand.

The constable had been fully briefed on the family and was able to give a detailed run down of their names and ages, finding himself offering as much information as he could remember, eager to appear helpful. He ignored the various bumps and thumps from inside the shed and found himself giving an outline of the murder itself.

As the elegantly dressed journalist shook his head in response to the dreadful story, his scent once again carried on the bracing air.

'I'll get my main establishing shot from 'ere.' Kane reappeared from the shed and brushed himself down. 'That's me done. We'd best be off.'

'Our helpful constable was telling me there are three generations of women heading homewards - even as we speak. Can you imagine?'

'Pure visual delight!' Kane agreed as they walked towards the car.

'Imagine what the editor will say if you capture these bereft womenfolk in their humble railway house? Tears, the little one clutching a teddy or doll in the snow as night falls.' Abel was enjoying himself.

They were next to the car and Kane had some keys in his hand. 'Constable, are you signin' off duty anytime soon?'

'I've been told to step down. I'm to return to Leicester as soon as they can send over a car. But they're talking their time - worst luck!'

'We have a car. With a working heater.' Kane winked. 'And there's a caff I know. Mainly for truck drivers and cabbies, mind, but it's on the way into Leicester.'

'That might be frowned upon.'

'What? Stay standing here in the cold doing nothing whilst we're heading that way. Twenty minutes of your time in the warm with a buttered teacake and cup of tea? Come on! We can drop you off near to your station, no problem.'

'And we won't say a word - if you don't,' Abel added, pointedly.

An hour later and young PC2166 had been dropped off a street away from his police station, positively glowing from the warmth of the greasy spoon cafe and having enjoyed two cups of tea and a bacon sandwich between doorstops of white bread fried on one side. These *Picture Post* boys with their expense accounts knew how to treat a fellow! He couldn't wait to get home and tell his mum about this fascinating experience. To have seen none other than Bert Hardy himself in action. Just think! He'd been sworn to secrecy, but they'd allowed him to share the story with mum. And besides, the philistines at work just wouldn't understand. They didn't appreciate an artist. They just looked at the sports pages and pictures of dolly birds. He chuckled to himself as he stepped into the station and met the desk sergeant's steely glare.

'You back already? Blimey, they must have put a move on cos' I only just sent the boys over...'

Kane and Abel returned the car they had 'borrowed' for the afternoon. A few moments with a set of skeleton keys and both door and ignition had yielded to Kane's practised hands. The petrol tank was a little emptier, but otherwise it was back where they'd found it and none the worse for wear.

Later that evening the real owner would stand in the street scratching his head with a bemused expression on his face. He and his wife had returned to Leicester after a weekend away with another couple, and even as he was lifting their suitcases from the boot of their friend's car, he was looking distracted.

'What's up, Harold?'

'It's the car, Mary. It's facing the wrong way.'

'Are you sure?'

'Yes. Look at those tyre treads in the fresh snow. There was no snowfall when we left. Well, the darned cheek of it. Someone's moved it...'

Not that The Debt Collectors cared one jot. They were seated in the restaurant of their hotel tucking into plates of indeterminate meat described as beef, accompanied by over-boiled potatoes and watery cabbage, washed down with pints of beer.

'That nice young copper gave us plenty to think about.'

'Well -.' Kane chewed with a look of consternation on his face, before extracting a piece of gristle which he put on the side of his plate. '- he's about to learn a hard lesson about blabbing his mouth off ten to the dozen. I've just put a call in. Arranged a hit and run after dark, so that way he can't cause us any aggro.'

'Oh, *Louis*!' The use of Kane's Christian name was reserved for moments of impact by Abel. 'Must we? How could you be so cruel?'

'You heard him! Singing like a bloody canary. Can't keep his trap shut for love nor money. Don't worry, I put one of the best on the job. Over in seconds.'

Abel made a sad face. 'But think of his dear mum!'

'I couldn't give a monkey's arse about his mum.'

'You're heartless, Louis. Heartless! I'm almost off my food.' Abel dabbed his lips gently with a napkin, but then thought otherwise and speared a spud and popped it in his mouth.

'Never mind that. We've got a list of names to check over, thanks to calling in a few favours with our contacts and from what that soon-to-be-dead constable told us, it sounds as though the pigs don't even have Leach on the scene. That puts us a step ahead.'

'He's awfully young and hardly privy to the inner machinations of the detectives, surely? He could be misinformed?' Abel raised an eyebrow and allowed his monocle to fall against his chest.

Kane shook his head and washed down the memory of the gristle he'd been chewing with some beer. 'Word gets around a police station like wildfire and you can bet your bottom dollar they'll talk about the juicy stuff. They might want to keep a lid on it, but they'll share what most interests them – and us. He seemed on the ball and from what he told us, I don't reckon we need have any interest in that tramp, nor the train driver.'

'He said they've reasons to suspect the driver?'

'Nah, I don't buy that.' Kane cautiously explored the over-boiled green mush on his plate. 'Listen, we do our research. We check our facts. We ask the right questions of the right people. People who *know*.' If sharks grinned, the effect would be similar to his expression now, as a row of sharp teeth were bared. 'Twenty minutes in a call box leaning on the right men and we're already streets ahead of the filth.'

'I hope you're right.'

'The house was cleaned out. The stuff we're after was gone. I knew where to look. I lifted the stair tread, the loose board under the chest of drawers and the trap in the shed floor. All the places the old bird stored her top merchandise. Zero. OK, so I found a stash of US dollars and some bits of trashy silver jewellery, but nothing that interests us.'

'What does this tell us?'

'That it was not done by a bloody choo-choo train driver, that's what.'

'Nor by a tramp...'

'Exact-o-mondo, Abe. The way I see it, we've got a couple of geezers who've muscled in on the racket having got wind of this special little stash she was holding on to.'

'And took what was not theirs to take.' Abel's eye widened behind his monocle allowing it to fall.

'Little monkeys. They need to understand there's a price to pay for that kind of cheek. And polishing off Palmer on top – quite out of line!'

Abel chuckled. His mood had lifted as he sensed fresh blood. 'I look forward to extracting a suitable confession. I'm sure I can dream up something fitting.' He screwed his monocle back into place.

'All in good time.'

'It was the track workers the pretty constable told us about, who robbed and killed her?'

'I reckon so. Leach came up here to make payment for safe keeping and collect the goods in return. Nice and discreet. And to be fair to the lad, there's no earthly reason why it should all go pear-shaped. Leach minded his back and kept his head down. But she'd been done over, and the stuff was gone when he got there.'

'His pleas of innocence were heartfelt after all?'

Kane drank some beer. 'That can't be helped.' Kane shrugged his shoulders with casual indifference.

Abel gave a slight sigh and a reflective pause. 'So, Mr Baylock and Mr Hind got greedy?' He gave a distasteful sneer at the pungent pool of watery cabbage.

'We know they did some fetching and carrying for her. Just minor stuff; knock off fags and bits and pieces. Pocket money.'

'But they fancied something stronger?' Abel licked his rather full and almost feminine lips as he considered the situation. 'They beat her up so she confessed where she'd hidden the stones then did her in.'

'Just as Leach turns up.'

'Awkward. You think they knew each other?'

'Not sure about that. I reckon Leach was aware of their involvement. They probably realised he was also part of the in crowd and needed to tread carefully. Leach offered them some of the funds he was carrying. Bought the two lads off so they'd not stitch him up and give him time to leg it back to London.'

'You think Leach never suspected the track workers?' Abel considered this idea. 'However, time was short. There was a dead body at their feet and the goods missing and Leach had to clear out before someone tried to pin the murder on him.'

'He'd have no chance of turning the situation around if he was banged up on a murder charge, so he gave them a wedge to keep schtum and he ran.' Kane abandoned the cabbage and tossed his knife and fork down on the plate.

'In exchange for calling for help and acting innocent? That way everyone thinks they're heroes and all the time Hind and Baylock are sitting tight with a a little bag of goodies and some spending money on top.'

'But they're not the brightest sparks. They were never paid to think, just do as they were told and now they're playing with fire.'

'We should spare a thought for Leach.' Abel also laid his knife and fork in perfect alignment on his almost empty plate. 'I did rather shock him to his core. I do hope you'll let me have a go at Baylock and Hind!'

'You will. But we need first need to think how we go about it.'

'I've already dreamed up something suitably *persuasive*. They don't have electric trains up here, do they?'

'I don't think so.'

'What a shame.'

Kane gave an indulgent roll of his eyes. His partner in crime was as camp as a Scout jamboree and smelt atrociously of lavender cologne, but he was the cruellest and most effective killer he'd met. Ruthless, unflappable and without the faintest trace of remorse. Abel seemed to positively enjoy meticulously planning ever more sinister means to cause the most pain and suffering before allowing the release of death. Not for him a swift bullet in the head or a knife through the heart.

'We'll put the frighteners on one of them and see where it leads.' Kane had pushed his plate aside, the greasy gravy already starting to congeal. He had his notebook open and was looking at the notes he'd made in a telephone kiosk earlier that evening.

'Divide and rule. Pick one and if he foolishly refuses to tell, the other is sure to do so once he realises what's coming.' Abel chuckled.

'I hope so. We need to collect on this.'

'We shall, dear boy, we shall. The Debt Collectors *always* collect what's due.' Abel looked satisfied like an over-fed cat. He'd been promised two fresh lambs to take to the slaughter and a warm inner glow of satisfaction was coursing through his veins. 'Are you ready for the tinned peaches and evaporated milk they are tempt us with for dessert?'

'Not me. I'm going for the rice pudding and prunes.'

Chapter Twenty-Nine

'There was nothing at Charlton's house?'

'Not a sausage and we went over it like my missus does our house at springtime. We found no gambling receipts, no stacks of unpaid bills nor anything to suggest a household living on the edge. There was nothing conspicuously new or ostentatious either. Just some rolls of Christmas wrapping paper, Santa Claus sacks and a new set of Christmas tree lights. That was it. The only anomaly was the missing cardboard Santa mask that Mrs Charlton told me they had bought a few days before.'

'And the relevance of this is what, exactly?'

'I don't know. But I found just such a mask lodged in a hedge close to the crossing. It was new and fresh.'

'You think it could be the one the Charlton's purchased?'

'Maybe. Or it's an irrelevance.'

Vignoles was unsure what to make of that piece of information. 'The way I see it, if Charlton killed Palmer, it was not because he was desperate for her money.'

'Nor in need of linen tablecloths and a set of spoons, either.' Trinder shook his head sadly. 'He had the opportunity; he's placed himself at the scene of the crime with only half an alibi as there were no dead rabbits on the compost heap or anywhere else nearby. And then there's the curious story about his new boots.'

'Not forgetting the forgotten knife and his unexplained movements that morning.'

'And yet there's no obvious motive,' Trinder responded.

'There needs to be a darned good reason for him to kill a work colleague, a friend and in such a violent manner. This was no accident or momentary lapse of reason - this was cold-blooded murder.' Vignoles chewed this grim fact over. 'Motive aside, Mrs Charlton did not offer a strong alibi for her husband. Her early evening sleeping and his ability to rise for work without disturbing her offers him a wide window of opportunity.'

'I think she's telling us an unadorned account. She only realised after she'd spoken that she was failing to protect her husband.'

'She had no reason to believe she needed to give him an alibi. Which suggests he is either innocent or a very devious character who hides his darker side effectively.' Vignoles replied.

'And don't forget Charlton was seen hurrying from the direction of Black Spinney about 4am that morning. His story of gong home to collect his clasp knife is surely invention.'

'I agree that's a fabrication. His wife was unaware he returned for the knife – and I think she would stir when the front door unexpectedly opened. Sleeping on when you hear routine sounds is very plausible, but introduce an unexpected sound, and we all tend to jolt awake.'

'Do you think all's well in their home?' Trinder asked.

'She's in the family way with a third child,' Vignoles replied. He was talking slowly, weighing up each statement. 'She looked healthy, content – at least until we started stirring things up. The house was clean and welcoming and had a nice feel to it. It was almost like a feature from one of the *Good Housekeeping* magazines Anna likes to read.'

'An idyllic image of the perfect family preparing for Christmas. But perhaps too good to be true?' Trinder's question was almost rhetorical.

'The perfect image of a happy couple with spicy apple pie baking?' Vignoles shook his head. 'Why go to the trouble to stage all that, and besides, she had no idea we were paying her a call. That was no set up.'

Both men looked baffled. Nothing was making sense.

'John, give me something that helps untie this granny-knot of a case! A story, no matter who far-fetched.'

Trinder filled his cheeks then expelled the air as he pondered the challenge. 'OK. There's nothing specific I can base this on. More gut instinct, than fact.'

'I'll take instinct for now.' Vignoles pulled on his pipe and stared at a spider's web in the corner of the ceiling.

'Mrs C was hesitant admitting she could not categorically say her husband was next to her all night. I'm not sure if she had even thought about this prior to our arrival, but once questioned, she was perilously close to telling a lie to protect her husband. Her loyalty to him runs deep, as we might expect.' Trinder now looked unsure where to go next with his story. 'I doubt she knew *why* she needed to lie, but something was telling her to be...wary. But we caught her unawares and so I think she told the truth.'

'She'll be ready and waiting the next time.'

'I think she began to realise she was making problems for him and wondering whether to lie.' Trinder looked troubled. 'What I'm going to say is dreadfully cynical.'

'Our job demands we are.'

'There were moments when I wondered if you'd punctured the surface of their happy life. She did not like you questioning her husband's relationship with Sarah Lake.'

'She thought I was implying something inappropriate in the relationship.'

'You touched a nerve,' Trinder replied. 'Perhaps Richard Charlton is fonder of Sarah Lake than his wife is comfortable with? Is his real motive for frequently helping the old lady on her allotment actually about spending time with her well-dressed and attractive daughter?'

'Who has a husband away at sea...'

'The old lady finds out – hardly surprising in a tiny place like theirs – and disapproved? She threatened Charlton, so he went around when Palmer was alone to - to do what?'

'For a heated discussion.'

'An argument flares up. He strikes her in anger, just as you suggested when we interviewed him.'

'No. The level of malice is too much to take. And don't forget this scenario does not explain how Charlton and his engine later rolled through the crossing if he'd already killed her!' Vignoles sounded exasperated and Trinder looked deflated. 'What about the even younger, Rachel What's-her-Name?'

Trinder raised an eyebrow in surprise. He'd not considered she could be involved. Vignoles took this as all the answer he needed. 'We need to speak to her. I presume she still has her married name?'

'I'm not sure.' Trinder looked worried. This was an oversight. He realised how very little they knew about this member of the family. 'Lansdowne said she was out when she went to Liverpool to accompany Lake back here.'

'No one has actually seen, let alone spoken, to this young lady? Find out when the family are due home. Get Rachel away from her mother and extract a statement from her as high priority. I'd like to know how interested she was in her granny's mouth-watering hoard of cash - and establish just how well she knows Richard Charlton whilst you're at it.'

Trinder gave Vignoles a curious look. 'You think she could be in on this?'

'No idea. I know practically nothing about her. What I do know is she's a young widowed mother living in a small cottage in the middle of nowhere. Sharing it with mum and grandma and with a little one to bring up. No privacy and far from any entertainment or distractions. A woman in the prime of life must want more. A life-changing haul of used banknotes could be a severe temptation.'

'But she was in Liverpool at the time of the murder. How could be she involved?'

'I don't see her wielding a mattock, if that's what you mean - but that doesn't stop her being implicated.'

'Through a proxy?'

Vignoles shrugged his shoulders. 'What about Hind and Baylock? Rachel would have ample opportunities to meet those two fellows who just might be willing to do some breaking and entering on her behalf.'

'Which then went wrong.'

'Neatly bringing us back to your initial interpretation. Is this a robbery that spiralled out of control?'

Chapter Thirty

Rain was falling steadily as it had since the early hours of the morning. Any romantic notions of a white Christmas were firmly on hold. Cobwebs lined with droplets of water sparkled and danced in the corners of the wooden crossing gates as they clonked into place and closed Desford Lane to road traffic. The relief crossing keeper was dressed in a long black waterproof that glistened as if freshly varnished, whilst his cap channelled water down his neck or dripped big droplets onto his reddening nose. A stub of a cigarette smouldered in a desultory manner in the corner of his mouth. He looked cold and miserable and unlikely to request the position on a permanent basis.

Engine 58148 steamed quietly some distance back, wreaths of slow-moving steam curling around the little coupled wheels and feeling its way around the curve of the boiler. The faces of the crew were pale smudges barely discernible through the curtain of pouring rain, both crew silently observing the mundane actions of the gates being pulled open ready for them to continue on their slow trip along the Groby quarry spur to drop off empty wagons before continuing on to West Wharf.

Driver Ashbourne was still struggling to come to terms with the sober reality that Old Janey was gone. Her body now lay grey and cold and stiff on a retractable metal bed inside a chiller cabinet in the city morgue. Every so often he would give a slight shake of his head as if this action would somehow help his comprehension. Ashbourne was so used to steaming up to the signal protecting the crossing and exchanging a few friendly words before the gates were opened and the signal pulled 'off', that this morning he'd done just the same. Only this time, all he got was an impatient flap of a hand from the taciturn relief man as he stomped out of the cottage door and unhitched a gate. The regime had changed and there was to be no idle chat from now on.

Not that it was weather for standing around. Earnshaw edged closer to the boiler backhead on the footplate and soaked up more radiating warmth, eager to keep as dry as he could. There was much to be said for a roaring fire on days like these, although a more generous cab would not go amiss. A few years earlier, the fitters in the engine shed had rigged up a tarpaulin stretching from the back of the cab roof to two metal poles welded onto the tender sides to create a tent-like covering. This held off the worst of the rain, but it still dripped unpleasantly along the edges and had a habit of suddenly emptying the pool of water that gathered in the middle down Earnshaw's back at unexpected moments as they jolted down the undulating track.

He remained unenthusiastic about the new-fangled diesel locomotives starting to find their way onto the railway, but the bright and shining example he'd recently watched trundle around the goods yard in Leicester, had a fully glazed cab and a door that closed against the elements - and apparently even came with an electric heater and a comfy padded seat! Perhaps sitting in one of those on a wet winter's day would not be so bad after all.

'Looks like the police are back.' Ashbourne observed. 'I thought they'd packed up.'

Earnshaw flipped open a wet spectacle plate to get a better view from his side of the cab. 'That's DS Trinder and WPC Lansdowne. I've met them. I wonder if the family have returned?'

'I'd heard word around the shed they were back from Liverpool.'

'Perhaps the detectives need to check a few things with them.'

'They can't think they've anything to do with it?'

'I couldn't say. But police question everyone, just to be sure. Perhaps they've got a suspect in mind and want to ask if the family know of them?'

'Pity they can't just leave the poor girls to their grief.' Ashworth looked unimpressed and perhaps made his feelings known by giving a particularly sharp screech on the whistle as the signal dropped and they were given the right of way. Trinder and Lansdowne both reacted to the shrill sound, with Trinder lifting a hand to show they'd heard the warning and were standing clear to let the train roll past.

Lansdowne recognised the fireman eagerly peering down from the side of the cab and gave him a slight nod of the head in acknowledgement, but she looked preoccupied; tight-lipped and impassive as the engine and its open trucks banged and boomed and complained as they passed close to where she was standing.

'The ladies are all upstairs. Unpacking.' The two detectives were shown into the kitchen-cum-signal cabin by the crossing keeper, who was already shaking off his coat and hanging it from a clothes dryer above the roaring range which was kicking out a wall of heat. The water draining from his coat started to add to the puddles collected on the quarry tiled floor. 'It's not my house and it's not my business and I've work to attend to.'

'And it hardly feels like ours either. Not now.' They found Sarah Lake slumped in an old armchair in the corner of her bedroom. An unopened suitcase stood in the centre of the floor, its presence adding to the feeling of impermanence. 'We've been given four weeks to get out.' Lake was holding a letter from the British Railways Board. She shrugged her shoulders in resignation and tossed the letter aside and it fluttered to the floor. She lit a cigarette.

'What will you do?' Lansdowne asked.

'Move out, of course. What else do you suggest?' Lake narrowed her eyes as she inhaled and gave the WPC a challenging stare.

'Do you have somewhere to go?'

'I've only just opened the letter, me duck.' There was no affection in the soubriquet. 'I need a while longer to decide. You know, what with having so many options.' Her voice was sarcastic.

Lansdowne gave a weak smile, unsure what to say. It was a cruel situation.

'We'd like to speak with Rachel if we may?' Trinder asked.

'She's a grown woman, she can decide herself if she wants to talk. You'll find her in the next room.'

The bedroom door had been closed as they had ascended the stairs and they were aware of the sound of a young girl's voice from inside and the quieter tones of her mother answering. Saving them the trouble of knocking, the door flew open at that moment and Daisy stood looking at them with a doll clutched close to her side. She did not seem at all surprised by their presence outside the door and with big blue eyes looked them over before asking 'Have you come to see Gerr Gaa?'

'Sorry?' Lansdowne smiled back.

'Gerr Gaa!' Daisy repeated it with the tone of someone who thought them foolish at not understanding. 'Mummy says she's dead. So you're too late.'

Lansdowne was momentarily floored by the directness of the little girl's statement once she realised that Gerr Gaa was Daisy's Great Grandma. 'We've come to see your mummy.'

'Dolly says a bad man hit her too hard.' Daisy gave Lansdowne a wide-eyed look and thrust her doll upwards as if to help Lansdowne hear this statement from the painted lips of the wide-eyed doll. 'Have you caught the bad man?'

'Daisy, do be quiet!' An attractive young woman appeared behind the little girl, but her pretty face was marred by a scowl. 'You the police?'

'Rachel? Mrs Rachel...Lake?' Lansdowne asked.

'Corrigan. It's me married name. I'd have thought you lot would have finished nosing around by now?'

'We'd like to ask you some questions. It might be better if you were alone.' Trinder was letting Lansdowne lead. A WPC was more likely to win her confidence. A brief frown crossed Corrigan's brow. 'What about? I know you're investigating – you know what,' she glanced down at Daisy who seemed unperturbed by the presence of the police. 'But what can I tell you? We were away.'

'If we could speak to you alone?' Lansdowne glanced at Daisy.

Corrigan made an impatient snort, 'Daisy, go to Granny Sarah, I need to talk to these people for a few minutes.'

'But dolly wants to know who -.'

'No, dolly does not want to know anything of the sort!' Lake appeared behind the detectives and deftly steered the young girl, still clutching her inquisitive doll down the narrow stairs. 'We'll go to the parlour. We can freeze in there until you've finished. Hurry up as there's not been a fire lit since dad's wake.' Her pointed remark was fired upwards as she clomped down the wooden stairs, a loose step squeaking under the stair runner as she did, her hands guiding the little girl before her.

'Go in there. There's more room.' Rachel Corrigan indicated Palmer's bedroom which was fractionally larger than her own and had the advantage of having only one bed in it. Lansdowne and Trinder stood to one side of the bed, Corrigan leaning her back against a low dressing table that stood before the small paned window. Rain rattled against the little square panes and ran down in rivulets like streaming tears.

'What makes you think I can help?' Her antagonistic attitude had not thawed.

'How old are you?' Lansdowne smiled.

Corrigan frowned. This was not perhaps the question she'd expected. 'Twenty-five. What of it?'

'Your husband, Mr Corrigan, is the father of Daisy?'

'Was. He's dead.' Lansdowne waited for her to elucidate. 'Once Daisy came along he didn't want to hang around. Sharing a room with a baby wasn't what he wanted. There I was with a babe in arms and he just walked out with not so much as a goodbye.' She looked faraway and gave a shake of her head at the memory. 'He drank most of his wages, so it was no great loss.' She glared at Lansdowne. 'Are you married?'

'No.'

'Best stay that way, love.' She sighed heavily. 'The idiot moved up north and got himself drunk as a skunk one night and thought he could take on a speeding lorry. The lorry won.'

'Where were you and your husband living?' Trinder asked.

'Over Ratby way. We rented rooms. Look, what's this got to do with anything?'

'You moved here once your husband left?' Trinder answered her question with another.

'What choice had I?'

'Do you work?' Lansdowne changed tack.

'Part time. Work does not exactly grow on trees around here,' she sounded defensive. 'It's like the back of beyond. Just with trees and cows.' She almost smiled.

'Where do you work?' Lansdowne sensed they were starting to coax her into opening up.

'The brick works. I do light office work. Which is a way of saying my typing's not that fast and I can't add up for toffee.' She made a rueful expression that was not unattractive. 'The boss seems to like me, so that helps.' Corrigan touched her hair in a self-conscious manner then leaned back, her long legs stretching into the room as if better to show off her fine physique. Trinder could imagine her boss approved and probably for all the wrong reasons. Her dress was perhaps surprisingly well-made and expertly fitted, which combined with the thin and only partially buttoned cardigan, served to enhance her youthful, hour-glass figure.

'I'm not the brainiest with numbers, but I'm learning.' She actually laughed and looked prettier for it. 'Mr Carruthers, that's my boss, he says that if I improve my typing and numbers I might be able to go full time. But... everything's a bit messed up now. I'm not sure what will happen.'

'Where are the brick works?' Trinder wanted more detail.

'This side of Glenfield. "The Premier Brick & Terra Cotta Works" to be exact, but no one calls it that. It's just the 'Brickie'.'

'How do you get to and from work?' Lansdowne asked.

'In the nice weather I use my bicycle.' She hesitated. 'But I most often hitch a ride on the train because the roads are awful.'

'In the brake van?' Trinder quizzed. He knew that no passenger service had run on this line since before the war.

'Mostly. They go right past the works all the time. They've got sidings and a branch line turns off there and often pick up or drop off wagons there. I mean it's the easiest way to and from the works.' She sounded defensive.

'Is Mr Charlton one of the engine drivers who stops to pick you up?' Trinder felt this to be significant, but was unsure why.

Corrigan ignored the question by fiddling with her hair and giving an ambiguous shrug of a shoulder.

'Was it hard having to give up your own place and move back in with your family?' Lansdowne asked.

'I had no choice.' She looked at the floor. 'I'd never have been able to keep up the rent on my own.'

'I understand you and your mother have been given notice to leave here. Do you have any idea where you will go?' Lansdowne continued.

Corrigan made another dismissive gesture with her shoulders.

'Probably to Liverpool. I've made friends there and there's a better chance of work that will pay the rent in a city rather than a dead-end place like this.'

Trinder gave her a long look. 'Until this case is resolved I would like you to remain in the area.'

'It's all very well you saying that but I need to find a place to live! I'll do what I must to find a home for me and Daisy!' She stood up and paced once (it was a small room) then spun on her heels. 'You march in here just as you please and question me about something I know nothing about and now you tell me what I can and can't do.' She almost stamped her foot in frustration. 'You're not the one being kicked out on the street!'

'I appreciate that, but this is a murder investigation and as such I would rather you did not leave the county until we are satisfied you are not implicated.'

'Implicated? What do you mean *implicated*?' She put her hands on her hips, eyes flashing. It was not an unattractive sight. 'This is ridiculous. I left here with mum and Daisy on Saturday and in case you've forgotten, that was days before the old coot was attacked!'

'You left for Liverpool on November 27th?' Lansdowne wanted the date confirmed.

'Yes! Are you deaf? Look here, Miss Detective What-Ever-Your-Name is, you know this. You even came snooping to Liverpool, prying into our lives, so give it a rest.' She turned away and stared out of the grubby net curtains. 'How could I be in two places at once? That proves it's nothing to do with me.'

Trinder and Lansdowne let that hang in the air for a beat. 'Did you know your grandmother kept her savings in this room?'

'Savings?' Corrigan said it as if the concept was novel.

'Cash put away for a rainy day. A considerable sum.' Trinder was not fooled by her attempts to sound dumb. 'She kept it locked in that draw.' He indicated the damaged chest of drawers, the fresh splinters where it had been forced bright and harsh in the dim light. Trinder felt Corrigan was making an effort not to look where he was pointing.

'No.' The detectives remained silent. 'She didn't go around discussing her savings, more's the pity. Daisy and I might have been able to use some help.' She sounded sulky and school-girlish in her denials, folding her arms across her ample bust, creating a dark cleavage whilst slightly lowering her head so she had to look at Trinder through her heavy eyelashes.

'Your grandmother never said a word? With you and Daisy needing a roof over your heads and forced to learn new skills to have any chance of enhancing your work prospects and get a better wage, I'm surprised.' Lansdowne was not convinced. 'Grandmothers usually dote on grandkids – and I imagine on great grandkids even more.'

'Not her!' Corrigan wrinkled her nose. 'Believe me, she was a proper old Scrooge. A few shillings for birthdays and Christmas and that was it. She counted every penny that came in and every penny spent in this house.'

'Can you give us any idea how much was stolen?' Trinder suddenly asked, hoping to catch Corrigan out.

'I said I didn't know about no savings,' Corrigan was starting to look rattled and fiddling with her hair again. She gave Trinder a sulky, or perhaps, sultry, look.

'Have you identified anything missing?' Trinder piled on the questions. 'From your room or elsewhere in the house? We need to know everything that was taken so we can hopefully get it back.'

'I dunno. Some stupid spoons and a few bits of cloth. That's what mum says. I lost nothing. I've got nothing worth stealing I suppose.'

'Your mother did not mention the considerable sum of money?' Lansdowne was starting to feel her hackles rise, not liking the way this obviously attractive woman was trying to use her looks to charm her DS. 'She only told you about the spoons and Irish linen?'

Corrigan narrowed her eyes. 'That's what she said.'

'How well did you know Mr Charlton?' Trinder asked.

'Charlton?' Her attempt at pretending not to recognise the name was worthy of The Belgrave Player's Amateur Dramatic Society on a bad night.

'Richard Charlton. He's an engine driver. The one I mentioned earlier, in case you have forgotten.' He paused a beat. 'But you know who he is, as he's a good friend to the family and often comes over to help in the garden.'

'Oh, you mean Richie. I didn't make the connection.' She laughed rather too loud and her eyes flashed, not uninvitingly, towards Trinder.

'Now you've made the connection, could you answer the question?' Lansdowne gave her an icy look.

Corrigan hesitated a fraction as if she was trying to decide whether to admit something. Or lie.

'The truth, Mrs Corrigan.' Trinder advised. 'We'll find out anyway and it will not look good if we discover you attempted to conceal information, especially in a murder investigation.'

'I wasn't *going* to lie!' Her eyes flashed. 'I know him. He just works in the garden out the back. He gets on with digging and whatever it is he does out there. It's none of my business. I don't take any notice. He waves from the train sometimes. They all do. The lads on the engines. They all look and wave when they pass.' She smiled innocently, her cleavage deepening.

I bet they do, Trinder mused. *And no mention of hitching rides squeezed next to him on his engine.*

'Do you know if your grandmother ever discussed her savings with Mr Charlton?'

'I've no idea what they talked about. I keep telling you I don't know anything about the hundreds of pounds she had squirrelled away.'

'Why did you say hundreds of pounds?' Lansdowne fired back the question.

'I just said it. I-I invented a number. You know...as something to say.'

An uneasy silence fell in the small room. They could hear the faint sound of Daisy laughing downstairs.

'Thank you for your time.' Trinder was quietly formal. He touched the brim of his hat. He handed her one of his cards. 'If you remember anything that might help us catch the person who killed your grandmother, please telephone.'

They let themselves out, both detectives feeling Corrigan's eyes burning into their backs whilst she pensively curled her long hair around a forefinger and chewed the inside of her lip.

* * * *

'A house without tears.'

Trinder gave Lansdowne a quizzical look as they settled into the police Rover. 'How do you mean?'

'Mother and daughter didn't shed one tear, nor had they recently. The little girl also, come to think of it.' Lansdowne looked straight through the many diamonds of raindrops on the windscreen as she expanded on her observation.

'Perhaps they don't show their emotions in front of strangers.' Trinder fired up the motor and then the wipers, which started with a painful squeal of rubber on glass. 'I can understand that.'

'The English stiff upper lip and all that rot?' Lansdowne folded her gloved hands in her lap, an oddly prim gesture that managed to convey her lack of belief in this quality. 'Not even a balled hankie tucked up a sleeve - and the lovely Rachel's make up was perfect. No tear-smeared mascara on her. Not even a catch in the voice.'

'It has been a few days since they heard the news.'

'Sorry, Sarge, but there was a distinct lack of heartbreak. Something I sensed about Lake when we first me, if you remember.'

Trinder did. 'Corrigan thought her granny was mean.'

'If she had hundreds of pounds secretly tucked away, then it was probably true.'

'She sounded bitter. Do you think relations were strained between Palmer and Corrigan?'

'Or has resentment started to build now she's discovering Palmer was loaded?' Lansdowne was trying to be balanced despite her feelings of antipathy. 'I noticed she called Palmer an 'old coot'.'

'Hardly the worst insult in the book,' Trinder was also trying to maintain balance. 'Palmer comes across as a strong character, but well-liked by everyone who passed her crossing - or so we're led to believe. Being cooped up in that little cottage for many months, a young woman might develop a different viewpoint however.'

'Perhaps.' Lansdowne stared at the wet hedgerows passing the car window for a moment. 'You're right, calling her a mean old coot hardly sounds like motivation for murder.'

Trinder laughed. Lansdowne looked out of the rain-streaked side window at the ragged hawthorn hedge that formed a boundary to the road. 'Corrigan is probably a distraction. However, I noticed her dress was expensive, her cardigan was lamb's wool or even merino and that's got me wondering.'

'Bought by an admirer who enjoyed how they flattered her figure?'

'You noticed?' Lansdowne gave Trinder a sidelong glance. Why was she feeling such resentment towards this young mother? 'One thing I do know, a part-time office junior with a little child couldn't easily afford that dress,' Lansdowne continued. 'Her mum flogs Avon in the afternoons and evenings and I doubt makes much in this area, whilst granny is mean with her cash.'

'An anomaly over her spending power.' Trinder nodded agreement.

'Why do you think she tried to hide the fact she knew Charlton?'

Trinder considered this a moment. 'She knows something about Charlton she wants to hide from us.'

'That he buys her nice dresses?'

'Perhaps...'

'She claimed it was hundreds of pounds stolen. What do you read into that?'

'She tried to cover up the admission instantly. Perhaps it was just a figure of speech, but I'm not convinced. We need to keep an eye on her.'

'And her mother. I don't think either of them are telling us all they know. There are secrets in that household.'

Trinder looked sceptical. 'Many families have secrets, but how does this impact on the case? Are we really thinking Lake and Corrigan are involved in the death of Palmer?'

'Put it like that and I'm not sure. Mother and daughter conspiring to kill an elderly relative?' Lansdowne pulled a painful expression. 'I can't see it.'

'Neither can I. But more digging might be instructive. The brickworks must be close.' They were motoring along Desford Lane towards Glenfield. 'It might be interesting to see what Corrigan's boss thinks about his part-time office assistant.'

After some minutes of frustrating wrong turnings, doubling backs and peering at metal finger posts through the teeming rain, they eventually found a narrow and badly pot-holed road that wended its hedge-rowed way towards a cluster of low buildings whose presence was marked by a clutch of sulkily smoking red brick chimneys. The car suspension creaked and groaned as the tyres sank into deep pools of muddy water. Trinder cursed.

He liked to keep the Rover looking immaculate, and with each sploshy rise and dip, the once gleaming paintwork was being coated in more pinkish mud that lay like a sticky blanket across the unmade track.

'A Devil of a place to get to.'

'Corrigan preferred to hitch a ride on the train. I can see why. It would be easier to hop onto that loading dock than wade or pedal your away through all this.' Lansdowne was unenthusiastically surveying the quagmire surrounding the raggle-taggle collection of buildings and privately admitting that Corrigan was being pragmatic on this point.

The rain was making deep splashes in the pools of water standing amidst the churned surface of the yard. Two men in long sopping-wet brown cotton warehouse coats were wheelbarrowing towering stacks of newly baked roof tiles out of a smoky building with a roof that looked in danger of imminent collapse. Trinder warily stepped out of the car, feeling his polished shoes sink into the mire as hailed them.

'Hullo! We're looking for the manager; Mr Carruthers?'

'Over there, matey. Straight through the main door.' The man barely paused in his barrowing and nodded his head to indicate a small building that stood out as more important than the others due to it having some decorative terracotta tiling on its upper sides and moulded flourishes around the windows and doors. When first built, the intention had no doubt been to make this modest construction an advertisement for their wares. Unfortunately, the exuberant designs entirely out of scale for the scale of the building, were now chipped at the lower edges and stained green due to leaking gutters, whilst browning stems of ragwort and buddleia clung around the base of the walls and poked from gaps in the mortar. The impression was of a company struggling to pay the bills. Corrigan's part time status might be more a reflection on the financial state of the Premier Brick & Terra Cotta Company, than her typing abilities.

A number of rusting and over-grown railway sidings lay hard by. The siding adjacent to a concrete loading dock held three open wooden wagons. All but one of these appeared to be fully laden and sheeted over, and the wheelbarrowing men were busy steering their excessively laden barrows along a succession of duck boards that dipped and waddled in the mire until they reached the door of the partially laden wagon. The freshly baked tiles were then manhandled into neat stacks inside. It was wet and arduous work, but the wagon was at least nearly full. There was an obvious sense of urgency about their work because in the far distance, almost masked by a silvery veil of rain, stood one of the ancient black locomotives so particular to the line, stopped on the long goods loop that served the works. It was smoking quietly from its chimney as it waited with a motley collection of wagons in tow. Loitering and killing time seemed to be a full-time occupation on the 'Swanney'.

Both detectives were eager to get out of the rain, already regretting leaving the cosy warmth of their car. They felt no envy for the bustling workers in their sodden coats nor for the locomotive crew sipping tea hunkered down in their inadequate cab.

The front door opened into an open-plan office that smelt heavily of wood smoke and poorly combusted coal. A desk that had seen better days stood squarely in front of the door. A massive typewriter, telephone, bottle-green Anglepoise lamp and letter trays occupied most of the desktop, the remaining space taken up by untidy piles of receipts, bills and other papery office material awaiting filing or paying, or perhaps ignoring in the vain hope the debtors might quietly fade away.

A tired desk chair had been made to look more comfortable by the addition of a threadbare cushion, but nobody occupied it. The office appeared under-staffed, with just two men visible. A thin man in the right-hand corner was kneeling on the floor and ineffectively fiddling with a pot-bellied stove that was creating the pungent smell and faint haze of smoke that filled the room whilst failing to lift a depressing damp chill from the air.

'Mr Carruthers?' Trinder fired the question towards an older gentleman seated behind another desk covered with yet more untidy piles of paper. The man looked up slowly and without any obvious sign of surprise, nor indeed expectation they might be potential clients about to place a substantial order for complex terracotta tiling.

'How may I help you?' He slowly sat upright and equally slowly placed his fountain pen on the blotter on his desk. He was checking something in an account ledger and this task did not appear to have given him much reason to be cheerful.

Carruthers stood up and shook hands as Trinder made the introductions, revealing his warrant card as he did so.

'Police. Dear me, not more vandalism? Another runaway truck on the track perhaps?' Carruthers looked weary rather than overly concerned by their unannounced arrival. 'The local raggamuffins tend to get bored and have recently taken to letting the brakes off wagons and giving them a push. Luckily, we have few significant inclines along the line to allow these to gather any real momentum and there are trap points guarding the main line. We keep these locked of course -.'

'Actually, we're here about something quite different,' Trinder interrupted. 'Is there somewhere we can talk?'

'Don't mind Simpson. He's my finance manager.' There was a snort of derision from the kneeling man, or perhaps he was just blowing on the unenthusiastic fire. 'Alan and I have no secrets. Although I sometimes wish he'd find a way of hiding the deficit in our accounts a little better!' Carruthers laughed, and it was a warm and generous sound that lacked any malice or bitterness.

'Please, take a seat, take a seat. Tea?' He nodded towards the pale, slight figure of Alan Simpson who was already dutifully sloping away to a partitioned off section at the back of the office that screened a small kitchenette. A water geezer banged and whistled out of sight just as Trinder declined the offer. Tea was evidently on the way irrespective of whether they wanted it or not.

Carruthers sat back down in his chair and idly flipped the ledger closed. He might joke about the accounts but that was no reason to let the police take a surreptitious gander. 'If it's not boys playing pranks, then how might I be of assistance?' He tried to ask the question of Trinder, but his eyes were pulled to Lansdowne in her neatly buttoned police winter coat and trim hat balanced on her fair hair. 'I don't think I've ever had the pleasure of meeting a lady policewoman. I must say, you bring a most welcome ray of light into the office on a gloomy Winter's day!'

Lansdowne could find nothing sensible to say in reply to this patronising comment, especially as she was dressed from head to toe in midnight blue and the wool was damp and in danger of smelling like a wet Labrador dog, so she gave a coolly polite smile, hoping this would not encourage any further comments.

'I expect you have heard about the murder of Mrs Palmer at Black Spinney Crossing in the early hours of Friday morning?' Trinder could see a fresh newspaper folded to one side of the manager's desk.

'Yes. Dreadful business. I read about it on the way in this morning. The Leicester Mercury gave it quite a splash, although there seemed precious little detail. But word spreads quickly up and down our little branch line and we'd actually heard the shocking news before the weekend. Unsettling. Most unsettling.' Although Carruthers did not seem especially perturbed. 'How do you think we can we be of help?'

'Murder investigations demand we look into the lives of all the people involved or affected if only remotely. You should not presume anything from our questions, which are routine, and I ask you don't share this conversation with others.'

Carruthers sat up straight in his chair and intertwined his fingers as he placed his hands on the edge of his desk. There was a spark of curiosity in his eyes. 'You can expect absolute discretion from us both.' He paused a moment as he considered his next words. 'I presume you came here in the hope of speaking with Rachel? Mrs Corrigan, that is, – whom you no doubt know is part of the family of the poor murdered woman.'

'We are aware of that relationship.'

'I'm afraid the poor girl is not expected back until tomorrow. She was away with her family on leave and I have extended this on compassionate grounds. She must be feeling the loss dreadfully.'

'We came directly from the cottage after speaking with her,' Trinder explained.

'Oh? Then I am at a loss how we can be of assistance.'

The sound of serious teaspoon stirring from behind the partition wall stopped as the pale finance officer perhaps strained to listen in.

'How long has Mrs Corrigan worked here?' Trinder asked.

'18 months or thereabouts. She'd found herself in a tight spot due to the loss of her husband and came knocking, so as to speak.' Carruthers was finding it hard to keep his eyes off Lansdowne's legs. She discreetly pulled the hem of her coat a little lower.

'She was looking for work?'

'Indeed. Somewhat fortuitous timing as it transpired. We'd just found ourselves without our previous girl, Miss Mannings. She'd moved away from the area to get married just a week before.'

'What is her work here?'

'Secretary. More glorified office girl, I suppose.' There was curious half-laugh from behind the kitchenette. 'She does a bit of typing, some filing, answering the telephone and general tidying up.' The dismal sound of rain drumming on the roof was loud and they could just hear the distant tuneless whistle of one of the men busy transporting bricks outside, but the phones were silent and the piles of disorderly paperwork clear for all to see. 'And greeting customers...' The list of her duties was running out. 'Rachel usually makes the tea when people call.' Carruthers coughed apologetically. There was a clattering of china from Simpson that suggested he was looking forward to Rachel's return.

'She works part-time?'

'Correct. Mondays to Wednesdays usually. We – that is to say, the company -,' Carruthers hesitated, perhaps prompted by the advance of Simpson carrying a tin tray laden with an ill-assorted selection of steaming mugs of tea.

'We don't need her here more than that,' Simpson interjected. 'There's not enough work.' His comment was blunt but devoid of any emotion or implied criticism.

'Quite so, quite so. Thank you, Alan. Please help yourselves -.' Carruthers indicated the cups and mugs on the tray. He selected a tired looking Queen Victorian Diamond Jubilee commemorative and blew across the top to cool the steaming tea.

'How does Mrs Corrigan get to and from work?' Lansdowne asked, choosing to ignore the chipped mug closest to her. 'It's quite a trek to get here by road, let alone by any other means.'

'I'm not entirely sure...'

'On the engine. Or smuggled inside the guard's van. Out of sight.' Simpson sniggered. 'The engine lads are always more than willing to give her a lift. They go out of their way to help the pretty young widow.' Simpson had already retreated towards the stove with his tea and a biscuit and threw this comment across the room. 'No slacking in that department!' He paused before adding quietly. 'Some of us have to make do with a scooter.' He returned to fiddling with the recalcitrant stove.

'She's popular?' Trinder asked.

'You're not kidding! At lunchtime the men flock around her like flies, all trying to get a smile.' Simpson sounded singularly unimpressed. It would take a lot to bring a smile to this gloomy individual. 'She might remember to do up an extra button on her blouse before coming to work.' He went back to staring at the recalcitrant stove.

Carruthers frowned at his assistant's comment. 'Let's not make too much of this, men will be men. It's just lads working here in the kilns and sheds and so she rather, er, um, stands out in her summery dresses and make up. A solitary rose amongst thorns, ha ha!' He seemed to be having a similar problem with Lansdowne. He was finding it hard to not look at her even though it was Trinder asking the questions.

'Does she ever discuss her home life? As the granddaughter of Mrs Palmer, it would be useful if you can offer any insight.'

'She's never said anything much except about her own little one, and that was mainly in regard to taking her to a doctor if ill or ensuring she got away in time to pick her up from nursery school.'

'Both of which she does often enough. Always an excuse to slip away early.' Simpson shrugged his narrow shoulders and stood up, apparently satisfied that the stove was now burning adequately. 'Not to mention the extended lunch breaks when the weather's warm.'

'We understand you might increase her hours if she improved her office skills. Is that correct?' Lansdowne asked.

'Ye-es. I did hint at something along those lines. But it was some time ago. Not long after she first started, and we've not renewed the discussion since.' Carruthers looked across at Simpson, who rolled his eyes and dipped a Rich Tea biscuit in his mug.

'Is she good at her work?' Lansdowne asked.

'The work is not demanding and does well enough and she will improve.'

'She's lazy.'

'Now, now Alan, that's a trifle unfair. It's not easy to recruit in this area these days. The city pulls people away, you see.'

'Sergeant, if you want to know more about Rachel, I suggest you talk to those eager to take care of her every whim,' Simpson added.

'Anyone in particular?'

'There are a number, but one stands out.' Carruthers coughed, and it sounded almost like a warning, but Simpson ignored it. 'Driver Charlton. Or "Richie", as she always insists on calling him.' His tone was sarcastic.

Chapter Thirty-One

'Have I done something wrong, miss?'

'Not at all. I just need to ask you a few questions about last Friday morning, the 2nd December. Answer as accurately as you can, please.' WPC Benson smiled reassuringly at young Sammy Chambers who looked as nervous as a cornered deer.

'Of course.' Chambers was fiddling with his cap and looked excitable. 'I never tell lies!'

'Glad to hear it. Can you tell me what you did from the moment you woke up on Friday morning?'

'Gosh, that's easy, miss; I stopped the alarm clock and got dressed – I always lay out what I am going to wear to have it ready you see, and then I had a bowl of Corn Flakes and then cleaned my teeth.' He grinned enthusiastically.

'OK, that's good, but I'm more interested in what happened after you left the house, I don't need to know the details about breakfast.'

'I thought you wanted to know everything?'

'You're the knock-up boy?' Benson tried a different approach.

'That's right! I also light the fires on the engines and other duties around the shed. But first I have to cycle all over and make sure as everyone that's on earlies is awake and getting up.'

'Good. So perhaps you could tell me the order in which you knocked and awakened the crew on Friday? I'd like to have an idea of where you cycled, who you called on, and the timings.'

'Righty-o...' Chambers furrowed his brow and made a convincing expression of someone trying to remember details accurately. He then started to give a minutely detailed description of his exact route he'd taken, illustrated with plenty of extraneous detail. Benson felt sure he would make an outstanding witness, but it was also slow going, and so far had offered nothing that sounded remotely useful. She interrupted him mid-flow feeling the need to get onto something useful before she filled all the pages in her notebook.

'Excellent, your memory serves you well Mr Chambers, but I'm particularly interested to hear about anything you saw as you approached Desford, and especially when you knocked up Driver Charlton.'

'Mr Charlton?' His eyes widened. 'Why would you want to know about him, miss? He's a senior driver!' The way he said this, it was evident he held the man in high regard.

'Just answer the question.'

'Right... well... now here's a funny thing. You see Mr Charlton is never late. Not once. I'm quite pleased, as I feel a bit nervous throwing stones up at the windows of the more senior men. They get a bit shirty if the stones are too big and I worry I might break the glass!' He grinned, sheepishly. 'Can you imagine if I did?'

Benson encouraged him to continue.

'Mr Charlton told me on my first day on the job, that if I saw the bedroom light on and especially if I saw the hall light on, I was not to throw stones or even loudly knock on the door. The light meant he was up and dressing and soon on his way.'

'I see.' Benson was not feeling any more enthusiastic.

'I ride past and seeing the lights are on every time, I just give the knocker a very light tap, because you see Miss, I'm paid to knock the men up and it doesn't feel right to do nothing so I just give it a little gentle tap to prove I was there and whizz off on me bike.'

Benson took a deep breath, she needed patience. 'And is that what you did on Friday morning?'

'Yes. I saw the hall light. That meant Mr Charlton was up and so I freewheeled up to the door and lifted the knocker - and then the door opened! It nearly frightened the life out of me!'

'Who opened the door?'

'Mr Charlton, of course, who else at that time of day?' Chambers looked puzzled. 'He looked surprised.'

'What do you mean?'

'He looked startled to see me. He was a bit gruff – almost as if he was annoyed I was there, but I was supposed to be, and at that time.'

'Was he fully dressed?'

'All ready for work and with his jacket on and cap. I think he was just about to open the door and go and maybe my knock startled him.'

'What time was this?'

'About quarter past three.'

'Was this normal?'

'He's always up when I pass, but to be leaving so soon was a bit eager I suppose.'

'Did you speak to Mr Charlton?'

'I just said good morning. He growled something in reply and that's about it and I cycled away towards Ratby where I needed to -.'

Benson felt deflated. This was not proving to be a revelation. The man was an early riser and left the house promptly? Hardly evidence he was a murderer. 'Was there anything else you can tell me about Mr Charlton?'

'But this is not the interesting bit, it's just that I thought you wanted me to tell you everything about when I was in Desford and knocked him up.'

'There's more?'

'It was about ten to four or something like that and I was whizzing along on my way back to the shed from Glenfield when I saw Mr Charlton again.'

'Where was this?'

'Near Black Spinney.'

'You are sure it was him?'

'It looked like him. Ok, most drivers wear much the same clothes and caps, but I'm dead sure.'

'What was he doing?'

'I was pedalling along pretty fast so I didn't get the best view, but with all the wind in the trees I suppose he didn't hear me and although it was really dark my eyes are used to it so I was sure I saw someone close to the hedge at the side of the lane. He was staring back towards the railway.'

'Then what did he do?'

'He'd stepped onto the road as if through the hedge, but at that moment as I was about to cross the line between the gates, I freewheeled, but the bike makes a ticking noise and my mudguard rattles and he must have heard and darted back into the hedge.'

'As if he didn't want to be seen?'

'Or I made him jump.'

'What did you do then?'

'I slowed so I could get a better look and approached the spot about ten or twenty yards past the crossing, but I couldn't see anyone, so I stopped, hopped off my bike and peered through the hedge and there was Mr Charlton hurrying along the track towards Desford Junction.'

'How can you be sure it was him?'

'You get to know how people look and walk. It was his back view and he was in a hurry and had his cap on and a scarf around his face, but I'm sure of it. I mean, he had to hurry as he should have been on shed. It was odd, because he'd been up and ready to leave early and I couldn't work out what he was doing all the way down there.'

'Did you call him?'

'No. I got straight back on my bike as I had to be on shed as I had an engine to light up. I couldn't waste a minute.'

'Did you see anyone else – Mrs Palmer for instance?'

'There was light in a window, but to be honest I never looked. Not properly. I was more interested in Mr Charlton hurrying along the track.'

'When you got on shed did you see Mr Charlton?'

'I was straight on the footplate of the engine and getting kindling and oily rags into the firebox, but I seem to remember hearing him call out to his fireman and their engine was soon off shed.'

'You are certain it was Mr Charlton you saw? You could be mistaken.'

Chambers looked thoughtful. 'I do think it was him, miss. Honest.'

'Did you mention this to anyone on shed?'

'I was on my own and things to do and then when I finally got a chance to go for a cuppa in the bothy, that's when we heard there was something wrong down the line, although we didn't know what, and it went out of my head because I was that upset and confused about what we'd just heard.'

'Did not strike you odd that Mr Charlton was there when he should have been on his engine?'

Chambers chewed his lower lip. 'I don't know why, but he must have had a good reason. I mean he's one of the senior men, so he's not a trouble-maker or anything.' There was an innocence about Chambers in his unshakable belief in the innate goodness of a senior driver and Benson suspected he was telling the truth.

'Have you told anyone else about this?'

'No. I was taught that you don't go around telling tales. Especially about the senior men.' He paused. 'Is Mr Charlton in trouble?'

'That's for us to decide.' Benson stood up, the interview was over.

Chamber's eyes widened as realisation dawned on him. 'Do you think he might have something to do with the old lady who...?'

'I cannot say.' Benson closed her notebook and was about to leave the Shed master's office which he'd allowed her to use for the interview as one of the few private places in the open and draughty engine shed, when she stopped. 'I know you were taught not to tell tales, but have you ever seen Mr Charlton with Mrs Corrigan who lives at Black Spinney Crossing? It could be really important and really helpful if you told me.'

Chambers stared at her in silence, as the sounds of the shed intruded into the office; the clang of a hammer, the rattle of fire irons, some tuneless whistling. He looked as though he was trying to decide whether to speak or remain silent. 'Miss Rachel?'

'Rachel Corrigan.'

'She's awfully pretty.'

'I believe so.'

Chambers looked as though he regretted mentioning her looks.

'Have you ever seen Rachel on the footplate of Mr Charlton's engine?'

'That would be against the rules.' He shook his head solemnly.

'It would, but I'm not interested in that and have no intention of telling anybody. What I want to know is if you have seen the two of them together on the engine or - off.'

'Maybe. Once or twice.' Chambers went red. 'On the engine one time. Together. She was giggling and trying hard not to get her dress mucky.'

'And the other time?'

A long silence. 'Near the brick works. A few months back. A hot sunny evening and I was walking my dog in the fields at the back.'

'And?'

'It might not have been Mr Charlton or Miss Rachel...'

'You were sure it was him in the dark, so I am sure you could tell in sunshine.' Benson urged him on. 'Tell me what you saw. It could be very helpful to us.'

'They were kissing. Really kissing. You know...Right up close and...' He looked embarrassed. 'I tried not to look, but she...'

Benson waited patiently.

'She had her dress undone.' A pause. He looked at the floor. 'I could see - *everything*.' His eyes were like saucers, two red blotches appearing on each cheek. 'Not that I was trying to look!'

'And the man?'

Chambers stared at the dusty floorboards and his ears glowed. 'He was kissing her. And lifting her dress. And, you know...'

'They were having sexual relations?'

He nodded. 'I had to hurry along really quietly and not let them see me.'

'And did they see you?'

'No. Leastways, if they did, it didn't stop them.' His voice went quiet and Benson wondered if she detected a note of bitterness.

'You are sure this couple was driver Richard Charlton and Rachel Corrigan?'

Chambers nodded.

Chapter Thirty-Two

Anna Vignoles answered the telephone in the hall of their house in Birstall, a leafy suburb on the northern edge of Leicester.

'It's Gwen!'

Vignoles appeared at the door.

'She sounds upset.' Anna covered the mouthpiece and mimed the words almost silently, then handed the instrument across to her husband with a sympathetic look. He'd only just returned home after a long day at work and had hardly time to put his slippers on. Vignoles felt weary and cold and been looking forward to sitting beside the fire in their living room for a few minutes with a pipe. But this sounded urgent and he immediately pushed aside any personal considerations, long used to telephone calls at any time of day or night.

Anna went into the kitchen intending to finish preparing supper, but hearing her husband's guarded responses down the line, decided it was best to delay food and take a couple of bottles of beer into the lounge. He might need some alcoholic fortification after facing whatever new trauma had erupted.

'I see...'

Gwen was rattling off her complaints down the line like staccato machine gun fire.

'Slow down.' His head was starting to ache. 'Take a deep breath and let's take this one stage at time and do try not to fly off the handle -.' He instantly regretted the phrase.

'I am *not* flying off the handle, Charles. I don't think you appreciate how serious this is.' She sounded cross. The line crackled with static but could just as easily be her anger. 'You must see them for yourself and then you will appreciate why I am furious. And shocked. They're disgusting. The most terrible magazines I have ever clapped eyes on. I'm appalled that a son of mine would even glance at such things.' Vignoles thought she was starting to sound like a politician. He seemed to remember there had been some rambling parliamentary debate about these particular horror comics imported from the USA that were allegedly corrupting the nation's youth.

'They are just teenage comics -.'

'They are *not*! They are packed full of awful drawings of evil creatures killing and torturing young girls, and blood and – Oh, I don't know what. Ugly things! I could hardly bare to look.'

'It is possible you may have over-reacted if you took just a cursory glance?'

'Don't try to be clever, Charles. One short look at a few pages and my stomach was turned. I did not need to study them in detail. I want to know where Maurice got them from!'

'From his school chums, I suspect. That's what they do, share things around the dorm. I hardly see that takes much working out.' Vignoles was trying to be sympathetic but this hardly sounded a matter to prevent him from eating his dinner.

'Not with my son, they won't!'

'Boys will be boys and they're all the rage, at least if one believes what the more populist newspapers say. Not that I read them as a rule. The red top that is, not horror comics.' Vignoles laughed in the vain hope it might lighten the mood.

'Then you'd better see for yourself. That's why you are taking this far too flippantly. You will be outraged.' Gwen's voice was clipped and curt.

'I know very little about them, I admit. But let's try and put some perspective on it. I'm sure they're just foolish nonsense. I can't believe they are quite as disturbing as you believe.'

'Humph! Well, I was disgusted. Hellish creatures everywhere, limbs being dismembered, blood dripping from gaping mouths, things coming out of open graves carrying knives and...'

'Sounds like a typical Hieronymus Bosch. And they're considered high art.'

'Really, Charles, you're not taking this at all seriously. I do not want my son corrupted by these abominations.'

'I'm sure you don't. But I would not dissuade him from going to an art gallery to see Bosch, nor indeed going to the cinema to see a Boris Karloff film, no matter how foolish the plot. I'm not trying to be flippant, but I can't help thinking all the images of the Nazi death camps and these horrid nuclear tests and the Korean War are far more disturbing that fantasy horror stuff.'

'That's real life, not something packaged as entertainment. There is a proper place to learn about the less pleasant aspects of real life but reading blood-thirsty comics in bed is not one of them.'

Vignoles took a deep breath. 'What would you like me to do?'

'Talk to Maurice. You need to explain to him why I've confiscated these things and will be burning them as soon as you have had a chance to confirm for yourself how corrupting they are.'

'Is that not a little extreme?'

'The content is extreme.'

'A matter of opinion, perhaps.' He heard a sharp intake of breath down the line as his sister prepared to launch another ear-bashing. 'I'm not sure Maurice is especially receptive to my views about anything at the moment.' Vignoles ran a hand over his forehead. He was finding extended contact with the lad an increasingly trying experience if he was brutally honest. It was not that he didn't like the lad, but all this teenage gloom and silence was hard to cut through. Maurice was not sharing his enthusiasm for railways and their respective tastes in music and books was not easy to bridge. He shuddered at the very thought of suggesting they look over some of John Clare's nature poetry.

'He's interested in your police work and respects what you do.'

Vignoles felt now was not the time to mention that this work could also involve ugly scenes of mutilation and gore and plenty of blood. The photographs from the police labs of poor Jane Palmer were a case in point. He doubted if any cheap American shock comic would come close. 'I shall try, but I'm not sure it will count for much - and do please keep father out this.' That was the last thing they needed. 'Send Maurice down to Leicester. It might be easier to have a quite talk away from the vicarage.'

Gwen wanted Anna and him to rush over that evening, but much as he loved his sister, this he steadfastly refused to do. The fog was thickening, and it was no night to be out unless absolutely urgent and, quite frankly, this hardly qualified as an emergency. And besides, he'd heard the welcoming tink of bottle against a glass. He needed a beer (or two) with his wife in the comfort of their own fireside.

He calmed his sister down with a vague promise to meet Maurice at Central Station tomorrow, work permitting. As he walked back into their cosy lounge, his ears long since tuned into the sounds of the railway, caught the distant crack of a fog signal set off by a passing train.

Chapter Thirty-Three

Robbie Trinder was helping his mother stick coloured paper chains together. He was diligently licking the shiny end of the paper with the funny-tasting glue on it and managing to get so much spittle over the paper in so doing that not all were bonding together. Those that did hold were a bit wonky and misshapen. Despite these setbacks, the chains were steadily growing in length and snaking across the wooden kitchen table and down onto the quarry tiled floor. The paper was making a gentle rustling sound and Violet's voice was tender as she coaxed Robbie into making links that were actually usable or laughing when they had to be discarded as useless soggy strips of paper. The radiogramme was playing carols from Norwich Cathedral and the room was warm and felt cosy, a sensation increased by the thin layer of snow gathered on the frame of the kitchen window.

It was a perfect picture of those anticipatory days before Christmas and John Trinder was struck by the potency of the image as he opened the door and stepped in, bringing some of the cold air and the smell of the railway carriage with him. He removed his hat and ran a hand over his neatly slicked hair, then started to unbutton his heavy winter coat. All actions that were perfectly normal and accompanied by a smile for his beautiful wife and little boy. As he gave Violet a kiss on the cheek and patted Robbie on the head, an action that caused the boy to burst into a giggle, he was doing what he usually did, but this evening he was using these familiar actions to disguise a feeling of anxiety welling up inside.

Trinder had steeled himself on the train journey home to finally confront the situation and take out that fateful letter and pass it across to Violet. She had to know what was inside and they would face it together, for better or worse. He was a seasoned copper able to deal with almost anything that life, or death, could throw his way, and yet here he was almost quaking in his shoes. But there again, what was about to happen was going to affect this beautiful domestic scene. Nothing would be quite the same again.

'What a lovely set of paper chains you've made! Shall we put them up?' Trinder had hung his coat up and now took a seat and started to loosen his tie.

'We were waiting for you to come home to do just that. Daddy can reach the ceiling easier, can't he Robbie?'

'Righty-o. I was thinking we could get a Christmas tree on Saturday - what do you say to that Robbie?' Trinder could not help hearing Mrs Charlton saying the same. It was a faintly unsettling memory.

'Ooh yes!'

'Good. Then I'll go into the loft and fetch down the lights and the decorations. I can start checking over the lights after dinner as they always seem to go on the blink between putting them away and when we next need them, no matter how careful I am.' He was stalling for time.

'A year of sitting in the cold up in the loft wouldn't do you much good,' Violet replied with a smile as she licked another paper link. 'How about we have a glass of beer each and then we hang these up? I can quickly get the food hotted up after.'

'Good idea!' Trinder needed a drink.

'Beer!' Robbie gave a thumbs-up sign. 'Daddy loves beer!'

'I do, but not for you, young man. Stick to your milk for now. Beer is for when you're older.'

'How soon is older?' Robbie seemed to find his question amusing as he reached for the glass of milk on the table.

Trinder sat back in his chair and watched Violet standing beside the kitchen sink skilfully pouring the beer into a glass. His eyes wandering up the curve of her back and the roundness of her shoulder clearly delineated by the fashionable roll-neck sweater she was wearing. The fullness of her breast made his heart beat faster. He liked her long fingers with the gold wedding band glinting in the warm kitchen light. She sensed he was looking at her and turned her face and gave him a questioning smile, her eyes playful. 'What?'

'Nothing. No, that's not correct. Far from nothing. I was just thinking how lovely you look.' He chose flattery rather than say what urgently needed saying.

'John! You've not even had a beer yet,' but Violet looked pleased, despite trying to brush aside the compliment.

'I'm a lucky fellow. I have a beautiful wife and a lovely son and a decent house – even if it is rented. I'd say I've done ok.'

Violet walked over and handed him the pint glass and laid a hand on his shoulder. He caught a slight hint of the perfume she was wearing. 'I'll drink to that. What's brought this on?'

'Probably the carols on the radio. They have a way of making one feel content.'

'And sentimental!' She laughed. 'I do love it when they start playing carols.' Violet went over to Robbie and suggested that he made a few more links in the chain rather than stick them along the table edge where they would only fall onto the floor. 'I've grown quite fond of Woodford. It's a lovely community. It'll be strange to leave.'

Trinder looked startled. 'Were you thinking of leaving?'

'Of course not. But saying that, it's not my work that's likely to drag us away.'

'But mine is -.'

'We know that.' With Robbie back on the chain gang and making good progress, Violet poured her own beer. Robbie was humming along tunelessly to the radio.

'John –.'

'Violet –.'

They both spoke at the same time, stopped and laughed, but for all that something had crept into the room. Silently, stealthily, like a black cat on the prowl. Perhaps this unseen, invisible presence was a witches' familiar, for it was perceptibly altering the mood, not helped by the aching dissonance and heart-rending sadness of 'The Coventy Carol' being broadcast.

'I'm not sure if now is quite the time -.'

'For what?' Violet looked at her husband across her glass of beer.

Robbie sensed something was in the air and had stopped humming.

Trinder put down his glass in a movement that suddenly felt more significant than he'd intended and reached into his jacket for the envelope. 'I received this.' He handed it across the table to Violet. 'It came a few days ago.'

'Christmas card!'

'Not this time, Robbie.' Trinder gave his son a wink, but he was actually watching as Violet started reading. It was short and took her little time.

'Oh!' She clapped a hand over her mouth and stood up as if stung. Her eyes were wide with surprise. 'What news.'

There was a moment of silence as the carol on the radio ended.

'It is rather - surprising.' Trinder sounded apologetic.

Violet glanced at the letter one more time as if to confirm what she'd just read. 'No, it's marvellous! Really, it is.'

'You're pleased?' This was going better than he'd hoped.

'Pleased? I'm delighted. And so proud!' She clapped her hands joyfully and Robbie joined in, gleefully clapping his sticky hands despite having no idea what about.

'It will mean big changes. And soon.'

'Of course. I realise that. Oh but, John...' Violet ran around the table and kissed her husband. 'I need to read this line again and savour it.' She smiled. '*Detective Inspector John Trinder*. You're going to be a D I!'

Trinder felt a flood of relief course through his body and gave Violet a grateful smile.

'Daddy is going to be a really important detective, Robbie! He's passed all the exams and tests and interviews and has been given promotion, what do you think of that?'

Robbie waved his arms above his head and cheered as he did when listening to the football on the radiogramme, but then decided this event needed something more significant to mark the occasion and dropped down off the chair and ran into the other room, hurtling back moments later brandishing his favourite red Dinky Toy tractor. This was placed reverentially on the table in front of Trinder as if it's presence somehow confirmed his promotion.

'Thank you, little man. I will be the only Detective Inspector on British Railways with a red tractor.'

Robbie thought this extremely funny.

'You realise we must move away.' Trinder grimaced.

'There is that.' Violet took a breath and considered her response. 'We always knew one day we would have to. It comes with the job. And you deserve the promotion and we've both hoped and longed for this day, so we can't complain now it's happened.'

'I get posted to wherever they decide.' He gave his wife a guilty look. 'And in our case, it's Wales. Real Welsh-sounding Wales.'

Violet was re-reading the letter 'What other sort is there? How do you say the name of the place?'

'Beats me! Landydiddlydo Junction or something like that.'

'Land-Did-No? Why do you think they have two LL's at the start of the word?'

'We'll soon find out. We'll be living there by February, although I need to find us a place to live before then and I've already been told to go over straight after New Year to make preparations in advance of the move.'

'That soon?'

'I'm afraid so. I had better write and accept the position and hand my notice in sharpish.'

'You've not done so?'

'No...'

'Why on earth not?'

'As you can see from the date I've been carrying the darned letter around and not had the nerve to tell you. You had to know first, of course. Then this serious case came up and has kept us all busy and somehow the time never felt quite right.'

'All this time and you didn't say?'

'I had to summon up the nerve -.' He looked around the kitchen. '- to take all this apart. It means wrenching us away from everything we've made together. From Jenny and Tom and from your old mum in Leicester.'

Violet was silent for a moment as she took in the significance of what the letter implied. A few lines of formal type, but with such a profound effect. 'Putting it like that I cannot pretend that side of things will be so easy. It will take some adjusting to. But as you said, you have no influence over where you went.'

'None.'

'Then we shall take what we are given and be thankful. Good policemen work up the ranks and if they want promotion they take whatever posting is offered and give their best to whatever is thrown their way. I've seen you study in the evenings and packed you off to goodness knows how many training courses and to go and sit exams in London. It's hardly such a shock.'

'I appreciate that. But Wales? In an unpronounceable place in the back of beyond.' Trinder winced.

'Wales is very beautiful, so I've heard and from the pictures I've seen.' Violet frowned. 'Is it north or south?'

'North. I looked it up. Close to the sea. On an estuary filled with boats.'

'Robbie, did you hear that? We're moving to the sea!'

'I want a boat!'

'Yes, why not have a boat? We could learn to sail. That's the spirit.' Trinder needed to be encouraging, as much for himself as his family.

'Our last Christmas in Woodford.' Violet lifted her glass of beer. 'Then we'd better make it a good one!'

'Cheers!'

'Cheese!' Robbie lifted his glass of milk from the table and joined in the toast, unsure as to why the sudden mention of cheese.

Trinder drank a long draught of beer and this had a calming effect. One major hurdle safely jumped. He just had to tell the guvnor now. What was Vignoles going to think? He felt as though he was letting Vignoles down by leaving. He just hoped he could at least help close the Palmer case before he had to leave.

He was excited about the promotion. It was a massive feather in his cap and a decent wedge of salary going into his bank account on top, but it brought tremendous responsibilities both in the new office and at home. He was going to need to be strong and decisive. Everything he'd failed to be this last week. He'd waited a week to tell his loving wife he'd got a new job. Well, let that be a lesson learned. He couldn't afford to be so wet once he moved to Landydiddiyno or whatever it was called. He was being sent into a strange town in what might as well be a foreign land where he would be on his own with men he didn't know, all expecting him to know what he was doing whilst ready to snigger and complain behind his back if he messed up.

He'd better tell the boss in the morning. The most intelligent thing he could do right now was get as much advice and guidance as he could from the man who had taught him all he knew about the detecting business.

Chapter Thirty-Four

The dense fog muffled sound like a heavy woollen blanket, but instead of bringing warmth and comfort, the dank soupy atmosphere made muscles ache and arthritic joins complain. The poor visibility was made worse by the mercury dropping by the hour. Frost was already starting to rime the steel of the many metal-bodied coal wagons and pick out the point rodding and linkages that snaked beside the rails as if waiting to catch the unwary and twist an ankle. The sleepers and the creeping weeds crouched between amongst the cinders and stones of the ballast looked as if an artist had dry-brushed them with pale grey to accentuate their edges.

The fog men were out. Every so often a passing train triggered detonations under their wheels, whilst their hand lamps flashed signals. Some carried burning flares that stank of Paraffin oil in their hands in an attempt to help the fog-blinded crews see their way around the shunting yard with their engines. Lights and whistles, shouts, calls and great rippling sequences of clanks and percussive strikes crossed the yard as the wagons were bullied into order. Goods need delivering, trains needed making up and fog or no fog, the men had to work

Danger lurked on every track. Free-rolling wagons were rendered almost invisible and deadly quiet until too late, their wheels scything along the tops of icy rails in an unstoppable moving force. Long snakes of vans and coal trucks were propelled along sidings, their buffers closing like immense vices on those of the waiting wagons, whilst shunting engines angrily snorted and yanked at their coupling chains as they urged the heavily-laden trains into movement. This was no place for the fainthearted or the inexperienced.

Neither Louis Kane or Jesse Abel were the least bit faint-hearted. Despite their deceptively dapper appearance, both preferred to undertake their lethal work near railways, operating with a confidence and callous precision that was chilling. They were men who had spent their lives watching their backs and staying one step ahead of the pack. They knew how to avoid a knife in the back or a blackjack to the jaw - or dodge a line of rolling wagons in the fog.

George Baylock was a seasoned railwayman, brought up since he was barely 13-years-old in the ways of the railway. He'd spent his working life tramping the edges of running lines, oiling fishplates and signal cranks or packing dipping rails and fixing broken signal wires between trains. He knew when to step aside and raise a hand or flashlight to an approaching engine to show he was aware of their presence. He knew when to seek refuge in the special hollowed out recesses in tunnels to let trains pass barely a hand width away. He knew not to dice with death yet could walk confidently beside even the busiest lines in the foulest of weather. He had no specific fear of the railway, aside from that constant respect such a dangerous environment demanded. And so, he trudged with little concern between two of the fog-bound sidings on his way back to the Permanent Way Gang bothy where he could finally put down his tools and clock off.

Unfortunately, Baylock had no experience of how to anticipate and avoid sudden ambush by a pair of professional killers.

He was walking slowly, one weary leg followed by the other, his mind focussed on a warm mug of tea and a biscuit to dunk. There was nothing much to see except the almost impenetrable wall of pale vapour and strange looming shapes of wagons and the faint glow of a solitary signal lamp like an unblinking eye of a mythical beast. He was feeling his way forward as much as using his eyes, but his senses were dulled by weariness whilst a complacent feeling of being on familiar territory allowed his mind to drift away to thoughts about the weekend's football fixtures.

The gloved hands and face masked by a scarf gave him no warning. Leather-clad fingers clutched at his throat like a vice, the other hand clamping his mouth shut and forcing his chin upwards as he was propelled between two uncoupled box vans standing a few feet apart. His bag of tools thumped onto the ground with a clatter that sounded like coupling chains unloosed.

'Make a sound and the knife goes in your heart!' The voice hissed close to his ear. 'One second - and you're dead.'

Baylock made a mangled noise in his throat and started to struggle despite the warning, then saw a second figure draw close and realised it would be wiser not to resist. Even if he could somehow evade the threatened blade and escape the hand severely constricting his breathing, he could never hope to beat off a second man. That stunt only happened in cowboy films and despite his own strength born from years of hard labour, he'd been caught unawares and was now trapped like a fly in a spider's web.

'Good lad. Now we're going to have ourselves a little chin-wag.' Kane pushed his face up close, eyes cold and unblinking, breath clouding through the thin cloth over his mouth. 'We'll ask, nice and polite like, and you're gonna give us a straight answer. No funny business or the blade goes between the ribs. Got it?'

Baylock nodded his head as best he could.

'I'm going to ease off so you can speak. Shout out, and you die.' Kane held up the knife so Baylock could see what he was up against. Even in the poor light the slivery-blue blade looked cruel. Baylock's eyes widened. He nodded acceptance.

The other man, who reeked of flowers and hair oil took one of Baylock's arms and with an expert move wrenched it behind his back and upwards, making him wince with pain. 'Aaah! What d'you want?' He was gasping for breath as the pain bit hard.

'Steady, Abe, I think he's got the message.' Kane and Abel lowered the scarves so they could speak more easily, but this did nothing to lessen their menacing appearance. A shunting engine tooted somewhere distant and there was another cascade of buffers clashing down a line of wagons. Normal life was continuing. His work colleagues were close by, but they were smothered in a cocoon of night and freezing fog and Baylock realised he was as far from help as if on a lonely moor.

'Tell us about Palmer.'

'Eh?'

'The dear old lady. The one you nobbled.' Abel gave the arm another tug. 'Don't pretend or this will just get worse.'

Baylock winced. 'W-what about her?'

'Why d'you kill her?' Kane sneered.

'I never! I tried to save her. I swear!' Another wrench on the arm and his face crumpled in pain. Despite the bitter cold, a drop of perspiration formed on his brow. 'We found her like that and got her warm and -.'

'Liar!' Kane slapped him hard across the cheek. 'Ain't you the kind one? Moving her inside and calling for help?' He spat on Baylock's boots. 'I don't believe a word. Tortured her, got her to squeal, then finished her off. That sound familiar?'

'A rather messy job you made of it. Tut tut.' Abel sounded like he was admonishing a school boy for poor homework. His lavender scent mingling oddly with the smells of the railway yard.

'Clever though. I'll give you that. You and the other geezer had the perfect excuse to go inside, collect what you wanted, then sit tight in the warm and wait for the pigs to show up. Nice.' Kane's face formed a sneering smile as he leaned in closer, his breath hot on Baylock's face.

'No, that's wrong!'

'So how was it?' Kane pressed the blade against Baylock's donkey jacket, the cloth starting to part as the point eased closer to his skin.

'We found her. Outside. Honest!' The whites of his eyes were showing as he flicked from one face to other, then strained to look down in horror at the knife as if staring might halt its progress.

Abel looked at Kane with an expression of gentle surprise. 'He's very persuasive. Do we believe him?'

'No. He's a bloody liar.'

There was a blast on a little whistle of an engine and a muffled shout in response followed by a series of exhaust beats. A line of indistinct shapes started to move in the adjacent siding. There was the sense of activity all about and yet it blanketed by the pea-souper. Wheels sang on rails and an improperly loosened brake block screeched unpleasantly.

'I swear I'm not lying!'

'Cut it out.' Kane had lost patience. 'We know about you and Hind. You're runners for Palmer. Mules. Fetchin' and carryin' for her, so don't try to pull the wool over our eyes.'

Baylock tried to swallow but his throat was too constricted by Kane's hand.

'You fancied something richer? I get that. We both do. We know 'ow it goes. You're making a bit on the side, but then you get to thinkin' as how you're taking risks, day in, day out and its others making loads of dosh. It's just not fair!'

'You fancied a better return for your troubles. You can tell us...' Abel was sounding like a sympathetic friend. Except they were in a fog-bound yard, with a naked blade closing in on Baylock's' heart.

'How d'you know this?' The resignation was audible and Baylock slumped. He'd lost the will to resist.

''cos it's our business to know,' Kane gave a throaty chortle. 'You did the old bird over and took something rather tasty. Trouble is, it weren't yours to take and we need it back. Small, sparkly and valuable. You know what I'm talking about.'

'There was nothing there!'

Abel smiled his sickliest smile. 'I'd probably do the same, old bean. A little bag of sparkly, pretty things. So-o tempting.' He rolled his eyes theatrically.

'So just tell us where we can we can collect what you thieved, and we'll be off. Debt settled.'

There was another metallic cascade of sound rippling towards them until suddenly the van they were pressed against jolted sharply and they were rudely shaken by the movement. As the shock wave reached the end of the line the less powerful counter-movement went back along the line and then all was still.

'Ooh, that was close! One's got to be awfully careful around here.' Abel readjusted his hold on Baylock.

'So me and Hind did a bit of this fetching and carrying as you call it. Ok? Just fags and I dunno know what in packets wrapped up. Sealed. I never asked, I never looked. I didn't want to know. We just delivered and took our money. We never killed her. She was lying there when we arrived.'

'How does Leach fit in?' Abel asked.

'Who's he?'.

'Maybe he never introduced himself, but he was there. Surely you remember the gent?' Abel twisted the arm higher.

'Did he kill her?' Kane pressed the blade in harder and could feel some resistance, but not much. It would cut into the skin with just the slightest pressure.

'There was someone. You don't need the knife! Stop. He was there. We saw him over the body but he ran off. He must have done it!'

Kane shook his head. 'Not good enough. He never took the stuff. So why kill her then hoof it if he was empty handed?'

'Makes no sense.' Abel agreed, a gleeful glint in his eyes.

'He knew we'd be onto him. We'd tell the cops.'

Kane looked as though he were weighing up the odds. 'Still not making sense. What convinced you to keep quiet? How much did he pay you to keep yer traps shut?' Silence. 'No matter, Leach's goose is cooked anyway. Come on, where've you and Hind got the bag of stones? Tell us, and we're gone.'

'I keep telling you the place was cleaned out.'

'Oh, so you *did* have a look? Lyin' toe-rag!' Kane and Abel exchanged glances and with that almost telepathic understanding that existed between them, Kane pulled the knife away, allowing Abel to manhandle Baylock from between the vans.

'You robbed her and even got paid off by Leach. Trouble is, you never factored us in old boy. So close and yet snatched away at the last moment! Life's hard like that sometimes,' Abel almost breathed the words in Baylock's' ear.

'Meet The Debt Collectors.' The blade was ready to flash forward at any moment. 'And we can't let this debt go unpaid. There's a big fat geezer in the Scrubs getting agitated and he wants to know his investment is safe. Understand?'

'I don't know what you're talking about!'

'You don't get it, do yer?' Kane looked almost sad. There was another series of distant calls and shouts and an engine whistle. 'There's no place you and Hind can cash that stuff in. What were you thinking? Flying down to Rio? A ship to Barbados? Or gambling and drinking yourself to an early grave?' Kane looked at Abel whilst Baylock remained silent, his breath coming in anxious gasps. 'He's not playing ball.' The blade was put swiftly away in a pocket. Baylock wondered if the sting had somehow been drawn.

Perhaps they believed him, and it was over. He felt his breathing start to slow.

'Unfortunate,' Abel shook his head sadly. The line of wagons started to move, the wheels grinding unpleasantly on the rail heads, the rotten sleepers dipping and rising in the clinker and ash ballast. 'Best step clear,' Abel's mellifluous voice made it sound as though he was concerned for their safety as he directed Baylock into the space between the sidings, but the upward pressure on his twisted arm increased and the platelayer stumbled forwards, his back painfully arched in an attempt to relieve the excruciating pain.

'*C'est la vie*, old boy!' Abel, deftly aided by Kane on the other side, lifted Baylock off his feet then swung him through the air as though he was as light as a few bags of flour. This slick move was made just as another line of wagons rolled at some speed towards them on the opposite track. They were about to collide with a row of massive hopper wagons that lay in waiting, the hand brakes in place to offer resistance. Baylock was taken completely unawares and was helpless to resist, his legs for a brief moment kicking in the air as he stared in horror as his head was dangled in front of a buffer head all sticky with grease, now advancing mercilessly towards him. Baylock started to make a noise like a yowling fox but was cut off in a flash. Kane and Abel let him go and the immense force of the moving train took over. They quickly stepped out of range.

The sound was sickening, but apart from fractionally softening the soud of the metal buffers clashing, it was inaudible to those working the yard. The wagons chattered without hindrance and the now lifeless and almost headless body of Baylock was dragged under the wheels like a rag doll, then sliced apart as the heavy train – shunted a little too hard - slammed into the waiting wagons with a rippling clash that pushed them a foot or two backwards. His mortal remains lay hidden in the impenetrable gloom underneath.

The two assassins slipped away, unobserved, unflustered and unmoved, but not before Abel had picked up a shunter's wooden pole used for uncoupling wagons that he'd previously noticed lying beside the tracks. It had been forgotten by a careless worker, and he now tossed this artfully on the ground close to where they had interrogated Baylock.

'Tut tut. You could trip over that. Someone could get hurt!' They both chortled into the scarves back across their mouths.

The lines of wagons continued to be broken up and re-marshalled. The shunting engines continued to potter about whilst the crews stayed warm in their cabs drinking tea from their billy cans and dreaming of ending their shift and getting home to a warm bed and their warmer wives. The men on the ground pinned down brakes, unpinned brakes, flashed their signal lamps and called to each other. The fog detonators sounded like gun shots as they exploded their warnings below the wheels of freight trains passing on the Coalville line. It was many hours later before the mangled bloody mess was discovered.

Chapter Thirty-Five

'Now here's something special,' Vignoles had just finished wiping specks of snow from his glasses. The early morning fog enveloping Leicester had lifted to reveal a city white with iron-hard frost and now a few exploratory flakes of snow silently tumbling from the sky. 'What class of engine is that?'

Maurice stared with a blank face at the highly polished green locomotive gently easing its long train of blood and custard coloured coaches along one side of the island platform at Leicester Central. 'It's more interesting than the last few we've seen. They were just black and looked the same.'

'A trifle harsh,' Vignoles gave the lad a quizzical look. 'There are many detail differences between the classes of six-coupled goods locomotives on this line if you take time to observe carefully.'

'If you say so, uncle.' Maurice was trying to be generous. 'Oh, this one's got a name!'

'Excellent.'

A squeal of excitement erupted from a small group of young trainspotters close by. They were seated on a trolley used for carting parcels around the station and apparently oblivious to the wintry conditions despite their short grey school trousers revealing legs mottled like Corned Beef. Vignoles doubted they had permission to leave school over their lunch break to watch trains, but he had more important things to worry about than naughty schoolboys. 'We all love a namer - as you can judge from their reaction.'

Maurice read the nameplate. 'Royal Lancer'. Is that mounted cavalry?'

'What about the locomotive?'

'Well, it's a *pacific* type. An A1 or perhaps an A3 class.'

'Bravo!' Vignoles gave his nephew an approving look as the gaggle of spotters ran cheering towards the engine that had now stopped a few yards away. Vignoles judged it was time to offer Maurice a reward, he dared not push his luck too far. 'I think the arrival of this fine engine deserves celebrating with a cup of coffee, what d'you say?'

'And cake?'

'I'm sure we manage that. It's nearly Christmas after all.'

Vignoles was trying his best. The lad needed to be drawn out of himself rather than moping about in the vicarage lost in his own almost silent world. Vignoles appreciated such behaviour was understandable under the circumstances and was making an effort to be considerate. Losing his father was a devastating shock, although Maurice had said little on the subject. Despite the obvious sadness of the situation, they had to find some way of relighting a spark inside, and if not exactly cheer him up, then at least offer a diversion from dwelling on what could not be changed.

Vignoles had promised his sister he would talk to Maurice and even broach the subject of those stupid comics she found so distasteful. This had the potential to be a tricky conversation and risked building yet more barriers and forcing the boy further into his shell, so Vignoles was in no hurry. Diversionary tactics were the order of the day for now.

Truth be told, Maurice was not Vignoles' most pressing problem right now. The lad had turned up at the station as pre-arranged on the telephone the night before, although Vignoles had completely forgotten this. Events during the night on top of the already tricky Palmer murder enquiry had quite pushed it from his mind. As a result, the unheralded arrival of a rather cold teenager in the Detective Department office reception had prompted a puzzled Mrs Green to interrupt Vignoles mid-flow during a briefing session with his team. Vignoles had little choice but to hand over to Trinder and pretend he'd been expecting him. Vignoles could only imagine how furious Gwen would be if he just sent the poor lad straight back to the vicarage.

The timing however was awkward and Vignoles was distracted by what felt like more pressing matters, although he reminded himself he had a duty as an uncle to make time for Maurice. The sudden death of Baylock had thrown a massive spanner in the working of the Detective Department, not least, because the victim was a witness in the Palmer murder inquiry and possibly even a suspect. The effect was not unlike stamping on a nest of wood ants. The discovery of Baylock's mutilated body had seen everyone working flat out since first thing to collect information and report back as quickly as they could. Their urgency compounded by the knowledge that Chief Inspector Badger was heading their way from London to 'find out what the Hell is going on there,' as he'd thundered unceremoniously down the telephone an hour earlier.

Under the circumstances it was hardly surprising Vignoles had neglected to put Maurice off until a quieter day. Well, he was here now, and Vignoles had told Trinder to take over and get a briefing document of some description on his desk before Badger turned up.

Time was tight, so train spotting was the most practical suggestion, allowing Vignoles to remain close to field urgent calls or queries. Better still, Vignoles could soon hand Maurice over to his wife, who'd agreed to take him into the city later that afternoon as soon as she could escape her own duties as a despatching clerk at the same station.

Maurice had at least responded with at a modicum of enthusiasm to the idea of improving his appreciation of steam locomotives. He retained enough respect for his uncle to not just refuse and sulk. It was likely Maurice had picked up something of the almost electric atmosphere in the office, alerting him to the fact that something important was happening. Added to this, his solo train journey to Leicester whilst only short, had none-the-less held an element of excitement for someone his age and he had been quite animated when telling his uncle about this minor adventure, which in turn led them to them spending a tolerable time together watching trains.

Vignoles now brought steaming cups and a large piece of Victoria sponge cake and a mince pie to the table. It was hot inside the station buffet and for about the 100th time that day Vignoles had to polish his glasses to remove the condensation. He envied Maurice's youthful eyesight at moments like this. The buffet was decorated with loops of Christmas bunting and there was an emaciated Christmas tree in one corner covered in gold, silver and blue tinsel and some cheery fairy lights. Bing Crosby was adding to the seasonal atmosphere by gently crooning something

Christmassy from the glowing radio set on a shelf at the back of the serving counter.

'I've underlined 'Royal Lancer' and also 'Blackbuck' we saw earlier. I think the red ink looks best.' Maurice was dutifully transferring numbers and names written down in pencil in a small note pad into his brand-new *ABC Combined Volume* that Vignoles had handed to him as an early Christmas present. This came with two Biro roller-ball pens, one with red ink and the other blue.

'I prefer using red.'

This was promising, thought Vignoles. Maurice seemed to be taking to the task, busy skimming through pages searching for the locomotives that just had numbers and no names. Whilst he did so, Maurice asked a question.

'Have you found who did it yet, uncle?'

'Did what?'

'Killed the old lady.'

'Ah.' Vignoles sipped some coffee. 'No, as it transpires. In fact, it's proving to be trickier than we first thought.'

'Why's that?' Maurice looked up at his uncle. 'Surely it's just a case of gathering lots of facts and evidence then searching through it until you find what you're looking for. Like I am now. There's absolutely mountains of numbers in here, but I just need to sift through until I find what I need – and there we go – got it!' Maurice pointed at the number he was searching for.

Vignoles smiled. 'If only real life was as perfectly ordered as that book.'

'Trains are real life.'

'They are, but the locomotives listed there are but one tiny aspect of the hugely complex world of the railway including all the people who work and travel on it, and railways are but a fraction of society.' Vignoles found his mind flashing back to the dead bodies of Palmer and the mangled remains of Baylock. Two railway workers, both now dead. He watched as Maurice used his new red biro to make an underlining. Two members of the 'railway family' taken away, their names metaphorically struck through with a blood red line. Their deaths stung that bit sharper and motivated everyone that bit harder in their investigations. He saw it in the frenetic energy and steely looks in everyone's eyes that morning.

'It needed a lot of hard work just to create that book you have there. Months and months of checking and re-checking data, and yet it's easy to make a list once you've done the ground work. In a murder investigation there can be confusing and contradictory pieces of evidence that don't appear to make sense and won't fit neatly into columns and tables. We often find information that turns out to be deliberately misleading and which can distract and send one off one quite the wrong track.' Vignoles noticed he had Maurice's full attention. 'And then, there are the things one does not know, but which could be crucial to making sense of what happened.'

'Where do you look for something when you've no idea what it is?'

'A good question.' Vignoles bit into the mince pie. It was warm and spicy and offered a welcoming hug of homeliness on a day that had started so bleakly, standing shivering in the freezing fog looking at the wrecked remains of what once had been a man.

Maurice considered this. 'Is that what you've been doing today - looking for something you don't know?'

Vignoles hesitated before answering. His mind was crowding with questions that needed asking about the death of Baylock and how this may, or may not, impact on the killing of Palmer. Tempting though it might be to sound out ideas spinning around, he was unwilling to share this turn of events with Maurice. He bought himself time by sipping his coffee and taking another bite of mince pie, in so doing realising how hungry he was. The rush of sugar was pleasing. Maurice had now carefully put his *Combined Volume* to one side and was attacking his slice of cake with gusto.

'We are asking questions of many people and probably need to ask a whole lot more before we can be confident of understanding what happened.' It was a deliberately guarded reply.

'But you will get him? The murderer.'

'I sincerely hope so.'

'Do you know why she was killed?'

'That is always the first place to start. Find out why someone felt the need to do such a dastardly deed, then determine whom amongst the possible suspects most closely fits the motive and has the weakest alibi, and so you close in on your prime suspect.'

'What do you think was the reason?'

Vignoles placed his cup on the saucer with almost exaggerated care. 'I'm really not sure. We have ideas, but I feel dissatisfied with any of them as a convincing motive and hence the trickiness of the case.' Vignoles was hardly understating the situation. So many aspects felt unresolved or contradictory.

Had Baylock been killed? This was a startling question. If so, then by whom and equally importantly, why? What possible reason could there be for such a brutal death? Vignoles felt as though he was trying to convince himself this was just another tragic accident. A fatal trip over a carelessly discarded shunter's pole in the dark and the fog on icy ground. It had a horribly authentic ring to it. Such accidents were all too common when men and rolling stock were close together and he must be careful not to allow his imagination to run free.

He returned to his mince pie and as he looked up his eyes caught the front page of the *Leicester Mercury* held open by a gentleman at a neighbouring table.

Young constable killed by speeding car
– Knocked off his bike and left to die. Police seek witnesses.

Vignoles had not heard this news and felt an icy chill down his spine. Another ghastly twist of fate. The same treacherously foggy night and it took just one momentary lapse in attention for tragedy to strike. He felt sure the motorist had no evil intent and was now wracked with guilt for causing a fatality. It would be proven to be an unfortunate accident, just as the men on the engine and the shunters in that foggy yard were guiltless for their actions as Baylock tripped...

'Uncle, do you like catching killers?'

Vignoles snapped out of his reverie. 'Most of my work is quite mundane. It's not nearly as thrilling as you might imagine. There is a lot of paper work and report writing and mostly of this is about petty crimes and minor incidents. Typically, it's just hard slog proving that -,' he tried to remember something suitable, as it was time to curtail further discussion of current investigations. '- that a shed foreman is skimming off stock he handles to sell on the blackmarket; or that a ticket clerk is fiddling the books. Not very glamorous!'

'Of course, I know that, but you've done some exciting work too. I've heard the stories! Guns and spies and child killers.' Maurice rolled his eyes in mock horror.

'I can't deny there have been moments of high drama. Nor indeed that I'm investigating a suspicious death at present. Might this be a line of work you want to explore? I can see it captures your imagination.'

'I might. Although I'm not so sure about the report writing and that boring stuff with ticket clerks.' Maurice wrinkled his nose with displeasure. 'I like the sound of the Flying Squad! Fast motorcars racing across the city with blue lights and bells ringing as they race off to catch really hard, dangerous criminals!'

'I bet you do. They're a new innovation in London - and a far cry from Leicester, I can tell you!' Vignoles sipped his coffee and was momentarily reminded of the young policeman struck off his bike by a car. He leaned forward conspiratorially. 'I'll let you into a secret about the Flying Squad. They do their fair share of routine work and still need to do paperwork. Oh yes, a lot of paperwork, I suspect!' Maurice groaned. 'It's a fact of policing and there's no avoiding it. Those Flying Squad chaps will have slogged away for years on the 'boring stuff' – quite possibly directing traffic - before they earned the right to drive their fast cars.'

'I suppose so.' Maurice became more interested in his cake.

'Now, if you look out of the window, you'll see something rather splendid. I was hoping out luck would be in.'

They both watched as a handsome engine with much gleaming brass and copper work and with a brightly polished curving nameplate slowly eased past the condensation streaked window. 'That's a Great Western engine, or at least it was before Nationalisation. One of the 'Hall' class.'

Maurice nodded approvingly, he liked the look of what he saw. 'Shotton Hall. I wonder where that is?'

'Shropshire, I think.' Vignoles gazed at the engine which fortuitously had drawn to a halt outside the window. 'We don't get many of these over this way, but every so often one strays up via Banbury and Woodford and are taken off here to be sent back down to their own region.'

'You can tell they're not from here. Strangers in a strange land...'

'I've not thought of it like that before.' Vignoles mused, not hearing the subtle change in Maurice's voice. He was still studying the distorted view of the locomotive through the rivulets of condensation on the window pane and watched the fireman step out of the cab to uncouple the engine. 'They have quite a distinct style. Easily recognisable.'

'You bet! They're known as 'New Edwardians'.' There was awe in Maurice's voice.

'No? That is not correct...' Vignoles looked back at Maurice in puzzlement.

'Not the engine! I mean those two cool cats over there.' Maurice licked his fingers free of the sugar left after demolishing the last of his cake whilst nodding towards two striking characters in their early twenties who had just taken a seat in the corner. Both were wearing shockingly bright but perfectly tailored suits that were long in the jacket, off-set with straight and narrowly cut trousers. One was dressed in a garish electric blue, the other in wine red, both with black velvet collars and lapels. Vignoles stared in horror at their candy pink and yellow socks just visible between the deep trouser turn ups and their crepe soled shoes.

'Good God!' He kept his voice low. 'They look like they've escaped from a pantomime at the Palace Theatre!'

'Oh uncle, don't be so *square*. They're Teddy Boys. It's all the rage in the Smoke.'

'Oh. I see.' Vignoles sat upright and pursed his lips. So these were the so-called 'Teds.' He'd read about them and it didn't make pretty reading. They were gaining an undesirable reputation for robbery with violence, having a particular love for flick knives and razor blades. They hunted in packs, terrorising whole neighbourhoods at night. At least, that was what the newspapers said, and of course one should not always believe everything in print. They were an unknown quantity in Leicester and Vignoles had not yet met anyone with first-hand experience of these strange, exotic creatures.

'They're really the tops. Just look at their suits.' Maurice could hardly pull his eyes away whilst speaking in an almost reverential tone of voice.

'Humph! And just look at their hair. It's right over their collars and worn in that ridiculous swept back affair.'

'That's a DA.' Maurice responded with obvious admiration.

'A what?'

'A Duck's Arse.'

'I beg your pardon?' Vignoles stared at his nephew in surprise. 'Yes, it does somewhat resemble a wet duck from behind. Fine on a duck on a duck pond, but most ill-advised in a station buffet.' His contempt was barely concealed. He frowned, then turned his scrutiny towards Maurice. 'Your hair needs a trim.'

'I like it like it is.'

'A regulation number three all over won't take long.'

'I'd rather not.' Maurice pulled a face.

'When I was your age, I did as I was told.'

'There've been two world wars since then, uncle.' Maurice retorted. He quickly sipped his tea knowing he'd been rude and kept his head down. However, his eyes were still drawn to the two candy-coloured dandies seated in the corner, now lolling in their seats with their legs stretched in front of them, displaying their finery and smoking with an arrogance that seemed to dominate the room. Vignoles was annoyed with Maurice, but the buffet was hardly the place to admonish him and instead observed two middle-aged ladies in coats and dresses that looked woefully drab in comparison with the Teddy Boys. One of the women nervously glanced at her watch, perhaps willing their train to arrive so they had an excuse to leave.

Vignoles decided to let Maurice's comment pass. For now. But the lad's hair was too long and Heaven forbid he should try to emulate those two men in their ridiculous garb. Thankfully his pocket money would never stretch to one of those vile suits, so this was unlikely. Still, he'd better keep an eye on the lad. Oh God, he was starting to sound like Gwen. Vignoles wanted to change the subject, but suddenly felt at a loss. He unconsciously tapped his fingers along to the sugary tune playing through the loudspeaker.

Maurice noticed. 'They need a Juke Box in here.'

'A what box?' Vignoles was starting to feel old. For the second time in minutes he had no idea what Maurice was on about.

'For playing music. You put money in and select a record. They fill them with those 7-inch single records that are all the rage now. They're always full of cool songs. Or, at least, so I've been told.' His increasing use of slang was awkward, but energetic. 'Not like this horrid old stuff that grandma listens to.' He stopped.

'Or your uncle.'

'Sorry.' Maurice went red.

'Do the boys at your school follow modern music?'

'Not half! There's a gang who really dig it. Older boys mainly, of course, as they have loads to spend on records. They've set up a Jazz Club and they've got boxes of long players and our Prefect – he's called Simon Harper-Tarr – has got a smashing record player! The House Master lets them use it for an hour before lights out and we can sit in and listen as long as we stay quiet. One of the boys has a father who works on transatlantic ocean liners and can get rare records from America. You've just got to hear some of those!'

Vignoles lit his pipe. Maurice was becoming exuberant and enthusiastic and it was good to see. At least he was no longer staring longingly at those two idiots blowing streams of smoke into the air as they continued to exude their brand of over-confidence and arrogance into the humble surroundings of the station buffet.

'There's this new sound in America they call 'Rock and Roll'. Not really like jazz at all. Lots of drums and guitars and with a wizard rhythm and funny words. It's going to be all the rage.'

'I've not heard of that.'

'It's only just coming over the Atlantic. But you'll absolutely love it, uncle.'

Maurice's wish to include him in accepting this new-fangled sound was appreciated and acknowledged with a non-committal smile, although Vignoles was not sure he would be quite so keen. Music trends came and went, and it was harmless enough, he mused. The school Jazz Club might not offer a decent career path, but it clearly brought enjoyment. It might be good to introduce John Trinder to the boy. He had an extensive record collection and piles of music journals. Damn poor timing though...

Or perhaps Benson could introduce Maurice to her outrageous trumpet playing boyfriend? Vignoles silently winced. Bad idea. Gwen was unlikely to approve of that particular heavy smoking, hard-drinking 'jazzer' and especially once she learned of the controversial 'arrangement' with Jane. It was wise that Benson kept him in London with only rare appearances in Leicester. Tongues had a habit of wagging and what they said was not always complimentary.

'Is there a particular song you like from this rock and roll sound?" Vignoles asked, eager to keep the conversation alive.

'Oh yes. The best is 'Shake, Rattle and Roll'. It's by someone called Bill Haley and his Comets.'

Vignoles laughed. 'Halley. Its Halley's Comet.'

'He's American. They say things differently.'

'True. However, you have me intrigued. It sounds like a song written about one of those long goods trains we've just watched rumbling and shaking and rattling through here!' They both laughed.

Chapter Thirty-Six

'Guv?' Trinder put his head around the office door. 'News just in.'

'Good or bad?' Vignoles looked up from a number of typed reports he'd found waiting on his desk after leaving Maurice with his wife for the remainder of the afternoon.

'That depends on one's point of view.' Trinder stepped into the room. 'Two leads that wipe McMullen off our suspect list.'

Vignoles leaned back. 'That has to be good news as we've too many suspects. What do you have?'

'Lansdowne has just taken a call from a District Nurse, Mrs Sylvia Bainbridge, who says she was called out to one of her expectant ladies in Botcheston on Thursday evening. She went out in her Morris Minor, travelling from her home in Leicester along Desford Lane and she remembers passing through Black Spinney Crossing not long after nine o'clock. She was specific on this point as she was aware the last train of the day was due and remembers being thankful the gates were still open.'

'Nurse Bainbridge seems to have a remarkable knowledge of the railway.'

'That's her patch and has been for many years, and she makes a point of learning when the crossings might be closed as sometimes she's in a frantic rush to reach one of her ladies who's started labour!'

'A sensible lady. Her observations are probably reliable.'

'I agree. As she continued along Desford Lane just before she was to turn off right onto Botcheston Road she remembers seeing a shuffling tramp of a man – those were her words. She felt rather sorry for him as the night was raw, but duty called and hurried on.'

'That would be what - ten or fifteen past nine?'

'That was her estimation. Before Palmer allowed the last train through and before the first assault.'

'If the man described was McMullen, he could still have doubled back.'

'There's more. Howerth has been continuing his door-to-door work and found us something of interest. Newtonlea Farm lies a short way off Desford Lane, almost exactly where Nurse Bainbridge turned off towards Botcheston. The farm had been visited by the Leicester civvies, who met the farmer on that occasion and drew a blank, but in a stroke of fortune, Howerth encountered the farmer's wife pulling into the farm in a van. He hailed her on the off-chance. He asked specifically if she had seen either McMullen or Charlton in the area between Thursday night and Friday morning. She confessed she'd seen McMullen outside, loitering about and looking miserable. She discreetly directed him to a hay barn and told him to stay in there for the night and out of sight. She took him some bread and cheese later and told him to make himself scarce early the next morning and not let her husband see him or he'd get a hiding.'

'What time was this?'

'No later than half nine when she first saw him and around ten thirty or a little later when she went out again with the food.'

'Did she notice his footwear?'

'As it happens, she did. Old boots falling off his feet. That was one of the things that made her decide to take pity on him.'

'It's unlikely that having found shelter, food and a kindly face, McMullen would then slink off and assault Palmer. I can think of no good reason for him to do so. Strike him off the list.' Vignoles was toying with his unlit pipe and pointed the stem towards Trinder. 'This seems to confirm the boot prints on the door and around the cottage were made whilst worn by Charlton and not McMullen. That would explain the driver's sudden charitable desire to get shut of them.'

'Charlton's not coming out of this well. He's still top of my suspect list.'

'I harbour got doubts over Baylock and Hind. All logic tells me it was an accident last night, but I can't escape the thought that Baylock's death was deliberate.'

'But why?'

'Because he knew too much. Did he see Palmer's killer?'

'What about Hind? Is he an innocent bystander in this or is he implicated too?'

'What do you think?' Vignoles wanted to hear Trinder's thoughts.

'Did they rob and kill Palmer but then there was a falling out? Tension mounting and each blaming the other perhaps. We need to speak to Hind. Perhaps we've just elevated him to prime suspect.'

Vignoles sucked on his pipe and looked more worried than pleased by his sergeant's analysis. 'It feels like we're going around in circles. It's time to force a hand or two. Flush out whatever is lurking in the undergrowth. Start by bringing Charlton and Corrigan in. Ask the Constabulary if they can send two cars and some constables. Make a song and dance about it so the neighbours see. They're not under arrest, but I want them to feel the pinch. Let them sweat in an interview room for a while. But keep an eye on Hind. Let's see what he does when he hears things are starting to get hot. We'll interview him once we see what we get from loverboy and his girl.'

'With pleasure!' As Trinder left the office, he had to step aside to allow the trim, compact frame of Chief Inspector Badger to pass. Badger gave Trinder an odd stare as if surprised to see him, then strode into the centre of the office, laying his swagger stick along the edge of Vignoles' desk and tossing his expensive cap and soft kid-leather gloves onto a heap of paperwork tottering on one corner.

'Right, tell me what's been going on with our railway!' His opening gambit was every bit as perfunctory as Vignoles feared. 'I was all set to run my eyes over your report on Palmer when I was informed about this plate-layer chap getting squashed. Please don't tell me these events are related.'

Badger eased himself down into the empty chair whilst speaking, but not before carefully easing each trouser leg up half an inch up to prevent removing the creases and creating a bagginess around the knees. His uniform was immaculate with silver buttons gleaming like baubles on a Christmas tree. Mrs Badger clearly spent a lot of time with the Silvo polish and a soft cloth. His hair was cropped short and his moustache shaped to perfection. The very model of a Chief Inspector, complete with a sharp tongue, but an equally sharp mind. Not the easiest man to work with and perhaps harder to like, but Vignoles had learned that for all his irritating mannerisms, conceit and barely controlled impatience that seemed to crawl over the man's skin like an infectious disease, he had the ability to cut to the chase and reach the nub of a problem. Vignoles was not expecting an easy ride as he tried to explain the current state of their investigations but might benefit from some of Badger's brutally direct observations.

'It is possible they are.'

'Bloody Hell! Then we need coffee.' Badger grabbed the intercom (a relatively recent innovation for the Detective Department). He punched the key that took him to Mrs Green on reception. 'Be a dear, and rustle up some coffee, toot suite? Strong and plenty of it!' The squawking sound of her voice in reply was cut short. 'Give me the worst. Two deaths in a week. What's going on?'

'A murder, most probably for a significant sum of money, and what on the surface looks like an accident in the fog. Of course, if it really *is* an accident, then things are not quite so sinister.'

'But you're not convinced this squashing incident was an accident?'

'On the face of it everything points to a trip in a busy yard in poor visibility. The man, George Baylock was a seasoned railwayman walking his usual route and apparently stumbled and lost his footing at exactly the wrong moment. No one was seen acting suspiciously at the time.'

'In the dark and fog? Hardly surprising nobody saw anything! Neither should it surprise anybody it was hours later he was discovered. That proves nothing either way.'

'My thoughts entirely.'

'What suggests suspicious circumstances?'

'Baylock, together with his friend and work colleague Hind, found Jane Palmer. They were the first on site and claim she was still alive. They moved her indoors to keep her warm, tried to administer first aide then raised the alarm once she died.'

'Or so they claim.' Badger's eyes were like that of a hawk as he looked at Vignoles. 'You have suspicions?'

'We are questioning their story and both men were on our list to interview. We'd taken statements but wished to press them harder on certain points.'

'And one ends up dead before you can get to him.'

Mrs Green unceremoniously barged into the office at this moment with a tray laden with a steaming coffee pot and two mugs, a small jug of milk and a sugar bowl. Vignoles hurriedly dropped yet more papers onto the floor beside his chair to make room as the tray was set down with a rattle. Badger drummed his fingers impatiently on the desk whilst Mrs Green poured aromatic coffee into each cup, the colour an impressive shade of brown. She was learning. It looked an improvement on the pale, insipid hot water of years gone by. Once she'd left they took up their discussion.

'Why do you think these two men are not telling you the truth?'

'I think they're hiding something, although I'm not sure what. If they are the perpetrators of the Palmer killing they created a bold alibi that is hard to crack. They moved her body and had ample time both inside and outside the cottage to remove whatever they wished and alter the way you interpret the crime scene.'

Badger nodded agreement.

'Their prints are everywhere, but fully explainable according to their story and ample time to turn the cottage over.'

'It needed turning over? A poor gatekeeper's residence?'

'Palmer is believed to have over £500 in the cottage.'

'Strewth.' Badger looked incredulous. 'Ample motive. One of these two could struck the fatal blow?'

'It's possible. If it was Hind, perhaps Baylock was losing his nerve and threatened to run to us. Perhaps he thought he could pin all the blame on Hind.'

'And so Hind staged an accident to remove the threat,' Badger sipped his coffee.

'We're watching Hind to see how he reacts as we step up the investigation. I want him to feel the pressure build, then pull him.'

'But That implies Hind is not your number one suspect?'

'We have others...'

Badger didn't like that. 'I'd stick with the platelayers. They went for the money. It makes complete sense. But look here, is it plausible an old crossing keeper had such an amount?' Badger raised an eyebrow. 'Legitimately.'

'It's frustrating we have only the word of her daughter and grand-daughter to go on, but if the hundreds being quoted are correct then something is wrong. Even the most frugal worker could never hope to save this kind of money. And hence my concern that this is not quite as straightforward as it seems.'

'Hmm. She'd be on a pittance in that job. Was this Palmer woman on the fiddle?' Again that hawk-like stare.

'We have no evidence yet to support the idea. We're still digging into the family history to see what we can turn up. If she was up to something illegal, possibly Baylock and Hind got wise to the fact?'

Badger drained his cup and refilled it. He took a deep breath in advance of shifting the focus of his questioning. 'What about Charlton? From your report, it's clear he's trying to explain away his very visible tracks by giving his boots to some old tramp. The man's a bare-faced liar.'

'The question is, what is he trying to cover up with his lies?'

'It's your job to find out!'

'Trinder's on his way to pull him in, and also Palmer's Grand-daughter, Rachel Corrigan.'

Badger looked puzzled. 'How does this Rachel Corrigan fit in? Wasn't she supposed to be miles away on the other side of the country?'

Vignoles also refilled his cup. 'What I know is that Charlton is a family friend, especially to Palmer. As such, I'm struggling to see him violently mutilating and murdering Palmer. Avarice can make people do many things, but Charlton is not struggling financially. Robbery for money does not seem sufficient motive for Charlton to violently murder a close friend. However, he was there at some point that evening. He admits it and we have evidence backing that up. He kicked the door, although why, is unclear as it was not locked. He was quite familiar with the use of a nail to hold it shut. He admits to using the mattock identified as the probable murder weapon, but he claims he used it for killing sick rabbits and not Palmer.'

Badger spluttered and nearly spilt his coffee. 'Poppy cock! Rabbits! In the dead of night?'

'We have found no evidence of the dead rabbits he claims he threw on the compost heap.'

'Pure fabrication...'

'These anomalies tell us something is wrong.'

'We can agree on that at least.' Badger sighed. 'So, if money is not behind Charlton's actions -,' Badger sipped his coffee before continuing, giving Vignoles a curious look, '- are you suggesting the next most likely motive?'

'Sex. Desire - and Rachel Corrigan.'

'What's she like?'

Vignoles understood perfectly what Badger was asking. 'Young. Widowed. Pretty and dresses to accentuate the fact.'

'Ah ha! Is she a flirt?'

'Trinder gained the impression she was certainly the centre of attention at work, but in fairness, she works in an all-male environment and can't help her looks.'

'Humph! You've hauled her in for questioning, so you suspect she's complicit and she sounds the sort to catch Charlton's eye. Spill the beans.' Badger looked quite animated.

'We have a witness who claims to have seen Charlton and Corrigan having sexual relations.'

'There you go!' Badger grinned. 'The oldest motive in the book.'

'This was not far from the brickworks where Corrigan works. We've learned she regularly hitched a ride to and from work on the trains, either in the guard's van or on the footplate with Charlton.'

'Hitching a ride in all meanings, eh? A married man having his way with the pretty young grand-daughter. Right under the nose of mother and grandma Palmer. One, or both, must have known about this, surely?'

'My money is on Palmer. I think she worked out what was going on - and didn't much like it. What's the betting she told Charlton to back off or she'd spill the beans.'

'Mrs Charlton was not going to like that.'

'Quite. Mrs Charlton is also expecting another child. He'd lose his job on top of his wife and family.'

'Darn right he would. We'd thrown the book at him, Vignoles! I'd see to it personally.' Badger put his mug down with some force, making the tray rattle. 'The impudence of the man! I've never tolerated this kind of behaviour on our line.'

'However -,' Vignoles spoke calmly. 'Is this sufficient motive for murder?'

'Losing his wife and family, his house, job and keeping his bit on the side? I'd say he was fighting for his life by finishing off an elderly lady, all dressed up as a house-breaking that went wrong. I'd say that's motive enough.' Badger snarled like a fox about to pounce on an unsuspecting vole. 'He's going to have to fight a lot harder in court to save his neck now. He's your man, Vignoles! Give him the works - and don't spare the punches. You were right to call that little minx in too. I bet she'll blab the whole story and deliver his head on a plate like Salome.'

'I hope you're right.' Vignoles looked worried. 'There are some aspects not adding up. Timing issues that are causing us serious headaches.'

'Don't worry. It will all come out in the wash, just you see. So that means Baylock made a foolish mistake in the fog. It was an accident. Darned shame, but he should take more care. No, you'll have this all sewn up before Christmas and you can spend time with that lovely wife of yours.'

Badger shifted his position, signalling that the discussion of the case was closed as far as he was concerned. He flipped open a carton of expensive Park Lane cigarettes and popped one into his mouth. It was signal that Vignoles could fire up his pipe. Smoke was soon spiralling up towards the roof light.

'Now, what about you man, Trinder? He's got his marching orders and will be gone in the New Year. Remind me where we've sent him?'

'Llandudno Junction.'

'Really?' Badger winced. 'Bad luck...'

'He'll be a big loss. A hard man to replace.'

'Plenty more fish in the sea. But you need a replacement and look sharp about it.'

'Trinder has not told the others yet. He's not broached the subject with myself.'

'Darned strange behaviour. Is he getting cold feet? I can't stomach a man who shows weakness. Mind you, if was being posted to Llandudno Junction I might stall.' This last part was spoken *sotto voce*.

'I don't doubt his resolve, sir. I expect he's feeling unsure how we'll take the news.'

'Policing is a tough business. There's no place for pussy-footing around and worrying about the sensitivities of others. He wants promotion and he's got it. He'd better just pack his bags and then stand everyone a drink at the bar! I'm more interested in his replacement.' Badger's expression was curious. Challenging. Vignoles felt a sinking sensation in the pit of his stomach. He sensed what was coming next. 'Who've you got in your sights?'

'I have someone in mind.'

'Excellent. Who is he?'

'Not the man you put forward.'

'Why not?' Badger looked surprised. 'I must remind you, DC Mellor is a darned good copper and hungry for promotion. Hard as nails and bright as a button. You'll have no problems with Dicky Mellor backing you up, trust me, Charles.'

'I had no problems with John Trinder.'

'Maybe, but he's history. Mellor's as strong a candidate as you'll find by a long chalk.' Badger lent on his elbow, cigarette burning in his hand. He spoke more softly, in a confiding tone as one colleague to another. 'With Mellor watching your back, you'll have more time to do the interesting stuff. He'll whip your team into action and clear that stack of papers off your desk in double quick time.'

Badger even offered a playful smile rather than delivering the usual admonishing. 'The work he's doing down Paddington way is remarkable. He'll take the daily burden off your shoulders. You'll have time to do more of those activities that could smooth the advancement of your career.' Badger puffed in his Park Lane with a satisfied look on his face, his body almost relaxing. 'A round of golf or two could do you no harm, y'know? I could take you on an introductory round. Get your foot in the door, so as to speak. A few brandies in the club house and good word with the secretary would soon you right...' He actually winked.

Please God, no! Vignoles tried hard not to let his face betray his is abject horror at the idea. Golf! With The Badger! The awful clothes, the dreadful hierarchy and social positioning of the club house, never mind the silly act of whacking a ball down a characterless green. Badger meant well, and in his own way Vignoles could appreciate this was a generous offer, but he knew he could never accept.

'Let me consider Mellor and the other candidate I have in mind a while longer. Give Trinder a chance to break the news. I'll put forward my recommendation once the Palmer case is closed and the Baylock death satisfactorily explained.' It was a tactful answer that Badger could not reasonably argue against.

'Just don't take too long about it or else I'll have to force your hand. Remember, Mellor's your man! Why not take a trip up to town and see him in action on his home patch? You'll be impressed.'

Chapter Thirty-Seven

Trinder knocked lightly on the open office door. 'Charlton's in the interview room. He's asked for a lawyer.'

'Drat. I hoped we'd get a chance with him alone. You've sent for one?'

'Mrs Green put the request in and they're sending a man over now.'

'Then leave Charlton to stew until the duty brief arrives. What about Corrigan?'

'Not good news. She and her little girl have left home. Packed their bags and gone.'

'Gone where?'

'To Liverpool according to her mother. House-hunting. They've been given their marching orders by the British Railways Board to quit by the 2nd January. I saw the letter, so that much is straight. I'm not best pleased they've broken our request to remain in the county.'

'We can hardly blame a young mother wanting to seek a roof over their heads either. With Christmas approaching she does not have a lot of time to spare. People go on holiday, offices close for the duration. We must hesitate before reading anything sinister into this action. Do we know where she is staying?'

'Mrs Lake was unsure. She and Rachel did not discuss this sudden development. She just upped sticks and left without even saying goodbye.'

'Should we find that curious?' Vignoles pondered.

'It's an odd way to carry on. Lake sounded put out, but by the same token didn't seem worried either. Corrigan is an impetuous and headstrong character, apparently. Lake has given us an address of a girlfriend in Liverpool as the most likely place she will stay and we're chasing this up.'

'Keep on top of this and once you make contact make sure she's brought in for questioning. Request the Liverpool City Police help track her down.'

'Righty-o!' Trinder turned as if to leave.

'John. A moment. Close the door and take a seat.' Vignoles had his feet on the hot water pipe that ran beneath his office bay window. His chair was tipped backwards, and he'd been idly watching a B1 Class locomotive steam through Leicester Central on a local stopper. He scribbled down it's number, 61063. It was an engine he'd seen many times as it hailed from Annesley shed close to Nottingham, but when he next saw Maurice he would encourage the lad to check to see if there was a red underlining in place in his own spotter's book. Vignoles felt he had made some small progress and it would be wise to keep the momentum going.

Trinder sat down. They'd worked together since 1944 and had a good relationship that spilled over into friendship, but despite this, he sensed something in the tone of the Guvnor's voice that made him wary.

'Should we plan our strategy for the interview?' Trinder decided to take the initiative.

'We know what's needed. We'll needle him over his relations with both Corrigan and Palmer and demand answers and clarifications on his activities that night.' Vignoles was filling his pipe. Probably a good sign, Trinder decided. He struck a match. 'No, I want to know what *your* strategy is.'

'In respect of what, sir?'

'Surely you know?'

'Are we talking in riddles?' Trinder extracted a carton of Black Cat cigarettes and popped one in his mouth, using this action as an excuse to look away.

'I believe I'm being direct. I'm just wondering how long I must wait for you to tell me straight whether you have written and posted your acceptance of your promotion.'

'Ah.' Trinder's lighter flared and he momentarily paused, before lighting his cigarette. 'You know?'

'I'm a detective! And besides, who do you think put your name forward in the first place? When were you thinking of telling me?'

Trinder took a grateful lungful of smoke and then exhaled. 'I should have said something earlier but what with the investigation taking up so much time and -.'

'You've sent off your acceptance?' Vignoles cut across his excuses.

'The letter is on my desk.'

'Then hand it to Mavis before the final post collection today. Don't dilly dally a moment longer.' He pulled on his pipe. 'What does Violet think? You have at least told *her*, I hope?' Vignoles gave Trinder a stern look.

'Of course. She's delighted at my promotion.'

'Glad to hear it. And, John, this is good news. Congratulations are in order. We must find time to raise a glass or two together before you leave.'

'That would be nice. It's going to be strange to leave.' He took a long drag on his cigarette. 'I suppose I've delayed breaking the news to stall for time. Held back the moment of truth so I could have time to think privately about what means. Don't misunderstand me, I'm pleased to achieve promotion, but I've been here a long time. We're a team.'

'And like every good football team it evolves. Players move on and new ones come in. It is vital that change is embraced.'

'Of course.'

There was the sound of a man's voice outside the office. The duty solicitor had arrived and was being shown into the interview room.

'It will be tough for Violet at first,' Vignoles cautioned. 'Despite her enthusiasm. Your little boy is young enough to adapt quickly, but she might find it harder. Leaving her own work, her customers and friends in Woodford; and finding her way around a new community without a badge of office to open doors and make introductions.'

Trinder nodded sagely, as he smoked. 'I'm not sure I won't find it difficult! North Wales is a place I barely know. A different culture and starting up a whole new detective office on top.' He sounded worried.

'You'll manage. That's why I proposed your name for that position.'

'That was kind.'

'You were far and away the best candidate.' Vignoles looked out of the window in response to a chime on a locomotive whistle, but perhaps to avoid embarrassment to either.

'I just hope I can solve a few quick cases to get my feet properly under the table. Show the others I can do it.'

'Concentrate on building a decent team and developing trust and everything else will follow.' Vignoles watched a V2 class locomotive gently roll to a standstill. The Manchester express had arrived. 'Crime will happen of its own accord, so no need to go looking for it.'

'Who will you bring in?'

Vignoles continued to look at the V2. He liked these engines and the distraction was not unwelcome. 'You won't be so easy to replace - but don't let that go to your head. I have someone in mind.' He paused a beat. 'As does Badger...' He swung around to face Trinder. 'I might have a fight on my hands to get the candidate I want. Badger's put forward someone from London. A "whirlwind of efficiency and driven ambition", apparently.'

'Then he might be just what's needed.'

'Perhaps. I've not met him.'

'You don't sound convinced.'

Vignoles paused a beat before answering. 'If he convinces me he will enhance the team then he might win my vote, but from Badger's description he sounds too full of himself. Perhaps not the sort to drop into our team without causing ructions. We're lucky here, we rub along quite well and have developed friendships, but that's unusual.' Vignoles paused and considered his next words. 'I shall attempt to be fair in my assessment of the dynamic PC Mellor, but if his working style threatens to disrupt the efficiency of this office, I will resist his introduction,' Vignoles gave a wry twist to his mouth.

'I won't forget working here, sir.'

'You'll be far too busy to think about us. Right. We've work to do.'

* * * *

'Mr Charlton, you understand why we've brought you in for questioning?'

'No comment.'

'A little soon for adopting that line, if I may say so.' Vignoles looked from Charlton to the duty solicitor, who gave a blank look in return before making a note on his legal pad in crabbed letters impossible to read upside down. 'We wish to ask you about certain events that took place in the between the evening of the 2nd and the early hours of the 3rd December in the vicinity of Black Spinney Crossing. You previously told us you were at that location that evening. Is that correct?'

'No comment.'

'Are you now denying you were at Black Spinney Crossing on the evening of the 2nd December?'

'No comment.'

Vignoles took a long slow deep breath. 'It will considerably help your cause if you answer our questions. We can prove that you were there, and your denial will not play well out with a jury.' The solicitor leaned towards his client and mumbled something inaudible.

'I was there, what of it?' Charlton's voice was flat and emotionless. 'I never killed her.'

'We didn't say you did.' Vignoles gave Charlton a steely look. 'What were you doing?'

'Helping. Helping Old Janey, like I often do.'

'In what way were you helping her?'

'Killing rabbits. The sick ones.' The solicitor made an effort to conceal a look of disbelief as he made a note.

'Interesting activity for a winter's evening.' Silence. 'When did you arrive and at what time did you leave?'

'I think it was about six fifteen and I left at seven thirty.'

'Different times from when we first spoke with you?'

'My client has considered the matter in more detail since that first, *impromptu* interview, and has refined his recollections of the evening,' the solicitor added.

'I see. It was only a short visit. You're confident it was no later when you left?'

'I said so.'

'That means you left Black Spinney Crossing before Mrs Palmer let through the last train and closed the section for the night?' Trinder took his turn to make notes as he asked the question.

'Obviously.'

'And Mrs Palmer was alive and well when you left?' Trinder continued.

'Yes.'

'How was her mood? Was she anxious or nervous about anything? Did she give you any reason to suspect she was worried about being alone, perhaps?'

'I didn't speak to her.'

'Not even a greeting?' Vignoles responded. He and Trinder had agreed to press Charlton from both sides to ensure he never felt at ease, never sure from whom the questions would come. 'You just turned up at her home and started...doing exactly what? Please explain.'

'I already said, I was killing rabbits.'

'In the dark?' Trinder was incredulous.

Silence.

'We find you explanation hard to understand,' Vignoles added.

'They were sick. They just sit there. Dying. You see their eyes reflecting.' The solicitor was giving his client an odd look.

'How many did you kill?'

'Two. Three. I'm not sure.'

'You cannot remember? I find that odd.' Trinder made a note. 'Not remembering how many creatures you killed...'

'What did you do with the two, or perhaps it was three, dead rabbits?' Vignoles kept his voice gentle.

'Threw them away.'

'Where?'

'No comment.'

'We searched the area around the cottage at Black Spinney Crossing. We even took apart the compost heap and found no evidence of these rabbits.' Trinder challenged Charlton.

The solicitor mumbled something in Charlton's ear. He shrugged his shoulders. 'Foxes must have took them.'

'How did you kill the rabbits. Was it using this tool?' Vignoles slid a photograph across the table of the mattock.

Charlton barely glanced down at the print. 'If it's from the shed, it will be. But they all look the same, don't they?' There was a slight upturn to his mouth. 'I use the tools all the time. I'm in and out of the shed all the time.' He sounded confident.

'You admit to using this to strike rabbits?'

'My client can hardly be expected to say whether this is, or is not, the tool in question from this photograph,' the solicitor intervened.

'We found your fingerprints on it, and also fresh blood and hair. Can you explain why that would be?'

'My client has already given you a perfectly clear explanation of how and why he used that tool. You have your answer.' The solicitor's eyes were hard.

'When you finished killing whatever number of rabbits, all of which subsequently vanished, what did you do with the actual blood-stained tool you were using?'

'I put it in the shed. I always put tools away tidy.'

'A careful and thoughtful man. I find it strange that you did not think to clean the unpleasant blood and gore from it before returning it to the shed.'

Silence.

'You say you finally came home at 8-o-clock in the evening. Did you leave your house again at any point before you had to rise and go to work?'

'No, why would I?'

'Can your wife confirm that you did not leave your house later that same evening.'

'Of course, because I never left.'

'Interesting. We have asked her if she can confirm your movements and she is struggling to corroborate your story to our satisfaction. Mrs Charlton explained that being heavily pregnant, she tends to fall asleep easily and did so that evening.'

'I cannot see how her present condition can have any bearing on your investigation,' The solicitor intervened.

'Establishing when Mr Charlton was at Black Spinney is central to our questioning. I would have thought you would be equally keen to help confirm his alibi for the time we understand Mrs Palmer was attacked. As it stands, Mrs Charlton was not able to help,' Trinder replied, curtly. He'd met this particular duty solicitor before on a number of occasions and he did not like the man. 'Did anyone apart from Mrs Palmer, see you whilst you were at the crossing cottage?'

'I doubt it.'

'That's unfortunate.' Trinder made a note. 'Did you go inside the cottage?'

'Why would I?'

'Can you explain why your boot print was found on the front door, as though it had been kicked with some force?'

Charlton's left eye twitched slightly in a spasm and he looked as though he was straining hard not to blink. 'No comment.'

'Do you know why a pane of glass was broken in one of the lower windows?'

'I never saw that.'

'Can you explain why the blood-stained mattock that you put back in the shed was found under the same broken window?'

'No idea.'

'At what time did you go to work on the Friday morning?' Trinder was consulting his notebook.

'Three thirty.'

'No earlier?' Vignoles chipped in.

'Of course not.'

'How well do you know Mrs Corrigan?' Trinder changed tack. The solicitor visibly reacted. He'd not heard this name before. Charlton made a non-committal grunt.

'Rachel Corrigan. Daughter of Sarah Lake, grand-daughter of your friend Jane Palmer. Come now, Mr Charlton, forgetting the number of rabbits you killed is almost plausible, but this young woman is impossible to forget. She lives in the same small cottage.' This last sentence was said for the benefit of the solicitor who was frantically making notes.

'I-I'm a bit flustered. Being interviewed like this...'

'We understand.' Vignoles smiled indulgently as he took over from Trinder. 'People often stumble and get confused in these situations. Starting again and taking a moment to gather your thoughts before answering, how well do you know Rachel Corrigan?'

'We say hello from the engine. A wave and a greeting, being polite. But she keeps herself to herself and I can't say I know her as such.'

'Are you sure that's all'

A pause. 'Sometimes she gets up on the train.' The solicitor was looking annoyed. It was clear he was angry his client was dropping this information on his lap. 'She works in the brick works and it's the easiest way to get her to and from work.'

'Very kind of you. Does she ever get into the cab of your engine?'

Charlton swallowed. 'Once or twice.'

'Against regulations?' But Vignoles smiled and implied he was prepared to overlook this irregularity. 'No doubt you enjoy her standing close to you on that hot footplate?'

'A pretty young woman. I'm sure you enjoy that.' Trinder took his turn to appear almost sympathetic.

'Where is this leading, exactly?' The solicitor could almost have been directing the question at his client. He looked severe.

'It is leading to the fields at the back of The Premier Terra Cotta & Brick Works. To a quiet spot your client thought was out of sight.' Trinder answered the solicitor, who then blinked a few times as he tried to take in the information. 'Mr Charlton, you were seen having sexual relations with Rachel Corrigan. Our witness was quite graphic about the nature of the relationship.'

A long silence. 'They were wrong. It was not me.'

'You deny having sexual relations with Corrigan?'

The solicitor whispered something. Charlton frowned, chewed the inside of his lip. 'I might have kissed her. Just once or twice, that's all.'

'It was more than kissing according to our witness.'

'We – cuddled a bit. An arm around her waist. It was a foolish moment, I admit it. Then I stopped and saw sense.' The detectives waited and watched. Charlton mopped his brow with a handkerchief. 'It's a bloody lie if anyone says it was anything more. Who was it who told you?' He drummed his fingers nervously on the table, but Vignoles and Trinder held their silence. 'Look, I made a mistake, alright? It was last summer and... I'd had a beer or two. It went to my head and she's a pretty lass. Everyone knows she's a looker! She's flirty and a tease and...' he was floundering in his attempts to deflect the blame onto Corrigan. 'Come on, you've seen her!' He tried to include Vignoles and Trinder in his expansive gesture. 'She shows herself off in her short summer dresses and flutters her eyelashes and...' Impassive silence from the detectives. 'I'm not the first man to make a mistake like that. Maybe my hands were wandering a bit.'

'I think you're lying.' Trinder's voice was steely.

'It was just the once. It was nothing.'

'I'm sure Mrs Charlton won't see it that way.'

Charlton swallowed. 'Listen, I was stupid. I know. I felt so bad I can't tell you. I never went near her again. I swear I didn't!' He slammed a fist on the table.

'I think you've been having an affair with Rachel Corrigan for at least six months.'

'That is pure supposition. My client has been very clear that this was a solitary error of judgement and unless you have proof otherwise, you will withdraw that allegation,' the solicitor barked.

'Mr Charlton, your affair with a young woman is not a criminal offence and our interest is purely in establishing what impact – if any - this ill-advised dalliance has upon your actions on the night Mrs Palmer was murdered.'

'I can hardly see how it can.' The solicitor responded, but Vignoles continued. 'Was your secret discovered by Mrs Palmer? We have one witness and I am sure we will find more who knew about your liaisons with Rachel. People talk. Were you in fear of having your secret exposed?' Vignoles decided it was time to land some metaphorical punches. 'I imagine Mrs Palmer would be quite protective of her grand daughter. Especially when it turns out to be a trusted friend of the family who is leading the vulnerable young woman astray. Did she threaten to tell your wife?' Vignoles locked his eyes on Charlton. The slight twitch above his eye was back, but otherwise Charlton was maintaining his composure well.

'No comment.'

'Did you argue with Mrs Palmer that night?' Trinder took over. 'Did she challenge you? With the cottage empty as the whole family were away in Liverpool, it was the perfect opportunity to have her say without the others overhearing. One to one. Did she tell you to back off or she'd ruin your home life - your work life as well?' Trinder followed up the attack: 'I think she goaded you. Told you off like a naughty boy caught in the act. I imagine it was humiliating. Embarrassing, and it made you angry. A little old lady pointing her finger at you and telling you what a disgrace you were, whilst you realised your whole world was on the brink of collapse.'

'She turned her back – and your struck her, with the mattock you'd been using.' Vignoles added.

'No!' Charlton looked like he was having trouble swallowing.

'She was dazed and confused, but she knew it was you who'd attacked her. You were in deeper trouble now. There was no turning back.'

Charlton was shaking his head.

'But you ran off at first. Scared by what fear and anger and humiliation had made you do. But once home you realised you were in great danger. Palmer was alive and would soon tell the police. You'd be hauled in here on a GBH charge and even if you ended up with a suspended sentence, you'd still lose all that was dear to you. Your family would be gone. Your status as a driver.'

'It was not like that.'

The solicitor made notes. A slight smirk played across his face, Trinder noticed. It was time to introduce another revelation and see if he could get Charlton to crumble. 'The signalwoman in Desford Junction box saw you hurrying along the railway line away from Black Spinney Crossing just before 4am. You were racing to get on shed to drive your train. Why would you be doing that? Was it because you hurried back to the cottage to finish the poor old lady off?'

'No.'

Trinder could feel his blood starting to boil. 'I'm sure you only wanted to threaten her, to make her shut up. But you lost your temper. You're a strong and fit man. But once you'd hit her, you had little choice but to go back in the early hours to kill her and set everything up to make it look like a violent robbery.'

'It was a clever move. Rifling through the house, smashing drawers, breaking a window. It was a neat touch.' Vignoles allowed a generous smile. 'You nearly fooled us.'

'I didn't kill her.'

The solicitor cleared his throat in a portentous manner that suggested the two detectives were going to be brought down with a bump. 'Most interesting. In a different context I might even quite enjoy your little flights of fancy. It's rather like something out of one of those trashy crime books my wife is addicted to.' There was no attempt to hide the supercilious smirk on his face now. 'If Mrs Palmer lay dead at the hand of my client sometime before 4am as you claim, how was he able to return to his locomotive - as your witnesses clearly attest – and then be signalled down the line at 4.30? The line section was open, the gates also to allow my client's train through. The signals stood at clear! Mr Charlton saw Mrs Palmer standing near the crossing as they passed.'

'The fireman did not see her,' Trinder felt a cold prickle of unease down his spine and his voice was flat.

'You need to do better than that. His failing to see Mrs Palmer who was dressed in black on a dark night standing on the far side of a footplate whilst partially blinded by the glare from his fire does not undermine the startling fact that Palmer was quite obviously alive and well. I fail to see how the section could be opened and everything as they should be if Palmer was dead. Unless ghosts can undertake such functions, of course.'

It was a strong argument.

'If that is all, gentlemen?' The solicitor made a point of replacing the cap on his fountain pen with a flourish and closing his note pad with a firm slap. 'I see no reason for you to hold my client a moment longer. I am surprised my client has been subjected to this inconvenience as after only the most superficial consideration, I can find many flaws in your argument.' He was standing and urging Charlton to walk ahead of him. 'Good day.'

* * * *

'Jumped up little pip-squeak.' Trinder let fly. His dislike of the duty solicitor had intensified.

'It's his job.'

Trinder smoked a cigarette in a series of short, angry puffs. 'Perhaps my annoyance is because I fear he's got a point.'

'I agree.' Vignoles was also looking frustrated. 'We cannot explain how Palmer can open her section of the line – and Laura Green's log book makes it clear she did – if Charlton killed her before 4am. After that time, he was on the footplate of his locomotive accompanied by Mitchell until long after the investigation commenced.'

'We're missing something vital. But what?' Trinder paced across the room, literally scratching his head. 'Palmer was still alive when discovered by Baylock and Hind. Is it possible she opened the crossing after that horrific injury?'

'Partially blinded and probably brain damaged? Impossible! Her injuries were too severe.' Vignoles paused. 'If she had any strength left it would be to call for help, not go about her normal duties. Or at least flag their train down for help.'

'It feels like we're trying to force a piece of a cardboard jigsaw puzzle into the wrong place,' PC Blencowe observed with a dead-pan voice. 'It won't fit no matter how hard we press it home and mangle the edges.'

They were clustered around Trinder's desk, smoking and finding little solace in the activity. WPC Lansdowne and PC Blencowe were seated behind their own desks, invited to join the impromptu meeting. WPC Benson was carrying in a tray of much-needed teas and coffees. PC Howerth was out, tasked with bringing Hind in for questioning.

'Either Charlton didn't kill Palmer, or he had an accomplice who knows how to use the block instruments and opened the section?' Lansdowne suggested.

'An accomplice gets around the timing issues,' Trinder replied.

'I thought Charlton's falling out with Palmer was about keeping secret his affair with Corrigan? He's hardly likely to rope someone else in. He'd be leaving himself open to blackmail,' Blencowe's quiet observation hit home.

The room fell silent. Benson quietly delivered mugs of tea or coffee. There was a collective sense they'd failed. Charlton had walked free. A key witness was dead and perhaps under suspicious circumstances, whilst Corrigan had slipped away to Liverpool, a fact that only added to the sense that everything was spiralling out of their control.

'Any news on Hind?' Vignoles addressed the room.

'Howerth says he didn't report to work this morning and is not at home. His missus says he left the house for work as usual. She can't offer any explanation.' Benson almost felt guilty passing on the news.

'What?' Trinder shook his head in exasperation. 'Get on to the constabulary and request their motorcycle patrols keep a look out. And telegraph word along the line - all stations, depots and signal boxes in the county on alert. Hind can't have gone far and if we mobilise everyone we'll soon run him to ground.' He sounded more confident than he felt.

'Blencowe. Wipe that chalkboard clean!' Vignoles suddenly barked the order. 'We need to start over.'

Blencowe looked unsure. The board in question was covered in names, dates, arrows and observations all chalked in his open, school-masterly hand. It was the product of many hours of work and the distillation of a lot of evidence. 'Everything, sir?'

'Wipe the slate clean! Then put Palmer's name in the centre. She's at the heart of this, and not just because she's dead. I'm wondering if her death is blinding us to something else. Something that runs deeper.'

'Everything circles around her like ripples from a stone tossed in a pond.' Trinder was narrowing his eyes and thinking hard.

'Now, put Charlton on one side, Baylock and Hind on the other. All three were at Black Spinney Crossing at various times between the night of the 21st and the early hours of the 22nd.'

Blencowe wrote their names, circled each, then traced an arrow pointing towards Palmer. Without prompting, he wrote the names of Sarah Lake and Rachel Corrigan below Palmer's. A double-ended arrow lead from Corrigan to Charlton.

'That relationship is important. Charlton and Corrigan were having a sexual affair, of that there seems little doubt despite his denials. We have the knock-up lad to confirm the fact.'

'An appropriate title...' Blencowe muttered and there was a gentle ripple of laughter that offered a welcome release of tension. 'Sammy Chambers'- he placed the name on the board and made a dotted line that ended in twin arrow heads pointing at Charlton and Corrigan.

'Draw two tracks through all this to represent McMullen and nurse Bainbridge in her car, both of whom passed through the area that evening.'

'What about Miss Green and Mr Weatherall?' Benson suggested.

'Yes. In one corner place those two. Signalmen are careful people with good observational skills. Fortuitously, they were together when they saw Charlton hurrying on shed. We can have no doubt about the veracity of their testimony and the timings. We should start with their story and the moment Baylock and Hind telephoned in the death of Palmer as two fixed mooring points. Everything else feels open to question.'

They all stared at the board looking for inspiration.

'What about the daily log Palmer kept in her cottage?' Vignoles asked.

Trinder inspected his notes. 'Up to date until 9.30pm on Thursday evening. But nothing for the Friday morning.'

'Implying she was attacked for a second time and lay dying shortly after the train passed at 4.30am, but before she had time to go indoors and complete her log.'

'Which fits with Charlton's testimony he saw Palmer alive outside her cottage,' Trinder reluctantly conceded. 'We might get GBH and robbery charges to stick on Charlton, but not more.'

'Then who's the killer?' Benson asked. 'What sits uncomfortably with me, is that Palmer was attacked twice in the same night. Why not just kill her outright the first time?'

'Good point. Thoughts?' Vignoles looked around the room.

'Our initial explanation was that Charlton attacked Palmer because she'd threatened to tell his wife about his affair. He struck out in anger then ran off in a panic. We've been trying to argue that Charlton's odd behaviour in the early hours implied he went back and finished her off, but unless he had an accomplice, which makes little sense, that won't wash.' Trinder tailed off. 'All right, so Charlton did not kill Palmer. He assaulted her in the evening but could not have been responsible for the second attack.'

Blencowe chalked in 'G.B.H' on the board beside Charlton's name.

'The question is, why was Charlton seen hurrying from the direction of the crossing when he was supposed to be rushing back from his house with his forgotten knife?' Vignoles threw the question out.

'Beats me,' Trinder looked flummoxed.

'What if...' Lansdowne spoke up. 'No...' She sounded unsure of herself and stopped.

'Say it, Lucy,' Trinder urged her to speak. 'We need ideas; good, bad or down right bizarre!'

'What if there are two unrelated crimes here. Quite separate from each other, but both focussed on Palmer.'

'Hard to credit, but not impossible.' Trinder was cautious.

'Have you a scenario?' Vignoles was encouraging.

'Charlton has a run in with Palmer for the reasons discussed. However, I wonder if their crossed words actually took place some days earlier. Charlton claims he did not speak to Palmer on the Thursday evening and he might be telling the truth. People who are lying to cover their tracks will put as much that is correct into their story as they can. We now have a man feeling resentment towards Palmer and also fear. It boils over, and he goes out to assault her. A swift unannounced attack from behind. Was he intending to kill her or just scare her? Or was he not thinking at all? I don't know.' Lansdowne shrugged her shoulders.

'That could work.' Benson looked interested. 'Once he's laid her out on the ground the stark reality confronts him. He's been hot-headed and foolish. He's in hot water now. But then he has an idea about how he can deflect attention away. He kicks the door, smashes a pane of window glass then rifles through the house to make it look like a break in, although he takes nothing.'

'As a friend, he could have robbed Palmer in broad daylight. His actions were done to look as though it was done by someone unfamiliar with the house,' Trinder added.

'Charlton thinks he's left a convincing crime scene and heads home where his wife is sleeping and unaware he ever left the house for a second time. But he can't sleep. His whole world is still in the balance. What if we don't buy the idea it was a spur of the moment robbery?' Benson stopped.

'This is good.' Vignoles interjected. 'Once home, it's obvious he's in a bind. Perhaps he feels remorse for what he's done, so he sneaks back just before 4am to see if she's recovered from his assault.'

'With what intent?' Trinder asked.

'I doubt he's thinking clearly. I believe he was an unstable frame of mind. He observes she's alive and readying to open up the section and feels satisfied that perhaps no serious harm has been done.'

'Hoping Palmer will think it was the robber who hit her?'

'I imagine so. She is walking and presumably not badly hurt, so he runs back to his engine and later steams past her cottage. All looks in order. He starts to believe he can recover the situation and has time to dream up a plan of how he can perhaps mollify Palmer with offers of condolence and concern for the awful assault and robbery she's suffered. Perhaps he can find a way out of this mess. They get to West Bridge and Charlton hears the news Palmer has been murdered.'

'The second crime.' Lansdowne added.

Everyone exchanged glances. Trinder picked up the story. 'Charlton hears of this brutal killing and the eye gouged out which he knows he was not responsible for. And yet he did strike her, and even entered the house and smashed it up.'

'He's committed a crime against the same woman and in the same location, but not murder. There's every chance he's going to hang for a crime he didn't commit. No wonder he's lying!' Vignoles stood up. They were getting somewhere. A new energy started to course through his veins. 'Then who killed Palmer, and why?'

'Let's look at Baylock and Hind again.' Trinder was jabbing a finger at their names on the chalkboard. 'I've never liked their story. Moving her body and their first aid attempts destroyed the crime scene. They muddied the waters perfectly.'

'The death of Baylock takes on a sinister aspect', Vignoles agreed. 'We can quote statistics about how many railwaymen die each year in accidents and factor in the fog. Even that poor copper getting knocked off his bike in Leicester the same night highlights the dangers, but it all feels too convenient.'

'And now Hind's buggered off! Excuse the French,' added Blencowe.

'These two killed her and robbed the house. They made a lot of money.' Trinder looked convinced.

'If they learned of the cash tucked away in there, then they had motive. Perhaps they were waiting for the right opportunity, and in a stroke of good fortune they find Palmer befuddled after the earlier attentions of Charlton and realise now is their chance. She's let the first train through, gone back to put the kettle on, but she is also pain and distressed and vulnerable,' Vignoles was puffing away on his pipe. The story was flowing.

'And Charlton had already set the scene for a robbery!' added Lansdowne.

Vignoles nodded. 'That could work. One of these two is a killer and the other an accessory. If Hind struck the blow, Baylock could have become jittery and in danger of putting a noose around Hind's neck. We need to search their houses. Look everywhere as money is easy to conceal. In their garden sheds, work bothies, anywhere we think they might have hidden their stashes of cash.'

Trinder agreed.

'And so we get back to Palmer. Why had she so much money in the first place?' Vignoles asked

'On the fiddle?' Blencowe chipped in.

'Doing what?' Benson asked.

'Stolen merchandise. Stuff lifted off the trains or out of goods sheds. Faked station and goods receipts? There's plenty of angles if you're willing to take the risk,' Trinder suggested.

'It will be something like that. Perhaps for a great many years.' Vignoles inspected his pipe. It had burned out. He'd been putting in a lot of thinking. 'I think she was the banker. Looking after the ill-gotten gains earned by the actions of others. I can't see her holding boxes of knocked off goods in that tiny cottage, undetected by the others she shared it with. Money can change hands unobtrusively and can be stored under floorboards, in lofts, in a garden shed.'

'In jars and packets at the back of a kitchen cupboard?' Benson added.

'They'd been thoroughly searched!' Trinder was excited. They'd picked up the scent and the hunt was back on.

'She was thorough and meticulous. Reliable. She almost never left the property and looked like the last person you would ever suspect.' Vignoles was also looking pleased. 'Search the cottage again but this time look for places for concealing small items. Floorboards with bright screws holding them down, trapdoors and hidden spaces. False bottoms to wardrobes. You get the picture.'

There was a murmur around the room. It was action stations and a renewed sense of purpose gripped the team.

'And find Hind. I want him in our sights ready to interview. But we need some evidence first to throw at him.' Vignoles was about to walk back into his office to call Badger when he suddenly stopped. 'What's that?'

He pointed at a cardboard mask of Father Christmas lying on Trinder's desk, partially covered by the brown paper bag it had been placed inside.

'I found it near Black Spinney Crossing.' Trinder paused. 'Mrs Charlton told us she and her husband purchased one a few days earlier. But we could not find it in their house.'

'The implication being?'

'That this is the same one.'

One again everyone stopped what they were doing.

Vignoles gingerly picked it up. Careful to touch only the edges of the card and peered at the glossy printed surface at an acute angle. 'It looks brand new. There might be finger marks. It's a long shot but try and lift them. It cannot have lain there long in this weather if still so pristine.'

'That was my thinking. I cannot imagine too many people passing by and dropping such a thing.'

'Show it to Mrs Charlton. And Mrs Lake. Perhaps she also bought one and it's missing.'

'I have a feeling this is the one from the Charlton house.'

'So how did it get where it did?' Vignoles stared at it a while longer. 'Why does someone wear a mask?'

'To conceal their identity.'

'Charlton wore this on the Thursday evening when struck Palmer. It's the equivalent of the classic stocking over the head.'

'That fits with Lucy's idea he went there to surprise her and not reveal his identity,' Benson added.

'But once home again he realised he'd dropped the mask,' Trinder took up the story. 'He knew it was incriminating and rushed back, but he can't find it in the dark, not helped by the fact Palmer is up and about. He can't risk being seen and is forced to run back to get on his train.'

'As observed by young Chambers,' Benson added.

'Once on the train he also realises his boot prints are a giveaway -,'

'- and in a moment of inspiration he sees Irish Mick, who is always lurking around the crossing and hands across the incriminating boots. A penniless vagrant is going to be a favourite to be framed for the robbery.'

'It will be something like that.' Vignoles agreed. 'It's starting to come together. Trinder, I know you said Charlton was comfortably off and didn't seem to be in debt, but £500 is a huge temptation. He, of all people, is probably as likely as anyone outside the family to have stumbled on her secret.'

'What about the family, sir? Do we believe they knew nothing about this money?' Benson was sceptical.

'It is hard to believe. She may have good reason to leave, but we need to speak to Corrigan as a matter of extreme urgency.'

Chapter Thirty-Eight

Rachel Corrigan was grateful the compartment was empty. She needed time to think. She shivered and ran a hand over her forehead which felt clammy. She hoped she and Daisy could be alone. She didn't think she could stand the thought of strangers in that cramped space watching her every move, perhaps sensing her guilt. Because she was guilty. Her plans were in mortal danger of being blown out of the water by the insane actions of that idiot Charlton. How stupid

to imagine getting Richie to do her dirty work would let her off the hook.

What on earth had possessed him to kill her grandmother and in such a repulsive manner? Corrigan had been physically sick when the full horror had been made known to her. The cruelty of gouging out an eye whilst the old lady was still alive and presumably staring back up at him had turned her stomach. What disturbed her more was the knowledge that the man who'd done this vile act had been her lover. He'd kissed her and those same hands that had brought that weapon down on granny's face had, so gently and erotically, removed her clothes.

She squeezed her eyes closed for a moment to prevent stinging tears welling up and dropping. Why was she even thinking of shedding tears? Not because she mourned the loss of that mean old bitch of a granny, that was for sure. It was a hideous way to go, but good riddance! She'd always been a mean old crow, and dishonest with it. A grasping criminal, dressed up like a comedy character from an Ealing Comedy film. Underneath that stupid tin helmet and her lank grey hair, Corrigan had half expected to find Alistair Simm in full character. A proper Ealing Comedy crook. Old

Janey had been a bad 'un, no matter how much the dumb engine crews had fawned all over her and considered her the salt of the earth. Stupid men. They fell for her lock, stock and barrel.

No, what was upsetting her was a mixture of revulsion at what Richie had done and selfish anger and frustration at the pickle it had put her in. He'd dropped her in at the deep end and she was fighting hard to keep her head above water.

But why had the idiot killed her? All he had to do was clonk her on the head to render her senseless for a short time whilst he kicked and bashed the door to make it look forced and threw a few things around inside, and then go. She could not have made it any easier. *Aagh!* She could strike *him* with that bloody mattock right now!

Why? Why? Why? Her head was banging but the fruitless question kept repeating. Charlton was surely going to be charged for murder and things were going to get complicated, and she was scared.

Corrigan snuggled in the corner, staring through the smutty window glass at the balls of steam billowing from the engine, swaddled in her fine new winter coat. The coolness of the glass was oddly pleasing on her flushed cheek and throbbing temples.

The coat was an extravagant item and the fit surprisingly good. She'd allowed Richie many opportunities to explore her body and he'd made it obvious the delight he took in caressing her every curve and hollow and drinking up the sight of her naked form, but she'd never once thought this would have converted into being able to accurately guess the right size and fit of a piece of clothing. She'd had been both horrified and delighted, in equal measure when he'd handed her the coat. It was too expensive, and it was going to be impossible to explain how she'd come to afford such a thing on a part-time office junior's pay. Everyone would notice and ask questions and it was going to be hard to maintain a convincing lie. Worse still, she could imagine the ructions it would cause back in the Charlton home when the significant loss from his wages was noted. She and Charlton had argued badly over this, and the coat, unworn until today and kept furtively furled up inside an old suitcase in the bottom of her wardrobe, had effectively become the tipping point that made Corrigan realise she needed to end this foolish dead-end dalliance.

'Your wife will notice the loss. How will you explain that?' Corrigan knew she'd hit a sore point.

'I give her the housekeeping and the rest is mine. It's none of her bloody business!'

'There's so much left over? And with a family to feed and another on the way? Aren't you the generous one.' Her voice had been heavy sarcasm.

'That's not your problem.'

'I think it is. It's our problem. Everyone's problem!' She'd flashed her eyes at him in anger, a mixture of guilt, fear and desire mingling into a potent mix of passion that suddenly felt the need to boil over. 'If you do something stupid and spill the beans, then it'll be my problem too!'

'It won't, I promise. Rachel love, I've been right careful.' He'd tried to reach for her and draw her close, but she'd pushed him away, although she was still clutching the deliciously soft coat which exuded a gentle scent of new wool. It was dangerously intoxicating.

She now closed her eyes and allowed the rocking of the train to lull her close to sleep, eager to forget the arguments, forget all about Richie Charlton and his pregnant wife and thoughts of her murdered grandmother, and instead the savour the caress of the coat fabric against her body and imagine that all was going to be all right. She needed to escape from all the worries and fears and rest. Her mind was sore and spinning and she needed sleep.

Daisy was seated opposite and also enjoying her own sense of luxury by spreading herself out across the whole width of the compartment bench seating. She was lying on her tummy, sometimes pretending to sleep with her face against the slightly scratchy moquette that covered the cushions. It was oddly pleasing. She had her favourite dolly lying beside her, its painted, staring face close to her own as she whispered private thoughts in a voice too soft for her mother to overhear. The quiet murmured conversation appeared to include responses from the doll. Whilst she couldn't catch the words, this gentle confessional reminded Corrigan of her own secrets. Of the things she must hide and never tell.

Richie was in deep trouble and she was unsure if he could be trusted to keep her out of the story. Those detectives had warned her not to leave town, but she had no choice. She had to get away. Corrigan knew she was not strong enough to resist them if they dragged her away from Daisy and put her in a cell or whatever it was they did in police stations and started questioning her. They'd probably put her on a hard chair and shine bright lights in her face and lean across an ugly little table whilst shouting at her until she broke down and admitted to everything.

The train was clicking and clacking along smoothly, the engine beating time with a deep regular sound that was soothing. Corrigan felt her eyelids become heavier. Drowsily, through half-closed eyes, she watched her daughter open a tiny drawstring cloth bag. This had once held some sugar-coated eggs as an Easter Sunday gift. Dolly was dutifully watching with a glassy gaze as Daisy handled the little bag. It was making tiny clicking sounds from something inside. Was it possible after all these months that Daisy had managed to save some of the speckled eggs, painted in pale pink and blue and yellow? Corrigan allowed herself a little smile. That was a pleasant surprise. Her daughter usually snatched at sweets and gobbled them down like a dog with barely a gasp for air. She was always arguing with Daisy whenever she did this and trying to teach her how to appreciate things and learn how to save up treats and savour them. Another tinkling sound. Perhaps Daisy was learning.

Daisy opened the bag and was carefully allowing the contents to slide into her hand, adjusting her tipping motion to the swaying and hunting of the coach as the train puffed its way through the rugged Pennine valleys. The little girl held the small brightly shining objects in her palm, her eyes transfixed by the colours; the flashes of brilliance as the whites, reds, greens, blues and yellows twinkled like the Christmas lights now going on in houses all over the land. Daisy pulled the doll closer with her free hand so even her mother could not get a glimpse.

The little stones glittered so prettily. 'We must keep them a secret or else Father Christmas will come and take them away!'

Through heavy eyelids Corrigan watched her daughter. Daisy looked content and pre-occupied and they had many miles to go before their destination, so she had no desire to break the spell and intervene and ask what she was doing. There was more than enough time for Daisy to alter her mood and become fractious and demanding and restart her endless questions of 'Why? Why? Why?'

The wild, snow patched landscape dipped and rose fell away again on the other side of the sleet-streaked glass. The hillsides were covered in lank yellowing grass that look stiff and unyielding behind the seemingly endless yards of Millstone grit field walls; the highest hills were topped by scars of exposed rock and the whole landscape dotted with solitary stone houses blackened by soot and surrounded by sprawling yards of clutter and rubbish. Many black fingers of mill chimneys pointed towards the snow laden clouds from the narrow depths of the crowded valley bottoms. Corrigan jerked awake from a dream about being pursued by some very large policemen and stated almost sightlessly at the darkly unwelcoming landscape outside for a few moments, trying to remember where she was.

She'd chosen to travel north to Sheffield Victoria and then across to Liverpool via Manchester through these northern hills but was unsure exactly why. They were not on the run from the police. Or were they? She chewed on the inside of her cheek. Why was she taking this route if not because it was part of an ill-thought out escape plan? Why lie to her mother about where she was staying in Liverpool if not to try and cover her tracks?

The detectives had told her not to leave, but time and tide waited for no man not even for that odd old king who's name she could not remember, who tried to stop the tide coming in. She had every right to leave. They would be homeless by 2nd January, so '*excuse me Mr Detective, but I need to get a roof over my head for me and my daughter*.' Corrigan felt a comforting glow of satisfaction as she rehearsed this response. '*Put that in your pipe and smoke it!*'

They really did need a home and she was travelling to Liverpool for that purpose. Yeah, and with a staggering sum of money waiting for her there! Hidden in a place only she knew. They were rich beyond their wildest dreams. Corrigan had almost fainted that first time when she'd found the barely-concealed key whilst her grandmother was busy with the crossing gates and opened the top drawer of her dressing table. £500 pounds. Perhaps even more, as her hands had started trembling as she'd tried to hurriedly count them all. Even in work she rarely saw money on this scale. And to think the old Scrooge had hardly spent a penny on any of them! Too mean to buy a slightly better brand of tea and always sponging off the men on the trains who fell over themselves to help this poor old lady in the over-crowded cottage. Pah! What a fraud!

Corrigan adjusted her position and closed her eyes again. She'd considered this incredible discovery in the locked draw for weeks, careful to leave everything as she'd found it despite the urge to simple pocket it all. The next few days it had been all she could think about. It had become an obsession. But Corrigan had also started to feel a cold trickle of fear down her spine and a weird sensation as though the floor was moving under her feet. So much money spelt trouble. It was far too much to be legitimate. Granny was up to something, and whatever it was, it paid well. Far too well. And even Corrigan with her limited knowledge of the world (most of which was gleaned from the *Daily Express* at work and the trashy women's magazines she sometimes managed to read) knew that if people were paid that much for doing something they shouldn't, then it was very bad. It was better to proceed with caution. And so, over the next few weeks she'd hatched a plan.

Corrigan would lift the money in a move that took but a matter of moments, just before they left the cottage for Liverpool. With all the hustle and bustle before departure and Daisy running about making a noise and losing Dolly and the old bat busy with her trains and her bell and signals and saying goodbye and wishing them well, it was easy to do. She had to take the chance that her grandmother would not notice the loss until the second part of the plan was put into action. That was a risk, but she'd taken comfort in that when she came to open the draw the second time, the contents were exactly as she'd last seen them. That was promising. Then, once Richie had faked the robbery as instructed, he could reward himself with the £20 she'd generously left in the drawer for him to find as he removed some of the other odds and sods stored there and disposed of these as he saw fit to help convince the police it had been an opportune robbery. When gran re-awoke with a sore head, she would know what had gone but was unable to make much of a fuss. How could she? £500 of ill-gotten gains told Corrigan that the old witch would keep her trap shut, or at best moan about an opportunist burglary for items of little consequence. Palmer would never suspect her own granddaughter had robbed her blind. It all sounded so perfect and easy...

Daisy was holding one of the little sparkly stones between thumb and forefinger and allowing the weak Yorkshire light to shine through it. As she turned the stone it flashed and glimmered and burned inside with a yellow fire the colour of a wasp, with one strange stripe of almost black. It was mesmerising.

Corrigan did not see. She was dozing as a new plan started to form. She could afford to relax for an hour at least. They had money. Plenty of it with twenty pounds in her purse and that great horde safely tucked away ready for when she needed it in Liverpool. They would rent a place for six months to start with. Somewhere a bit shabby and poorly furnished so nobody would think they'd come into money. Avoid too many questions and raising suspicions. Then, when the fuss had died down and Charlton had faced whatever music was coming his way, they'd splash out on somewhere special. Move much further away and start a new life.

She stirred again, trying to get comfortable. Perhaps it would be sensible to cover their tracks? Just to be on the safe side. Why not get out at Manchester and take a room in a hotel. She was flush with cash and nobody knew her there. Luxuriate for a couple of nights in their own posh room and take time to properly plan the next step. Read the papers and keep an eye on how things were developing back in Leicestershire. Not that she expected it would make the Manchester news.

Her chest rose and fell more slowly and steadily as the heat in the compartment and the gentle lullaby of wheels on rail joints rocked her to sleep.

Daisy was still whispering to Dolly. 'It's like a bee! Buzz, buzz!' She giggled softly. 'Look how pretty they are.' The little jewels twinkled. She made them roll around in her hand enjoying the mesmerising colours and the smallest of sounds as the skilfully cut facets touched. 'Shhh, Dolly! It's our secret. Don't tell anyone, not even mummy.' This last statement was accompanied by a serious nod of the head towards the attendant doll with it's vacant stare. The little girl had enough understanding of the moral complexities of the world to appreciate that she had taken these stones without asking. That was naughty. But they looked so pretty and so irresistible. It was a shame to keep them hidden in that little envelope she'd found lying under those bits of white cloth in the drawer no-one was supposed to ever look in. Gerr Gaa had once opened the draw and shown her some little spoons and said these were special to her, but Daisy had not been allowed to play with them and felt disappointed when the secret drawer was closed and locked shut again. Daisy had seen where the little key was kept, however, and often snuck upstairs to take a longer peek in the forbidden drawer. It was actually rather disappointing and held very little of interest. The dirty banknotes smelt funny and the spoons, though tempting for a dolly and teddy bear's picnic, had instantly lost their appeal once she'd stumbled upon the envelope of sparkly stones. If Gerr Gaa didn't want to look at them, then she would. She'd put them back, of course. But then Gerr Gaa had died, and they were moving away, so it didn't matter. But perhaps it was still best to keep them secret.

Daisy gave her sleeping mother a glance, then carefully put the stones back in the little bag, drawing the neck tightly closed, using the looped draw strings to tie the bag around the doll's neck. Daisy was proud of having learned to tie a bow and although it took two goes and needed her to partially stick her tongue out in concentration, it was done. The doll was propped up against the seat cushions. Daisy sat up.

'I'm hungry!'

Chapter Thirty-Nine

Passing the crossing cottage that guarded Glenfield Station was going to be difficult. Not only was his face familiar to the old gent who staffed the crossing, but everything about the look and location of the octagonal cottage reminded him powerfully of the one at Black Spinney, and his jangling nerves were starting to prey on him. Hind felt his pulse quicken and the sensation of being watched, of his every step being monitored by an unseen enemy took hold with a force that almost immobilised him. He was not sure if he could walk along the cess beside the track and through the wooden pass gates to cross the road towards the abandoned station without his fear and his guilt betraying itself on his face.

Hind pulled his scarf over his mouth, readjusted his canvas work bag and took a deep breath. He forced his legs to move and prepared himself for the raise hand in salute and the voice asking ''ow he was doin?'.

The wind brought another flurry of snow and the crossing gates that barred the line rattled against their fastenings. A face was dimly visible behind the window, but sensibly the crossing keeper had better things to do right now than step outside of the warmth of his cottage.

Hind envied him his fire and envied him his boring, safe and secure job. Ring a few bells, open and shut the gates. Drink tea. Read the paper. Nothing to worry about. No need to keep looking behind to see who was following. No need to keep fighting down the nausea inside. No reason to feel insecure at home, at work. No need to be on the run.

The crossing safely passed, he approached the station which presented a sorry state, especially on this bleak winter's day. The little wooden station building had ceased to be used as a ticket office and waiting room since 1928 and lain unused and unloved ever since, although it had occasionally been opened to serve as a coal merchant's office. However it was too draughty and leaky. The wooden structure groaned too loudly and the merchant felt it was unwise to remain there for long. His little hut beside the tracks near the short coal siding served him better, being closer to his mounds of coal and coke and far easier to keep warm. The wooden planking of the station building was covered in peeling paint that once had been cream and maroon, but now faded to almost milk white and pale pink where it had not blistered off to reveal the silver grey or rotting wood beneath. The curved topped windows had once been charming and no doubt let in a lot of Leicestershire sunlight, but now admitted only rain and pigeons through broken glass or were shuttered tight like closed eye lids with nailed sheets of plywood. The slate roof was at least intact and sat like a broad hat on top with a deep valance of prettily carved wood that ran around the edge to let the rain drip away, lending the whole structure the air of something one might see at the seaside, on a pier.

The single platform was a mass of weeds even in winter, and some of the edging stones had been removed. The coal merchant's siding opposite was not much more inspiring as he seemed to trade as much in abandoned scrap metal as he did in coal, with an ancient pre-war flatbed truck resting on its axles and tyre-less wheels. A sycamore sapling growing up between the bonnet and the front fender suggested it had been these sometime and was not likely to be moving any day soon. More rusting junk in heaps leant the place a depressing air of melancholy only slightly relieved by the presence of a surprisingly clean and very new, steel coal wagon in the final throes of being emptied. A skein of smoke trailed from the merchant's little wooden shed suggesting there was at least a glimmer of life in this desolate place, but the merchant's delivery wagon was nowhere to be seen. Perhaps this cold snap was making extra demands on coal and he was out. Hind debated taking refuge inside the office, but he barely knew the man and such bare-faced cheek would surely only result in him being reported to Desford shed.

Hind slumped down on a weather-beaten wooden bench against the far end of the station building, grateful of the chance to sit and get his back out of the wind and to be out of sight from the crossing cottage. He had a lot to consider. The man who'd smashed in the head of Old Janey had killed his mate Georgie, Hind was sure of it. This man had paid them off and said they'd be alright - but why believe him? He was a cold-blooded killer! He'd changed his mind, God knows why, but perhaps he wanted his money back? Why should he trust a blood-thirsty murderer? Or perhaps had Georgie done something stupid and word had got back? Either way, Hind was petrified. He was next. He was sure of it but in spite of all the danger he couldn't tell the cops.

He needed to lie low. Mind his back and watch out for that deadly assassin. Hind shivered and fished out a cigarette. If in doubt, have a smoke. He sat hunched on the bench and gloomily surveyed his surroundings. The cold started to numb his brain and he felt unable to think clearly what he should do next. He'd legged it that morning with barely a thought for what he was doing. His head was pounding, and he closed his eyes barely noticing the sound of a motor vehicle close by, the engine ticking over.

A woman in a maroon coat and wellington boots over her pale legs, trotted along the road from the pub, one of the few oases of welcome to be found in the tiny village of Glenfield. She had curlers in her hair and an unlit cigarette dangling from her mouth and carrying a dinner plate with another upturned on top to serve as a cover. Hot lunch on its way to the crossing keeper. She was a shrewish, busybody type who spotted everything and wanted to know more. Nothing escaped her watchful eyes, including the two men in the smart motorcar sitting with the engine running on the weed-infested station yard entrance. It made a convenient place to pull over as the yard had not seen traffic in years. Perhaps they were waiting for her to open the pub? They might be good customers judging by their car and their good top coats and hats, but she still barely repressed the down turn to her bright red lips. She didn't like the look of them. Out of towners. Probably Southerners by the way they sat wasting their petrol with the engine on.

She clomped past the crossing gates and walked into the cottage without knocking. This was her regular delivery and the customary niceties had long been abandoned. Her first words were not of greeting, but questions fired in a brash voice. 'What are those two up to? Sitting there like they own the place? And what's he doing skulking about an' all?'

'If you mean the fella having a smoke, he's one of the gangers. Just stealing a quiet moment to have a smoke. No harm in that.'

'Dodging work, more like. Skiving and thinking nobody can see him!'

'I can't from where I'm sitting.' The crossing keeper tried to make a joke of it. He was long used to her stream of observations of the comings and goings of the village.

'Well I've seen him and there's something fishy about him. He looks like he's up to no good.'

'I thought that was the two in the car.' He winked.

'Them an' all!' The plate of food was slapped down on the desk beside the crossing keeper. 'You know him, then? The work-shy ganger?'

'Only by sight.'

The telephone clattered into life and cut short the exchange. 'Yes? Uh huh. Is that so? Funnily enough I can help. Yeah... He's here... Yes, right now! Leastways I reckon as it's him. On his own just having a quiet fag... Understood. OK.' He put the receiver down. The inn keeper's wife was almost agog with anticipation. 'Well I never! That was Desford shed. They're trying to find a Mr Graham Hind who's gone missing without leave.'

'And who's he when he's not at home?

'The lad sitting out there.'

'What did I say? I told you he was up to no good! I knew it straight off!' She folded her arms across her chest and gave a triumphant look of self-congratulation.

'They're sending some police officers over now. They want to talk to him. It was his colleague who was killed in the fog over at the junction yard.'

'I reckon they're already here. That's those two plain clothes fellas in the car. They're detectives!'

Hind was unaware of what was going on inside the crossing cottage. He was trying to stir himself. Despite the cold and his acute state of anxiety, it felt as though his body wanted to retreat into sleep. His head drooped a few times but then, with a shock, he'd realised he was nodding off. He shook his head and surveyed the scene that lay in front of him, trying to decide a course of action.

The station, with its two under-used sidings thick with dying weeds was dominated by one curiously inescapable presence. Just a hundred or so yards away the land suddenly rose into an escarpment and bored straight into this steep hillside was a narrow tunnel. More mouse hole than railway tunnel and shaped like an inverted horseshoe. Its brick faced opening was black, smoky and dangerously constricted. It was too small for the modern railway; indeed it had always been too small even since the opening day of the Leicester & Swannington on 17th July 1832 when the celebrated engineers, George and Robert Stephenson proudly stood on the footplate of the locomotive named 'Atlas', hauling the first train to traverse the line with a string of open carriages packed with important ladies and gentlemen all decked out in their finest. This joyously laden train of the great and the good had chuffed between verdant fields and hedgerows whilst the passengers condescendingly waved at farm labourers and excited shoeless urchins who chased the new-fangled train on its maiden voyage, until suddenly the locomotive chimney struck the top of the tunnel. It clattered to the ground having somehow missed the locomotive crew and father and son engineers on their open footplate, but not before showering the expensively clothed guests in cloying wet soot, burning cinders and a fountain of steam as the train was forced to halt ignominiously just inside the tunnel and the boiler released its pent-up steam, scouring fresh mortar and brick dust from the walls that encased them all like a coffin.

Even the great engineer George Stephenson must have been forced to wonder how his measurements were so far out. The tunnel proved navigable with a cut down chimney, but as locomotive designs improved, so did their size and by the time British Railways inherited this ancient curiosity in the form of the 'World's First Railway Tunnel', it was clear that few locomotives would fit. When groups of enthusiastic duffle-coated men with cameras and notebooks and haversacks stuffed with corned beef sandwiches and flasks of tea arrived to study this fascinating survivor from the earliest days of railways, they were always given dire warnings that under no circumstances must they enter the tunnel lest they be trapped by an approaching train. The few refuges built in the tunnel walls were dangerously slim and to traverse the tunnel was something only those intimately acquainted with the operation of the line dare take on.

Hind was aware of the danger it posed. He'd only entered when accompanied by his work chum Georgie Baylock, the elder and more experienced of the two, and he felt his mouth go dry as he contemplated the constricted opening and the faintest drift of smoke that still lingered from a train now long past. Inside, he would be safe from view and could shelter out of the falling snow and even the worst of the wind for a few hours. It was a considerable risk but compared with the threat posed by that killer on the loose, he reckoned it was still the better option. He could hunker down and take cover, but he needed to remain vigilant and ready to press himself hard against the back of one of the shallow refuges and pray not to be struck by a passing train. It was just unfortunate that in his hurry to run that morning he'd not thought to check if there were any extra trains movements timetabled in.

* * * *

A police car sped towards Glenfield, its blue lamp showing but the bell silent, the headlights on to help warn other road users of their approach, the heavier snow flurries now falling from the iron-grey sky catching in their yellow beams. They needed to make good time but felt it prudent not to make their approach too obvious. Hind, according to the observations of the crossing keeper, was unaware of their approach and they stood a chance of nabbing him with little effort if they could just get there quick enough.

* * * *

Kane and Abel smoked a second cigarette each.

'I say, he's walking into the tunnel.'

'Unwise.'

'Limits his options, don't you know.'

'Yep. He can either pop out the far end – in which case we can be waitin'. Or double back if has a change of heart.'

'Why would he do that?'

'Why even go into the tunnel? He's not thinking straight. The sign of a man with something on his mind.'

'Perhaps he's thinking to sit tight inside?'

Kane sucked air in through his teeth and unhurriedly studied his expensive watch. 'I'd take my chances in the old station. Ah well, it's his funeral. This beat up old railway does not appear to take much notice of timetables, so choosing to enter the tunnel certainly introduces an element of risk.'

'A certain *frisson*, shall we say?'

'We shall, Abe, we shall. Now, If I was in his shoes, I'd not spend too long down there right this minute. Not by my reckoning...'

'Insufficient time to reach the far side?' Abel's eye was wide and staring behind his monocle.

'If he walks fast, maybe he can make it.'

'He appears to be almost strolling,' Abel smirked.

'Then it's going to be a tight squeeze.'

* * * *

The police Rover stopped with a crunch of tyres on the lane beside the crossing cottage. Trinder, Blencowe and a uniformed constable stepped out briskly, all three surveying the scene with practised eyes. Trinder indicated to Blencowe and the bobby to start walking towards the station, whilst taking a moment to watch as a car suddenly on the other side of the line pulled out and accelerated away, he rapped his gloved hand on the window overlooking the railway. The casement slid up and the crossing keeper and a woman with startling lipstick and curlers in her hair, peered out.

'He went in the tunnel.'

'Are you arresting him?' The woman's voice was strident.

Trinder ignored her question. 'When was that?'

'Minutes ago. But it's not safe in there. I've a train due anytime. It's an extra and he might not know about it.'

'Get it stopped. No, wait.' Trinder was rapidly making a calculation. 'Can you hold the train on the other side of the tunnel and talk to the guard or driver on the telephone?'

'I suppose so. There's a telephone in a box on the signal post guarding the far entrance. The signal box can put the board at danger.'

'Good. Hold them there and speak to the crew. Tell them there's a man on the line and they're to proceed into the tunnel at a crawl, with extreme caution. Whistling frequently. They're to halt part way in and not think about moving either way until I give the command!'

'I'm not sure that's wise? It's highly irregular.'

'Of course it's irregular! Just do as I say. They're flushing him out like a terrier set down a rabbit hole, and we'll be waiting. And tell them to whistle! Frighten the living daylights out of him!' Trinder strode off to join the others, leaving the bemused crossing keeper looking anxious as he started dialling the signal box. Hind was going to be driven out and into their waiting arms whether he liked it or not.

* * * *

'Bloody Hell, the pigs!' Kane instantly threw his cigarette out of the driver's side window and engaged first gear.

Abel did the same with his menthol cigarette. 'Retreat is the better part of valour.'

'Let's clear out. They're onto to Hind. Damn it!' Kane glanced in his mirror and saw the men climbing out of the police car. 'They want him good and proper.'

'Looks rather like they've caught up with us. Most unfortunate; I was looking forward to dealing with that little rat snared in his trap.'

Kane's mouth was set in a line. He was thinking hard whilst powering their stolen car away. 'They've nabbed him before we could. Still, mebbe it won't matter. He might be a red herring anyway. His mate was no bleedin' use.'

'A crushing waste of time.' Abel giggled.

'Let's have a think. You know what, I'm not too gutted about losing this one to the filth. I feel it in my bones that he's a waste of space. I can't help thinking that his mate was no hero and he had nothin' to tell us. It's time we cast the net wider. Try someone fresh.'

'Who'd you have in mind?'

'It's a long shot, but what about the old dear's family? They've got the opportunity, day and night.'

'Not sure I'm with you, old chap?'

Kane's shark teeth were revealed in his chilling variation on a smile.

'Me neither when it comes to the details, but I can think of a bargaining chip that will soon get tongues wagging.'

'Do tell! I'm all ears...'

'The little girl. The one with the pretty mum. Nobody likes a missing girl. I mean, that focusses the mind like nothing else.'

'I'll say! A splendid idea. She can be our hostage to fortune.' A strange silence filled the car as both men considered the implications of what they were planning. 'I've never had the pleasure of persuading a young child...'

Kane, although used to his partner's evil ways, still winced. 'No. We need her alive and kicking, unharmed. She's only useful if she's alive. It's to get the mother talkin'.'

Abel fell in to a sulky silence for a few moments as the wiper blades fought with the falling snow. 'But Louis, if she proves terribly stubborn we can always nudge things along. A little finger delivered in a box, perhaps?' The snow fell on the windscreen, the tyres rumbled on the muffled snow.

'It wouldn't kill her...'

* * * *

Hind entered the tunnel and instantly felt his world close in around him. He was out of the snow but the damp air, thick and noxious with trapped fumes was almost worse. Icy drips of water plopped on his shoulders. It felt more claustrophobic than he'd remembered it. Not having his colleague to guide them through was more of a loss than he'd expected. He could feel his nerve failing, and even more stupidly he'd stumbled and fumbled his way quite deep inside without even getting his torch out of his bag. Idiot! He stopped, standing in the centre of the single track and turned towards the small pale shape of the opening crossed by diagonal traces of falling snow whilst he felt blindly for his torch.

Was that someone approaching? A man in a long black coat. It was hard to see properly at this distance and through the snow. There was another with him. He squinted to focus his eyes and now could make out the silhouettes of two men walking towards the tunnel entrance. He could see flashlights winking in their hands. Police. And they were coming after him.

He stumbled deeper into the tunnel. He dared not use his light as it would betray his whereabouts. If he could just get out the other side.

* * * *

'I don't like this one bit, Eddie lad. Not one bit.' Driver Ashworth was inching his locomotive forward into the tunnel. 'I dunno what they're playing at asking us to take this in when they know there's a man and a bunch of coppers and whoever else running about on the line. It's plain daft!'

'They said it was so we block one end and force them out the other?'

'Or squash them trying, more like.' Ashworth looked grim. 'Why can't we just wait at the mouth for whoever the poor sod it they're chasing?' He yanked on the whistle cord. 'They wanted whistles and we'll give them it. Open your fire. Flood the walls with light!'

Earnshaw obliged, and the searing orange-white light threw powerful shadows and shapes on the tightly curving brick tunnel lining that was moving past the almost open cab at a snail's pace. Steam was billowing around the cab, making the two men look like wraiths in some diabolical painting, the vapour coloured yellow, orange and red like a scene from Dante. As they drew in deeper the sound of their engine puffing slowly and the line of empty wagons rattling and banging behind started to reverberate louder, filling their ears with unpleasant noise despite their snail's pace. Smoke and loosened soot combining with the steam was starting to make their eyes water and both men tied their neckerchiefs tight around their mouths. It was hard to breathe.

'Hells bells!' Hind could hear the roar of the engine. The sound was funnelled towards him after the first icy cold wave of air flooded around him like a river, pushed forwards by the train that now effectively plugged the narrow gap. He could smell the sulphurous smoke and there was an ominous red glow behind a trapped cloud of vapour. A piercing whistle rang around his head. It hurt his eardrums and he clapped his hands over his ears. He had to get away from this advancing train but spinning about, he could see three beams of light playing across the entrance. The police were calling out, although he could hear nothing they said because of the awful ringing in his ears caused by the repeated whistling. Hind lurched towards a slim recess in the side of the tunnel wall. It was barely a brick length deep and his chest was rising and falling with mounting panic and he was starting to cough, the deep, wracking attack on his lungs jerking his head forwards. If he coughed when the train passed, then he was a dead man. He doubled over, clasping his chest, There was no air, the smoke was being pushed forwards in a broiling cloud and enveloping him. If he stayed like he was then he would tangle with connecting rods and the pumping cylinders or be dragged into the spinning wheels. He would be mincemeat.

'Help! Help!' He started running towards the lights, waving his arms frantically. A police cell had to be better than this nightmare.

Chapter Forty

Rachel and Daisy Corrigan disembarked their train in Manchester Central. Although her tickets would allow for a connection onwards to Liverpool, she chose to leave this portion unused. She'd managed a few fitful moments of rest in-between worrying and Daisy's demands for food and being 'bored'.

Corrigan was frazzled and tired. The teeming snow and biting cold were not helping her mood and state of mind. With her heavy suitcase in one hand and her daughter's little hand in the other she slowly fought her way through the crowds and onto the noisy city streets. The day was fading fast and the city looked huge and forbidding. Great buildings black all over with soot loomed over her, the streets packed with cars, shiny black taxi cabs, heavy lorries with grinding gears and smoking exhausts, buses and then yet more buses. How many buses did they have in this place? A few horse-drawn delivery vans clopped by. There was noise and light all around and the pavements seemed full of confident people eager to get somewhere and in a hurry, pushing and barging past her at a dizzying pace. When a particularly sharp elbow nudged her in the back and she almost lost her footing, she felt the tears start to prickle in her eyes. 'I can't do this.'

'Why have we stopped, mummy?'

Corrigan searched the oncoming headlights, urgently taking some deep breaths. She saw what she wanted and dropping the case to the ground waved an arm, stepping almost off the pavement such was her desire to hail the cab.

'A hotel. A nice one, please. Somewhere respectable - and comfy.'

The burly cab driver seemed pleased to have such a pretty young woman as a fare and her little girl was delighted to be helped into the back of his cab. It was going to be a meagre sum as there were hotels all about, but the good money came later in the evening and this was his slack time. And besides, he was always ready to give assistance to a young lady. It made a welcome change to smug businessmen.

The Midland Hotel was warmly lit by yellow lights and had coloured glass in the doors and lower windows and a small cast iron and glass portico. A liveried employee stood waiting, hurrying to help them from the taxi. He was perhaps surprised at their youth, but the woman tipped the cabman well and her coat was new and of quality. She was different from the usual clientele. She looked very young and tired and with suspiciously few suitcases. He couldn't quite place her on the social scale. But her little child clutching a doll and a bag of beads was charming and he decided to overlook his scepticism as to whether she could afford their establishment, and warmly welcomed them both, opening the varnished wooden door and carrying her rather shabby case as though it contained the travelling wardrobe of a film star.

Hours later, after warm baths with plentiful scalding hot water that didn't run out and delivered through pipes that didn't bang and without a queue of impatient guests standing outside the door demanding they hurry up, Rachel and Daisy Corrigan were both feeling refreshed. Their room was large and comfortable and warm, the carpet underfoot was deep and looked almost new. The Midland Hotel clearly had pretension to quality and had reinvested now the severe years of wartime and austerity were coming to a close. The Corrigans had spent the past hour sitting companionably on the large bed discussing the various details of the wallpaper, the wall lights, even the softness of the towels. These alone were a world away from the two threadbare examples folded in the bottom of her suitcase that must be ten years old if not more.

This was the life. Corrigan was slightly uneasy about how much it was going to cost but the greater part of her twenty pounds still resided in her purse and this gave her confidence she could meet any costs incurred that night. Perhaps she should go to Liverpool and retrieve the rest and they could spend the next few years living like this. Moving about without a care in the world; no shopping, cooking or washing; no dull office work for a failing brick company on a meagre wage. The sheer indulgence of this luxurious experience was temporarily building a cocoon around Corrigan. The place she'd called home only that morning seemed like something from another world, from another life. She couldn't bring herself to reflect on what might be unfolding back there. It was too alarming, and too darned inconvenient. She wanted no part of it. She and Daisy were rich - and free. What did she care now about Richie Charlton on a murder charge? Served him right, the double-crossing cheat! He would have to deal with it. It was not her fault he chose to kill her. The comforting feeling of having money in her purse and being warm and cosy in their elegant room as the snow fell on the sooty Manchester streets outside blinded her to the very real dangers that lurked outside, dangers that even now were circling closer like sharks scenting blood in the water.

They had been shown a table for two in the restaurant and both ate heartily, the waitress charmed by Daisy who was on her very best behaviour, and if the Maitre'D was sniffy about a somewhat tatty doll in his restaurant, he managed to restrain himself from actually forbidding its presence.

Later, they sat in a lounge beside a roaring fire, Daisy's attention shared between the huge Christmas tree covered in lighted candles and loops of sparkling tinsel and by the shapes of falling snow beyond the stained-glass windows. Her questions about where they were going and when they would next see Nana, were for now put on hold as she drank in the wondrous new experience, Dolly safely tucked under one arm.

A gentleman approached the empty wingback armchair on the other side of the fireplace. He was clean shaven and smartly dressed in an expensive-looking sports jacket that had brass buttons and pale trousers with a severe crease down the front. His shoes were brown and cream brogues that shone as if yacht-varnished. He was wearing rimless spectacles that made him look very clever.

'Excuse the intrusion, but might I join you, madam?' His voice was soft and gentle. 'The log fire is most inviting on such an evening.' He held a perfectly folded copy of the *Manchester Guardian* in one hand and raised this slightly as he spoke. 'I have my paper and I promise not to intrude on a mother and her charming daughter.'

'Of course.' She could hardly refuse. It was a public space.

He was fastidious in his movements. Precise and careful, adjusting the lie of his trousers with the air of a man who knew about expensive tailoring. He carefully placed the newspaper on a side table and extracted a carton of cigarettes that looked very posh from the inside pocket of his jacket. Corrigan was not familiar with the brand, but the twin gold bands on the cigarette he held in his manicured hand, spoke of expense. How the other half lived.

She smiled to herself. *But now I can do likewise. I can buy nice dresses and smoke expensive cigarettes if I want to.*

'May I take the liberty of inviting you to join me in a smoke?' He stopped and gave a slight cough. 'Forgive me being so forward, but it struck me as being awfully impolite to light up and not extend the offer to a lady.'

'Oh. No. I mean yes, that's awfully kind.' Corrigan was unsure how to react. Was he being too forward? Should she rebuff him? But his manners were polite, and he looked unthreatening. 'Please. Thank you.'

She extracted one of the slim cigarettes being proffered and the gentleman gallantly lit this for her using a gold lighter. Once his was alight as well, he sat back in his armchair. Corrigan felt more at ease. They could converse and yet the distance between them crossed no awkward boundaries. She inhaled and was pleasantly surprised by the menthol flavour on top of the tobacco. This was like no cigarette she'd ever had. Better than the furtive Woodbine with Richie Charlton as she quickly pulled her knickers up and re-buttoned her blouse, behind the brick kilns.

'If I may be so bold, you seem quite content with the world?'

She jumped. He was speaking to her and she had slipped into a semi-trance brought on by tiredness, a full stomach and the warm crackling fire.

'Forgive me, I startled you.' The man made a slight bow at the waist and as he did so both eyes momentarily closed a fraction. His eyes looked limpid behind his glasses which were perfectly round in shape. Corrigan thought they did not quite suit his face and noticed that one eye looked slightly wider than the other and there was a slight red mark above and below this eye as through it had been rubbed by something hard and this had left an impression on the skin. He probably did something awfully clever with microscopes or perhaps looked through a telescope all day and it had bruised his skin.

Daisy however, was taking no notice of the man and was now busying herself with her little bag of eggs or beads or whatever it was she had in that draw string bag. As long as it kept her quiet and distracted.

'I could not help noticing a smile on that pretty face of yours.' He flapped a limp wrist as he spoke and puffed a stream of scented smoke towards the ceiling.

Oh God, he's a pansy. Corrigan realised she could smell a sweet, floral scent that was different from the cigarettes as the man adjusted his position in his chair and fussed with the lie of the cuff on his startlingly white shirt. She was sure he was. Not that she'd ever met one. But she'd heard about them as the men at work sometimes made comments about how disgusting it was and the tell-tale signs to look out for. She gave a vague smile by way of a reply.

The thought suddenly struck her that if he really was a pansy, then he was perfectly safe. She was certainly in no mood for men drooling over her, but male company for an hour or so was welcome, even useful. She was aware that she and her daughter stood out as unusual in this room filled with middle-aged couples and stiff businessmen nursing their balloon glasses of brandy. It might help her blend in to be sitting – not too close of course – with an intelligent and well-dressed gentleman who could have no carnal interest in her.

'I was just enjoying the fire and remembering the meal we had. The lamb was good.' She could not think what else to say.

'They always deliver a fine spread here. Even in those trying times of coupon-counting and rationing they managed to pull out all the stops!' His watery eye widened a fraction. 'I always stay at the Midland. I would not dream of seeking an alternative when in town. May I ask, is this your first time with the establishment?' He paused. 'Forgive me, my questions are too intrusive! My natural inquisitiveness has let my mouth run away without pausing to consider your wish for privacy. Forgive me.'

Corrigan laughed. 'Not at all.' She realised how much she wanted to talk to a grown up, someone adult to offer welcome distraction. More than that, she realised she could say what she liked to this stranger. It could be the truth or half-truths. Or down-right lies. It wouldn't matter. They'd never meet again. It was time she started to create a new version of herself, a reinterpretation of the woman she'd been that morning but could never be again. If she and Daisy were going to live in expensive hotels and travel from one city to another then she was going to need a story. An explanation that would deflect suspicion. Now would be a good time to start practising a few white lies to see how they fitted.

'It is our first visit. I rather hope it may not be our last. We find it most - welcoming.' Corrigan was feeling her way forward. So far so good. But what next? If he asked her who Daisy's father was, what should she say? Why were they both here in Manchester without her husband? She needed to start imagining a new background story.

They smoked and exchanged non-committal comments for a while. It was almost as though this effete man with the perfect manners and limp wrist knew not to press her too hard on anything awkward or too intrusive. Or perhaps he was skilled in the art of conversation and knew when to draw back and not stray into being considered inquisitive. Corrigan felt under no pressure to give much away and she felt herself relax with this unchallenging conversation. He in turn said a lot in his flowery and fancy manner, but it was 'everything and nothing,' and whilst she listened she learned nothing definite. She was unclear what line of work he was in, although she learned a lot about his constant travelling for business, and whilst she knew he lived in a fine place in London, the location remained vague although she could probably describe some of the fabrics and ornaments he collected in exact detail. He suggested they took a glass of wine and clicked his fingers and a waiter duly delivered almost before she had time to refuse. A Coca Cola was supplied for Daisy who sat contentedly sucking the fizzy drink through a straw.

Mr Jones, as he called himself, was easy company. He smiled at Daisy and politely batted back some of the little girl's questions in a manner that suggested he was sympathetic towards small children. He even managed to laugh convincingly when Daisy suddenly announced that he looked like an owl. Corrigan flushed red with embarrassment, but no offence seemed to be taken.

She felt strangely secure in his presence. It had been her intention that Daisy and she retire early to their room, but the chance to smoke a second fine cigarette and drink a glass of excellent wine was alluring. However, she now needed to visit the ladies. Daisy was deep into telling a rambling and utterly incomprehensible story about Dolly and her adventures. Mr Jones was patient and polite, nodding and smiling and saying, 'Oh golly gosh' and 'well I never' at appropriate moments. He too appeared relaxed and was indulging Daisy, who was clearly revelling in the attention. Corrigan knew she was often guilty of closing her ears and barely taking notice when Daisy got into one of her interminable tales. It was good for her to have different adult company. Male company. Something she'd hardly ever experienced.

Corrigan pushed aside all common sense and caution, perhaps aided by the large glass of wine which took the edge from her guard. 'Mr Jones, would it be an awful imposition if I asked you keep Daisy amused whilst I go and powder my nose? I will be straight back.' Looking at Daisy, 'Mummy will be back before you even know I've gone.'

Daisy looked unconcerned. 'Yes Mummy. Then Dolly said...' Her interminable story recommenced almost without interruption.

'It would be a pleasure and a privilege. Have no fear, Daisy will not leave my sight for one moment!' Mr Jones' honeyed words dripped, and he gave her a winning smile.

How that look would haunt her.

* * * *

The sofa was empty. Devoid of any clue that a little girl had been there save for the almost empty glass of Coca Cola with a striped paper straw that had been chewed at the end on the table. The wingback armchair Mr Jones had been occupying was also unoccupied. Even the newspaper was missing. That was an odd detail. Corrigan looked from one to the other, stupidly. It was clear as day that neither Daisy or Mr Jones were still there, but blind panic and almost heart-stopping fear gripped her so hard she could not properly comprehend, let alone accept the possibility they were gone. In those first terrible moments as she felt like she was being dropped in a vat of icy cold water. Stupidly she found herself wondering why the man had taken his newspaper along with her daughter. Why did he need his paper?

She stumbled and staggered about the room as if she were inebriated, staring into the startled faces of everyone she encountered. She could hear a strange whimpering sound like a small dog in severe pain, then realised it was she who was making the sound.

'Daisy? Have you see Daisy? Oh, please God, you must have! She was sitting there with the man...'

The room started to murmur with a contrasting mixture of the irate wondering what that mad woman was banging on about and the concerned. A waiter took her gently by the arm, the barman paused in polishing a glass and listened, then lifted a phone to the front desk.

A terrible howling wail of pain filled the room and stilled conversation. Heads turned, glasses were placed back on tables. A newspaper dropped to a knee.

A rush of people to help as the young woman collapsed in a heap onto the carpet. Frantic conversations at the front desk whilst a brandy and a cup of sweetened tea were found.

Staff running up and down stairs and along corridors. A back door was found swinging free, the tiny drift of snow already gathering on the floor just inside. Two sets of footprints rapidly being masked by fresh, heavy snow, one set small, that of a child. A piece of paper lay close by with a terse typed message:

We have the girl.
You have what we want.
Do as we instruct and the girl lives.

Chapter Forty-One

Graham Hind sat behind the plain wooden table in the interview room, his shoulders hunched, head dropped as if seeking comfort and protection from his shirt collar. He was staring at the tin mug of tea in front of him, looking a perfect picture of misery. His right leg was twitching nervously. He didn't look like a man with much fight left in him. The duty solicitor beside him stared equally unenthusiastically at his legal pad upon which he'd written a few remarks. Despite his best efforts at stoic professionalism, he looked like a man who knew Hind's defence was built wholly on sand, towards which, a tidal wave of seawater was fast approaching.

'Mr Hind. We searched your digs and we found these.' Trinder placed two crisp ten-pound notes upon the table between them. 'Freshly minted by the look of them. Hardly a mark or a crease and an awful lot of money for a lowly member of a track gang to keep in an envelope stuffed behind the cistern in the outside privy. Can you tell me how you came by such riches?'

'I don't know nothing about that money.'

'Really? Well your landlady certainly didn't and was deeply shocked at the discovery.'

'Someone else put it there!'

'It was a shared toilet. Anyone using it could be responsible.' The solicitor suggested.

'We also searched your room. My men crawled all over the place, indoors and out and took everything apart. Your landlady has served notice on you as a result. A shame, but that's what you get for being dishonest.'

'You have no right to cause such unwarranted distress to my client!'

'Actually, talking of warrants, that was exactly what we had. Warrants to search both Mr Hind's property and that of his friend and colleague, the recently deceased Mr George Baylock. And guess what we found in his place?' Trinder was about to deliver the knock-out punch. He silently laid another pair of notes on the table. 'Equally new. And would you believe it, these four notes are all in number sequence. Now what are the odds of that?'

The solicitor's mouth opened and closed like a fish. Hind said nothing but his shoulder's sagged even lower.

'This money was not honestly earned, Mr Hind. You know that, I know that and your learned friend sitting beside you knows that -.'

'Pure conjecture! You cannot put words in my client's mouth, let alone mine!'

Trinder gently waved the solicitor's complaints away. 'Let's not play silly games and waste time. You were on the take, so let's cut the play-acting and have a proper grown-up talk, man to man.' Trinder's voice was soft and easy-going. 'No-one tramping a weed-infested, underused little branch line tightening fishplate bolts earns this kind of dosh. That's a fact. Even if they did, they don't stuff it behind the cistern in a shared toilet. Nor for that matter do they rent a shabby room in a shabby house with a battle-axe landlady.' The solicitor took a breath as if about to launch into another defence of his client, but Hind effectively stopped him by muttering, 'It started 'cos I wanted a scooter. To get to work that bit easier.'

His solicitor almost groaned aloud.

'And you were lured into some illicit money-making scheme?'

'Something like that.'

'I suspected as much.' Trinder actually smiled. 'Look, Mr Hind, it may surprise you, but I have a suspicion you didn't kill Jane Palmer.'

'I never! You can't say I did. I never laid a finger on her except to try and help keep her warm, I swear to it!'

'I feel inclined to believe you. Cigarette?' Trinder shook the carton of Black Cats to release a couple. 'Go on.'

Hind took one and mumbled something but kept his head down as he leaned forward to accept a light. Trinder lit his own. WPC Benson and the solicitor were not offered one. This was all part of Trinder's strategy. He wanted to form a bond with Hind. Get him to open up and confess.

'In situations like this, we are, as your learned friend next to you can confirm, able to cut you a little slack. You see, I think you got yourself into something that earned a bit of pocket money on the side. Am I right? Both you, and your friend Mr Baylock were in on it.'

Hind looked at Trinder, his face pale and he swallowed, but he also nodded agreement.

'He might have led you on. Encouraged you. He was the older man after all. Did he make promises that it would be easy money and there'd be no – unpleasantness. Yes?'

Hind smoked but his eyes betrayed him. He looked on the edge of speaking.

'Now, we're not here to talk about these lovely twenty-pound notes lying here. Not directly. We're interested in why a poor crossing keeper was brutally murdered.' Hind was pale as a bed sheet. 'We're in a position, where, frankly -,' Trinder deliberately smoked slowly, keeping the words hanging in the air, '- where in return for complete honesty, we can help improve your situation. You are in trouble, but there are many levels of trouble and I feel sure we could improve your situation.'

They both smoked. The solicitor's pencil made scratching sounds on paper. The solicitor then whispered something in Hind's ear. Hind nodded, gratefully.

'I didn't kill her. I swear to God.'

'So, just supposing we accept that you didn't, how about telling us exactly what *did* happen. It would help your cause to be fully co-operative. If we discover that you lied to us now, that could put you in a very tight spot indeed.' Trinder gave an encouraging look.

'It was Georgie. He suggested it. A few months back.'

'That would be George Baylock?' Benson asked.

'Yeah. He told me that Old Janey could pay us a bit extra. All we had to do was collect and deliver stuff.'

'What kind of "stuff?"'

'I dunno, we never looked. We knew not to. Packets. Small things. Parcels taped and tied up so they'd know if they'd been opened.'

'Who are "they"?'

'The people who pay for the stuff, but I don't know who they are.'

'You didn't meet these people?'

'Never. I wouldn't know if I had, if you see what I mean.'

Trinder smiled in a kindly manner. 'How did you know where to collect the goods and where to take it?'

'Georgie looked after all that side of things. I think Old Janey told him. We went to funny places that were hard to find and there was what we had to fetch and carry waiting and we put in our knapsacks or jacket pockets and then as we passed Janey's place –.'

'Black Spinney Crossing?' Benson wanted clarification.

'Yeah. She took it and gave us payment.'

'Twenty pounds?' Trinder was sceptical.

'No! Nothing like that. A quid per delivery. Tops. Sometimes less.'

'So where did this money come from?'

Hind paused and licked his cracked lips. 'The bloke gave us it. To keep quiet.'

'What bloke?' Trinder looked serious. They were getting to the important part now.

'I dunno who the Hell he was. He was there and suddenly he was saying how we'd killed her and we hadn't. But he said he'd fix it on us and...'

'Take it slowly. I need to understand the sequence of events.'

'That morning we had to get to Desford sharpish. Georgie said we had a delivery to make. We clocked on as usual and then slipped off, quiet like a bit previous to get down the line in good time. We made a show saying good morning and all that to a few of the lads so they'd remember we was there then were off.' He shrugged his shoulders.

'What time was this?' Benson was making notes.

'Not long after four.' Hind finished his cigarette and drained his tea. 'We got to Janey's place but there was summat wrong. She was sitting on the ground outside and looked in a bad way. She was acting all strange and confused and was not making sense.'

The solicitor perked up and was writing furiously.

'Are you saying that Jane Palmer was alive when you and George Baylock arrived at her crossing?' Trinder asked.

'Yes! I just told you! She was alive but in poor shape. She was sitting in the cold with a hand on her neck and mumbling. Gibberish stuff about Father Christmas. It was all a bit weird to be honest. We tried to help her stand but she was wobbly on her feet and next thing she fell down, right sudden with a thump. She was on her back on the ground.'

'She fell over and the fall killed her?' Benson queried.

'No. There's more. We were worried about her. Honest. And a bit anxious, because we had some stuff to deliver. We knew we had to hand it over or else there'd be trouble. But she was not making any sense. Then suddenly this fella appears. Standing in the doorway of her cottage and he says 'Gotcha' Red handed!' and he starts to laugh.'

'There was someone else at the crossing apart from Baylock and Palmer?' Trinder and Benson exchanged excited looks. The solicitor was also all ears.

'I never seen him before. A sharp looking fella with a London accent. He looked mean and very angry. He looked like he could handle himself as well. He said we'd robbed her and attacked her. We told him that was not true, but then he said he knew who we were and what we were doing there. Said we were 'dumb mules' and shouldn't mess with what we don't know about.'

'And you had not seen this man before?'

'Never clapped eyes on him before. But he said he knew we were carrying a delivery. He frightened the life out of us. And he was saying we'd attacked Janey.'

'There were two of you, one of him. Did you not think to overpower him and turn him over to us?'

'He started talking. He knew all about us. He even said if we tried anything on he'd sell us down the river and we believed him. I mean, we *were* up to no good. And if we killed him, how were we going to explain that? He said that the real bosses, the big men who ran the operations would be after us if we tried any funny stuff. They'd get us wherever we went.' Hind rubbed his temples and looked green. 'And it's true. Georgie's dead! They nobbled him.'

'That's why complete honesty now will be the best. We can protect you. Tell me what happened next?'

'This fella was angry, saying that something really valuable was missing.

He'd come to collect it and not only was it gone, but Janey had been assaulted. He tore into us. Next thing, Janey starts mumbling and raving and this man starts shouting at her. Demanding where the stones are.'

'Stones?' Trinder sat upright.

'That's what he said.'

'What do you think he meant?'

'No idea. I don't know anything about no stones.'

'What did Palmer say?'

'She was rambling. Saying all sorts of weird stuff. Next thing we know this bloke is waving a bloody axe at in her face. Threatening her.'

'An axe or a mattock?'

'Er...yeah, maybe it was a mattock. A garden tool anyway. I think he had it in his hand the whole time, but I can't really remember. Next thing I know, he hits her. Whack! Just like that. He bloody well kills her. Christ. It was horrible.' Hind shook his head in disbelief. 'Right in front of us. There was no warning. He looked savage. Then he chucks the mattock in the grass under the window and would you believe it, he smiles and says we're part of the murder. Says we're in it up the here.' Hind put a hand next to his neck. 'Says we're going to prison or worse unless we help him sort things.'

'What did the three of you do next?' Trinder asked.

'He pulls out this great wad of money. Fresh banknotes, Jesus, there must have been hundreds. He peels off twenty each for me and Georgie. Blood money he calls it. We took it. I mean, I didn't know what I was doing. I was all over the place. I thought I was going to sick. I took it. I was scared, and so was Georgie. Then he says he needs time to get away and think what to do to sort this mess out. Says we should act as though we've just arrived and found her dead. Tells u we have to call the police and act innocent and nobody would ever know, as he'd keep his trap shut and that was a promise. If we all played our part we'd be OK. But if we blabbed our mouths off it would not be the police we should be worrying about. Then he was gone.'

'You believed him?'

'What choice did I have? We never said a word. Leastways, I never. But someone killed Georgie. They got him, didn't they?'

'We're still investigating his death. It could be an accident.'

'Fat chance!'

'What did you do after this mysterious man left the scene?'

'We realised that to make the story look better we should arrive later. By later, I mean after the first train had gone down. Otherwise people might start to ask questions why were we there so early. We had no choice but to make this look good. Georgie has a long black coat and said if he wears the old woman's tin hat, in the dark nobody would tell the difference from Old Janey. He could probably fool the train crew. So, we drag her inside and he takes her hat and I open up the section whilst he gets ready to open the gates.'

'You communicated with Desford Junction box to open up and then accept a train?' Benson was sceptical.

'No problem.'

'How is that possible?' Trinder also looked surprised.

'Before I got a transfer here I worked at Groby Quarry. I was the points man. You know, a kind of signalman working the signals and ground frames there. I know my way around. And my dad is a signalman up Burton-on-Trent way. I spent years sitting in there watching and learning. I know the drill, especially on a tiddly place like Black Spinney.' Hind almost looked pleased with himself.

Trinder looked at Benson. 'Driver Charlton and the guard would only get an imperfect view of a figure in a long black coat with a distinctive tin helmet on their head.'

'With no reason to doubt who it was, they'd think it was her,' Benson agreed.

'After the train went through, what did you do?' Trinder continued.

'We closed the gates. Told the box the train had passed. Put her helmet back on her head, then gave it half an hour before phoning through to say we'd just arrived and found the old lady dying. Once you lot had finished and sent us back down to Desford we ditched the packets of whatever it was we were delivering to her in the brook along the way. Good riddance!'

* * * *

'Mr Charlton, I'm not going to waste time with the niceties.' Vignoles sat down opposite the engine driver. 'I don't have time to waste on someone like you. No, I shall rephrase that; the quicker we get little Daisy Corrigan back safe and alive, the sooner we can all breathe easier.'

Both Charlton and the solicitor stared back at Vignoles.

'Are you telling me you know nothing about Rachel Corrigan's little girl being taken hostage?'

'What? How could I?' Charlton stared at Vignoles then licked his dry lips. 'I was too busy being arrested and holed up in here!'

'For you to say that, you would need to know at what time she was abducted.'

The solicitor staring at his client with a look of extreme consternation.

'Well I never had nothing to do with it. I'd never hurt Daisy. I swear to God I wouldn't.'

'I'm glad to hear that, because I can advise you going to prison for taking a young girl and mistreating her is to be avoided at any cost. Some crimes offer no protection in prison. None of this 'honour amongst thieves' rubbish when it comes to hurting children.' Vignoles was cold and stern and glared at Charlton with unblinking eyes.

'Neither my client nor I are aware of this new development and my clients' assertion that he was incarcerated in a holding cell would seem to count against his involvement unless you can provide strong evidence to suggest otherwise...'

'Spare it. We need to get the little girl back and every minute is precious.'

'I have nothing to do with this!'

'But you have a lot to do with her mother, Rachel. And her grandmother, Jane Palmer. You are very much involved, Mr Charlton. You are right at the heart of all this.' Vignoles leaned closer across the table. 'Right this minute, I want to know what you've been up to. On the night in question and in the days leading up your assault on Mrs Palmer. You might not have taken Daisy, but you have information that might help bring her back alive.' Vignoles waited a beat. 'Unless you want her death on your conscience, speak up!'

'You are over-stepping the line, Detective Inspector.'

'Am I? Then I hope your precious law books offer you sufficient comfort if the worst happens to that little girl!' Vignoles turned back to

Charlton. 'It's time to come clean. You've got yourself into something deeper than you intended. You're no kidnapper, but someone's taken an innocent victim because of actions by others. Get talking.'

Charlton scratched the back of his head then rubbed his eyes as if trying to scrub away the reality of where he was. He looked for help from his solicitor, who had paled and appeared to be wondering exactly what kind of man he was defending. Vignoles knew the solicitor had twin daughters. He was not a particularly pleasant man, but he was a father and had been stung by the chilling news. The solicitor gave a slight nod of the head. 'I think it wise to offer any information that might help to ensure her safety.'

Charlton took a deep breath, looked up at the ceiling as if seeking support then started talking.

* * * *

Badger, Vignoles and Trinder were corralled in Vignoles' office. The air was blue with tobacco smoke, the desk littered with empty cups. Half-eaten sandwiches lay abandoned. Hunger was taking hold and yet nobody could swallow the sliced white bread and ham. Anxiety was almost palpable in the air.

'We're convinced Charlton did not kill Palmer?' Badger was slumped uncharacteristically in a chair, his tie loosened and the top button of his shirt undone. Clear signs he was worried.

'Yes. Charlton gave us a full confession. He slipped out of the house once the children were in bed and leaving his wife snoozing soundly beside the fire. He took with him this cardboard Father Christmas mask they had bought the Saturday before.' Vignoles indicated the item in question.

'To disguise his face?'

'Correct. He waited until Palmer had allowed the last train through and closed the section for the night. She was outside, and he approached her and struck her once from behind as she retreated towards the safety of her cottage.'

'Using the mattock discovered on site?'

'Yes. He was familiar with the tool shed and could readily find this in the dark. He had previously, a few days earlier used this to kill a sick rabbit and this inspired his initial defence. His boot prints found on the scene back up the movements he describes. He says the first blow was cushioned by her helmet and he needed to hit her twice again to render her unconscious. Which was the plan.'

'A plan hatched by Charlton and Corrigan.' Trinder added.

'To do what?' Badger wanted everything clear in his mind.

'To stage a breaking and entry. It had to look like a convincing ransacking of the premises, the idea being that we would confirm that a robber had perhaps speculatively forced entry and searched and removed anything of value. Palmer lived on site and was almost never away, they had to knock her out first.'

'But Corrigan had already taken the money and was in Liverpool at the time of the assault?' Badger queried.

'Correct. Charlton was acting on her behalf. He wanted to help her as she was in a rotten job, in a cramped little cottage and with few prospects.'

'What a kind-hearted fellow,' Badger snorted with derision.

'He's steadfastly denying sexual relations with Corrigan.'

Trinder also now made an expression of disgust.

'He's lying.' Badger dismissed this with a gesture. 'If he thinks a jury will believe he'd do all that just to be friendly to the young woman, then he's naïve.'

'I think she leaned on him, sir.' Trinder chipped in. 'She held all the cards. Do this for me or else I tell your wife, or words to that effect.'

Badger grunted assent.

'It was enough to ensure his compliance,' Vignoles continued. 'He ransacked the place, ensuring the locked draw in Palmer's bedroom is forced and takes some worthless items and discards these to help reinforce the faked crime scene.'

'Did we ever recover the Irish linen?'

'Probably blown by the winds across the fields and lying in a ditch covered in snow by now. The spoons were found by a passing tramp.'

'But how on earth does this lead us to that poor little girl being kidnapped!' Badger was getting impatient. He was trying to concentrate on the investigation, but his mind was crowding with imagined horrors being inflicted on Daisy.

'Corrigan took a considerable sum of cash held secretly by Palmer. The old lady traded in valuable stolen goods and probably handled 'hot' money. Once recovered from her assault Palmer would not be able to report the true loss. The Rachel and Daisy Corrigan would move away using their illicitly gained funds and Charlton could go back to his wife.'

'But Palmer died.'

'But not by the hand of Charlton,' Vignoles continued. 'Charlton hurried home, slipped in without anyone stirring and presumably went to bed and tried to sleep. Except he couldn't sleep. The adrenaline was pumping; he was feeling remorse for assaulting a friend.'

Badger shook his head dismissively and impatiently flapped a hand.

'But even worse for Charlton, he realised he'd dropped the Father Christmas mask. It was evidence and he needed to retrieve it. He had to find this mask before daylight and the alarm was raised by a sore-headed Palmer. But he was hampered by the knock up lad who was due and it was important he gave the lad a sign that he was up and ready to go to work. If he was not in there was every chance Chambers would knock and wake the household. Things were starting to spin out of control, so Charlton dithered and planned a ruse to allow him to sprint to Black Spinney and get back on shed before his engine was due off.'

'The forgotten knife?' Badger asked.

'Yes. He came on shed, spoke to his fireman then made a fuss about forgetting this essential tool. It was dumb enough to sound plausible. Charlton left the shed and sprinted towards Black Spinney. It's possible for a fit man to do it. But as he approached, careful to avoid being seen by Palmer who would be up and about, he was shocked to see two men outside the cottage apparently helping Palmer who was lying on the ground.'

'The platelayers?' Badger asked.

'Yes. Hind has given a confession that fits this story,' Trinder added.

'Charlton claims he heard the men talking to her. He swears Palmer was alive.'

'You believe him?'

'Hind's statement backs this up.'

'Charlton sees Palmer apparently receiving attention for the blow to her head. She appears to be recovering. His plan is working - aside from the missing mask.' Badger was thinking it through.

'But he can't look for the mask with those men close by and time is short. He retreats along the road, observed by Chambers, then clambers through the hedge and makes his way to the shed beside the railway line.'

'And is hailed by the signalwoman as he does so,' Trinder added.

'He returns to his engine and by 4.30am he is steaming through the crossing. Charlton distracts his fireman, then looks across to see how everything is playing out. Instead of police and an ambulance, he glimpses Palmer in her helmet going about her business. Surprising perhaps, but he's not going to complain. He no doubt feels like he's accomplished his part of the deal. They proceed to West Wharf and Charlton thinks everything is OK, until he hears the shocking news that Palmer is dead.'

'Sitting at West Wharf he has time to chew over the mess he's in, and think about the dirty great boot prints he's left all over the place,' Trinder added.

Badger slapped his hand hard on the desk. 'All well and good. He cheated on his wife, committed GBH and aided and abetted the theft of ill-gotten gains. But why is that little girl being held ransom? Give me some answers!'

'Charlton is a side show. This is really about Palmer and her illegal activities. She was holding something desirable. Something worth even more than the considerable sum of cash Corrigan had taken.'

'How do you know that?'

'Hind and Baylock were accosted by an unidentified man as they were trying to help Palmer. He'd been inside the cottage and presumably searching it. He knew they were carrying illicit goods for Palmer and threatened them, accusing them of taking what he'd come for.'

'He even paid them a decent wedge from a stash of ready cash he was carrying to cover got his presence, laced with ominous threats if they didn't comply,' Trinder added.

'Who is this man?' Badger asked.

'We have no idea, nor where he is,' Vignoles was unhappy with this admission. 'But he's the third man present at the murder of Palmer.'

'Like in the film...'

'Humph! Then we'll call him Mr Welles.' Badger's jaw was set firm.

'You think Welles has taken Daisy?'

'Yes.' Vignoles removed his glasses and rubbed the bridge of his nose. 'Palmer was holding something of considerable value. Corrigan took her money – but perhaps she also took something else? Mr Welles with the London accent did not travel up here in the dead of night to relieve her of the cash as he was carrying what sounds like an even more considerable sum. Corrigan had taken what he wanted. Leaving one very angry man, who killed Palmer in a last-ditch attempt to get her to explain what had happened.'

'Welles killed Baylock? Was he trying to get him to confess?' Badger asked.

'It's possible. I think neither Baylock or Hind had any idea, but perhaps Welles went back to try and squeeze out a confession. Welles then changes tack and tracks Rachel and Daisy Corrigan. He takes Daisy and leaves the note, hoping Corrigan will do a swap?'

'He thinks she has what he wants and is prepared to trade the girl's life for it.' Trinder looked sombre.

Badger stood up. 'Damn the man to Hell and back! We've got Corrigan under arrest in the Midland Hotel?'

'Yes. The local force stepped in and have uniforms and plain clothes covering the building. The kidnapper will presumably send his next order through the hotel.'

'But the fly in the ointment is that Corrigan has no more idea what Welles wants than we do?'

'No, sir.' Vignoles looked equally exasperated. 'She's confessed to everything she knows – the money, the plot to stage the robbery and her dalliances with Charlton. But has no idea what it is Welles wants. The only good news is that she has given us a good description of the Mr Jones, aka Welles, the man who took Daisy.'

'We throw a ring of steel around Manchester. Roads, rail and the ship canal. We mobilise everyone and anyone. All leave cancelled!' Badger was pacing around the office. 'He's made mistakes. Mistakes in allowing us such a good description, and he can't go far with a young girl in tow. And he needs to stay close to make the exchange. Get a photograph of Daisy and a pen-picture of Welles to every station, every signal box, every guard on every line leading out of Manchester. I'll put the City Police and those in the surrounding townships on high alert. We've lost hours, but no more. My bet is he's lying low in Manchester. Well? What are you waiting for!'

Chapter Forty-Two

It was probably anxiety working on his imagination, but Vignoles was sure he could see in the faces of the station staff at Manchester Central a similar level of heightened tension. The drawn faces, the eyes restlessly casting backwards and forwards across the great spread of platforms beneath the magnificent over-arching train shed. The porters leaning on their trolleys, watching each passenger with suspicious glances. The station master in his formal attire complete with top hat was strutting about like a crow, his movements sharp and sudden; spinning about on his squeakily clean leather soled shoes and changing direction with no obvious reason to do so. He was restless and felt the need to walk to try and quell the churning in his stomach. The guard standing at the back of his train that was soon to depart for Marylebone, was staring with piercing blue gannet-like eyes at every small child and their innocent parents as they passed.

Every child drew stares and knitted brows and with the schools breaking up for the holidays, there were plenty of children to be seen. Parents gave stern and reproving looks in return, uncomfortable at the unwarranted glares their child seemed to be garnering. One large lady in a shocking lilac coat and matching hat found the ticket inspector's insistence on knowing her daughter's name infuriating and a scene erupted as cross words were exchanged. The ticket inspector offered a weak apology, unwilling to discuss the true reason for his interest. Lilac hat and coat stomped off, daughter almost dragged behind, fortuitously uncomprehending of the real reasons that lay behind the encounter.

Vignoles drew again on his pipe and returned to looking, watching, waiting. It was almost certainly a futile task as they had mobilised as many railway employees as feasible in a catchment area over a hundred miles around Manchester, including the ferry ports. The main lines to London, Glasgow and Scotland and down towards Bristol and the South West were in readiness. The eyes of many hundreds of railway employees were looking for Daisy and her abductor. Motorcycle patrols were roaring along the roads around Manchester and the Cheshire plain.

'Call the hounds out and put the fox on the run!' That had been Badger's description and it was apt. The local police forces had willingly weighed in to help. There was something about the taking of a little girl that cut across boundaries, threw budgetry caution to the wind and mobilised everyone in the desire to bring her home safely.

'Make as much noise about it as you can. All bells and whistles and make it obvious we're on the trail of the nasty piece of work responsible. Get their nerves jangling. Force them from cover as we can reel them in once they go on the run.'

It was as good a plan as anyone could conceive and at least everyone could lend a hand. Vignoles stood impatiently outside the Stationmaster's office, ready to be called back if any news came in or to jump aboard a departing train if so needed. He felt he had to do something. Anything. He could not just sit and state at a silent black Bakelite telephone willing it to ring.

With so many on the lookout, it had to be just a matter of time.

But how much time did they have?

Just one terse call to Rachel Corrigan had been the only communication to date. The message had been stark. 'You know what we want. Hand it over, or Daisy suffers. Wait for our next call.'

Corrigan was accompanied by trained officers from the Manchester City police and was practically under house arrest. Everyone had picked up on the words 'we' and 'our'. There were two or more abductors. A team who meant business. A gang. It was an unsettling realisation. A criminal gang might be more inclined to violence. As each hour passed, the options for the kidnappers were becoming more limited, but that in turn meant that Daisy was an increasing liability. And worst of all, the police had nothing to offer in exchange. Corrigan was utterly distraught but adamant she had no idea what was being demanded of her. It as an appalling impasse.

Chapter Forty-Two

A whistle blew and a B1 locomotive named after an obscure African breed of gazelle, answered back. An all stopping train to Sheffield huffed into motion. Vignoles barely looked. He was still staring at every face, at every small child. Wondering. Analysing. Had they disguised Daisy? Put her in boy's clothes and a schoolboy cap? Cut her hair and coloured it? Anything was possible. He could not endure the idea that she might slip past his nose undetected. How would he forgive himself?

The same feelings were being replicated across the railway. Trinder paced up and down Liverpool Lime Street, acutely aware that the probability of stumbling upon Daisy and her abductors was minute. He too was within hailing distance of an office, ready to answer a call when it came. He concentrated on watching the station staff bustling about with more energy and drive than usual, knowing that each pair of eyes was focussed on the same objective. He'd not told Violet the real reason he was in Liverpool. He knew it would upset her. He wished this could all be over, and he could hurry back home to see Robbie. He tweaked the brim of his hat a touch lower and pulled the scarf a bit higher over his mouth. It was foolish, but he felt better keeping his face partially covered. That was the risk one took in this business. He dealt with cruel men with no morals who'd not think twice about hurting his own family if they thought it would advance their needs.

That depressing fact made him wonder about the Detective Inspector role he'd just accepted. Was he crazy? Was he just placing himself and his family in even more danger? Trinder moved his shoulders and paced aggressively around the broad station concourse with its giant clock face high overhead on the train shed curtain wall. He really had to stop worrying about things that had not yet happened and may never happen.

WPC Benson was seated on a platform bench at Sheffield Victoria, cold to the bone but determined to stay put and watchful. The station was quiet with few people about, but that was no reason to drop her guard. She sat and watched and waited and her feet started to complain with the biting Pennine cold. The snow fell harder. A goods train clanked past, the locomotive caked in snow around the front buffer beam and over the tender. Each loaded coal wagon looked like it had been decorated with Royal Icing on a Christmas cake.

WPC Lansdowne was at Chester General. Vignoles had advised her this was a busy junction with lines branching off to the four points of the compass, yet within striking distance of Manchester - and Rachel Corrigan. Chester offered a variety of options for escape routes, perhaps into Mid-Wales or southwards down the Welsh Marches through regions peppered with small halts and sleepy country stations. Farmhouses high in the hills or unseen down snow-filled lanes would make the perfect hide out and opinion seemed to favour this as a likely option. Trains were surprisingly frequent, entering the station from all directions and keeping Lansdowne and the station staff on their toes.

However, the wind off the Cheshire plain was cutting like a freshly sharpened knife. Lansdowne was shivering, and chilblains were forming on her toes. Her eyes watered but she stood and stared and prayed. *Please God, don't let them do anything to her.*

The hands on the station clocks crawled. Time passed interminably slowly.

A signal dropped and the Tannoy crackled. A train was announced. Lansdowne paced the long platform once again, her feet complaining with the constant pounding on the unforgiving surface and the attentions of Jack Frost. She listened to the perfectly enunciated vowels of the woman reading out the train details and watched as a man in uniform selected a long black painted wooden board with white letters that listed the next stations along the line. This one was coming from Wales and Lansdowne felt her shoulders sag. That was unlikely to bring good news. Nevertheless, duty compelled her to stand and watch the green engine with its brightly shining copper and brass details steam merrily into the platform and come to a halt. It bore a long name of a grange, located somewhere in Wales by the sound of it, but Lansdowne gave it no more than a cursory glance. Her eyes eagerly scanned the passengers disembarking. She realised she was holding her breath. There was a boy in shorts, but he had ginger hair and freckles and was too old. The boy sprinted towards her and then ran on past, without giving her a glance. He shouted out the locomotive name to his mother, who walked behind.

Lansdowne turned away. She felt a sudden jolt of anger welling up inside. Someone had broken Rachel Corrigan's heart by taking her innocent little girl. Whatever Corrigan had been up to, Daisy did not deserve this, nor did her mother. Nobody should endure this torment. Lansdowne was once again fighting down the sense of frustration that all this standing around was futile.

A telephone rang in the porter's room close by. This was her point of contact with the greater railway network. A young porter with a bright red nose stood at the doorway. 'Miss Constable,' He stumbled over her title.

'What is it?' Lansdowne fired back. She was in no mood for foolish young men.

'There's a call, miss. On the phone. For you.'

'Is it news?' She realised stress was making her sound harsh. She ran towards the door and barged past the young porter who had to hold onto his cap to prevent it falling off. She grabbed the heavy receiver that smelt atrociously of years of sour spittle. 'WPC Lansdowne. Yes? What can you tell me? Yes... Her name... That sounds like her!' *Please let it be her.* 'Is she unhurt...? Where are you now...? Don't let her out of your sight for one second! Hold the train... Don't let anyone leave... I don't care if you're blocking the line or if they're kicking up a fuss! The train does not move and that's an order!' Lansdowne didn't care if she hadn't the authority to deliver this command. This was no time to pussy-footing about. 'We're on our way.'

Lansdowne realised that silent tears were streaming down her cheeks. The young porter was shuffling his feet and staring at her with a confused expression.

'Was that good or bad, miss?'

Lansdowne stared at him, cheeks streaked wet. She hurriedly blew her nose. 'Sorry. Foolish me.' Then she beamed her broadest smile. 'That was good news. Very good news!'

Chapter Forty-Three

The Great Central Hotel had seen better days and was run by an infamously crotchety landlord who appeared to regard with suspicion almost everyone who dared set foot inside the place. His loyal customers were treated only marginally better, receiving stony glares and monosyllabic replies to enquiries about his good health, although he might vary this with the occasional rant about business, the weather, the Government, the railways and anything else he could find in the popular press to moan about. However, for all the failings of both building and landlord, it was warm and close to Leicester Central; nestling as it did hard against the elevated course of the railway on the junction between Soar Lane and Great Central Street. The over-riding saving grace – at least in the eyes of Vignoles and Trinder – was that it served a fabulously good pint of Everards. The local brew was a favourite of both men. Furthermore, as the Hotel was rarely full, it made an excellent alternate meeting place where work could be chewed over with the welcome help of some alcoholic lubrication to get ideas rolling more freely and little chance of being overheard. It also meant that newly promoted Detective Inspector John Trinder could take over the place at a modest cost and cause little inconvenience to what passing trade dared risk entering the premises.

Violet Trinder and Anna Vignoles, with help from Benson and Lansdowne, had strung up paper chains from the nicotine-coloured ceiling and added a few more Christmassy garlands to the shabby rooms to try and lend them some welcome cheer. They also strung a shiny gold banner that declared 'CONGRATULATIONS JOHN' in red letters above one of the fireplaces. A jazz band was now unpacking instruments and plugging in cables and placing loudspeakers in front of the small, low stage reserved for the infrequent occasions when a band played. Trinder suspected the last time live music graced the Great Central Hotel was VE Day but was prepared to concede the acidly delivered riposte from the landlord that 'they'd put on a splash for the Coronation.' Either way, the seven-piece band Benson had rustled up from London were going to be pressed cheek by jowl as they performed. The band were already proving to be a slight bone of contention.

It was one of the worst kept secrets around the Detective Department that Benson was taking advantage of every free weekend to travel down to London to spend time with Mr Max Hawkes, the rakish, if charming trumpet player in the band. Lansdowne knew more than the others, but loyalty demanded that she remained silent on the subject, but despite her best efforts, it was generally accepted that Benson was 'seeing' Hawkes.

He was a divorcee – but there was some ambiguity on this point. Stories abounded, with varying degrees of accuracy and degree of lurid detail, about an irate wife banging on the door of the lodgings Benson and Hawkes had briefly shared and of Hawkes apparently seen running down a back alley in a state of undress. Or even naked, depending on who was telling the tale. The rumoured details of Benson's involvement with this colourful character had entered the whispered folk law of the department, although any attempts to bring the subject up with Benson met with stony silences or a sudden change in subject.

'He's just not the sort a WPC like Benson should be seen with.' Blencowe's disapproval was thinly disguised. He liked, indeed respected Benson as a work colleague, and as an older man he believed he could adopt a proprietorial approach and offer a 'voice of reason', based upon his years of unremarkable marriage to Mrs Blencowe. His ham-fisted attempts to warn Benson off had threatened to cause irreparable damage to the relationship between the two officers. They had eventually found an uneasy equilibrium by steadfastly refusing to allow any mention of Hawkes, London or even jazz music. Blencowe's early arrival at the Great Central Hotel had been accompanied by a disapproving stare towards Hawkes, replaced even more quickly by a look of horror as he realised that five of the seven-piece band were coloured. Apparently unable to comprehend this shock to his system, he had beaten a hasty retreat to the bar where he muttered all manner of less than complimentary observations with the landlord. Blencowe had never met such people before and felt the need to settle his nerves with a couple of swift pints. He and the landlord discovered brotherly companionship in their narrow-minded complaints, thankfully out of earshot of Benson, Hawkes and the band.

If Benson's 'man' was an intriguing subject for whispered debate, the sense of wonderment at the sight of the band members in their sharp suits, neat porkpie hats and gleaming instruments was palpable. 'Blacks' were a rare sight in Leicester and Benson aside, none of the Detective Department had spent any time in the company of these exotic recent arrivals from the West Indies. Trinder was unabashedly delighted. He had high hopes for the evening and was clearly impatient for the band to strike up and get into their swing.

PC Howerth and his beau, Laura Green, were seated in a corner accompanied by Eddie Earnshaw who, despite scrubbing his skin until almost raw and now dressed in his best jacket, still had something of the locomotive shed about him that Howerth envied.

He was still working for the railway and had daily contact with its machinations, but there were moments when he remembered the days of Eddie and himself clambering over the lines of quietly steaming giants, cleaning and scrubbing, oiling and firing the locomotives in readiness to leave Woodford Halse engine shed. It was dirty work and badly paid, but he missed it.

However, any such thoughts were instantly pushed aside by the captivating presence of Miss Darling. Still in her bus conductresses uniform having come straight from the depot, she was both surprise and delight to Earnshaw's friends. A few subtle clues that there was 'someone of interest' in his life had been dropped in advance, but this was the first time Miss Darling had been introduced. She was self-conscious, perhaps all too aware she was a new person introduced into a group who knew each other well. She was glad to get a gin and tonic in her hand. Earnshaw seemed slightly nervous in her presence, but Laura Green was soon chatting to Darling about the weather and how the snow affected the running of the buses and other inconsequential subjects as they started to get to know each other.

Both women were aware the two men were now talking about an investigation that was coming to a conclusion and it was hard not to listen in. Miss Green tailed off in her observations on frozen points and they both turned their attention to a more compelling subject.

'They found the girl, Eddie. Safe and sound,' said Howerth. 'I can't tell you how pleased we are.'

'She was unharmed?' Green interjected.

'Yes, Laura. Daisy was found in a carriage on a train travelling towards Chester from Shrewsbury. She was not able to explain exactly what route she'd taken to arrive there, but with a little time and patience that will become clear,' Howerth explained.

'Shrewsbury to Chester? The kidknapper took the girl in Manchester, which offers a direct route to Shrewsbury.'

'That's right, Ed. We suspect the kidknappers – we now know there were two - got her to Shrewsbury then bundled her onto a local just as it was departing. They then hoofed it, leaving her unaccompanied.'

'There are plenty of options from Shrewsbury they could have taken to escape,' Green added.

'Including London,' Howerth agreed. 'Or Holyhead and the ferries, South Wales, the Midlands. We've got a fair bit of work to do to track their movements. But we'll get them. One day...'

'But the little girl is OK?' Darling asked. She felt nervous intruding into what was a work conversation.

'Yes,' Earnshaw replied. 'Whatever it was the kidnappers wanted, they got it. They no longer needed her as a hostage.'

'Strange? To go to all that trouble and risk then just abandon her. Isn't that rather odd?' Green was puzzled.

'We're still working on why. But if we can take the word of a young girl in a state of shock, then we have an explanation,' Howerth explained. 'Daisy says one of the men took her jewels. Leastways, he took a little bag of what she calls 'jewels'. She was most indignant about it!'

'Jewels? Gem stones? But they will be just worthless paste, surely?' Darling laughed. She felt levity was permissible as the girl was safe and sound.

'Now this is where it gets interesting. The mother – Rachel – says she knows nothing about jewels, gems or paste stones, call them what you will. She remembers Daisy was fixated with a tiny drawstring bag – the sort of thing you put chocolate money in at Christmas. She assumed that her mother gave a bag to Daisy with something inside to amuse her. It's plausible.'

'I'm not sure I understand?' Earnshaw was just as intrigued as the two young women.

'Daisy somehow picked up a haul of real gem stones. Diamonds perhaps.' There was a collective intake of breath. 'We know the old lady who was murdered was trading in stolen goods. We think she was sitting on a clutch of diamonds or such like of spectacular value. The sort of things someone would travel a long way to collect and who would kill and kidnap to ensure their return.'

They all looked at each other around the table.

'The kidnappers seized Daisy to use her as a bargaining tool, thinking the mother has the stones?' Green was thinking it through. 'They reckoned she had taken these diamonds along with the money?'

'That is our thinking. Rachel Corrigan, the mother, claims she was innocent of anything to do with the gem stones and we believe her. However, somewhat fortuitously, the kidnappers discovered that the little girl and her faithful Dolly had the very things they wanted. Literally in the palm of her tiny hand!' Howerth continued. 'The biggest stroke of luck ever.'

'For the kidnappers,' Earnshaw exclaimed, bitterly.

'No, for Daisy!' Darling added.

'Of course. Now the hunt for the diamonds and the kidnappers, one of whom is almost certainly a killer, is our priority.'

Earnshaw was chewing all this over. 'What happens next? The mother is in trouble?'

'She is. Theft, conspiracy and obstructing a murder enquiry. The charges mount up.' Howerth answered. 'But the feeling is that with full co-operation and sufficient expressions of remorse, she'll get a suspended sentence. With a coaching, she could make a favourable impression to a jury.'

'You mean she's pretty!' Green smiled pointedly at Howerth.

'Tolerably...'

'Will the little girl be taken from her mother?' Darling looked horrified.

'That remains to be seen. She's a decent enough mother on balance, and if she gets a suspended sentence it might be possible to keep them together.'

This was a good moment for Earnshaw to visit the bar to refresh their drinks just as the band struck up the first number. The party was starting. Once seated again, talk turned to Trinder.

'It's come as a complete shock,' Howerth explained. 'He's a good sergeant. Decent. He works me hard, mind. But I'm awfully sorry to see him go.'

The girls could see Trinder across the room deep in conversation with Vignoles and Badger.

'I just hope we get a good replacement.' Howerth supped some ale.

'Any ideas?' Earnshaw asked.

'None. The fact Trinder's leaving is news enough for now. Say, Laura, fancy a dance? We need to get this joint jiving!'

'Charlton will be charged with GBH and conspiracy, but he and Corrigan are both sticking to their denials of an affair,' Vignoles was explaining. 'Both he and Corrigan will get suspended sentences is my best guess.'

'And lose his job,' Badger was drinking a pint. 'The railway can't tolerate cheats and crooks in charge of its trains.'

'Losing his job will be a heavy blow,' Trinder added. 'Mrs Charlton will have to decide if she believes his story of selflessly helping the young and pretty Rachel Corrigan,' He winked.

'Along with his heart-warming gifts to poorly-shod tramps!' Badger laughed and they all joined in.

'Hind might wriggle out of anything serious. He offered us a full confession and we can't stop him talking now. There's not enough he can tell us in the hope he'll be shown some leniency. I think he's inventing some of it in the hope of being seen to be helpful,' Vignoles continued. 'But he's a minnow. It's the mysterious Mr Welles we want and his accomplice. One of these two is the killer. They're who we want and so far they've have evaded us all.'

'You'll get them. Welles is the so-called Mr Jones who abducted the girl aided his accomplice. You have an excellent description from Corrigan to work with. Given time and good policing, we'll nab the pair of them.' Badger lifted his glass in anticipation.

'Kind of you to say, but it will be that bit harder without John here to help!' Vignoles wanted to steer the conversation back to the reason they were gathered.

'I'm not sure about that, sir!' Trinder held up his hands as if miming surrender. 'I got a lot wrong. My first murder case and I didn't collar the killer.'

'This won't be the first and won't be the last murder you investigate. We can all tell similar tales of letting someone slip through their hands,' Badger addressed Trinder. 'You put in some decent work amidst a complex muddle of conflicting stories. And don't forget, the little girl was found alive.'

'I'm not sure I can take any credit for that!'

'You don't need to tell everyone that,' Badger winked. 'We can collectively sigh with relief and be thankful.' Badger emptied his glass. 'I can't find it in me to feel sorry for that old lady. She was a nasty little crook and doing it on railway premises. She was inviting all manner of evil to her door.' He stated at his empty glass. 'Enough of this. We're here to celebrate you becoming a Detective Inspector, not to talk shop. Now I see the ladies have glasses that need refilling. High time I stood everyone a drink.' Badger moved towards the bar, but then stopped and looked at first Vignoles then Trinder in turn. 'If anyone leaves this place sober, I'll have them arrested!'

The party warmed up. The drinks flowed and Trinder talked with Benson's trumpet-blowing friend and after much laughter and nodding of heads, the band struck up again but at a much faster tempo and with more gusto. Even Blencowe was starting to lose his sniffy attitude and loosen up. The extensive collection of empty glasses in front of him and a fresh pint no doubt playing their part. His mood had noticeably lifted and his fingers were seen tapping along to the beat.

A couple of hours later and the party was becoming a riotous success. Badger had made it clear to the landlord that a lock-in was appropriate as this was a private party, whilst the band were letting loose with more up-tempo songs, the beat and rhythm taking on and drowning even the regular rumbling and roar of passing mineral trains high above their heads on the viaduct, Hawkes' trumpet soaring and cutting across the excited chatter and din.

Benson had been dancing for hours, but now hot and weary, she had retreated to the gloomy back yard filled with stacks of beer barrels and hemmed in by brick walls topped with curls of barbed wire. She stood on the back step and lit a cigarette. She rarely smoked, but a cigarette break was exactly what she needed now. Her ears were ringing.

The skies had cleared to reveal a moon drenching the snow-shrouded city with its cool light. Benson looked up at the stars.

It had been a risk inviting Max to play and she knew she'd get a lot of leg-pulling, knowing winks and curious questions next week. Never mind. Everyone was enjoying the entertainment. Perhaps it was time she faced the music and let people think what they wanted? She was tired of keeping Hawkes quiet. But for all the obvious enjoyment their relationship offered, there could still be consequences. A woman was expected to set an almost spotless example to have any chance to get on in the police. The slightest blemish against her name and her chances were effectively ruined. Had she just destroyed any chance of promotion?

She realised she was not alone. 'Oh! You surprised me, sir!'

'May I join you in a quiet stolen moment?'

'Please do. It's quite nice to hear the music from a distance.'

'It is. They play awfully well, but I am perhaps showing my years and a short breather is welcome. These last few songs are new?' Vignoles had his pipe alight. 'I understand it is of a type they call *Rolling Rock Music*.' He looked pleased with himself.

Benson laughed heartily, so much so she felt tears in her eyes.

'I judge by your reaction, I got that wrong.'

'I think you mean *Rock and Roll*,' Benson was still laughing.

'Precisely! My nephew is trying to educate me, but clearly I'm a slow learner.'

'It's very new. Fresh from the States. Sergeant...I mean DI Trinder, is enjoying it immensely.' There was a pregnant pause. 'It's going to be tricky to replace him. He's a hard act to follow.'

'Everyone is replaceable.' He puffed a smoke ring. 'But you're right. I need someone reliable, intelligent and hard working. Someone who knows their own mind and isn't scared to stand by what they believe.'

'That's quite a list.' Benson smiled in the moonlight. 'Good luck in finding him!'

'I think I know who I want.'

There was an odd silence. Benson was relieved when a steam engine whistled high above and they both looked up to see it's dark outline dimly etched by the slight glow of the station lamps and the rows of lighted carriages as it rumbled by.

'I have my eye on a candidate, but there are many bridges still to cross. There will be forces stronger than me working against me.'

'It sounds like your man is not an obvious choice.' Benson had an odd feeling in her tummy. Perhaps she'd not eaten enough and drunk too much bubbly.

'The obvious is not always the best. Good policing is almost a dark art. I need someone loyal and yet who can blend convention with a fresh and different approach. Unafraid of challenging conventions.'

'I like the sound of that person.'

'Each case is like a puzzle. Often a very complex puzzle, and two quite different minds united in the same cause can crack it that bit quicker.'

'I love a puzzle.'

'Don't we all?' Vignoles laughed and Benson concentrated on her cigarette. 'But we are neglecting our friends and colleagues and you will catch a chill in that dress.'

'I'm warm enough, sir.'

'Perhaps, but I need you fit and well. It's going to be a rocky road ahead.'

'I'm sorry?'

'With Trinder leaving. It's going to be different. There will be a lot of re-adjustment. I'm going to need you, all of you, in tip top shape!' He smiled. 'Come inside, Jane, the music is calling...'

Violet Trinder sat back in a chair, glad to catch her breath after a number of dances. He husband flopped down beside her, setting two fresh pints of beer on the table.

'Are you enjoying yourself?'

'Very much so.' He took a long draught of beer. 'The music is fabulous.'

'They can play.'

He nodded approvingly. 'Whatever one might think of the of her situation, you cannot fault Jane's choice in musicians. Max is a darned good player.'

'And Jane looks so happy. Just look at her.' Violet used her glass to make a slight indication towards the dancing WPC. 'She's in her element.'

'It's good to see. She deserves some fun. I sometimes worry she takes he work too much to heart and forgets she's allowed to cut loose and enjoy herself.'

'And who are we to question with whom she finds happiness,' Violet was thinking of her own grown up daughter, now married. She had been unplanned and conceived out of wedlock, and at the time a potential time-bomb that could have caused almost untold sadness and suffering if the situation had been handled carelessly. Society would have been harsh and uncompromising in its condemnation. Cruel in the 'solution' it would inevitably have imposed. A sleight of hand and years of lying and evasion had followed, but events had dramatically brought all into the open. Her secret was out – and John Trinder had stood by her, and now all was well. But it could have been so very different.

Trinder seemed to guess what was going through his wife's mind. 'Sometimes one just has to take a chance. Make a decision, then jump in and start swimming and jolly well make it work.'

'Like moving to North Wales.'

'Exactly. It's a big leap for us both and a wrench to leave these lovely people...' Trinder hurriedly supped more ale. 'But I was actually thinking of us. Do you remember that time when the Guvnor was laid up in hospital back in '46?'

'How could I forget?'

'He was going stir crazy cooped up in that ward!'

'Smoking his pipe in bed and the matron going spare!'

They both laughed.

'I had to summon up all the nerve I could find to ask you.'

'Don't be silly!'

'It's true. I needed something to hang the invitation on. Then I saw the concert at the De Montfort hall advertised and bought two tickets.'

'They played this tune.'

'"American Patrol" by Glenn Miller.'

'We danced to it.'

'We did.'

'So, what are you waiting for, Detective Inspector John Trinder?'

'Shall we dance?'

The End

(To be continued in the next Inspector Vignoles Mystery, 'Murder on Broadway')

The Inspector Vignoles Mysteries

'The best of the railway detective novels on the market. The series continues to grow from strength to strength with every new release. First rate.' *Steam Railway*

Smoke Gets in Your Eyes (1946)

The Murder of Crows (1947)

The Torn Curtain (1948)

The Marylebone Murders (1949)

The Last Train (To Brackley Central) (1950)

New Brighton Rock (1951)

Blood & Custard (1952)

The Mountsorrel Mystery & Other Stories (1953)

Cold Steel Rail (1954)

Coming in 2019: Murder on Broadway (1955)

Every book is available from all UK booksellers and online via Amazon and other suppliers. The GCRly shop in Loughborough Central stocks all titles, as does the Glous Warks Rly, Vale of Rheidol and Severn Valley Railway, all sales of which actively support the respective heritage railways.

Books direct from the author.

Individual, signed copies are available at £8.99 plus £2.75 p&p (total £11.74). A selection of 8 books in a 'catch up bundle' are available at the special price of £48.00 plus £4.99 p&p (£52.99).

Please send a cheque to: Stephen Done, 28a Holland Road, New Brighton, Wirral, CH45 7RB. Or email Stephen.done@gmail.com to arrange bank transfer.

Any book suppliers interested in stocking the Inspector Vignoles Mysteries, please get in touch and I can arrange attractive rates.